2211

UMBRA

A Future History Novel

Grigor Fedan

2211 Umbra
A Future History Novel

Copyright © 2015 by Grigor Fedan

Hafiz Publishing

978-0-578-15940-9

I dedicate this novel to Divija.
Thank you for being in my life.

Thanks to all who provided valuable feedback
and helped me shape this novel.

Author's Note

While reading astrophysicist Brian Greene's books to write this novel, I became aware that modern String Theory is aligned with ancient knowledge: Hinduism, Zaroastrianism, Gnosticism, Hermeticism, and Neoplatonism all speak of the energies that comprise creation, and the parallel universes discovered by modern scientists.

The ancient texts also describe the cycles of evolution that humanity is going through. They do seem to hold the secret to where our world is heading. With this in mind, I decided to write about the future of our society, using the ancients' wisdom.

1

One hundred and eighty-five years after Obama, and fifty-four after the end of the Dark Years, on a sunny summer afternoon in New York City, two men in their late forties or early fifties walked briskly across a university campus, dressed in ill-fitting but brand-new suits. One of them was very tall, around six-eight. They stole admiring glances at the imposing buildings and ample green, perfectly manicured lawns. They looked up to gaze at the cars cruising above their heads, hundreds of them, crisscrossing paths silently, in invisible corridors. The lower ones glided leisurely along, some of their occupants standing near the wide windows looking out at the city. There were a few sleek, elegant ones with one or two occupants, and the tall man pointed out that these were obviously the ones used by first tiers and regents.

They went by a corner restaurant, its patrons sitting outside under magnetically- controlled plasma shade canopies that hung like clouds above the tables. A small army of android waiters served food and cleared tables at breakneck speed.

The taller man took in the scene with apparent disdain, but his companion looked appreciatively at the food being served.

"It all looks real good," the shorter of the two said, "and like everything else in this city it's all free. Why don't we stop and order us some?"

"We don't have time," the taller one said as he picked up the pace, "their central computer wouldn't let our van drop us off

1

anywhere near the lecture hall, so the time we could've spent eating we spend walking. Besides, I don't want any part of their evil atheist socialism. Let's do what we came here for and get out."

The shorter man quickened his pace to catch up. "Yeah, well, anyway, I want to get it right, Reverend Reilly."

"Don't call me 'reverend' here in New York, Bob," Reilly said without breaking stride.

Bob smiled nervously as a woman on an autowalker sped past them. "Okay, Mister Reilly," he said, out of breath, "But anyway, you want me to sit a couple of rows from you and then at the right moment—"

"This is important, Bob. We've already gone over it." Reilly raised a hand as he studied the group gathered in front of the lecture hall some distance away. "After I say, 'We need to bring God back into the government,' and I give my spiel about what that would mean, you say your piece. Don't let me down. This is going to be big."

"Okay, I got that. Then what happens? What do I do?"

"At that point all those in that room who are good Christians will rise up and applaud and cheer; that'll be all the opening I need. Once they do that, we make sure they keep at it. We'll start a movement that no board of regents will be able to stop. The whole world will be watching. I'm sure I'll get millions of followers, and not just in Texas. We'll change the world."

They approached the large crowd slowly making its way into the auditorium. Soon they would be within hearing distance of others.

"That's outstanding, Mister Reilly. I am sure you'll get your following. But what about all those people?" Bob looked at the crowd. "I bet they figure there's nothing wrong with the way things are." At this, Reilly stopped suddenly and turned around to face him, his eyes staring hard. Bob was taken aback. "What I mean is, why, most folks who are ignorant, and like you said, not in tune with the word of God, but if they are living comfortable lives…I mean, why would they want to change anything, you know?"

Reilly drew closer. "How would you like to be a slave to the board of regents, Bob? To have one of those chips planted in your head so some bureaucrat can control you? Those people are nothing but slaves to the regents, working so the privileged few can live in luxury. That's what their government is all about; they take power away from the people and give it to the board of regents. That's all. And the regents want nothing better than to invade Texas so they can reinject us all with their chips and have us at their beck and call. They know most folks in Texas had their chips removed. All they need is an excuse that we are a threat and they'll come right in. We gotta stop them Bob. We must get rid of the whole rotten bunch." Reilly paused for a moment, then he turned to look at the gathered throng some hundred feet away entering the auditorium. "Look at them, Bob. Those are second tiers, and they dream of becoming first tiers so they can be elected regents. That's the bait dangled before them. But most of them will never make it, no, sir. The board of regents handpicks who they want to join their privileged ranks."

Bob studied the well-dressed men and women of all ages and races, no different than the patrons at the restaurant. They seemed excited and eager to get inside the auditorium. "That's real sad, Mister Reilly, how they are being fooled."

"You're damn right they are being fooled. So let's go in there and do our work for the Lord. We'll start my movement so fast it will take the regents by surprise. In no time at all, we'll have us a revolt that will make their New Paradigm look like yesterday's news."

The two made their way toward the entrance to the auditorium and the crowd waiting to get in.

"One thing I don't get," Bob said. "We are supposed to be second tiers and have all kinds of credentials. How did you manage that?"

"Don't worry about it. You are a chemist. If someone asks, just bamboozle them with your knowledge. These people are no better than us. Remember that."

The two men merged in with the second tiers slowly making their way into the auditorium, a huge rounded building shimmering in the sun. Bob nodded at a slim and intense-looking woman who came up beside him. She smiled, but before she could say anything, he quickly turned toward Reilly, who was now engrossed in a virtual document from his phone. For a moment Bob's attention was drawn by the sheer presence of the man: very tall, imposing, with a strong chin, high forehead, riveting bright blue eyes, dark brown hair, and a small beak of a nose that somehow seemed to add to his looks. Then about his voice…it just made you listen. Yeah, Bob thought, people are bound to follow him.

They flowed past the scanners at the doors. Bob felt himself hold his breath as his biometrics were scanned, but no one stopped them, and they made it to their seats, four rows apart. For some time Bob studied his surroundings, the big hall that even smelled important. There was nothing like it back in Texas. Everything, every surface, seemed so shiny, so new. This was the place every second tier wanted to come to study under the big man himself.

A dignified man in his sixties climbed up to the dais. He had that unmistakable air of authority about him. Bob recognized Regent Louis Sagan, the famous genius. There he was, the top regent in the world! If anyone could be a match for Reverend Reilly, he would be it, thought Bob. Not quite as tall or good-looking, and a bit older, but he carried himself with a certainty, a sureness about him that was impressive. He had a big mane of gray hair, which contrasted handsomely with what looked like a deep tan. His facial features, which many in Texas thought spoke of his African descent, denoted an intense focus. A superior type of smile seemed to hover in his mouth and eyes.

Sagan stood by the lectern briefly, and then looked down at his notes. "The Thornton administration instituted reforms in 2082…"

Sagan was talking about history Bob knew nothing about, so he started thinking about his wife and what she must be doing at that moment back in Houston. He was tempted to reach for his phone and check in on her, maybe watch her play with the new baby, but knew he had to pay attention.

After two long hours of presentation by Sagan and a lengthy discussion, Bob finally heard Reverend Reilly's distinctive voice. "Pardon me, regent, but you are forgetting a key element," the deep and resonant voice spread through the large auditorium. Everyone in the room seemed to perk up. Bob's heart pumped hard…"We need to bring God back into the government," Reilly said as he stood up to his full imposing height. "This government has put aside the Word of God that has kept humanity in line. We need to follow the Bible to the letter! God says we should earn our living by the sweat of our brows. It doesn't say anything about providing free food and free everything for everyone. That's creating a lazy population with no incentive but to sit around and sin."

Bob quickly pressed the comment button in his chair. "Yes," he heard himself say, "the Bible is our real constitution and God is our president." Bob waited…there was a heavy silence in the room. No one cheered, no other person followed. Then he saw Sagan smile. It was the ugliest smile he had ever seen. It made him feel small and stupid.

"You two gentlemen must be from Texas," Sagan said, and the whole room exploded with laughter.

On the television monitor to one side of the room, Bob saw his own life-size image and that of Reverend Reilly as real and clear as you can get. And the whole world was watching!

Bob glanced at Reilly, who rose quickly from his seat and then rushed along the long row as people stared at him, laughing and grinning. Bob followed suit, and felt his face grow beet red.

On their way back to Texas Reilly paced back and forth inside their borrowed church van, and kept saying, "Sagan is going to pay for that. He's going to pay. I've never been so humiliated."

Bob just wondered whether his wife had watched, and if so what she'd thought.

Reilly sat down, his eyes fixed on the floor. He felt his insides churning. Everything was now lost, he thought—Elizabeth, for sure. She was probably laughing at him right now, maybe after one of her snooty, educated friends called her with the news about what happened. Yeah, okay, Liz, go ahead and laugh at me for now, then go to New York, go ahead and study under your precious Regent Sagan, go ahead, become a first tier. But I'll show you one day. I'll show you I'm smarter than any stupid regent, especially that bastard Sagan, yes, sir.

After the longest time, Reilly looked at Bob. "You know, Sagan laughed at us because we are from Texas." He had his jaws clenched, a vein in his neck pumping hard. He made a fist and hit the seat beside him. "I'm going to show him what Texas can do; yes, sir, I'm going to show that dumb bastard a thing or two." Elizabeth, too, he thought. I'll show them both. No one laughs at William Omar Reilly.

That following Sunday, Bob and his wife, Myra, went to church. He was anxious to see what people's reaction would be to the "great embarrassment," as one of Myra's friends called it, and he also wanted to talk to Reverend Reilly and see what he thought they should do next. Surely he was planning another way to launch his world crusade.

In church Bob did find that some people smirked at him, and some made snide remarks about how silly the two of them had looked, but most were encouraging. One of his closest friends slapped him on the back, and said, "Way to go, Bob. Don't give up. You looked good among those pointy-headed New York jerks."

But Reverend Reilly was nowhere to be found. The other pastor gave the sermon instead, and when Bob asked for Reilly, no one could tell him where he was. It was the same thing the Sunday after that. After the fifth Sunday, everyone in church figured Reilly was gone for good.

The months and then years went by with no word or sight of Reilly. Then one day, and that was a full ten years after the "great embarrassment," Bob saw him on the news. Myra had put on a children's show while their four-year-old had played with his dinosaurs and giraffes and then gone to sleep, so Bob, who was eating lunch, switched the channel to the news. And there he was, Reverend Reilly being interviewed, but he was no longer the same person: he looked hard, tough. Still a handsome man, but there was now a deep line on either side of his mouth and a cleft in between his bushy eyebrows, which made him look fierce. And he was no longer a pastor, that's for sure. He wore a military uniform and had two other generals with him, and he talked about his army, and the Patriots, which was some kind of movement. Bob got up to study Reilly at close range and walked around his three-dimensional life-size image a couple of times; then he got a sick feeling in his stomach and was glad he had nothing to do with the man anymore. He went back to his chair and turned to look at Myra. "Whoa," he said. "What do you think? Oh, man." Bob rewound the program and listened intently. He heard the familiar rant against the board of regents, and Reilly talked of "smiting the heretics," and "punishing with the sword those who go against God's laws." Then he got to talking about Regent Sagan. He called him "the lead gangster, the Antichrist."

"Oh, man," Bob said, turning to Myra. "Reilly is going to make a whole lot of trouble. I just hope someone stops him before it's too late."

2

On a cold and crisp winter morning, a bit past sunrise, on a mountain in the Northern California Coastal Range, fresh, powdery snow covered the ground and dusted the pines. Near a cabin, on what used to be a road in the days of wheeled vehicles, stood a tall, slim man in his seventies with a big mane of tousled white hair. He stood there for some time in his shirtsleeves, impervious to the cold, lost in solitary thought.

In the near distance, somewhere in the woods, the man heard a coyote yap. Another soon joined from farther away, and after a moment the still, cold morning was full of the coyotes' conversation.

Footsteps on the snow behind him. He turned around to find his wife looking at him with a twinkle of amusement in her usually tired eyes. She had brought his dog, Yogi, along, an old and gentle-looking Rottweiler that sniffed his boots and looked up at his face.

She placed her gloved hand on his arm. "You'll catch a cold standing there in just your plain shirt, Lalo." She then nuzzled his cheek, cold nose against his stubble. "Are you thinking about the writer, how he probably stood on this same spot listening to the coyotes two hundred years ago?"

Louis nodded. "As a matter of fact, I was, Sharon. I was trying to imagine his life here." He turned toward the cabin, which was fifty yards or so away. "On a morning like this, he would follow the trail to the footbridge across the creek and through the cedars on to the meadow to meditate on the big boulder." He thought he'd got the words out without revealing the pain he was feeling.

Louis took Sharon's gloved hand firmly in his. "Are you up for a little walk?" he asked. When she smiled in assent, he led her gingerly on the path layered in new snow, downhill to the ancient concrete bridge that spanned the creek. Yogi followed two steps behind, his eyes apprehensive, sniffing the ground, apparently concerned about the coyotes. Louis made an effort to fix the moment in his mind: the bright blue sky, the cold air, the soft wind blowing through the pines, Yogi following close behind, the crunching sound of their boots on the powdery snow, and Sharon nearby, her warmth, her being…still alive. Yes, at this very moment she was still alive.

Louis rested his gaze on the top of the slope on the other side of the bridge. "According to his diary, the writer would sit very still on the boulder and, after some time, all kinds of animals would come around. He saw wolves, elk, bears, mountain lions, wild boar, and many coyotes. I'd like to do that."

"How often did he used to come here?"

"Once a month or so for the weekend. He and his son had to drive three hours to get here from the San Francisco Bay Area, as it was called back then."

As Louis talked about that life of so long ago—he trying to fill in the silence, she half-listening—they walked across the bridge and up the embankment to the edge of the meadow. The mountains rose in the background covered in fog, and the meadow stretched out serenely before them. Snow blanketed much of the dead grass and was sprinkled on the few bushes. The boulder stood some hundred yards away.

"How are you feeling, Sharon?"

She looked down at Yogi, who stood cautiously in between them. "Let's go back to the cabin, Lalo," she said in a soft whisper of a voice. "I have a doctor's appointment at noon. Don't forget that."

Yogi seemed only too happy to head back. The old black dog led the way this time, wagging his tail slowly in time with his steps, his massive head drooping down, confident they were close behind.

On the top floor of one of the tallest skyscrapers in Houston, the ornate and cavernous reception room fell uncomfortably quiet. The three men and two women dressed in green uniforms started exchanging impatient glances and whispering, and ignored the twelve civilians who had been told to sit on hard high-back chairs lined up against a wall. The five military sat on one couch and two overstuffed chairs that formed a semicircle facing the visitors.

One of the well-dressed visitors, a portly man, had started to perspire. Once again he glanced at the heavy-duty briefcase one of his car androids had deposited on the table in between the two big windows.

Forceful footsteps in the hallway outside, then the big, heavy doors swung open and the military types sprung to attention. The civilians tried their best to follow suit, and stood upright.

Reilly remained for a moment by the doorway, surveying the assembled group. He stood ramrod straight, and wore a spotless and perfectly creased dark green uniform. He walked briskly and came to stand beside the civilians. His retinue of ten or so men and women, all in uniform, stood a few respectful steps behind. The portly man nervously straightened out his tie while a woman next to him ran a quick hand down her skirt.

"President Reilly, sir. It's an honor," the portly man said in a shaky voice.

Reilly broke into a smile. The mood in the room lightened up. The military types relaxed, a posture here, a hint of a smile there.

"Tom Kennedy, so nice to see you," Reilly said, extending his hand in Kennedy's direction.

Reilly went around the group.

"Mrs. Sarah McNeal, descendant of the Vermont McNeals, and now lives near Austin," Kennedy intoned with an ingratiating smile as he walked meekly beside his host, "and Samuel Perkins whose family came from Ohio and is now from Galveston. His grandfather founded the Perkins-Stratton computers—"

"Yes, yes, yes," Reilly said as he shook hands and met the eyes of the visitors. Some blushed, others seemed to shrink in stature, as though trying to hide.

Reilly stopped. He didn't bother to shake the hands of the last three visitors. Instead, he turned to take in the whole group. "I am pleased you are all here showing your support for the Cause. In return, I promise to bring back the greatness the United States once held, and the greatness your families held for so many generations.

"I'm going to tell you my plan," continued Reilly as he stepped slowly in the direction of one of the windows, his deep brassy voice resonating through the room. "First, we'll take over Texas and keep the world government from interfering. That won't be a problem, once I come up with my well-armed five million soldiers. All they have are some police androids with stun guns. And we know how effective the Texas government is." Everyone smiled. "If it weren't for you folks establishing those protected areas, Texas would be a totally wild place, yes, sir...but now it's time for a new order, isn't that right?" The civilians made a point of agreeing vigorously.

He turned in their direction. "The Lord is always on the side of the righteous." Everyone assented. "Within a year's time, I'll end the world government, abolish the New Paradigm, and reintroduce money." He paused and appeared to reflect, staring down at the floor. "How, you may ask—how is he going to do all that?" The military types exchanged glances.

Reilly looked up. "Everything is in New York, and I can take over the city. Just march right in. After that, the entire world will be at my command. The regents never thought of that, I bet!" The colonel chuckled appreciatively and the other military shook their heads, smiling. "All those people who are getting a free ride at our expense, those lousy socialists, will have to work for a living!" At this everyone in the room applauded.

"All of you folks are from families that made their wealth the American way, by hard work, and the regents decided to rob you by doing away with money." Reilly sneered and shook his head. "They killed the incentive for anyone to work. That's not in keeping with the original US constitution, which their New Paradigm is supposed to have amended. An amendment? No, sir! It's an abomination. How can anyone pursue their own happiness like that?"

One of Reilly's aides stepped up and whispered in his ear. He listened and then turned to the group. "Yes, of course I know that the pursuit of happiness is in the Declaration of Independence, but that's unimportant. What's important is that the regents went ahead and blamed your ancestors for the Dark Years, and during the food riots incited those awful mobs to attack your families, the very ones who had made the US great.

"They dare call us—what is that term, Browny?" Reilly turned toward one of his aides, a balding middle-aged man who had been taking notes on his pad.

"'Atavists,' Mister President."

"Yes, yes! Atavists. That's the term they use within the government to describe us. It's the term they use for criminals, so they have categorized us along with murderers and thieves. Atavist means backwards, primitive. To them we are savages. Why? Because we want our rights back. We all want to stand proud on our own two feet, as the good Lord intended. I guess to them that's criminal. But not to worry—soon they will call us Patriots their rulers!"

Some of the civilians shouted, "Yes!" Others nodded. The military types smiled proudly.

"I'm happy your families had the wisdom to move to Texas, and helped us secede from the United States, and now we are all going to work together to get our country back! But this time, the United States will be part of the Confederacy! Yes, you heard me right. This is the start of a new age for the South."

With this, Reilly made his way to the briefcase and the big antique oak table. One of the military types came over quickly and opened it. The gold bars glistened in the light from the windows. Reilly casually glanced at the contents. "I can build ten tanks with this, but I need thousands of tanks."

Kennedy smiled nervously. "Yes, I know Mister President, sir. That's only the beginning. Within a month, we'll have ten times that!"

Reilly walked slowly over to Kennedy. "If you want to do away with the New Paradigm and get your country back, better think of multiplying that by the hundreds!" He placed a hand on Kennedy's shoulder and turned to look at the nearby group of civilians who stood in a cluster. Some smiled tentatively, others fidgeted with purses, pens, and rings. "I know you all will do your best for the Cause. This is your time to come forward and be counted! Tell that to your friends. You are either for me and a Patriot, or against me; there's nothing in between."

He gave the group another smile, and they relaxed. One woman had tears in her eyes as she came forward and took Reilly's hand. "Thank you, sir. We are all behind you, I assure you. All of my friends, the Vermont families, are with you!"

The rest of the civilians followed the woman's example and came forward to shake Reilly's hand.

"Good, good. Very good. I appreciate you all," Reilly said. "Now let's go downstairs and enjoy our parade, shall we?" With this, he started for the door. An android came out of an unseen door, grabbed the heavy briefcase, and stayed close behind him. Everyone in uniform followed, leaving the civilians to find their way out.

When Kennedy and his friends came out of the building, they were met by a bright Houston sky.

"Isn't he wonderful?" gushed the Vermont woman, looking down the street, waiting for the parade to start.

"Oh, we are all so lucky to have him!" a woman from a New York family said, taking her place by the curb. "Thank you, Tom, for bringing us to meet him."

Martial music wafted from some blocks down. "Just remember what he said, people," Kennedy said. "We need to hustle! I want you to raise a hundred pounds of gold by the weekend, or don't bother calling me again."

"No, no, Tom," the man from Galveston said. "We'll raise the gold, not to worry. You can count on us. Isn't that right?" He turned to look at the group, and they all did their best to agree.

Tom Kennedy, scion of a long line of blue-blooded American elite, smiled. Yes, indeed, he thought as he looked down the busy Houston street. It wasn't as modern as New York or Boston, but Houston was doing fine, thanks to the Patriots. Artificial sunlight radiating from some of the buildings bathed the street, just as in New York. In the two restaurants with outside seating, he could see dozens of diners—all of them in army uniforms—eating, being served, chatting, drinking, waiting for the parade to go by from their vantage point. Soon there will be a new world order, a return to what once was, the days of greatness, he told himself. Kennedy smiled broadly and stood straight, in case someone was watching. He was making a name for himself, and one of these days, he, too, would wear one of those army uniforms and watch a parade from a restaurant.

Once back at the cabin, having shed her coat and boots, Sharon settled into her reading chair. An android brought her a cup of tea and her slippers. She was thinking of that writer of long ago and the life he must have led. "I know race was very important in those days. I suppose you would've been damned in that world."

Louis took off his jacket and hung it on a peg. "You mean because of my black ancestry? Oh yes."

"Atavists today are still racist, right? I mean if you go to Texas…"

Louis walked over to stand by her chair. "Yes, tribalism is at the core of their pathology, but nothing today compares with what they were like back then." He told her how the writer described that world of seemingly unending conflict between the races, religions and countries. "But during his lifetime the world changed a lot. As a teenager he witnessed the civil rights turmoil of the 1960s, and in his old age he saw the long-range purging effects on the world after this country elected its first black president."

Sharon was enjoying her talk with Louis. Normally he was so busy with his work. His eyes were now soft and tender, instead of intense and probing. "Did the writer live anywhere else besides here and San Francisco?" she asked.

"Well, later on in his life, Hawaii. He says that's where he felt at home, for the first time in his life."

"Do you have copies of his books?"

"No, I don't even know his name. The graduate research assistant who found the diary, a real-paper document stored away in an old lady's attic, tried for a long time."

"But certainly, if you know he lived here, in this very cabin two hundred years ago…"

"Those records were destroyed during the food riots. We tried every avenue, just out of curiosity, but no, the diary is all that's left of that anonymous man."

Sharon turned her head to look out the window at the green trees and the white snow and was lost in thought for a moment, imagining what the writer had looked like. She felt a pang of sadness as she realized there was so little left of him. Only a diary. A whole life erased. In two hundred years, would anyone remember her? Not likely. She sighed and turned her gaze to her husband. "Well, Lalo, we must head back. House," she commanded, "pack our things." She put her cup down on the table, rested her head on the back of the chair, and closed her eyes.

Louis waited until she had dozed off and then walked across the soft cream carpet to the den and his desk. He reached into a drawer, took out a handheld body scanner, and made his silent way back to his sleeping wife.

He stood in front of her and aimed the scanner at her forehead, and a hologram of the inside of her head appeared before him. He located the tumor in the parietal lobe and studied it for a time. The tumor did not appear to have grown in the past week, but that was to the naked eye. Louis pressed a key and…it had grown.

Again he sent the query to Medical Central. A light blipped on the device, and the screen displayed the same diagnosis: *glioblastoma multiforme.* Perhaps for the hundredth time, he asked for a prognosis. It took several seconds, but the reply was the same: expected life expectancy eight months, conservative estimate; no surgery available due to age; palliative care only.

That was the problem with removing one's biochip; things could go awry, and a nasty cancer could do much damage. Too bad having an active biochip carried such a stigma. The irony was that now she had an implant to prevent seizures that was basically the same chip.

One of the house androids came from the den with Louis's briefcase already packed with his things, he assumed, and he handed it the scanner, then sat down on the armrest of Sharon's chair and leaned back on the generous back cushion. He brought his left arm to circle around his wife's head, and his hand gently touched her shoulder, frail and vulnerable. Her cat, Oscar, grey and white, climbed up on her lap and made himself comfortable.

Soon she would be gone, her presence gone from that room…from any room. He reached out his right hand to pet Oscar on the head, and the cat started purring. The illness had taken huge, sudden chunks of who she was in just the past few months. She couldn't work much of late. Her body seemed shrunken, defeated by the cancer; her once elegant gray hair now dry and wispy, her face worn out.

In time the pain of her death would dull, and eventually he might get used to being without her. But he knew he would remember her each and every single day for the rest of his life.

He withdrew his hand from Oscar's head and ran a finger gently along a vein in the back of her hand. But what if he terminated with her? He had lived enough, had accomplished

17

enough. They had done most things together for the past fifty-odd years: all the adventures of the mind, the excitement of the various projects, witnessing how their ideas changed the world. For all of that they had gone hand in hand. It would be only fitting to march into the great unknown as always, together.

Of course, she would say they already knew where they were going, that it was the state they reached in meditation. That had been a topic of one conversation not long ago, and it had made Louis realize his wife knew of a different reality, because for him the experience of meditation was too ethereal, too vague, merely a feeling of peace. For him, death was still the great unknown.

Sharon woke up and smiled at him. He bent over and kissed her tenderly on the lips.

A tall and distinguished-looking man with a goatee, thirty-five or so, walked along a downtown Houston street, trying his best not to appear conspicuous among the throng of onlookers, who were obviously all Patriots. He kept his gaze down, trying to observe without being noticed. The parade had already started and the martial music was unnerving…a reminder of the threat everyone was talking about. He found a group in a corner and decided to mingle among them.

He studied the people around him and tried listening to their conversations without being obvious about it. "Oh, I'm really worried Samantha couldn't come," said a man right beside him with a cowboy hat to a woman who held on to his arm. "Don't worry, she's a teenager," she replied, "I don't think they'll do anything to a kid, do you?" Her voice sounded tense, nervous.

"Stephen? Stephen Phillipiak?" the man with the goatee heard someone whisper to his right. Stephen turned his head and recognized his meditation teacher, a short middle-aged man now wearing a suit instead of his customary baggy clothes.

Stephen smiled and extended his hand. "Hello, Jorge," he whispered back. "I came to Houston for the parade."

Jorge glanced around, his eyes darting, not his usual calm self. "Yes, a wonderful opportunity to meet President Reilly," he said, perhaps a little too eagerly.

They could hear a military band approaching. The entire street was lined with spectators.

First came the band. Then the artillery, big guns pointed at the sky, and troops, many troops…and nobody dared move, everyone cheered, applauded, and smiled.

Finally, President Reilly's float rolled on by. He sat on a golden throne-like chair, surrounded by his generals, all in dark green uniforms, with ribbons and stars. Along the edges of the float stood an impressive armed guard, tall and muscular, men and women, all very serious.

People along the street broke into wild cheers and applause.

A television screen on the side of a building showed the real president of Texas, Julian Perry, and his cabinet officials sitting in the VIP booth. They looked somber, but forced a smile for the camera.

Stephen felt his insides tighten.

Once the parade had gone by, Stephen turned to Jorge, ready to say good-bye.

"Steve," Jorge whispered, "please come with me to the center."

Stephen nodded, thinking Jorge didn't feel safe talking out in the open.

They got into Jorge's car and flew at city traffic altitude along an avenue to Jorge's suburban meditation center without saying a word.

Once inside the austerely furnished, well-lit, and peaceful large room, Jorge gave Stephen a long hug. Now he had the serene look Stephen remembered.

"We face a great challenge, my friend," Jorge said as he made his way to the small kitchenette in one corner. Chairs and meditation cushions were arranged in concentric circles in the middle of the room, just as Stephen remembered from a year ago.

"We'll have to do something about the Patriots and Reilly," Jorge said, carrying a delicate white porcelain tray with two steaming cups of tea. He led the way to a low table by a window overlooking a carefully tended small garden with colorful flowers. "But we need to do it peacefully, without anyone losing their life."

Stephen sat down on a cushion with his back to the window. "What do you propose we do?"

Jorge looked at him from across the table. His dark hair was neatly combed back, his eyes beaming with peace. "I'm going to ask for a convocation in Los Angeles, to gather as many of our worldwide spiritual nation, real and virtual, that can fit in a stadium. We need to counter what's going on here in Texas."

Stephen took a sip of the herbal tea. He put the cup down on the table and looked at his friend and mentor. "I need to do more than just pray, Jorge. I can't see us stopping that monster by just sitting around."

A concerned look crossed Jorge's face. "Please, Steve. Don't use violence; don't even think about it."

Stephen shook his head. "The most effective form of prayer is action. I recall you said that."

Louis followed Sharon into his car, gray translucent glassite and silver stremptonite, long and narrow, with sleek stabilizing wings now shining bright under the sun. Inside, smells of filtered air, an ultraclean techno-place, made by machines, cleaned by machines.

Sharon carried Oscar in his cage howling in protest. Yogi made his own way, aiming for the space on the beige carpet between the two large opposing mauve-colored bench seats, front and back of the car's sanitized interior. As he sat down, Louis thought of the termination centers, of the possibility they could die together, and his heart felt lighter. Maybe he should do it. He watched Sharon settle down on the seat across from him. A safety harness came out of the back and buckled her down. He thought of how his colleagues and friends would react. Perhaps they would think he'd taken the cowardly way out, that he still had a good many years of productive life.

Sharon had placed her cat's cage next to her on the seat, which the car also secured with straps. She started watching a movie on a large virtual screen that popped up in front of her. From where Louis sat, her screen was just a big shadow in front of her face.

After Yogi was safely strapped down, the car lifted off gently. They kept rising in search of whatever air corridor Central had assigned. Through the ample window, Louis could see the California coastline in the distance. They entered a cloud bank, and the window became a display of the same coastline, the trees below, the scattered towns all conveniently labeled, all part of a massive urban sprawl surrounding the patch of forest they were leaving behind. The car found a corridor and gained speed, climbed to another one, and another. The speedometer read eight hundred miles per hour, then a thousand. They climbed again to fifteen hundred. Climbed once more and soon had reached a transcontinental corridor of two thousand miles per hour.

Sharon turned off her movie and studied her husband. The intense, intimidating look was back in his eyes. He was probably thinking about work. "Dear, you are always so busy. Why do you still teach that first tier preparatory class?"

Louis rubbed his chin. "Oh, for various reasons. It gives me a chance to foster those who truly want to serve, or have a particular vision for government." He thought for a moment. "It also keeps me in touch with the best and the brightest. And besides, it's a thrill to watch an occasional former student make regent."

Sharon smiled and closed her eyes.

Louis opened the writer's diary and found the part about the administration that preceded Obama when an ultra-conservative group called the neo-cons took over. Their natural proclivity for competition, control and aggression coupled with intense tribalism meant that war abroad and no-holds-barred partisan politics at home were appealing means to achieve their ends. Louis read for some time and occasionally shook his head at the predictable atavistic behavior.

Thank goodness the days when atavists were in charge are over, Louis thought as he watched Yogi chase something in his sleep, his legs twitching. But they are still in our midst, still inflicting abuse, pain, causing damage. Competitive, dominating, controlling individuals who stop at nothing to advance themselves. Oh, the suffering they have caused through the ages! The obvious ones are criminals. The less obvious are the ones that do the most lasting damage…their legacy from previous centuries evident, in-your-face: the fact that most wildlife is gone from the world, that a good portion of Earth is unlivable, and that natural clean water is hard to find. Yes, Louis concluded, that's what atavists do, and if we don't isolate them they'll try to have their way. The biochips can only prevent crime, not detect attitude, or values. The only logical recourse is to isolate them in a country of their own. But did he, or society, have the right to decide such a thing? Was that in essence acting like them? But then again, what other choice did he, or society, have?

3

Captain Cheney liked his job, but he didn't much care for Reilly, the so-called president. But what the heck, he thought, he made life a lot of fun. Cheney walked into the man's office, where he had been summoned. This was going to be another kidnapping, or maybe a hit.

"Ah, Captain Cheney," Reilly acknowledged the short, stocky, and ugly man who reminded him of a pit bull. "Did you find Elizabeth Stewart?"

Cheney hesitated. Word was Reilly had really fallen for that broad some years ago, and the man didn't like bad news. "Yes, sir, except she is now Mrs. Elizabeth Harding," he said as he came to stand in front of Reilly's desk.

"Is that so?" Reilly let out a derisive chuckle. Then he stood up and walked over to a window to look at the lawn, as though he were really inspecting it. After several minutes he turned around. "How's that special program of yours?"

"The torture-based deconstruction? Works just fine, sir. We got us nineteen walking idiots…just drooling all over the place." Cheney laughed.

"Well, I might have found us another target."

"Elizabeth Harding, sir?" Not that he cared; he was just curious.

"No, no, my boy. Her husband. Then I got us a real big fish to try it on, my old friend Louis Sagan. But for now, go fetch me the happy couple."

Regent Sagan? thought Cheney as he saluted and walked out of that room. That would be really exciting.

Louis, dressed in a temperature-regulating dark blue suit, stood on the sidewalk outside the World Government Headquarters. He looked up at the immense structure, all three hundred floors. The top of the building was lost in the clouds. He walked toward the glassite arches in front. The place always gave Louis pause. It was a feeling of reverence for the institution that held the world in its sway, but there was also some reticence. So many decisions were made here, so much at stake.

Today they would discuss the atavists.

He came through the entrance and stood still for the android to scan his DNA profile.

"Thank you, Regent Sagan, and welcome to Congress," said the male humanoid android dressed in a light blue uniform. Louis made his way to an autowalker station, lifted one shoe at a time for the small platforms to attach themselves. Then he "walked" at increasing speed down the long hallway, up a staircase and into the chambers. Seating units equipped with the latest devices and human comforts lined the room. The autowalker stopped at his chair in the third row from the front.

At noon sharp, the board on back of the stage announced a forum. All 2,004 regents were physically present. "We have come together to discuss the atavists," the regent acting as coordinator for that one meeting said, his virtual image up on stage. "Remember that the intent is not simply to isolate them, but to provide treatment."

Regent Gary Eagan's image took the coordinator's place. "The situation is direr than anyone here realizes," said Eagan, who was Louis's department chair at Columbia University and had made regent just two years before. "I move for immediate sequestration of all atavists, worldwide, before they rise en masse and hurt people."

Judging by the comments on the board in the back of the stage, most regents were baffled by Eagan's statement. Some noted that he had breached protocol as well. Louis had been slated to speak first.

"Let's just start with the basic premise that we are not going to sequester anyone," Louis interjected soothingly, as he watched his image appear beside Eagan's. "No one will be forced to go anywhere. Besides, we don't know who all the atavists are, and assuming they all pose a threat is a flawed assumption. If and when they go to Texas, it will have to be strictly voluntary."

"We know who most of the atavists are," Gary said. "They have active biochips, for God's sake."

Louis let out an involuntary chuckle. "Forty-two percent of adults over the age of eighteen have their chips still active. Are you suggesting we remove by force anyone with an active chip?"

Heavy and clumsy, but smartly dressed in a well-tailored brown suit, Gary turned to the audience. "What about the work at Columbia? I thought they were working on a predictive algorithm to screen those atavists who pose a threat."

Louis hesitated and stared at Eagan. How did he know about the algorithm? "You are right; Regent-Dean Joy Blass has some prominent people working on that." Louis saw Joy smile her assent, and he smiled back. "But there are a number of flaws associated with it," continued Louis, "what it boils down to, Gary, is that humans are a complicated species. Things are not as clear cut as we want them to be."

Gary smirked. "But quite a few subjects are clear-cut cases, right?"

"Yes, about two percent of the population—specifically, 300,485,732 individuals worldwide are defined as antisocial, and their actions are actively monitored by their biochips. In most cases we can detect the early signs and provide behavior modification interventions, but if they start committing a crime, their vital functions are curtailed and they go into a coma. That's what the chips were originally meant for."

Gary rolled his eyes and smirked. "But criminals can remove their biochips!"

"No, Regent Eagan. We intervene if anyone classified as anti-social tries to remove their chip. But atavists who fall outside this classification in outlying areas do remove them. Last year our police was asked by the Iraqi government to reinject over a million of its citizens with chips to prevent the country from erupting into sectarian violence. After we reinjected them we classified them as antisocial. We've done that in several countries over the years, often at our insistence. But the atavists who live in our jurisdiction have active chips, pose no threat, and have the right to decide where they live." Louis tried not to sound patronizing, but the man was being ridiculous. "Our only option is to make living in Texas voluntary. We plan on appealing to anyone who wants to live in an adversarial environment. I repeat what I told you three months ago: We estimate that the removal of atavists from our population will increase our wellbeing index by 37.46 percent…we are getting rid of a bunch of nasty people."

Mary Contreras, a regent who worked on natural resources, projected her virtual image onto the stage. "What if they don't want to go?"

"Well, we plan to make it very enticing, Mary." Louis said. "We have to make sure some key elements are in Texas, and if they are not, we'll introduce them. We plan to recreate fundamentalist versions of Christianity, Judaism, Hinduism, and Islam: who has the one and true book written by God, who is saved and who goes to hell, who is a heretic… definition of God, of a soul, of hell, of heaven, who is a true prophet, or avatar, or the son of god, what-have-you…all the significant stuff that created so much conflict throughout history." Louis turned to the audience. "Then, obviously, reintroduce money. People who don't work simply go hungry and perish. That should entice atavists to go to Texas, don't you think?

"Give them also violent competitive sports. Since the time of the Roman Empire, those sports have served as a catalyst to vent aggression and another means to identify one's 'tribe.' This will help create a culture that will lead to adversarial political and legal systems. What was in place before 2147."

"But Louis," Mary said, "won't they just reinforce each other? How will they evolve?"

"Just like we did," Louis answered. "Eventually, through trial and error, and challenges, their religions will change to what we have: an inclusive, benign, and non-dogmatic approach to spirituality. Their other atavistic traits will follow along. Then they can rejoin us."

Mary nodded thoughtfully, but Gary shifted his weight from foot to foot and appeared as though he had more to say.

One of the regents in charge of geographic apportionment projected his virtual image onstage beside Contreras's. "I thought Texas was almost dead!"

"Not anymore," said Louis. "Their congress asked us for help about twenty years ago and our Ecological Services Administration instituted the Basic Ecological Regeneration Program. Texas is now recovering."

"That program is a lot of work," said a regent who worked in education, "I assume Texans must be very grateful."

Louis smiled. "Actually, the Texas government is taking credit for it all. Recently, their president posed in front of one of the plants we set up, and told how Texas scientists figured out how to capture carbons and other pollutants from the atmosphere, and from deconstructed plastics, and blacktop, and then inject them back into the ground as reconstructed oil. And he was really proud on how his hydro geologists were extracting water from the air and restoring their aquifer. No, we are getting zero credit."

"But at least they are benefitting, right? Asked Mary.

"Oh, yes, of course, but mainly because we are also fixing the ecology all over the world. Global warming has stopped and is being reversed. Gradually, the long droughts punctuated by angry storms are giving way to a more stable climate. They are very happy about that. The air is breathable…and they now have water."

"Is Texas as wild as we hear in the news? Are there really warlords?"

"Yes Mary. The ultra-rich families who moved there do act like warlords; they have taken over large swaths of land and do what they want. But the big cities are fairly peaceful. That's what the Texas government controls. But out in the countryside, it's like the Wild West all over again."

Mary looked puzzled. "Sounds like Texas will be hard to control. Why not select Bolivia, West China, or some other outlying country as a test site?"

"In the past ten years about twenty million people classified as atavists have moved to Texas from all over the United States, Mexico, and Canada. I suppose because they heard the place is coming back. It obviously appeals to them and that's why we selected it as our test site. Of course, everything hinges on the Texas government approving our plan to move atavists from all over North America, but I see no problem; they have a history of welcoming anyone. And we'll assist with whatever is needed."

"Why not open Texas to atavists from all over the world?" Asked Gary. "Surely there's room."

"That would be a disaster for us, Gary. We can't transport that many people, yet alone feed them. If Texas works out, we'll replicate it elsewhere."

"It sounds as though you have everything figured out. Why haven't you presented your proposal to peer review?"

"No, we don't have everything figured out yet. There's still a lot of planning involved."

Before Gary could say anything else, the coordinator motioned for the atavist project to be tabled until Louis presented a formal proposal to peer review. He had four months.

A week later, a young man sat in his office at Columbia University in New York and stared in wonder at the virtual computer display floating ghostlike in front of his face. He couldn't believe what he had just come up with. All those long hours had paid off. He told his office to call the dean for research and development.

"Oh, Joy, could you come here for a moment?"

"What do you want Larry?" was the tart reply. "I'm busy."

"Please…It won't take but a moment." As he said this, Larry pressed a few keys and looked at the potted plant that stood by his window. He smiled again and tried to keep his excitement in check.

A few moments later, he heard steps outside his door. Larry's office recognized Joy and let her in.

She was met by a giant mechanical monster. It brought down a huge fist that pulverized the desk where Larry sat, tossing him violently against a wall. The robot lurched toward her…Joy screamed and spun around, only to be grabbed by an arm.

Joy froze, closed her eyes, and when she opened them again while still screaming, she found…nothing! She was sitting on the floor, and Larry stood with arms crossed, his tall and lanky frame towering over her, looking down and smiling. Joy looked around. There was no giant robot, no pulverized desk…everything was…normal.

"What? What the heck?" Several people had rushed in. Assistants, professors, scientists. They all stood by the door and stared at Joy, who remained on the floor, legs splayed. "Larry!" she started to yell, "You…" Then she noticed all the people and made an effort to control herself. "What did you do? What the heck was that?"

Larry grabbed her hand and helped her up. "Sorry, I needed to test the thing." He turned to the crowd now gathered by the door. "Oh, nothing happened, folks. I startled Doctor Blass, and she fell down."

The onlookers began to disperse; some studied Joy, others smiled in disbelief.

When the last person was gone, Larry turned to Joy, who now stood sternly with hands on hips. "Sorry, Joy. Maybe I should have waited to conduct the experiment at the lab, but I couldn't wait."

Joy took stock of the tall scientist, the famous "Doctor Cyborg." His laughing but frank eyes behind his steel-rim glasses, and those Germanic features she didn't quite like; good-looking, but cold, like a porcelain figurine, all rosy cheeks, blue eyes, firm chin. Too damn cute. But the kid was all right. His predictive algorithm was brilliant, and now he was on to something big. For the moment, though, she decided to make him pay. "Okay, but just tell me what the heck did you do? Where did that giant android come from? And where did it go? And what happened to the office? And—"

"Again, my apologies, Joy. I got ahead of myself. Listen, let me explain the whole thing over...some coffee?"

She stared him down, a hard, critical look in her brown eyes. She brushed back her bangs with one hand. "Okay, Larry. First thing, after I calm down, is you will explain in great detail what it is you did; second, we will go over the results...I believe you could kill someone like this. You were extremely irresponsible. Then we will review experimental protocol on my watch."

"Yes, ma'am. Again, I'm terribly sorry," Larry said, trying his best to appear contrite. She gave him one last hard look, then turned around and stomped out of his office, her thick dark brown hair bouncing with each forceful step.

The same moment when Larry had called Joy into his office, an astrophysicist in the Maryland labs of Macro Systems Inc. took a deep breath, rose from his desk, glanced at his computer display, and made his way to a shelf, where he picked up a cage with a mouse. He walked some twenty feet to a large glassite enclosure and placed the cage inside.

Across the room was another similar enclosure. His lab assistant stood beside it with a biospectometer in hand. The scientist took out his own biospectometer from his lab coat pocket and aimed it at the mouse. He closed the door of his enclosure.

"Well, let's try it one more time, Arlene."

Arlene stood tense and expectant by her glassite cube. "Very well, Alphonse. I'm ready."

Alphonse, his eyes fixed on the cage and the mouse he could see through the glassite, reached into his pocket, and pressed a button. The mouse and cage disappeared.

He turned his head as Arlene opened her enclosure and reached down. Alphonse held his breath.

And there it was in her hands, the cage, with the mouse very much alive. Arlene aimed her biospectometer at the mouse and nodded.

Doctor Alphonse D'Anjou let out an uncharacteristic "Yahoo!" It was followed by a "Damn, that's great!" He went over to hug his bemused assistant, picked her up off the floor, and did a dance while she still held on to the cage with one hand.

4

L ouis stood at the podium. He scanned the vast lecture hall bathed in a bluish glow. Many in the audience had changed their seating units to exercycles. His mind and then his heart veered to his wife, but he made an effort to focus on teaching the class. Life had taught him that the best way to maneuver around things his heart could not deal with was to plunge into the task at hand.

"How did we do away with money?" he asked the audience. He saw faces perk up. "And how did we bring about the first true democracy the world has ever known? You are about to discover the link between the founding of Switzerland in medieval times, the American Revolution, the French Revolution, and the New Paradigm."

Students looked at one another, some murmuring. Louis knew this was a much-anticipated session. All in attendance had been asked to sign confidentiality agreements, and they were about to find out why.

"Everything in our history, all events, are linked. One step leads to another...so what led to the New Paradigm? We all know about the food riots and the Dark Years that preceded them, so of course there's cause and effect, but it's not as clear as you think. What else came into the fray? How exactly did we decide that doing away with money and rulers was possible?

"It all started with President Obama two centuries ago.

"By the year 2000, most people in this country felt that race issues had been left behind—until Obama got elected. When he faced unprecedented opposition, the ugly truth came to the surface. A good many people could accept a black teacher, policeman, judge, senator, but apparently not a black in the highest office in the land. Barack Obama was an effective president, despite the corrupt system, but he would have done so much more had he not faced so much overt, but at times subtle, sick, opposition. It was then we realized how insidious racism was, and as a society we started the process to purge ourselves of not just race discrimination, but everything else we didn't like about ourselves.

"Central to this purging process involved a long hard look at money and how we dealt with it and the relationship between the powerful and the disenfranchised. The years during and after Obama saw a profusion of co-op ownership of businesses, and the concepts of fair redistribution of wealth, taxation as a voluntary contribution, and a moneyless society were avidly discussed. At this stage a good many of the ultra rich, rather than passing on their money to their children, donated most all of their wealth." Louis glanced at the podium's console display and noted with some satisfaction how a good many in the class were researching the topics as he mentioned them.

"But while we made some progress, the end of the twenty-first century witnessed a perfect storm brewing: enormous wealth concentrated in a small group of the ultra rich; an exploding population that reached an unsustainable twenty-four billion while food production declined. We had run out of oil and therefore we also ran out of cheap and abundant fertilizers; urban sprawl had gone unabated while climate change decimated what arable land and water reserves were left, and technology had not been sufficiently focused on alternate means of food production. Controlled-environment farming had been around in the form of 'vertical farms' in tall buildings, but the concept did not catch on until much later. And of course, they hadn't come up with the food synthesizers we now have. And so, for the three decades between 2080 and 2113, the world experienced mass famine, draught, and virulent diseases that wiped out entire countries at the time, the Dark Years you all heard about. As a result, the world population declined by almost half, down to fifteen billion. We knew whom to blame: the ultra rich who had profited from a booming population while they exploited natural resources to the point of extinction. Things came to a climax with the food riots in 2113, a disastrous bloodletting when the poor, who comprised eighty-one percent of the population, went after the ultra rich, who made up a scant one-thousandth of one percent. But the ultra rich had large private armies, and so the world descended into violence and chaos.

"Then a miracle happened.

"At this critical juncture, as in previous revolutions, a secret entity came into the picture to transform popular concerns into tangible change. It's apparent that their most immediate objective was a fair redistribution of wealth, followed by a cap on population. Millions of people the world over poured out in massive demonstrations demanding immediate action in these two areas, and not surprisingly, most nations readily agreed. With something concrete at hand, the violence stopped. Governments made sure everyone had enough to eat. They also made sure no one had more than two children, and ever since then we've kept our world population at fifteen billion. With the Dark Years safely behind us, we explored change in earnest.

"We then decided to select leaders on the basis of excellence and draft them into office." Louis heard chuckles around the room. "I know, it sounds so basic to all of you, but I guess you had to be alive back then to grasp how revolutionary the whole thing was.

"Then we dealt with wealth disparity. For many years the idea of a moneyless society was talked about as a far-fetched utopian ideal. The central tenet was that money corrupted; it conferred too much power on the wealthy, and the obsessive accumulation of money, pure greed, was viewed as an unfortunate human condition.

People the world over demanded permanent, radical change. With the memory of the Dark Years fresh in their minds, most world leaders agreed, and were willing to do anything to avoid another crisis. In this country the public pressure for change became overwhelming and the US Congress had no choice: We did away with money, removed raw survival out of the equation, and came up with our tier system to reward contributions to society: In the basic category, or third tier, an individual who for some reason does not contribute to society can still live in relative comfort. As second tiers, you do much better. Everyone in this room knows that. For first tiers and regents, the sky is the limit. But you do need to pass the first tier exam to qualify and the votes from your peers to get there.

"We formalized these concepts by amending the United States constitution, what people started calling the New Paradigm, because that's what it promised: a new world. Most other nations followed suit.

"These changes opened the doors to more progressive ways of thinking: boundaries lost their significance and ethnic and national identity less important. As a result, age-old conflicts such as the Palestinian and Israeli impasse, the Sunni versus Shia, and all manner of ethnic discords diminished. Muslims rose against the fanatics in their midst and stopped their terrorism. In fact, fanatics and fundamentalists of all stripes seemed to fade away. Worldwide our biochips have to intervene less and less with each passing year.

But what happened to the oligarchs? A lot of wealth simply vanished. However, some of the ultra rich had accumulated gold and they migrated to countries that had decided to stay out of the world government: notably Texas, Nairobi, Bolivia, West China, and New Arabia, and the dozen or so other smaller places that function as countries. As a result, a good portion of the gold in this country ended up in Texas, where our surviving oligarchs, around six thousand families, went to hide." Louis chuckled. "Who knows what they are spending their gold on. Maybe buying things from one another."

Louis saw in his podium's display that there were many comments. A good many had to do with the secret entity he'd mentioned. He picked one of the questioners at random. "Ms. Kutamala, you have a question?"

Lorena Kutamala's image came onstage to stand beside him. "Yes, regent. What evidence do you have that there were secret planners, the entity you talk about? Rumor mills are full of those tales, but you are saying they are true!"

Louis could see that the question had quite a few backers. Most of the class wanted to know. "We don't have documents, if that's what you are asking, but we do have very intricate studies that analyzed the French and the American Revolutions of the late 18th century as well as the New Paradigm in 2147, and found a common thread, an unknown causative agent."

"So it's circumstantial evidence," commented a man by the name of Johansen.

"No, it's not. There were definitively causative agents. They left a trail."

"Are you saying," a man in the back asked, "that the New Paradigm's Oliver, Johnson, Martinez, Zakaria…were all puppets? That they were doing some else's bidding?"

"No, I am not," Louis was quick to counter. "But they were secretly prompted and helped, or were themselves members of the secret entity. Everything points to the Knights Templar, who have a history of such meddling. We know they were secretly behind the founding of Switzerland in medieval times, the first democracy since the end of the Roman republic, a monumental step that was the ideological foundation for the revolutions to come. They were also instrumental in strengthening parliamentary power all over Europe. In the revolution of the late 1700's in this country, a good many of our founding fathers were Masons, an offshoot of the Templars. In the French Revolution, we know a similar group had a hand…and it behooves mention that the Latin American liberator Simón Bolívar was a Rosicrucian, another offshoot organization. So, yes, the evidence points to the Knights Templar in whatever guise they presented themselves. It's very likely they decided the time was ripe for a true democracy and devised the New Paradigm.

"Now why did I disclose to you the secret entity? You could have gone on believing the official story and become effective regents. But I, and the board of regents, want you to know the impact a concerted group of individuals, or even just one person, can have. So when you become regents, you, too, can change the world. Your present task is to learn how. In 1950 someone at the United Nations decided to write a paper titled *The Race Question*. It led to a Supreme Court case in 1954 called *Brown vs. Board of Education*, which called for school desegregation. The case was the catalyst for the Civil Rights Movement of the 1960s, which led to a monumental social change that eventually enabled a black man, Barack Obama, to become president four decades later, which in turn got us to where we are today.

"I want you to be that UN official who ordered the writing of that one paper.

"By the way," Louis said in closing, "since the New Paradigm, we've had the greatest output in the history of mankind, up and down, from the scientist to the baker."

The virtual image of John Phillips, a statistician sitting in the back row, came onstage. "But what about the oligarchs and those of the far right who migrated to places like Texas? Don't they pose a threat?" he asked.

"No, that's not possible," answered Lillian Mayer, a sociologist seated somewhere in the middle of the room. "They don't have the means. To do anything to us, the atavists must first organize, and by nature that's beyond their abilities, since they are so competitive."

"But do they have the numbers?" someone else asked.

"Potentially they do," answered Louis. "If they coalesce; but as Doctor Mayer pointed out, by nature they are competitive and not likely to organize. So we allow them to play in Texas, Bolivia, and Nairobi, and a dozen or so other places."

With the class over, Louis felt the weight of his wife's cancer resume in his heart. He took a deep breath.

Louis noticed his teaching fellow, Alex, standing a few feet from the podium, the look on his face a bit sardonic, his blond hair tousled every which way.

"That was a great session, regent," he said. "But I'll never agree with you about our government. I think it's a disgrace. A new oligarchy."

"That's fine, Alex," Louis said as he waved back at some students on their way out. "You can think that. You'll make regent one day, and then you can help reform it."

Alex stood with hands in his pockets. The sardonic smile became more pronounced. "Ha! They'll never let me join their ranks. They don't want me."

"Who are you talking about? Take the first tier exam and then be diligent about your work. You'll get noticed. You are smart."

"Oh, come on, regent," Alex said. "The board of regents handpicks who they want."

"No, Alex, we simply make sure the process is followed correctly. That's our duty. If you have enough votes from first tier social psychologists, you are in. By the way, let's go over this again in front of the class, on Monday."

Alex was about to say something when they both noticed a young, slim, and tall woman dressed in jeans and a sweater coming up the steps to the dais. Louis had noticed her before. She never spoke, but seemed not to miss a word. She came to stand a few feet away from them, hands folded in front.

Louis smiled at her, but she remained unsmiling. Her eyes studied Alex, and then she shifted her gaze to Louis.

"There are going to be many changes, regent. I can help you," she said in a slow and measured tone.

"Well, thank you, Miss..."

"I am Suzanne Martinez."

"I already have a teaching fellow," said Louis as he turned toward Alex.

"No, not like that," she said. "I have a doctorate in philosophy of science. I can help you with your project on space exploration. I am very proficient in physics."

Louis was taken with the young woman, a somewhat plain-looking brunette with a scrubbed face who was perhaps in her late twenties. Her hair was gathered in a ponytail, and she wore no makeup; in fact, Louis guessed she was oblivious to her looks, to the world around her. Throughout the years he occasionally ran across someone like her, somehow lost in a world where they didn't quite fit in. He was about to tell her he had a full staff at the Space Administration, Human Services, and at Columbia, but then something made him stop. Suddenly he felt so bad for her and didn't want to add to a possible long list of rejections in her life.

"Come by my office at the Human Services Administration and make an appointment with my chief of staff."

She nodded, turned around and walked away to join the throng leaving the auditorium.

Alex followed her with his gaze. He shook his head. "That's a weird one," he said. "She didn't even say thank you."

"I'll take an hour or so to talk to her. It'll make her feel good, as though someone listens."

Alex chuckled. "You are a soft touch, regent. Good luck with that. You may end up with more than you bargained for."

The following afternoon Suzanne Martinez was waiting for Louis in the sitting alcove outside his office at HSA. One of his chief of staff's assistants had not only brought her tea, but also cookies, which sat untouched on a side table.

Suzanne, clad in her customary jeans, T-shirt, and heavy boots, looked up at Louis as he approached. He smiled at her. She rose to her feet without saying a word and followed him into his office.

40

Louis sat at his desk in the middle of the well-lit suite. The back wall was solid glassite, and it overlooked the hundredth-floor plaza and its fountain, shrubs, and trees.

She sat on one of the two chairs facing Louis's desk and stared at the floor.

Louis smiled. "Hello, Doctor Martinez, how are you?"

"I am a highly functioning Asperger," she began, still staring down. "Have an IQ of 195. I am awkward socially and don't work well with others. Today, as we speak, there's a 78.58 percent chance that one of the 11,017 scientists working on space exploration will come up with a significant development that will revolutionize our ability to travel to other galaxies. I want to be a part; that's why I joined your class."

"I have well-qualified regents and first tiers working on space exploration—"

"My computational skills are well beyond the human bell curve," she said, her gaze lost in the floor somewhere, "and I possess reasoning abilities computers don't have. I can be very useful. As I mentioned to you twenty-six hours and thirty-three minutes ago, I am highly proficient in several fields of physics. I am currently conducting research in *two* projects in astrophysics..."

And she went on with her well-rehearsed delivery. Her voice was devoid of emotion, but somehow Louis heard a plea, and he realized how much effort it had cost her to be in that chair, facing him, making her case. Louis would not be surprised if she had obtained a position at some university, think tank, or lab, just so she could apply to be in his class.

Suzanne had stopped her delivery and sat motionless and silent, still staring at the floor.

Louis examined his hands, old and worn; and quickly glanced at hers resting on her lap...long, slender, smooth, full of life. "You may be right, Doctor Martinez. I could probably use your skills. Tell you what. Why don't I try you out as a teaching fellow at the university, and if that works out well, we'll work you into a research position with the Space Administration. How's that?"

Suzanne nodded, still staring at the floor.

Louis addressed his office. "Call Joy." In seconds, his chief of staff's holographic image appeared to the left of his desk. "Regent Joy Blass, I am offering Doctor Suzanne Martinez a position at the university as my second teaching fellow." He watched Joy turn to study Suzanne for a moment. "Can you see to it?"

"Sure thing, Regent Sagan."

The real Joy, a swirl of dark brown hair, flashing brown eyes, full figured in a flowing dress, marched into his office and smiled at the young woman. She was followed by one of her assistants, an official-looking man. "Come with me, Doctor Martinez. I'll have Bob here take you to the university, where I am the dean for Research and Development, so we'll be seeing a lot of each other. We'll get your application started, which I'll approve in my capacity as dean."

In the field below the presidential observation tower, the Blue Team took over the Red Team's headquarters. The war exercise was exciting, a lot of give-and-take on both sides, with a final push from the Blue Team led by Colonel Kristol.

General Horace Rumsfeld pulled the binoculars away. "Do we have what it takes to invade the United States? I mean those boys down below are doing fine, but what happens when they face the world government's police androids?"

President Reilly dropped his binoculars and turned around to face Rumsfeld. "Didn't you just watch the exercise? Those boys are good, I tell you."

"Granted, sir…but we only have eighty thousand troops, and they are armed with small weapons—"

"Don't you worry about that, general," replied Reilly. "But maybe if you doubt me, you shouldn't be here. Shouldn't be a Patriot. Maybe you'd be better off moving to New York."

42

The other four lieutenant generals in the observation booth fell very quiet. Then they moved away from Rumsfeld as though he had something contagious.

In her bed in the New York condo, Sharon decided she badly wanted to meditate. She sat up and, using her hands, scooted back on the big bed. She arranged the pillows behind her back and closed her eyes. Her head felt heavy, and she was dizzy for a moment, but she straightened out her back and started her breathing exercises. She was ever so grateful that she could meditate. She knew her mind was going, that she couldn't remember things, but she could still reach that state of bliss. So glad. Oh God, I am so glad I can still do this.

5

Larry walked into the cafeteria, a giant glassite enclosure inside a tropical garden with exotic plants; some could be seen growing right by the tall transparent walls, many with impossibly big leaves and dazzling flowers of all colors. A stream that seemingly came out of nowhere coursed around the outside, and likewise disappeared mysteriously into a wall.

He ordered a coffee and a croissant from the android behind the counter. With coffee and croissant in a tray, Larry looked for a table outside in the courtyard. His favorite place was a corner table by a hibiscus, but it was taken. The department head, Regent Gary Eagan, was using it. He was talking to one of the industrial psychology professors.

Larry noticed Alex and Suzanne, Louis Sagan's teaching fellows, at a table by an opening that looked out into a waterfall. He went over.

"May I join you?" he asked them.

Alex looked up, fork in hand. He had a plate with carrot cake. "Of course, Larry. I hear you may join the ranks of the ruling class soon."

Larry smiled. He actually enjoyed Alex's predictable barbs. He sat facing Suzanne. "Yes, Alex. The first thing I'll do when they make me regent is make all teaching fellows at all universities shave their heads."

Larry caught himself, but it was too late. He noticed the look of alarm in Suzanne's eyes. "It's a joke, Suzanne," he whispered in her direction. In the month or so she'd been a teaching fellow, he had already unnerved her at least once before.

"I do the same, Larry," Alex said soothingly. "Suzanne is good at putting up with me." Alex theorized whether it would be possible to teach Suzanne how to tell sarcasm and humor from serious statements.

Larry noticed the strange young woman kept staring at him, and he reminded himself that it was normal for her. "She's just fine the way she is." At this, he thought he saw a soft look come over her eyes.

"Doctor Zimmerman!" Larry heard Eagan say, just as Suzanne was about to speak. He'd never quite cared for Eagan; maybe it was his effusive manner that did not quite seem sincere, or his overfamiliar style that was far from appropriate.

"You are taking your first tier exam, I hear," Eagan said as he pulled up a chair in between Larry and Alex and plopped his solid frame down. His professor friend stood in awkward silence behind him. "I took mine some five years ago. Listen, now the fun begins: perform, perform, and perform! You have to show results and be noticed to get the votes and become one of us...a regent! Ha-ha. I bet that's what you dreamt about since you were a little kid, eh? It's like being God, ha-ha. Rule the world. What are you going to do, get a job in some obscure corner of the world so you can make a big splash and be voted regent? Ha-ha.

"So how are you doing, Doctor Zimmerman? Or should I call you 'Doctor Cyborg?' Ha-ha. How's the atavist work, doctor? Have you finished that predictive algorithm?"

Larry was taken aback. That wasn't exactly public knowledge. Now the department head was simply overstepping his boundaries. "Everything is coming along, Regent Eagan."

"When will you be done, eh? That's the question. Or are you too damn busy trying to become a first tier, eh? I bet you already have a house in mind, and a luxury car. Ha-ha. Yeah, all the goodies that will be within your reach, eh?"

"Ah…Well, you know…"

"Speak up, Doctor Cyborg, speak up. What's going on? Bring us up to date."

Larry looked down at the marbleized tabletop and followed the random pattern with his eyes. "I report to Regent-Dean Joy Blass on all matters pertaining to the atavist population project, so If you want information, you'll have to get it from her." He turned his gaze to Alex and Suzanne. "Alex, Suzanne, and I are talking about some private matters, Regent Eagan, if you don't mind."

Eagan looked surprised, and perhaps hurt, but left without saying another word and walked briskly toward the exit, ignoring the professor who trailed behind.

Alex watched him go. "I sure don't care for that man."

"I don't, either. Fortunately we all work for Joy, so there's no need to worry about offending Eagan."

They spent a few more minutes talking. By now Larry was used to Suzanne's style. She spoke very little but seemed to enjoy others' conversation. Presently she was trying to say something, for she had put her cup down and was staring at the ground.

"I want to go to the presentation next week," she blurted out.

"What presentation is that?" Larry asked as he leaned back in his chair and relaxed now that Eagan was gone.

"The one at the Space Administration," interjected Alex. "It's all she can talk about."

"Oh yes, of course!" Larry suddenly remembered the event. "You are qualified, Suzanne, no problem. I'll talk to Joy and make sure you get in. You can sit at our table with Regent Sagan. I'm not a first tier yet, but I'll be there as staff support." He stood up to leave and took in Alex's surprised look.

"But she's not a first tier!" Alex exclaimed.

Larry turned to look at Suzanne, who appeared oblivious, sipping her tea. "Actually she is in two fields, astrophysics and biophysics. Joy gave me the news when she requested her curriculum vitae."

"You are kidding! Why didn't she tell us she's already a first tier...twice!"

Larry smiled at Suzanne, still holding her cup. "Maybe she didn't want to explain what she was doing in that class." Suzanne seemed to smile back at him.

Alex stared at her, surprise all over his face. "What are you doing in that class, Suzanne?"

"A handful of first tiers take Regent Sagan's class, Alex," Larry said. "It's like no other first tier prep class. If you really want to become a regent, there's nothing like it. And because it attracts the best, you get to meet some amazing people. Besides, once Regent Sagan takes you under his wing, you are guaranteed he'll mentor you for years to come." He picked up his tray. "Wish me luck. I'm up to here with the exam," he said.

"Well, I guess I'll be doing the same this summer. Sagan talked me into it the other day," Alex said with a rueful smile while stealing glances at Suzanne, who seemed to be in another world somewhere.

On Tuesday, having prepared for the following day's class, Louis, wearing a temperature-regulating gray jacket against the chill air, rode an autowalker that propelled him along a busy street to his offices at the Human Services Administration. He felt his strides amplified by the two platforms attached to the soles of his shoes. For a moment he was mesmerized by the smooth gait. What should he do? What would he do with the emptiness? And the grief. Why go through it? Why not simply walk together into a termination center when she was still lucid, lie down in a bed together, and...let go? Maybe. Maybe that was good. Maybe he should plan accordingly, and see what happened.

In that case, and it made sense to keep a possible termination date in mind, time was running out. She only had another couple of months of lucidity left. He would have to present his proposal for the atavist project...and get it reviewed, make the appropriate revisions, and then finalize it. He had just finished three peer reviews and had one in the works. That was enough. He would have to tell Joy not to accept any more projects.

A woman coming his way smiled at him, and he smiled back. How he wished Sharon was like her: strong, vibrant...healthy.

That very morning he'd found her reading in bed with tears in her eyes. She turned from the document and said, "I don't understand a word in this paper." Louis came over and took a look. It was a proposal for an intervention for children who scored below sixty on the IQ test. It was all exciting and simple; something the old Sharon would have gone through in a minute.

No question, she was degenerating daily. Her friends, who used to visit often, were now dwindling, uncomfortable with the new Sharon, he figured. Even Kathleen, a childhood friend, now kept her distance. That was sad.

He was still half-lost in thought as he walked into the Human Services Administration building. He meandered his way through the long hallways to his private office and heard a woman's voice call his name. He turned to find Joy studying him, standing some twenty feet away facing someone he didn't recognize. On closer scrutiny he saw it wasn't the real Joy, but her holographic self.

"Where do you think you are going, Regent Sagan?" The fiery woman stood, arms folded across her ample bosom, while the person she had been talking with took a few respectful steps back.

Louis chuckled. Joy was always good at snapping him out of whatever ailed him. "To my office, if that's okay with you, Joy."

"No, it's not okay when I make a very important appointment for you, and you forget about it."

It took Louis a moment to remember. "Oh, shoot. Yes, that astrophysicist. Oh, Joy, you know, I meant to tell you I can't take any more projects."

"I'm sure at some point in time you'll tell me why. In the meantime, get your butt over here to the Space Administration's conference room, in your real self. No holographic cheating for you.

A whole roomful of extremely influential people are waiting to see your pretty face. Including me! Now get!"

Of course, she was right; there was no way he could not go. Louis rushed to his office, grabbed his coat on the fly, and boarded his car docked by the window.

Louis gave instructions as he sat down and was strapped in. The car took off and rose above the skyline, and he tried to think how to get out of the project, which enough people thought warranted a presentation to senior government officials.

There were some two thousand people waiting for him in the well-appointed meeting room of the World Government Space Administration. Louis stood on the autowalker that took him down the side of the big room to the front. Unlike his university lecture hall, which was designed for function, this place was meant to impress: a study of light, glassite, and techno-decor, full of subtle sounds, scents, and soft lighting meant to please the senses, punctuated by dramatic accents for design interest. A live shot from a space telescope currently viewing an exploding star was shown on the curved ceiling. Everyone sat in plush burgundy seats with retractable desktops, in concentric semicircles facing a U-shaped table, where Louis and ten others were slated to sit. Quite a few in the room appeared exasperated and gave him annoyed glances as he went past them, but others were engaged in scientific talk and smiled when they saw him. When he approached the main table, everyone came to life, straightened, and reached for their notepads.

Louis took the seat with his name on a holographic display, floating ghostlike where his torso would be. He sat down and the display moved in front of his eyes. It told him Joy sat to his right. The others around the main table were familiar names in space exploration, energy dynamics, astrophysics, quantum physics, and government. A young, tense-looking man faced them, reviewing his notes. This was to be the key presentation, the chief scientist of the project trying to get early buy-in from the big kahunas—regents and influential first tiers. To get to this stage, Louis knew the project already had the backing of many prominent names. He wondered who they were.

An android brought him a cup of coffee. The room fell silent as the young scientist rose and cleared his throat.

"Good afternoon, esteemed regents and first tiers. It's an honor to be here before you. My name is Alphonse D'Anjou. I'm an astrophysicist, and I have come up with a process that will open up outer space." The man came across as nervous, with a nasal voice that could belong to many an old aunt. Doctor D'Anjou went on to explain the current impasse in space exploration for the benefit of news media and the public watching the live broadcast. As he went on, he seemed to relax, his voice still old-auntish and nasal but more confident. He described the insurmountable distances involved in the known universe, the area forty-one billion light-years around Earth; he then zeroed in on Tolima, the planet five hundred light-years away that had characteristics similar to those of Earth. "Can we finally find out if Tolima is another Earth? We know there must be life, but are there humanoids like us? We have tried to access the planet for years, but found it impossible with our current technology.

"I have found a way."

People murmured excitedly.

"Starting in the late twentieth century, experiments with supercolliders showed that when protons were smashed together, some of the resulting 'debris' disappeared, meaning it went into a different dimension, a different 'reality,' or universe. As a result, we discovered we are one of many universes, part of a multiverse. For many years physicists speculated what these dimensions were like. Today we know that, put very simply, these are dimensions where different laws of physics apply. Using the Devries Accelerator, we have been able to detect some of them and deduce their properties, but up until now we have not been able to enter one in a controlled and deliberate way."

D'Anjou walked a few paces back and forth, apparently trying to clear his thoughts. "Travel, if you can call it travel, within one of these dimensions is so different, one could cover a million light-years of our universe in six weeks. You would have to enter another dimension, travel where you want to go, and then exit to our own dimension. The question has always been how to enter and exit the various dimensions successfully. I have found a way, using teleportation."

Louis felt increasingly uncomfortable, and judging by the shifting of bodies in chairs and clearing of throats around him, others felt the same way. There had been so many projects on teleportation in the past, and every single one had flopped. The process often destroyed the subject, be it an apple or a poor mouse, and left a small pile of carbon behind. The most successful ones ended up with something either resembling an apple, or the lifeless form of a mouse, sometimes horribly misshapen from having its molecules scrambled.

"My method is very different from what has been used up to now." D'Anjou quickly interjected. "In the past, teleportation involved the destruction and the reconstruction of a subject, but what I'm about to show you is different." He went on in his oddly undulating cadence. "There's no destruction, and no reconstruction, although it still appears that way, and I have no other way to describe the process other than calling it teleportation." He reached for the floor beside his desk and came up with a cage with a mouse, a rather large white mouse that moved nervously, whiskers aiming every which way.

D'Anjou walked to the far right wall of the room, toward a large cube-like glassite device with an opening to one side large enough to fit a man. He pointed to another device, much the same, at the opposite side of the room. He placed the mouse, cage and all, on the cube's floor. He pulled out a biospectometer, aimed it at the mouse, and the mouse genome appeared on everyone's virtual screens. D'Anjou pushed a button, a door slid close, and the cage and the mouse appeared on the device across the room. D'Anjou quickly walked the twenty or so paces over, aimed the biospectometer at the mouse, and the same genome data appeared on the screens. The mouse walked around just as nervously as before, his whiskers going every which way as before.

After a brief moment of total silence, as people absorbed what had happened, the room broke into enthusiastic applause. Louis shook his head in wonder. The man had succeeded where so many others had failed in the past hundred years. No question, the mouse had entered and exited some other dimension; otherwise it would be one fried rodent.

"In this case," D'Anjou intoned, "the distance covered in an infinitesimal fraction of a nanosecond was seventeen meters. Five hundred light-years would have taken approximately thirty minutes. In this dimension, identified as Kali 4, there are no distances as we know them. Outer space travel," he said with obvious pride, "has just become a possibility. Tolima is now within our reach."

Louis sat shaking his head. Just a few months ago, he would have found the demonstration probably the most exciting one of his life. Now, he just wanted to beg off from something that would demand tremendous work. He noticed D'Anjou's stare, and a silence descended in the room.

Louis realized they were waiting for his verdict.

He smiled. "Congratulations, Doctor D'Anjou. That's the most exciting advancement in your field I have seen in a long time." Louis heard his own voice—flat, noncommittal.

Applause rang through the room. "A project meant for you, Louis," he heard someone say.

His display exploded with positive comments.

"No, no, no," he managed to say.

To his right Louis noticed Joy staring at him. He turned to meet a surprised look on her face, her eyebrows arched, big brown eyes trying to read his face.

Louis stood up. It was all exhilarating, no question; that is, for someone whose wife wasn't dying. "I am truly impressed by what we just witnessed, but if you"—Louis's gaze panned the room—"are thinking of me to lead this project, I must beg off."

The conference room became silent. The virtual screen in Louis's seat scrolled with thousands of inquiries from across the world, from the regents and first tiers that were qualified to participate. After a few seconds, the screen displayed the summary, one word: *Why?*

Joy pulled on his sleeve and whispered "Dammit, Louis, what's wrong with you?"

"I...am very flattered everyone seems to think that I am the only regent left in the world." Laughter rang through the room, then silence, but a lighter silence. "There are over twenty regents with my qualifications." The screen came alive with new comments.

"So there's no need for me to get involved. Thank you for a tremendously engrossing and exciting demonstration, Doctor D'Anjou." With this Louis turned to walk away, but Joy would not let go of his sleeve.

"Just tell us why, Louis," Joy said in a crisp voice. "You owe us as much."

Louis smiled at her, studying her intense expression. "Joy...I will no longer be taking on any additional projects. I will finish the atavist project and retire for good, be done...It's personal, very personal...let's leave it at that, okay?"

She let go of his sleeve, her piercing stare following his every move, lips pursed. Louis knew it wasn't over; in her mind the fight had just begun. He stepped on the autowalker by his chair and climbed the interminable distance toward the back of the room amid the thousands of probing eyes. Joy would recruit many of his protégés and colleagues, and the barrage would begin...very soon. And they would be cheered on and backed by millions of concerned citizens, including D'Anjou, without a doubt. Well, let them try.

He would just shut off his phone everywhere: car, house, office, his clothes.

Louis made it out of the conference room, along the long hallway, then out of the building and stood on the sidewalk expecting the throng to follow him out. He tapped his breast pocket to activate his phone and summon his car.

His car came down and landed by the sidewalk. He got in and was immensely relieved when he felt the door close behind him. "Drive around, somewhere pretty, and turn off all incoming communications." He sat and stared out the window as the car took off. The car crossed Long Island and followed the coast to the north.

Louis felt himself relax. He took off his jacket and tossed it on the seat beside him. It was difficult to disappoint people, but he wondered why they wanted him so badly.

Louis tapped the car's window, and it became a computer display. He looked up the project using D'Anjou's name. The stats showed Regent Sagan way at the top, above all other contenders. His peers were still voting him in.

Louis read the comments and rationale people had used for picking him...and what stood out above scientific know-how and experience was common sense. Oh, and many had singled out genius. But then were the comments that offered more detail and described his history managing high-profile projects, and the "hundreds of projects where Louis has played a pivotal role." "To reach Tolima we need Louis," read a comment that had a lot of approval. Obviously he was well known. He had no idea he was thought of so highly; sure, he had some successful projects in his life, but...yes, that was pleasant to hear...he had done well, better than he thought.

But he still was not going to take the darn project.

He wanted to relax, take his mind off everything: Joy, Sharon, the hubbub that expected him the moment he returned to any of his offices. He tapped the display again to look up the writer's diary and produce a virtual-paper copy. He read for some time and noticed the computer display had disappeared from the window. The car kept flying north along the coast and Louis decided to read more about what happened when President Obama left the presidency. After a pleasant two hours of reading, the lights inside the car blinked, and a female voice announced, "You are home, Regent Sagan."

Louis looked out the window. They had docked at his New York condo. He looked at his watch. The car had decided to turn around at some point to arrive at home in time for dinner.

"Who programmed you?" he asked in wonder, staring at the car's display as though trying to see beyond it into the machine's inner works.

"I'm self-programmable, regent," the pleasant voice answered.

Louis stood and tried to remember whether he had ever noticed the car making a choice for him in the past. "Have you made decisions like this before?"

"Yes, regent. In the thirty-one years, three months, and six days I've been at your service, I have exercised my own initiative 162 times."

Over a hundred times? he wondered in amazement. "Well, I'm glad to be home…thank you." With that, he walked out of the car and into his living room.

6

"Did you get rid of Rumsfeld?" Reilly didn't bother looking up from his desk as Eagan walked in and stood at attention.

"Yes, sir," responded Eagan, stealing glances at the nervous couple sitting on the couch to one side. They looked like upper-class country-club types. The woman was very pretty, and the man tall and handsome. They were both pale. The man kept his gaze on the floor.

Reilly continued reading a virtual magazine. "Good. Notify his family he died in the service of the Cause." Then he looked sideways at the couple. "Elizabeth, meet another one of my loyal generals. He's one of your precious regents…isn't that grand?"

Eagan nodded at the woman, who in turn gave him a painful smile. He stood waiting to be dismissed.

Reilly turned to look at Eagan. "About Rumsfeld. I don't want this to happen again. I don't like surprises. I want to know what people are talking about, even what they are thinking. Rumsfeld began to doubt me and that's dangerous."

Eagan turned to leave.

"I'm not done yet."

"Sir?"

Reilly held up the magazine he was reading. "Look what they are saying about Sagan, will you?" And before Eagan could answer.

"I told you to keep an eye on him. That's why I got you that job at Columbia University and why I made you a regent. Remember that."

"Yes, sir."

"See that, Elizabeth?" Reilly said while looking at his magazine. "Now you know how powerful and smart your regents are, eh? Ha-ha. This one is at my beck and call. I can make and break regents at will…and I can do anything I want with you and your so-called husband. I'm wondering what I should do with the two of you. Good question. I just hate people who betray me."

Reilly gazed at the magazine for the longest time. Then he looked up at Eagan. "I know for a fact Sagan is a phony. Real dumb, too. He doesn't know anything about astrophysics. Soon we'll need to take care of him. You hear?"

Reilly dismissed Eagan, then turned toward the petrified couple and smiled.

The setting sun was somewhere behind the building across the street, streaking the little bit of sky Larry could see from his window when he looked straight up. He wished he had a top floor condo. Maybe when I make regent, he thought.

He told the house to switch the window off, and watched the glassite turn dark. He turned around to make his way to the kitchen-dining room, where his android had left a tray with two dinners.

Gingerly, so as not to wake her up, he walked into his bedroom. Larry paused in the doorway, tray in hand. Suzanne still slept and had hugged his pillow, her slim bare arms intertwined around it, her hair over her face. At the sight, Larry felt a sweet feeling in his heart and was surprised by his reaction. Was he falling in love? Was this how it felt? Carefully he placed the tray on the nightstand in front of the clock that read 6:10 p.m. He sat on the bed and softly lifted her hair so he could look at her. Her face, without the usual furtive looks and tension, was beautiful…flawless skin…thin, well-defined eyebrows…elegant nose…gracious lips. He fingered her hair, soft and silky and ran the back of his hand along her cheek. At this, she opened her eyes, smiled, moaned, turned on her back, and stretched. A breast came from under the covers, milky white, and he gently kissed it.

She reached her arms up and pulled him down. Their mouths met…her breath, warm, tasted somewhat stale, but he liked it…it was her taste. She surprised him; in fact she constantly surprised him. When he had first met her he had been curious about her. Her ability to process and retain information was not like his, but rather an instant understanding of the overall picture, where things belonged, their function.

Now all he wanted was to make sure she was always fine, that no one ever took advantage of her. She seemed to go along with it and accepted his friendship and protectiveness as natural. He had moved a small desk into his office so they could work together, and she thought that was also natural, didn't say a word. But there was the occasional way she looked at him, and it made him feel…good. Then a week ago she asked him to hold her. They had been talking in his living room, and her eyes became moist, as though something hurt. He put his arms around her, but she said, "No, not here. Let's lie on your bed." And she stood, grabbed his hand, and took him to the bed. She dragged him down to lie behind her. He hugged her. At first, Larry was mesmerized by her smell, like wild grass. Then it was more…it was how she felt next to his body. It was like holding…something precious, ethereal…from another world, a kinder, softer world. Larry wasn't sure whether he dozed off or not, but he ended up lying there with her for maybe an hour or longer, and for the first time that he was aware of his mind had been still.

For the next few days she didn't want to be touched, but that afternoon in their office she suddenly stood up, came up to his desk and said: "I want us to make love."

Now, as he looked at her, Larry realized he would want to be with her, even if sometimes she didn't want to be touched, and sometimes didn't want to talk and was silent for long periods of time…because overall he had never felt like this before…totally and utterly enchanted.

"Are you hungry?" he asked.

"No."

"Thirsty?"

"No."

"Do you want to make love?"

"Yes."

Louis braced himself as his car docked at the Human Services Administration. He decided to arrive at the VIP entrance, rather than his private offices. He was sure Joy was lying in wait with some ploy to get him to take on the space exploration project. Coming through the visitors' entrance would perhaps give him the element of surprise; at any rate he was sure stepping out of his car into his office would be tantamount to walking willingly into whatever trap she had devised. Surely by now she had come up with something clever.

Yogi, who had decided to come with him, went up to the car's door. He seemed to enjoy watching it slide open.

The departmental offices looked calm. A few staff ambled quietly about. In the lounge to one side, a few visitors waited for whomever they'd come to see. The usual plants in every corner, the almost imperceptible hum of computers, soft artificial sunlight emanating from the ceiling and walls, voices on phones. Music, faintly audible, could be heard from someone's office. Percy, the department director, came out of his office en route somewhere and gave him a passing glance and a quick hello. The slim, elegant middle-aged dark-skinned man walked on down the hall in front of Louis, a bit self-conscious, his steps quickening as though he were trying to get away, leaving a faint scent of cologne in his wake.

Louis, with Yogi trailing behind and sniffing everything in his path, made it all the way into his office without incident. No sign of Joy so far. He sat down at his desk, and the virtual computer display came alive in front of his eyes. He waved it aside with his hand, and it went to stand on the far right corner of his desk. Yogi had settled, as usual, under his desk and proceeded to get ready for a nap, grooming and grunting. Louis crouched down to pet his head and wondered how many years the dog had left; he was old, around fifteen or so, and his arthritis was getting worse. Louis wondered who would take care of him should he decide to terminate along with Sharon.

Louis turned his chair to face the window behind him. Visitors and staff ambled three stories below. A robotized mower went around the large lawn in concentric circles.

That previous evening Sharon had enjoyed one of her more lucid periods in a long time. She had called Kathleen and her husband, Juan, to come over, and they had sat down to one of Sharon's famous meals, hand cooked, everything naturally grown. "Veggies with their vitality intact," as she liked to say. They had some fabulous mushrooms in a creamy sauce with raw sliced carrots and vichyssoise accompanied by stuffed pastries. The dinner conversation had been about space exploration—"what everyone in the media is talking about," as Kathleen noted. Louis tried to divert the conversation, but they kept talking about it, shooting significant glances in his direction. Louis just nodded and smiled and ate his dinner. "How exciting it will be to find other beings in the universe," Juan said, apparently addressing them all, "and how probable it is that they could be very humanlike, since Tolima appears to replicate Earth in every detail." Louis took a sip of wine and smiled. Thank goodness Kathleen had decided the soup was delicious and asked how it was made, and where Sharon got the fresh leeks.

The phone rang, bringing Louis back to the present. It was time to tackle the latest problem in his life…that damn space exploration project. Tolima indeed. Louis turned around to face his computer display. It was Joy requesting a face-to-face.

"Come on in, Joy," he said in a resigned voice, and her virtual image showed up in front of his desk, sitting in her chair. "Louis, good morning," she said in a sweet voice, her face beaming.

"Good morning, Joy," he said, mentally bracing himself for the onslaught.

"We've been waiting for you for the past two days. Nice of you to show up." She twirled her chair back and forth with her feet, as if dancing.

"I needed a couple of days to rest and think things through."

"Well, you need not worry. I decided to recommend Regent Angela Hall as project director, and Doctor D'Anjou as well as peer review approved. You are off the hook."

Could it be real? Or was this part of her ploy? "That's terrific. That should make Regent Hall famous."

"Yes! She's a wonderful scientist. I've hardly been able to sleep since I made the decision. Angela was just thrilled." She stopped twirling in her chair, bit her lower lip, and her gaze turned intense. "But Louis, I need your help. Please, please, tell me you'll help her if the need arises."

"Of course, Joy. You need not ask; it's a given." She seemed sincere, and Louis was so relieved he wanted to hug her holographic image. "We need to celebrate. How about meeting for lunch?"

"I was just going to suggest that. Say, at one, at the trattoria by the plaza? We'll sit outside, so you can bring Yogi along," she said as she looked down at one black and beige paw sticking out from beneath the desk. "Oh, and I'll bring Regent Angela Hall and Doctor D'Anjou, if you don't mind."

In her office, Joy continued happily twirling her chair, this time feeling truly elated. It had all gone so well! She should try an acting career.

"Call Angela Hall," she told her office. Almost instantaneously, as though she had done nothing but wait for her call for the past two days, Angie's figure appeared in front of her desk.

"He agreed, Angie!" Joy exclaimed.

"Oh, Joy, thank you, thank you, thank you. Your plan worked. I'll call Doctor D'Anjou so we can get started right away." Joy noticed the relief that washed over Angie's face.

"Well, not so fast. We'll be having lunch with Louis at one. Let's see how far we can take him on this. Remember that peer review agreed, on the condition he comes on at least half-time. If he pulls back and wants to be in an advisory capacity, it's a no-go."

Angie nodded nervously. "We need him on board. We need him to get excited."

"I know, I know. You don't have to convince me. Relax, I know Louis better than even his wife. I know what will get him to commit. I have a feeling about this project." Joy studied Angie for a moment. "Don't be nervous. And try and act natural. I know he can be intimidating, so let me lead the conversation. See you at the trattoria, same one where we had dinner last."

The car left Louis in front of the restaurant. As he stepped onto the sidewalk and his car took off, he could see Joy sitting at a table by a terrace and in animated discussion with a human waiter. Probably haranguing the poor man about their bread or the wine, he thought, as he made his way through the swarm of pedestrians who, with the sun shining in anticipation of an early spring, were shaking off the last vestiges of winter, walking and chatting, coats optimistically swung over shoulders.

Joy smiled broadly at him. Regent Hall and Doctor D'Anjou stood up to shake his hand.

"And Yogi?" inquired Joy.

"Left him in the car," Louis said after he shook Hall's and D'Anjou's hands and sat down. "He's getting on in years, may need to pee often. The car will let him off at some park if the need arises."

Joy snickered. "They should build a special facility in their bathroom just for him; after all, Yogi is almost human." She turned to Hall and D'Anjou. "You should meet him. All he needs are thumbs and he would be a real menace." Then back to Louis. "How are his hips?"

"Oh, he's old. Just like his owner. What can you do?"

During lunch, Louis became more familiar with D'Anjou and Hall, although he faintly remembered her from his class...and he had helped her with something not too long ago. D'Anjou ate his lasagna somewhat absentmindedly, and Louis guessed he did that a lot, his mind on an experiment while he went about life. He appeared to be a quiet man in his mid-thirties, tall and lanky with brown hair, a wunderkind judging by his achievements, which Joy and Angela seemed to know all about. His voice and his manners suggested he was raised by a stern woman, one who taught him to eat carefully, mind his manners, and be very neat about his appearance. His voice and manner of speaking were female-like without necessarily being feminine. It was that odd intonation, an undulating quality that made it so. Angela, he noted, was a beautiful woman, perhaps too beautiful: all red hair, perfect figure, classic face and green eyes; and that was perhaps the reason why she tried so hard to compensate with highly technical comments to show off her expertise. But Louis knew she was good; he had read some of her articles on space exploration. And he had heard some of her talks on the atavists. She was a good bi-field scientist.

"I want to thank you, Regent Sagan," D'Anjou said as he put down his fork after Angela broached the subject of their project. "Your input will be invaluable. I have followed your career in space exploration since I was a child. This is quite an honor to work with you."

Louis picked through his salad. "Well, thank you, Alphonse. But let's be clear, I will be in an advisory capacity only, which translates into an hour or so a week. We can meet for lunch once a week, if you want, to review whatever comes up."

"Wonderful! Thank you, Louis," Joy interjected just as D'Anjou had started to stammer something. "Yes, I think lunch together once a week would be enjoyable." She turned her gaze toward the plaza with its meticulous small patches of lawn, walking paths, and benches. "I love this place. But say, do you have time to go to Alphonse's lab? We would like to present all the particulars."

An android waiter went by with a tray that held an appetizing-looking serving of pasta topped with artichoke hearts, and Louis wished he had ordered that instead of his salad. "No, not this afternoon," Louis said, thinking of the atavist project. He felt energetic and could make a lot of headway in a couple of hours at his HSA office. "How about tomorrow afternoon?"

"Great." Joy took a bite of her calzone and gave D'Anjou and Angela a meaningful glance. "Let's ride together. Angela and I can meet you at your university office at, say, two?"

"Yes, that would be fine," Louis said and noticed how Joy seemed to be making decisions for D'Anjou. The poor kid had already deferred all control to her without knowing how it happened.

"Wonderful," she said, putting down her wineglass. She studied Louis's eyes. He looked at ease. "Would you like to read the executive summary beforehand?" At this, his eyebrows tensed up.

"Yes, maybe I can read it in the morning," he said while taking stock of how much effort he wanted to spend on D'Anjou's project. He would have to read the thing so as not to sound foolish in the afternoon. But then, he would make sure Joy and Angela understood an hour a week is all he would give. Joy was stubborn, and he knew her well, but he had stopped her many times before. This time it would be no different.

7

That evening when he got home, Louis walked into a quiet condo and the usual pristine tidiness: the carefully arranged dark blue furniture, antique tables, and the ample expanse of white carpet. No human to leave cups or books around, disturb the pillows on the couch. He had hoped for signs Kathleen had visited, or that Sharon had at least made it downstairs.

"Is Sharon awake?" he asked the house.

"Your wife is sleeping. She had a turbulent morning, and we decided a sedative was in order."

"Has anyone come to see her?"

"Not since Drs. Kathleen Evers and Juan Milton were here for dinner."

Louis climbed the stairs to the second floor master bedroom, forgoing the autowalker.

Sharon rested peacefully in bed in her favorite fluffy blue pajamas; face-up, the covers up to her chest, her arms resting on either side of her. Oscar lay on top of the dresser next to the bed, examining Louis through half-closed eyelids.

Louis sat on the bed by her side and reached a hand to stroke her arm. The androids were doing well monitoring her, taking care of her every need, linking up with Medical Central whenever necessary, such as with the sedation. But still, she needed the human touch, and he wasn't with her most of the time. His own work was all consuming.

But what was more important, some project someone else could do, or Sharon? Louis took a deep breath and exhaled slowly. The ample bedroom of heavy blue velvet drapes, white carpet, two antique chairs against the wall, chest of drawers with her carefully arranged knickknacks...the intricately carved headboard...all were spotless...hospital clean...impersonal. He had to spend more time with her, a lot more time. These were, after all, the last months of their life together; how stupid to waste them working while Sharon withered away, cared for by machines.

How much could he let go of right away? His class, for sure. Joy could take over at a moment's notice. Well, there was no question the space exploration project would have to go; he'd never started, so there shouldn't be any problem. That left the atavist project.

Louis leaned forward and kissed Sharon's forehead. For the past week or so, she had been fully aware only once that he knew about. He stood up and tiptoed out of the bedroom and made his way to their study, the room next door. Her desk was tidy. His, on the opposite wall, separated by a window overlooking a patio with a Japanese rock garden, had virtual documents and his notes spread around, and Yogi's chew toy in one corner. He pulled out his chair and sat down. The display came alive, and the virtual keyboard appeared before him. He quickly typed a memo to his class with a carbon copy to the department chair, and Joy. "Starting as of this moment I will no longer be teaching the First Tier Preparatory Class, recommend Regent Joy Blass as replacement." The memo went out to all 3,217 registered students. Next, a memo to Angela, Joy, and D'Anjou canceling the next day's meeting and also announcing he would not be involved in any capacity in the space exploration project. The third memo went to Joy alone, telling her that from that moment on he would be working from home.

Louis shut down all communication inputs to the house and went back to his wife's bed. He shed his clothes and got under the covers, gingerly snuggled up to her, and wrapped one leg and an arm around her. She swallowed, opened her lips as though to speak, but then only smiled and continued sleeping. Louis smelled her hair and the nape of her neck, warm and cozy. She smelled wonderful, just like Sharon.

At eight the next morning, after breakfast and a walk with Yogi, Louis opened his display and was told there were over 100,000 urgent messages from individuals who had direct access to him. He read the analysis and summary: all of his students were complaining bitterly. Over a thousand had waited three years on the waiting list to get into his class. Apparently no other first-tier prep class would do. Another 506 had waited five years. Joy was clamoring for a talk. Most of the other messages were from peer review asking his reasons for what they termed as a radical withdrawal. The computer indicated that, all told, 2,011 regents and 52,105 first tiers were querying him. Surely that was the whole regent and first tier populations!

Louis sat back in his chair, suddenly aware of his aching neck and back. He had no idea people would react this way, no idea they thought he was so indispensable. But that was patently silly; there were many regents who could do his job. No one was indispensable. No one. That was the whole point of the system. Why did they think of him in such singular terms?

Maybe they were just being thoughtful, a way of telling him how much they appreciated his work over the years, and now that he was withdrawing this was their way of showing their appreciation. That must be it.

The calls to reach him kept up, but Louis ignored them. It was hard to ignore Joy, but he knew what she wanted, and decided not to answer.

Louis settled to finish the atavist project. A few days passed, and he fell into a routine. He would wake up, have breakfast and spend some time reading aloud to Sharon, sometimes reminiscing about their lives, the people they had known, places they had gone together, like the cruise they enjoyed five years before, when they had gone to the Mediterranean. It was then time to walk Yogi, albeit shorter than their old walks, and without any climbing. After the walks, Louis would make his way to the study. Almost invariably Yogi would bark, and an android would come over. Louis would stand on the landing to watch him, grateful he didn't have to carry the eighty-plus-pound dog. The android would carry the dog upstairs, where he would settle under Louis's desk. After working for a few hours, it was back to seeing Sharon and walking Yogi.

One evening after a long day, Louis went into Sharon's bedroom to check on her and read aloud an article from the magazine of the ashram in Los Angeles she enjoyed visiting for retreats.

Louis sat by her side, read aloud from the magazine for a moment, and realized how futile it all was; she would never talk again; his voice could not reach her anymore. He rested his head in his hands and felt sobs welling up inside, and tears flowed freely down his cheeks as never before in his adult life. The grief, the pain, was beyond anything he'd ever imagined.

After a short while, he began to feel Sharon's presence, as though she were talking to him. He felt her being, so close, as close as she had ever been, and he realized she was somehow able to reach out to him and console him. Mystified, but feeling much relief, he turned to look at her. She was still unconscious. He remained looking at her for a long time.

The following day, at the crack of dawn, two masked humans broke the front door of an apartment in Paris. The surprised occupants, a couple in their twenties, rushed from their bedroom to investigate. The masked men searched the small apartment for the two house androids and, after finding them on sleep mode, drilled into their brains, neutralizing them. The surprised man and woman followed the intruders, at first too shocked to say anything, but then the young man asked, "Who are you, and why are you doing this?" By way of response, the masked men knocked them both to the floor and handcuffed them hands to feet. Then they proceeded to ransack the place. Once they found a box containing the woman's jewelry, they left.

Twelve hours later, while Louis sat at his desk, he received an urgent text message from Police Services advising him they had detected a concerted effort from atavists, and they had branded it as terrorism. The message, labeled top secret, had been sent to the 337 regents in the atavist project. Louis was alarmed. Police Services had not used the term *terrorism* during his lifetime. Anxiously he read the summary.

In the past twenty-four hours, there had been over four hundred cases of criminal activity in all continents by "unknowns," which was used to designate those who had removed their biochips and whose biometrics produced no trace because they lived in an outlying country, such as Texas. The crimes were robbery of jewelry, sexual assault, and other violence against individuals, some resulting in serious injury. The perpetrators had managed to disable or neutralize house and car androids. House and car computers reported the incidents, but by the time police androids arrived, it was too late. Fortunately those computers' brains were so well protected that disabling them would require destroying an entire house or car.

Louis leaned back in his chair, but he felt the tension throughout his body like a taut wire. There was no way to tell how the public would react to the unprecedented acts of violence.

Louis watched his display. In a matter of minutes, there were calls to remove all atavists and incarcerate them. Fortunately Police Services had responded effectively. Police androids, armed with stun guns, were dispatched en masse to guard public places, and deployed to stand along housing centers. Police asked the public to keep communication channels open in houses and cars at all times and to maintain house androids on standby to make them hard to disable.

In case of attack, an armed police android would be at any given locale literally within seconds. The announcement was followed shortly with another announcement that the regents were taking the necessary steps to neutralize the atavist situation.

Louis turned on his communication system and told the house to place androids on standby. He looked at the display. The calls to remove the atavists were now several million…then hundreds of millions…one billion…then three…four. Louis held his breath for a moment; at that rate they could reach a public mandate. Someone somewhere had decided to make sure the atavists all over the world were sequestered. That was the only possible answer, and the only person with such an agenda that Louis could think of was Regent Gary Eagan.

Louis contacted Joy, who called back in a matter of seconds. Joy looked out of sorts. Her tired eyes darted about, and she kept running a nervous hand through her hair.

"Am I glad to see you, Louis!"

"Police Services seems to have everything under control." Louis tried to sound reassuring. "Is there anything else?"

"Well, the terrorism is bad enough, don't you think? If the public gives us a mandate to sequester all atavists, where are we going to put them? Bring them all to Texas, from all over the world?"

Louis tried to sound confident. "There won't be a mandate. We'll manage the crisis. Do you know who's behind it?"

"I don't. I just heard about it. Regent Gary Eagan was informed as well, and he's very upset. Keeps telling me he told us this would happen. Quite a few of the regents in the atavist project are saying the same thing; that we were warned by Eagan, but no one is of any help. They are just panicking. We need you, Louis," Joy said in a tense voice. "This thing can easily escalate, and we have no idea who is orchestrating it. These are not random acts of violence. Need I remind you the norm is 10.5 acts of violence per year, and in the last twenty-four hours we've had over four hundred? This type of violence belongs in Texas, or Nairobi, or any other outlying country..." Joy turned her head and talked to someone. A moment later Gary came in to stand behind her.

Joy's face registered annoyance, and she stared at Louis waiting for a reply.

"Joy, I am only a tired old man. You and the other regents who received the communication; you are all on top of this. Has someone sent out a public-address communiqué?"

Gary leaned forward on the desk, pushing Joy aside with his massive bulk. "Arkady, you know, one of those mediocre Russian regents, sent us his draft. Second rate, but maybe we should look at it."

Joy gave Gary a perplexed sideways glance. "Won't you read it, Louis? Put in your thoughts. All regents are extremely anxious, and they'll be reassured when they hear you are involved."

Louis agreed. After all, it shouldn't take long.

Louis read Arkady Grigorovich's draft communiqué: "A number of acts of violence have been committed by unknown atavists. Police Services have taken measures to ensure no further acts can be committed. Whoever is behind this orchestrated attack is attempting to manipulate the rest of us into rash action, to sequester all atavists. Please remain calm, be assured the regents are prioritizing this issue and will find a solution we can all live with, including the atavist population, most of whom are peaceful and productive citizens."

Short and to the point, thought Louis. He added a short sentence: "The public may monitor our progress via normal channels."

In a matter of minutes, the entire board of regents approved the draft, and the communiqué was issued worldwide. The calls to sequester the atavists had reached seven billion, but then they slowed down to a trickle, and then they stopped. There were no further acts of violence, and the first public mandate in history had been averted. But it was a tense and guarded environment, the kind of police state that had not existed before in people's memory.

Louis started a new routine. He would work for two-hour periods, and then spend an hour with Sharon, who remained mostly sedated. Her wakeful moments were now fraught with confusion, her eyes darting about, often not recognizing him.

Yogi seemed to enjoy his walks around the neighborhood less and less. Louis scanned him and found the arthritis was not just in the hips but also in the front legs and neck. He decided to keep up the walks but keep them short.

Five days after the communiqué was issued, Louis sat in the kitchen eating breakfast. As he watched an android clean the counter around him, he was alerted by the house that there was an urgent message from Police Services. He rushed to his study and his computer display. There was a response to the government communiqué consisting of a tract titled "The Seven Regents' Conspiracy," issued by unknown individuals calling themselves the Patriots. They justified the recent violence as a call to arms to stop the seven regents from dominating the world. The long article described how they were trying to take over the world for their personal gain, that they lived in luxury, had multiple palaces and the best of everything the world had to offer. They had as many children as they chose, some as many as twelve. Their intent was to create a plutocracy and pass on control to their children. The tract went on to say the conspiracy went back to the beginnings of the New Paradigm when parents of the seven regents connived to deny the world money, the means for individuals to assert their own power and control their destinies. Now the seven regents adjudicated power among themselves and Police Services was being transformed into an army at their beck and call. The seven were named, and Louis was first on the list. Five others were well known and respected individuals spread out across the world. The last on the list was Arkady Grigorovich.

And it was Arkady's name that struck Louis. Why would he be on the list? Louis pondered as he swayed in his chair, which helped to relieve his aching back. Could it be because he wrote the communiqué?...No, that didn't make sense. No one outside a small group knew he was the author. And why would that single him out?

The other six names, his own included, were easy; those were well-known regents to anyone who followed government activities, but Arkady would not be well known because, though an excellent administrator, he rarely authored anything. So the only people who would know about him were other regents and a select number of first tiers.

Louis stood up and walked around his study. He looked at the rock garden and the rake marks left on the sand by one of the house androids. Someone close to the government, either a regent or first tier, was in the Patriots' camp. Gary Eagan came to mind again as the most likely suspect. But how could a regent be an atavist? The biochips would flag someone with a proclivity to atavism as defined in the altruism scale, and the first tier exam was a fail-safe mechanism. However the case, it had been done, and if Gary was not the culprit, then someone very much like him would be...if only there was something to connect Gary to Arkady...he had called the Russian a mediocre regent and had said that his draft communiqué was second rate when it fact it had been excellent; so he had something against the Russian...and how did he know about Larry's predictive algorithm? At the time of the last congress only Larry, Joy, and himself could have known about it.

Yeah, Gary was the most likely candidate...and the only way he could have learned about the algorithm was...through some sort of secret surveillance. Oh, boy!

Louis decided it was time to meet with Joy to deal with the situation, in person, so no one could monitor their conversation. But he had to keep the meeting secret, particularly from Gary.

Louis thought how best to get Joy to come to his house. Gary would surely want to monitor calls between top regents, and he and

Joy were among this group. Louis figured he had to be careful. Somehow he had to make her understand what he truly wanted through an innocuous message only she would understand.

Louis sat at his desk, staring at Yogi sleeping on the floor. After thinking for some time, he hit on it. It was worth a shot. He called Joy, and she answered right away. Her anxious face studied him, probing, wondering.

"Louis. I was just going to call you!" she said as she looked him over, even peering discreetly over his shoulder. She was in her office at Human Services and he could see that her door was closed. Good.

"Joy, I'm fine, just resting a bit. I'm old, you know."

"Don't you talk to me about being old, you nasty old fart!" she said and smiled broadly.

Louis laughed. He missed Joy. "Hey, Joy, I need some of the virtual papers I left in my office at the university."

"I'll bring them over, no problem!"

"Yes. I want to bury myself in work. Bring a document called 'A Writer's Diary.' I made some notes on the office copy, and would like to have it. Enough of the atavist crisis. Let someone else handle it. You and I should also whoop it up. Bring some good liquor with you, maybe a single malt scotch."

Her eyes flickered with surprise then settled into a quizzical look. "Consider it done. I'll get over as soon as possible. You are right, let's cut loose, enough of this crisis stuff."

"Thanks, Joy."

"Yeah, the whole place is buzzing. I really need to get away."

"Come as soon as you can."

"Will do. Stay well and give my best to Sharon." She hung up.

Neither Joy nor he drank hard liquor. In fact they made frequent jokes about the poor saps who needed alcohol to cope. And once, Joy had said, "Maybe it will take the end of the world for me to drink the stuff." At that point Louis had quipped, "I'll give you a bottle of single malt scotch when that happens."

Louis was sure she remembered the allusion to the scotch.

8

Eagan's virtual image in civilian clothes came to stand before President Reilly and two other three-star generals in the presidential palace's lavish living room. Reilly, in his new gray Confederate uniform, turned to smile at him. "I've been following the news, General Eagan. Congratulations. You are making those people in the government extremely nervous."

Eagan smiled. "Thank you, Mister President. All for the Cause!"

"Good man, good man. Now, let's think how we are going to get Sagan. I've waited a long time to get back at that arrogant bastard. Any ideas?"

"Well, he's an old man. Should be easy to kidnap. But you know, he's thinking of terminating. That's what he keeps saying to his comatose wife."

"No, no. I don't want that. He's a big man in people's eyes already. All I read about is how great he is, and terminating would just add to his reputation, that he's leaving to make room for someone else. Did you read the *World News Today* article? They talk about him as though he's some kind of god. I want him humiliated, cut down to size. Can you help me do that?"

"Yes, sir!"

"Very well. I want Louis Sagan here in Texas. I will put that old man through some of our treatment. I'm sure we'll have him broken in no time at all, and then when we take him back he'll be just a foolish old man. Have him here in a week. Understood?"

"Visitors at the door," the house announced as Louis sat writing in his study. "Regents Joy Blass, Angela Hall, and First Tier Lawrence Zimmerman."

Louis looked up. "Please show them in." He was surprised Joy had decided to bring those two along, but she was an excellent chief-of-staff, always on the lookout for the best possible talent for whatever project came around, so if she had brought Larry and Angela, it was for a good reason. He checked his clothes. He was wearing his customary house attire: temperature-regulating gray sweatpants and top, and house slippers.

Not long afterward, he heard steps coming up the stairs. A house android walked into the study, followed by Joy, carrying the writer's diary, then Angie and Larry.

Joy placed the document on a side table. "Louis, let me explain why I brought Angie and Larry along, I…"

Louis raised a hand. "Thank you for bringing your friends. Time to party hardy, Joy!"

Joy studied Louis for a brief moment and then quickly exchanged glances with Angie.

"Let's go for a walk, shall we?" he said before Joy could utter another word. "Then we can open that bottle you talked about."

Louis led the small group out of his condo, down the hall to the elevators. A car had sensed their presence and opened its doors. They were quickly brought down to the building's foyer, right by the front door. Louis kept walking at a brisk pace, trying his best to keep Joy from saying anything else. A grassy area stretched in front of the building with concrete pathways, what in the old days had been full of honking cars. The sidewalk had its usual number of pedestrians, some going for a stroll, but most either coming in or out of cars or zipping by on autowalkers.

Joy pulled on his sleeve. "Louis, can you explain why we can't talk in your condo? From your message about the scotch I figured you wanted to talk about the Patriots, and that's why I brought Angela Hall and Lawrence Zimmerman along. I thought they would be indispensable for the kind of planning we need to do." She turned toward Angie, who walked behind them, all prim and proper. "I know you think of Angela only in terms of the space exploration project, but she's also a criminal psychologist and is on the atavist project. She knows the criminal mind. All and all, I think we need her." Joy extended an arm toward Larry, who seemed to be taking in the surroundings, the busy street, and the pedestrians with great interest. "You know about Larry's work on that predictive algorithm, and you remember I mentioned his idea of injecting plants in Texas with biochips to create a giant bio-computer. Louis—"

Louis raised a hand and interrupted her. "Joy, thank you. I'm familiar with Angela's and Larry's impressive work. I trust your judgment. Thank you for bringing them. You are right; we need to start planning. I don't think anyone else within the government can really move to counter this. We are—"

"But, Louis, what are we doing outside? Why can't we talk in your condo?"

Louis stopped and turned to look at Joy's anxious face, then at Larry and Angela. "Listen, people. My house may have monitoring devices."

Joy snickered. "Monitoring devices? Planted by whom? Louis, you've been reading too much about the twenty-first century."

Larry assented. "I beg your pardon, regent. There's no way someone could plant devices unknown to your house. Just ask it, the house will tell you if there are any."

Louis resumed walking and stepped aside to evade a boy on a skateboard, then a woman talking in earnest with a man's virtual image that floated beside her sitting on a chair. "Granted, it sounds a bit far-fetched. But we are dealing with atavists, and, yes, I have read extensively about them in the twenty-first century, and I am responding accordingly. I know how their minds work." Louis paused and again turned around. They all came to a stop, their gazes fixed on him. "Please listen to me. It's highly possible we are dealing with a highly sophisticated organization, and that they have infiltrated all levels of government. They would also want to keep track of key regents, which would involve surreptitious monitoring devices. That's likely, isn't it, Angela?"

Pedestrians skirted around them, some with annoyed expressions. An old woman with a bag stared at them inquiringly.

Angela nodded. "Yes, yes. If indeed they are organized along some anti-government scheme, then it would make perfect sense that they would want to monitor your house, regent, because you are such a key government figure. It would also make sense for them to embed their agents where you work. So I would expect a plant at Columbia for sure because we have high faculty turnover. Space Administration and Human Services would be extremely hard to infiltrate, given that turnover is almost nil."

"Who? Who could be a plant...at the Social Psychology Department?" Joy asked.

"Gary Eagan," answered Louis.

"Oh, c'mon," Joy said with a derisive smile.

"No, Joy," responded Angela. "I agree. That's a possibility. Let's hear Regent Sagan's rationale."

"But why suspect Eagan in particular?" Joy asked.

"He knew about Larry's predictive algorithm." Louis said and he turned to Joy. "How would he know about that?"

Joy thought for a moment. "You are right. As department chair he would've had to hear about it from me, and as a regent—"

"He mentioned it before I did at the congress. There was no way he could've known about it except from overhearing one of our phone conversations—"

"About a month before the congress when I called you at home."

"Right. Then at that congress he was trying his best to convince us to sequester the atavists, and I mean all atavists. It was bizarre."

Angela quickened her pace to keep up with Louis. "Yes, yes. And the recent terrorist attack almost made us do exactly what he wanted."

"Yes," Joy said, studying two men walking in their direction, but they appeared to be engrossed in their own conversation. "We came within a hairbreadth of a mandate to arrest and isolate the atavists on a massive scale. There would have been no other place for them except Texas…Gary wanted to force our hand, to speed up the project—"

"What concerns me most is that we would've antagonized the entire atavist population, Joy," Louis said.

"That's right!" Joy said, "They are already prone to anger and violence—"

"In their minds it would've meant war."

"Yes!"

Angela shook her head. "That's what Gary and his friends wanted, to create a war?…or at least a lot of anger. And that Patriot tract is good at planting that additional wedge of mistrust—"

"I'm sure those who view us with enmity are convinced everything in it is true." Louis said. "And it's highly possible that Gary and the Patriots' aim was for us to forcibly move a great number of atavists to Texas, thereby creating enough resentment so they would be willing to wage war against us."

They stood around in silence for a moment. A man came by talking on his phone. The virtual image of a young woman walked alongside him wearing a bathrobe. The man noticed Louis looking and hit the privacy button, making the image disappear.

"Do you think Gary wrote it?" Larry asked in his unemotional, even-keel tone.

Louis motioned with a hand for them to keep walking. "He was the main author. The tract mentions Arkady Grigorovich, and how many people know about him?"

"That's true..." Joy said, "and he was very disparaging of Arkady and his draft."

"For some reason he doesn't like Arkady," Louis said, quickening his pace again, and looking forward to the bench in the park. "Perhaps that's the only reason the Russian is on that list of seven. When you analyze the list, Arkady is out of place. Everybody else is a well-known regent."

They approached the park with lawns, benches, a fountain, and a basketball court. Louis added, "Let's be extremely careful. I can't ask my house if there are any monitoring devices, because if there are, whoever planted them will hear my query and be alerted that we suspect something. I'm concerned Gary and his friends must know we are meeting." Louis thought for a moment and led the others to a bench under a tree facing the fountain. "So let's use Sharon as an excuse. When you get back to your offices or homes, in casual conversation mention how I surreptitiously got you to come to my house because I'm beside myself." Louis plopped himself down on the bench with relief. Joy and Angela sat on either side of him. "Let's take some steps right away. Assume your offices, cars, and houses are compromised. Your computers, everything."

Larry stood in front of them, arms across his chest. "We need new phones until we clear this issue. I'll get us new ones and let's use them outside in the street or in restaurants to communicate between us. We'll continue using the other equipment for everything else."

Louis rubbed his knees. "Excellent. Once in a while call me or send me a message on the compromised equipment."

"Right, right. To avoid suspicion," Larry said.

They watched the fountain for a while. The water came out of a marble dolphin's mouth perched on top of a rock. The fountain was surrounded by a narrow band of purple and white flowers. The stone walkway went around the fountain and meandered out to various points in the park. One of Yogi's favorite places before his hips started hurting, thought Louis with sadness.

Angela broke the silence. "How do we know one of us is not a Patriot, a mole planted long ago…just like Eagan?"

"Because I say so," Joy said. "I know Larry and you, Angie…As for myself—"

"I vouch for you," Louis said with a smile, as he mentally reviewed what he knew about Larry and Angela: The week before he had gone over Larry's excellent work on the atavist predictive algorithm, and Angela's papers on the atavists were always to the point. And now she headed the space exploration work. They were both very good multi-field scientists and it would be hard to find more knowledgeable experts on the atavist issue…and from different perspectives. "Looks like we have a team. I trust Joy's judgment, and I know everyone's work. Now that I think about it, I couldn't ask for better talent." He turned his head to look at Joy. "Good job. But let's keep our team small. Don't include anyone else unless we absolutely need their expertise. As for security, it's possible any one of us could be a Patriot, but I would say it's very unlikely.

"But I do need to ask all of you: As of this moment, as far as I'm concerned, we are the only ones within the government organized to counter the Patriot threat. On a strictly practical level we have the access to information and resources as no one else, and we have the skills. But I don't know exactly what it will entail, how long, or where it will take us. Are you all okay with that?"

They looked at each other briefly then back at Louis. There was no hesitation; they nodded their assent.

"Fine. Thank you. Then let's get to work, shall we?"

"So where do we go from here?" Angela asked.

"We have to find someone who knows about this entire secret, surreptitious technology," Louis said.

Larry ran a hand through his short-cropped blond hair. "But how? I mean, if we go to the regent in charge of Police Services, we won't know if we are talking to a member of the Patriots."

"Right." Louis said. "Let's identify someone we can trust totally. The right way to do it is to contact the other six regents on the Patriots' list. We know they are safe, right?"

"That makes sense," Larry said with a laugh. "One of them will surely know someone with the right expertise."

"And what do we expect from that person when we find him or her?" Angie asked.

"To help us monitor Gary," Louis said. "We must find out his motives, assuming he's behind this whole affair. I'm sure he'll lead us to the rest of the group."

"Are you sure about Gary?" Joy asked.

"No, Joy, I'm not positive, but so far that's the only tangible lead we have. If he proves to be innocent, wonderful! Then we'll turn our attention elsewhere.

"By the way. Let's try and clear as many regents as we can. Larry or Angie, can you find someone to do that? "

"Of course." Larry removed his glasses and cleaned them with a tissue. "We need to know who is with us and who's against us."

Louis stood up to go back to the condo, but Joy held him by the arm. "Louis, listen to me. Please, please read the executive summary I sent you on the teleportation project. I know that under the circumstances, it's the last thing you want to read, but I have a hunch that it's important. So just to humor me, could you please read it?"

Louis promised he would read it first chance he got. "We have our work cut out for us. Let's proceed with caution," he said as he started walking.

Angie and Larry stood and looked for nearby autowalkers.

Joy followed Louis.

"Louis, wait up. I'd like to talk with Sharon for a minute or so."

Louis nodded and motioned for her to follow him.

When they got to the condo, Louis led the way up the stairs. He hesitated for a moment in front of the bedroom door, then opened it and walked in. Joy followed. He went to stand by his wife. Joy stood by the foot of the bed, surprised.

Louis reached out to touch his wife's hand. "Sharon is dying. She has a cancerous brain tumor. She has about four months left at the rate she's going, but she decided to terminate when she was still lucid. Maybe we already waited too long."

Joy stood in stunned silence for some time. "Sharon called about a month ago," she said staring at the prostrate form. "She wanted to meet for lunch, but then never called back. I figured she had gotten busy with a project...I never thought she was here, dying!" Tears started pouring down her cheeks. She sobbed and had to sit down on the bed, her head bent over. After some time she got up and walked over to where Louis stood staring at his wife and placed a hand on his shoulder. "I'm so sorry, Louis. I didn't know. Of course, you want to be by her side. Now it all makes sense."

"Regent Sagan," the house said, "I have a message for Regent Blass from your wife."

"Oh my!" Joy exclaimed. Her biometrics had triggered a sensor in the bedroom. Sharon's image appeared before them, on the other side of the bed. The date of the recording was a month before. Sharon was sitting in her favorite living room chair, dressed in her leisure clothes: a loose-fitting beige sweater and black pants of heavy fabric. She appeared relaxed and was smiling.

"Joy," her familiar voice began, "dear Joy. I probably won't get to see you again as I planned." Louis felt a lump in his throat and heard Joy's labored breathing. The two women had known each other better than he knew. "I don't have long to live, and that's fine, but what's not acceptable is that Louis plans to terminate with me. He made an appointment for both of us at a termination center for August twentieth. I don't know when you'll get to see this, but I hope it is well before then!" At this Sharon smiled, and Louis felt Joy grab his hand, and she held it tight as she looked at him with a shocked look. New tears flowed, her eyes riveted on him. "Please, dear Joy," Sharon continued, "do what you can to stop him. I tried, but he is so persuasive, and he refuses to listen to reason. He has so much to offer; he's such a wonderfully gifted man. I would feel terrible if he were to terminate his precious life because of me."

Sharon's holographic self froze. Louis turned to look at Sharon's placid features, her chest rising slowly in peaceful breathing. Very clever of her to enlist Joy, he thought.

"Well, very well…" he said in a hoarse voice, withdrawing his hand from Joy's tight grip. "That's a private matter, and we have things to do."

"Louis, I know it's your private business," began Joy hesitantly, "but are you going… really going to terminate on August twentieth? That's—what?—less than three months!"

"I am. I'm sorry, but I don't want to discuss it."

"What about those of us who care about you?"

Louis looked down at the floor. "Yes…well, I appreciate that, but—"

"But nothing!" Joy said. "I, too, love Sharon, I have been her friend ever since I started working for you some twelve years ago, and I do know you love her dearly—"

"Joy, please. I don't want to talk about it."

Joy brushed a tear with one hand. A heavy silence froze the room. Then after a deep sigh: "Fine, Louis," she said in a resigned tone. "It's your choice guaranteed by our constitution. You have the right to die whenever you want."

The following morning Louis sat eating breakfast at his desk. He heard Larry's voice, then his steps coming up the stairs. He showed Louis a thin wafer device a bit smaller than a regular phone, about the size of a fingernail.

"It's your new phone," Larry said. "It works like the rest. In a few minutes, it will recognize your voice and your body, and hone in to you so you can't lose it. It will replicate itself into all your clothes, your furniture, car, and—"

"I'm familiar with how phones work, Larry."

Later that morning Joy called on his new phone. Louis went outside in the street to answer.

"Louis, you were right about Gary," she said. "Arkady filed a complaint against him when they both worked as first tiers in a village in Africa. It was quite a case. Gary was accused of using undue influence in his relations with a subordinate. Eventually he was exonerated, but he came close to being classified as an atavist."

"Well, now we know what he has against Arkady. That would have been the end of his career; but how petty to include him on that hit list just for that."

"How fortunate, you mean. Now we know for sure that he's a Patriot."

That afternoon Joy and Angie called together on his new phone. Louis walked outside the condo to receive the call. He walked down the street along with a throng who seemed to be heading toward the park. Both women spoke at once, and were trying to dissuade him from terminating. Louis walked over to a building's doorway and stood to one side to let people go by. At that very moment it dawned on him that he couldn't terminate, not under the circumstances.

He let the women talk for a time, and then he smiled at them. "Not to worry, you two. I can't go ahead with it, at least not until the Patriots are no longer a threat." Louis felt a heavy weight in his chest. "I'll take Sharon to a termination center on August twentieth and…that's all I know at this moment." He read relief in Joy's face and resented it.

"We are sorry for what you have to go through," Joy said quickly, "truly sorry. If there's anything we can do, please let us know."

Angie gave him a painful smile. "You have my deepest sympathy, regent."

Louis nodded and thanked them.

Two days later Larry called. Louis went outside the building. "I found someone through Police Services who can help us with the surveillance equipment. It took a lot of work, and I had to go through a lot of people. By the way, the regent in charge, Alonzo Ross, is safe. The man he recommended is currently in Brazil, but he'll be assigned to me in a few days."

A well-dressed businessman came Louis's way on an autowalker and gave Louis and Larry a curious glance. Louis waited until he passed. "Let's have him look for surveillance equipment in our houses and cars as soon as possible."

Larry took a deep breath. "I'll get on it."

"After that we need to start clearing all regents. Let's find out who among them are Patriots."

Louis walked back to his condo, went into his study, and looked at his desk. The virtual display, the notepads strewn around, the note slips all spoke of tedious work. It was still early in the morning, and Louis wanted a distraction, but he didn't want to read the writer's diary, it just reminded him of the Patriot threat. Instead he decided to peruse Joy's teleportation document for an hour, take a hot bath and think about it, then call Joy and give her some cursory comments. Hopefully that would be enough to get him off the hook.

He read and got interested. D'Anjou began by describing energies identified two centuries before in what used to be called string theory. Back then scientists had identified eleven energies that were responsible for all matter in the cosmos. Then twenty years ago a key group of physicists had narrowed it down to seven, while other scientists theorized that, in actuality, the number was infinite, but agreed the seven were "a practical construct."

Then D'Anjou stated something quite revealing: The energies mixed in various combinations made up a yet to be determined number of parallel universes. The energies were constantly switching in our universe, and as the higher ones played a bigger role, there was a resulting higher output in technology and higher thinking by humans. D'Anjou stated that the current dominant energy in our universe was in the Meda Sequence, which was the fourth from the top.

In older times the number five energy, Petra, was dominant and the higher energies were at ebb, which made it so higher-thinking humans were in the minority and atavists were the majority. The reverse was true today. The transition had happened slowly over the centuries.

Louis remembered reading something about it some years ago, but D'Anjou was bringing everything into focus.

One day, while D'Anjou was helping a colleague with an experiment in teleportation, it had occurred to him that perhaps if he altered the frequencies of the equipment to match those of a particular parallel universe close to our own he might be able to access it. The question was how to go about it. To match a particular frequency, first he had learn what it was, and to learn what it was he had to enter it first to take a reading. So he did the best he could; he made an energy profile of our existing universe and started changing it ever so slightly toward the higher energies. He then tried sending an inanimate object, but ended up with carbon dust. He kept trying, every day, sometimes fifty times in a single day, making minute adjustments, until four months later when he teleported a piece of real paper. The paper disappeared without leaving a carbon trace, and D'Anjou knew he had entered another universe. He built a receiving station and was able to successfully teleport inanimate objects back and forth without alterations in their molecular structure. Based on the energy profile he used, he determined he had accessed a dimension in the Kali Sequence, what he called universe Kali Four hundred, or K4, where energy four was dominant. He went on to describe his other experiments, including the one Louis witnessed where he teleported a mouse. "In Kali Four, the time-space continuum is radically different. Essentially, from the perspective of our reality, there are no distances, there's no time. But in actuality, the time and distances are 'compressed' as we know them, to such an extent as to render them practically nonexistent."

Louis stopped to think. He stood up, circled his chair, and sat down again. To teleport the mouse, D'Anjou had identified its energy signature and altered it to match Kali Four's energy. Louis knew that the basis of all matter, including living things, was energy. So that made sense. D'Anjou had then projected the mouse's energy into Kali Four, together with the destination, which was the energetic imprint of the "Receiving Station," the mouse's destination. Louis read on. "The environment need not be sterile because the teleporter will transport only the defined parameters of the mouse's energy. Everything else is excluded, or included as need be, i.e., the cage."

Louis paused, his heart beating fast. The teleporter would transport only the defined parameters...everything else could be excluded. That was incredible! What would happen if the mouse got ill? Could D'Anjou identify the illness's energy and remove it?

Louis rushed out of the condo and down to the street and called Joy. She answered almost immediately.

"Joy," Louis said, walking briskly, "I want to meet with D'Anjou right away. Can you arrange it?"

Seated at her desk at Human Services, Joy seemed surprised, but she smiled sweetly. "Yes, Louis. I'll call you right back."

Louis strolled down the street and realized he was wearing his house clothes. It was a busy time of the day, and Louis felt self-conscious walking around in his bathrobe and slippers. He wished someone would come and get rid of whatever the Patriots had planted in his condo.

Three minutes later Joy called.

"Would an hour from now be too soon? He's at his Maryland lab."

"I'll be there right away," answered Louis. He walked back home and went to the master bedroom to change clothes. Sharon slept peacefully.

9

"Are you sure you can cure your mouse if we infect it with a flu virus?" Louis stared hard at D'Anjou, who stood before him in his lab coat, stiff and formal, like a soldier facing his commanding officer.

"I don't see why not, regent. It would be relatively straightforward," D'Anjou said without hesitation.

The two men stood in the middle of D'Anjou's lab. Joy, dressed in one of her customary flowing dresses, had found a chair by a desk a few feet away and studied them with apparent amusement. The place was a spacious room on the third floor of Macro Systems. To one side, lined up against the wall stood the two hulking glassite cubes D'Anjou had used in his demonstration some three months before. Equipment of all sorts was neatly arranged by function. Two lab assistants and another scientist had been with D'Anjou when Louis and Joy arrived, lingered for a minute or so studying Louis with thinly disguised awe and curiosity, but then politely excused themselves and left the room.

Louis couldn't contain his enthusiasm. "How soon can you run an experiment?"

"I don't really know," replied D' Anjou. "I need to get a hold of a biologist and some culture to infect the mouse."

Joy got up from her chair, straightened out her dress, and approached the pair. "I just got off the phone. I have a biologist ready with some culture. She'll be here in ten minutes."

D'Anjou appeared at a loss for words. "Well then…"

"If we inject the mouse in fifteen minutes," Joy said, "we'll be ready for the experiment in forty-eight hours."

Louis felt ecstatic. He looked at his watch. It was quarter to eleven in the morning. "Thank you, Joy…and thank you, Alphonse. I'll see you both back here in forty-eight hours?"

Joy smiled broadly. "You can count on it, Louis. Can I get Larry involved? I think he can be of help."

"Yes, of course."

Louis made his way back to his car waiting for him by the sidewalk, and knew the following two days period would be perhaps the longest of his life.

He didn't sleep that night, but tossed and turned in the guest bedroom downstairs. In the wee hours of the morning, he climbed the stairs using the autowalker and went to lie next to his wife. "Sweet Shari," he said as he snuggled next to her and caressed the side of her unconscious face, "you may be talking to me real soon. I may get to watch your annoyed expression when I interrupt your reading the newspaper at breakfast. Ah, Shari, that would be heaven."

Later that morning the house announced that there were two visitors at the door. Larry had come accompanied by an unknown guest. Louis told the house to let them in and went downstairs in his house clothes to find Larry with a short, slim, intense man in his thirties with long, shaggy blond hair. Louis signaled for them to join him on a walk out in the street. They rode the elevator in silence and walked out of the building's foyer. Once outside Larry introduced the man as Patrick Castelano, a Police Services officer and electronics expert.

They stood in the middle of the sidewalk watching a number of bicyclists go by in the avenue all wearing numbered jerseys. Louis shook hands with the odd little man who avoided his gaze and seemed preoccupied with a gadget in his hand. Pedestrians walking by, some whizzing by on autowalkers, seemed to ignore them. Up high, in between the tops of the buildings, the sky was blue.

"Patrick has come to scan your home and car, Louis. He's already done the same with mine. He found nineteen surreptitious devices!" Larry seemed perplexed, as someone who has run across an unexplained phenomenon.

Louis came up closer to the two, so he could whisper. "Oh! So we were right! That means the Patriots are quite sophisticated."

"Yes, seems that way," replied Larry also in a whisper, removing his glasses and rubbing his eyes.

Louis looked down the street at a nearby bakery. They were doing substantial business; there was a line outside their door, and customers came out eating pastries and sipping coffee. "What did you do with the devices Patrick found?"

Larry put his glasses back on. "Nothing yet. I was waiting to talk to you."

Louis gazed at Patrick, who stood next to Larry and seemed to pay no attention to their conversation. "Excellent. What types of devices did he find?"

"Monitoring of both visual and verbal, planted throughout the house and car, and inside my communication systems."

"How about the brains of the car and house?"

"No, those were intact. Apparently too well protected for whoever planted the devices…How do you want to proceed?"

"I want to leave the devices he found in place. Can Patrick install a disguise?"

"You mean a program to provide phony input?" replied Larry.

"Exactly," Louis said, stepping back toward the building to get out of the way of pedestrians. Larry and Patrick followed him. "That way they won't suspect a thing. The disguise has to be impregnable, so the surveillance bugs won't pick up our real conversations."

Larry gave Louis an appreciative glance. "How do you know so much about this stuff?"

"Reading about the twenty-first century."

It was odd to be talking without including Patrick in the conversation, as though he was an android of sorts, but Patrick seemed lost in his own world. Funny how Larry seemed drawn to savants; apparently he was quite fond of Suzanne. "Can Patrick also install a tracking system?"

Larry glanced at Patrick. "You mean, to tell us where and who is receiving the transmissions from the bugs?"

"Yes."

"Yes of course. That was a prime directive I gave him."

The bicyclists were still racing past out in the middle of the street. Number 2123 went by pushing hard on the pedals. "Excellent. When will he be done with my house and car?"

"Probably in about an hour. That's how long it took him with my place."

Louis became thoughtful. All of a sudden, he also felt very tired. "How did they manage to get into our houses and cars—"

"Without the houses and cars stopping them? In my case, they used a jamming device that temporarily interfered with my house's brain."

"Oh boy. Okay. Thank you, Larry. Let's head back to my condo and do what you need to do."

Larry started walking followed by Patrick. "Very well. And congratulations on how well you predicted it all; you saved us from God knows what."

Louis nodded. "I'm reading a diary from the twenty-first century that's a trove of information."

"I bet. By the way, I'm a regent as of this morning. You can officially keep me in the loop."

"Congratulations, Regent Zimmerman. That was quite fast."

"Yes," Larry said with a laugh. "You have to thank Joy for that, she can move mountains."

"Yes, she's quite capable."

Louis was lost in thought for a moment. "I notice you seem quite fond of Suzanne. Is that bona fide, or are you just being nice?"

A hurt or annoyed look came over Larry's usually calm eyes. "I am very fond of her. If you knew her better, you would know why."

Louis reached out a hand and placed it on Larry's shoulder. "Please don't be offended. I'm pleased you took her under your wing. I just want to know why."

Larry's appearance softened. "She's got quite a mind. I'm actually jealous of her. If I had her ability, I would be—"

"Exactly what ability is that?" Louis said as he led the way back to his condo.

Larry fell in beside him, with Patrick trailing them. "Her mind sees patterns at a macro scale. It's really astonishing. On a personal note, yes, she's awkward, but she's also like a...fairy."

"A fairy? What do you mean?"

"Oh, it's hard to explain, but when I'm with her, I feel...there's a softness about her, an innocence...she talks about—"

"She talks to you at length?"

"Oh yes, Louis. Once she warmed up to me, she became quite a talker."

Louis smiled. "Great. I'm glad you two get along. She doesn't seem to have any other friends."

"It's an honor to be her friend. Really."

Right before entering Louis's building, Larry instructed Louis that they would have to engage in some theater. Patrick was supposed to be a student of Larry's and he came along so that Louis could provide counsel on a problem they had in Brazil with a banana virus.

"It's called the bunchy-top virus, Louis," Larry said as they crossed the big ornate entrance, "and it's decimating the crop in the state of Bahia..." and Larry and Louis went on talking in the elevator, down the hall, and as Louis opened the door to his condo. They walked around from room to room, Patrick following them and nodding his assent from time to time, his attention on the phone in his hands. Louis took them upstairs to his study where they spent some time admiring the Japanese garden and talking about bananas. Finally, Larry asked to see Sharon, and they entered Louis's bedroom. They stood by Sharon's bed. Louis went into detail describing the cancer, how it was spreading, and how it was affecting his wife. After ten minutes or so, Patrick tapped Larry on the arm.

"Ah," exclaimed Larry. "We can talk freely now. The bugs have been neutralized. Now they are sending false input."

"Thanks Larry. I'll see you tomorrow at D' Anjou's lab."

"You bet. We'll make Sharon well again, I'm sure of that."

The next morning Louis tried to ignore the knot at the pit of his stomach. He took Yogi for a walk and watched him walk ever so slowly, his body swaying from side to side in a cumbersome, painful gait. And it occurred to him that it would be such a pleasure, such a miracle to have Yogi well again…and it was within his grasp. They were all going to spend some wonderful years together…again.

It took the longest time for the clock in the kitchen to read nine…then ever so slowly, so painfully slowly, ten. Louis, who had already shaved and changed clothes, made his way to his study. He went back to the bedroom and changed clothes again, to loose cotton slacks and a blue shirt. He thought better of it and changed his shirt to a temperature-regulating one, heavier but more comfortable. Did he need to take anything with him? He couldn't think of anything. Just his eyes to see. And hope, hope it would work. And he wondered whether he was just too enthusiastic; that his hope to see Sharon healthy again, to hear her voice, was leading him down a false path? No, Joy seemed enthusiastic as well. She was not just humoring him…no. Louis reviewed the evidence in his mind. Of course, it had to work! The way D'Anjou explained it, that's the way it would work. D'Anjou himself said it would work, right? Well, time to act like a scientist, he told himself. Let's just go and see what happens.

At eleven, they were all there: Joy, Larry, D'Anjou, the biologist, and one of D'Anjou's lab assistants, a pretty young blonde, and Suzanne, who Larry had brought along. "She understands computational processes better than anyone," he explained.

Louis was glad for their presence in that otherwise sterile and rather depressing lab; all shiny surfaces, machines, and various devices archived in shelves along the walls.

They went to look at the mouse. It certainly looked sick. The biologist, an efficient-looking woman in her mid-forties, pointed a scanner at the mouse, and it showed a fever. Phlegm filled the mouse's sinuses and lungs. It had the flu.

D'Anjou aimed a device at the mouse. A graph appeared on the display in front of them, showing concentric circles made up of a multitude of symbols. "This is the healthy mouse," he said, and he had the display change the color of part of the graph to blue. "And here, we see the virus in red and the dysfunction it causes on the mouse's body in green."

Joy bent over to whisper in Louis's ear. "He worked almost straight for the past two days on that algorithm with that assistant of his. Larry double-checked their work."

"Very interesting, Alphonse," Louis said, trying to hide his excitement. "Please go on."

"As you can see, I have been able to isolate the mouse's normal profile from the virus and the resulting ailment," D'Anjou continued. His nasal voice now sounded pedantic, annoying. "What I'll do next is program the teleporter to allow removal of what we see as the red and green elements, the virus and its effect."

Louis felt his insides churning with exasperation. The man was tediously meticulous. "Fascinating, Alphonse, go on," Louis said, casually noticing Suzanne was like a silent shadow quietly following the procedure, looking over people's shoulders with childlike curiosity.

"We can exclude anything we want, this process is very exacting." D'Anjou went on to describe in technical terms what he was doing. Fortunately the man could talk and work at the same time. "The matter we exclude is converted into energy and goes right into our building's energy conversion module," he said as he reached a hand into the display and removed the red and green strings.

Finally, D'Anjou placed the sick mouse in the sending station. After making sure all the readings were right and that it was indeed the same sick mouse for the umpteenth time, he pressed the send button.

They rushed to the other station, some twenty feet away, bumping into one another and the tables in their rush. And there was the mouse, a vivacious mouse, a healthy mouse! The biologist, apparently as excited as Louis, pointed her instrument. The mouse was indeed healthy, although quite excited, judging by its vital signs.

Louis felt like dancing. A huge weight had been lifted off his chest. He went over to Joy and hugged her. She hugged him back, laughing.

"Oh, Louis! This is the happiest moment of my life!" She turned to D'Anjou. "You said you could remove anything you wanted. Could you identify and remove the effects of aging?"

"Of course," he said without hesitation. "It would be the same as removing the effect of the virus."

The biologist, instrument in hand, stood shaking her head, her eyes wide, mouth open.

"Marianne, you realize this is very confidential, don't you?" Joy said.

"Yes, yes, Regent Bass, I know that."

"Alphonse, you already signed a confidentiality agreement, but what about your assistant?"

"Oh, she had to sign one for the corporation when she began working for me. I will vouch for Arlene."

"Thank you…Larry?"

"I already discussed confidentiality with Suzanne. You have nothing to worry about."

Joy turned her attention to D'Anjou. "How soon could we run another experiment to identify and remove the effects of aging?"

Louis laughed. Joy's scientific button had been pushed. "Joy, that's brilliant thinking. But I'm rather pleased with what I have seen so far…extremely pleased. If you don't mind, I would like the next experiment to involve my dog. He has severe arthritis, and I would like to see if the ailment can be removed before we try the teleporter on Sharon's cancer."

D'Anjou seemed flustered. "A human subject? Oh no, we are years away from that! I couldn't possibly go that far. I could lose my job."

Joy shot Louis a meaningful glance, then glared at D'Anjou. "Don't worry about your job, don't worry about peer review. I take full responsibility if anything should go wrong; and you can have all the credit if everything goes right. Is that understood?"

D'Anjou blushed. "Yes, Joy."

She smiled at Louis. "We'll be ready for Yogi first thing tomorrow morning."

That night, after a fitful attempt at sleep where the hours rolled by slowly and the covers felt stifling, he decided to sort out his concerns and got up. It was one in the morning.

He stood up and asked the house to turn on night-lights so he could see where he was going. He went to find Yogi. He didn't have to go far, found him sleeping at the foot of his bed. Louis got down on one knee to gently stroke the dog on his back and head. The poor animal had no idea what was going to happen, had no choice in the matter.

What if the teleporter simply made a facsimile? What if he was going to destroy Yogi and would end up with something akin to a clone, a dog that looked like Yogi but was not him? Well, that was the whole point of the exercise, wasn't it? Yogi's life was drawing to a close, he was presently miserable, so if everything worked the dog would be returned to health, if not…anyway, it was worth the risk, just for the dog's sake. In the process, he would find out if he could cure Sharon, and that was worth it, wasn't it?

Louis continued petting Yogi, who seemed oblivious and had continued sleeping. What else was bothering him? The Patriots. They were planning something, but what? What could they possibly want to accomplish? Obviously they wanted to be in control of Texas, have the place all to themselves, their rules, their way of life. But if they knew it was going to happen, then why the attack? To push things along. Okay. And the surveillance? To keep track of the perceived enemy. Ah yes.

It occurred to Louis that before they surrendered Texas to the Patriots it would be prudent to find out their plans. Joy and Larry were working on developing virtual technology in Texas that would help control the atavists if necessary. But it had not been tested.

Oh well, they would do what they could.

His mind cleared, Louis decided to sleep a few more hours. That day promised to be a full one. If Yogi is okay, we'll do Sharon right away, he thought as he got under the covers. The cancer was progressing, and her brain would turn to mush if he waited too long. D'Anjou needed a baseline measurement of healthy brain tissue. But when would it be too late? Another week could be too late.

10

"What's happening with Regent Sagan? It's been almost a week!" Reilly, in his gray Confederate uniform, shouted at Eagan, whose virtual image stood at attention in front of his desk.

"I have everything in place, sir. Next time he shows up at the university, my men will grab him. Very easy, sir, we'll just take him from his office, in his own car."

"When is he due at the university?"

"He'll be here tomorrow."

Reilly nodded, then stood up. "Just remember…doing away with Sagan is very important to me, almost as important as becoming president…do you understand?"

"Yes, sir."

In the morning, Louis went about his usual routine: he ate breakfast, read to Sharon, worked a bit, and then watched the two androids clean the house. He felt a bit nervous but excited. Yogi followed him around, and each time Louis looked at him, his heart sank.

At nine, he boarded the car. Yogi managed the short distance slowly, in obvious discomfort. Louis watched him settle on the floor in the middle of the car, with his usual grunts.

At the lab, he found Joy excitedly talking with D'Anjou, his assistant, Larry, Suzanne, and the biologist, all six standing in the middle of the big room. When Joy saw him followed by Yogi, she came up to greet them.

"We have to do things a little differently, Louis," she said as she bent down to pet Yogi.

"What do you mean?"

"Oh, nothing serious, don't be alarmed. I was concerned about the mouse yesterday when I looked at its vitals. It didn't make sense; the mouse was not scared or excited. Its adrenaline was normal yet its vitals showed extreme stress."

"That means the process—"

"Yes." Joy stood up and looked Louis in the eyes. "Somehow the process puts the body under considerable duress."

Louis studied the group, all of whom were expectantly looking at him and Joy. They wore the same clothes from the day before and looked a bit haggard.

"How…Wait. Yogi is old; he may die in the process. And so will Sharon."

Angie put an arm around his shoulders. "Yes, yes, that's what I concluded yesterday but didn't want to mention it until we solved it. We are going to make Yogi young."

"So that's why you were so interested in removing the effects of aging."

"Yes, Louis. We've been working on the new protocol since you left. We experimented on that poor mouse more than ten times, and it worked every time."

Louis walked over to the mouse, which sat in its cage looking much the same as it had the day before.

Joy followed him. "You can't tell by just looking at him, but he's half the age he used to be." Then after a pause: "Well, let's get to work on Yogi, shall we? The process is really extraordinary…we may be in the threshold of a revolutionary development…and that's putting it mildly."

D'Anjou grabbed Yogi by the collar and walked the lumbering but compliant dog to one of his worktables. He grabbed a scanner and aimed it at Yogi, who stood tense, his tail between his legs. D'Anjou ran it several times, inspecting his display until he was satisfied. He produced a keyboard and got to work with his assistant. Yogi walked away slowly, looking back at them over his shoulder, and went to lie down in a corner.

"Basically what I'm doing is cleaning this up," D'Anjou said, his fingers moving furiously across the keyboard. "Joy, may I request your assistance?"

Joy came up to the display accompanied by Larry and Suzanne. Three displays and keyboards showed up before them, and they began working as D'Anjou directed them. "Clean sector five-two, please...no, not that string, leave it be... the next one...Okay, sorry, I forgot. I'll color-code the strings."

The display turned into the familiar red, blue, and green colors Louis had seen the day before, plus a yellow one he didn't recognize. That turned out to be "the aging strings," Joy explained to Louis as he stood looking over her shoulder.

The biologist was just as intent as the other three, following each move with keen interest. "Look at that arthritis string!" she exclaimed.

"Yes, it's a big one," responded D'Anjou, completely lost in the work. "Poor dog, it's a wonder he could walk at all. Arlene, please disentangle it from the healthy tissue."

Larry reached a hand and touched an arthritis string. "Why don't you just give the computer a universal command to get rid of the yellow strings?"

"Eventually I'll have a program that can do this," D'Anjou said, eyes focused on the screen. "But for now we must do it manually. It's surgery after all, and we must be careful not to damage surrounding tissue."

"We'll develop the program," Larry said, smiling at Suzanne.

It had become apparent to Louis that D'Anjou was going beyond the scope of his normal work. "Thanks, Alphonse. I know I put you on the spot."

"No need to mention it, sir. It's such an honor to be able to help you."

"Yeah," Joy said, stealing a quick glance at D'Anjou. "You'll be a famous man when this gets out."

D'Anjou nodded and mumbled something.

After several hours they were done. D'Anjou kept examining the display, comparing it with the original scan he had taken, and then looking back. After Larry and Suzanne went over the data, he fed it into the teleporter.

"Well, we are ready," announced D'Anjou, turning away from the display. "Let's move the dog into the sending unit."

Louis inhaled deeply. "You double-checked—"

"Yes, Louis," Joy said reassuringly. "Everything has been double-and triple- checked by us all. There are no mistakes, nothing overlooked."

"How much younger will he be...I suppose you are restoring him to his optimum stage? Fully developed and no deterioration from aging, right?"

"That is correct," Joy said. "Around age four. "

Louis felt his heart sink. He went to the corner where Yogi had lay down. He bent down and grabbed him by the collar. "Come on, buddy," he said as he walked him over to the hulking glassite cube.

Louis had Yogi sit on the platform inside the cube. He felt his own heart racing and a lump grew in his throat. "Stay, Yogi," he told him as patted him on the head. "I love you, buddy."

Yogi stared back at him.

The door closed. Louis closed his eyes and felt Joy's arm around his shoulders. He heard Yogi's bark behind him. It was most certainly Yogi's bark! He would recognize it anywhere.

Louis turned around. Yogi was sitting on his haunches, looking around curiously. When his eyes met Louis's gaze, he bounded toward him, jumped up, and placed his front paws on Louis's stomach, almost knocking him over, something he hadn't done in years. There was no question; that was Yogi, a young, and healthy,

Yogi! Louis bent down and hugged him, his eyes welling up with tears.

Louis looked up at Joy's jubilant face. She, too, had tears running down her cheeks that she was trying to wipe away quickly with her hand.

"Thank you, thank you all so much!" Louis said, petting Yogi, but the dog ran off to look at something underneath a table. D'Anjou and the biologist followed the dog and started scanning him with their handheld devices with Larry and Suzanne peering over their shoulders. After a short while, they nodded to each another and smiled. Suzanne patted Yogi's head. Louis thought of asking them if he could bring Sharon over immediately, but looking at their faces realized how tired they were. He stood up. "Shall we reconvene tomorrow, at say, nine?"

"Oh, Louis. I know how anxious you must be," Joy said. "Give us a few hours to recover. Let's meet here this afternoon at three."

"Suzanne and I are fresh, we could do some preliminary work," Larry said. "Like writing the configuration program."

D'Anjou stared at Larry in wonder. "You can have something ready by this afternoon?"

"Oh, not a final version, but a program which will make the identifying and handling of those strings easier and foolproof. I already talked it over with Suzanne, and we can do it."

D'Anjou checked his watch. "Well, that would make the work go so much faster…Yes, three would be fine."

Louis noticed the man was smiling. He had never seen him smile before.

Louis approached D'Anjou and put out his hand. "You performed a miracle. Thank you, and congratulations. The world will owe you much."

D'Anjou blushed as he shook Louis's hand.

Louis looked for Yogi, who was happily sniffing something inside a closet. When Louis called him he came running, but this time he stopped short and sat down, looking at Louis expectantly, his eyes bright, not a trace of pain.

Louis went home to get Sharon and watched Yogi the whole way. There was no question that it was the same dog, only young and healthy. He did much the same things, same old habits; he lay down on his favorite spot in the car and got up to watch the door open or close. But also some habits he had left behind: he placed his head on Louis's lap and nudged him when he didn't get petted right away. When they got home, the dog went rummaging through the house. Louis was surprised and elated when Yogi came up to him with a piece of rope in his mouth. Years before they used to play tug of war with that same rope. Who knows where he'd kept it hidden all that time. Louis played with Yogi, but after a short time felt tired and was afraid he had thrown out his shoulder. "Sorry buddy, I guess I'm too old for you now."

Louis went up to Sharon's bedroom. She was sleeping, as usual, sedated, but he knew she could still hear him. Since that time that he felt her console him, he had talked to her all the time.

"Shari, sweetheart, we are going to get you well. Look at Yogi!" Louis turned around. The dog was sitting by the door, hesitant to come in. "Doesn't he look great? We'll do the same for you, dear."

He asked the house for the two androids to help him.

The androids came in, and he instructed them to carry Sharon into the bathroom. He watched as one, who was made to look like a young woman in her twenties, carefully reached one arm under Sharon's legs and another under her back, lifting her. The other android, a young man, also twenty-something, reached over and together they stood Sharon up and walked her into the bathroom. Louis undressed her, and they placed her in the tub.

Louis spent the next two hours with the androids caring for his wife; they bathed her, washed her hair, and dressed her. He then asked one of the androids to apply the makeup the way he had watched her do so many times in the course of their life together: "foundation to hide the wrinkles, a little accent on the eyelashes, some blush on the cheekbones to make them stand out," he recalled her describing one time when he'd watched her getting ready to go out, "and some subdued lipstick so I can feel young again."

When done, he examined Sharon. It was a sad sight—not her at all—but there wasn't much he could do, and he asked the androids to carry his unconscious wife to the living room and place her on her favorite chair, where she slumped like a rag doll. He tried not to look at her and waited impatiently for almost two hours until two thirty, attempting to read a magazine.

Two-thirty finally rolled around, and he told the androids to carry Sharon to the car. He watched as the male android carried her in its arms and placed her in her usual seat. Then the female android gently smoothed out Sharon's clothes, folded her arms, and propped her head with pillows. Louis sat next to her. Yogi lay down by his feet.

After a twenty-minute ride, Louis made his way into the lab with his wife, carried by one of the car androids, followed by Yogi wagging his tail.

D'Anjou sat at a desk with his assistant by his side, and Larry and Suzanne stood behind him peering over his shoulder.

Joy, with the biologist in tow, walked over from another room looking fresh and perky. She motioned for the android to place Sharon on a chair next to a table with the scanning equipment and other devices Louis didn't recognize.

The android lowered Sharon onto the chair. She was limp, her torso bent over, arms to the sides, her head tilted, drool on her chin.

Louis took a handkerchief out of his back pocket, dabbed her chin, and tried to straighten out her body, make her look more like herself.

"I thought of having Sharon's oncologist join us," Joy said, placing a hand on Louis's arm, "but I decided we have all the expertise we need. We all know how to identify cancer cells. But I can still call him if you want me to."

Louis thought for a moment. "No, I agree. The task doesn't require specialized medical training. We have all the expertise we need: Larry has the computer knowledge, Alphonse and Suzanne both have degrees in biophysics, both you and I have studied applied physiology, and we have Marianne along, who I suppose has a doctorate in biology."

"Yes, she does," answered Joy, looking at Marianne. "She's a professor at Harvard, and a first tier."

"Very good. If anything unexpected comes up, I'm sure between us we'll be able to figure it out. The fewer people we involve the better."

They set to work on Sharon. D'Anjou ran the handheld scanner along her body, all the while observing the computer display, which was filling up with codes. He reached for the keyboard, tapped a few keys, and the codes changed color. Louis could see the tumor, the unaffected brain tissue, and the effects of aging.

D'Anjou and Joy started cleaning the strings, this time assisted by the program Suzanne and Larry had written.

Louis turned his gaze to Sharon, her comatose bland features; her body slumped every which way. Watching her he felt afraid, afraid something might go wrong. It was one thing to teleport a dog, but what about a human? What right did he have to experiment with his wife? What if something went wrong and she ended up not herself, but...something else?

"Stop...Joy, stop...wait," Louis blurted out. "I think I should go next."

Joy looked up from the keyboard, her eyebrows arched, eyes quizzical. "Louis, why?"

"We haven't done a human subject. If anything goes wrong, let it be me instead."

Joy stared at him wide-eyed. "No way...if anyone is to be a test subject, I'll do it!"

"No, Joy. Let's be reasonable—"

"Yes, Louis, be reasonable, you are invaluable…do you get it? Invaluable."

"Joy…I don't want to argue; time is wasting. If anything happens to an old man…and listen, the experiment would not be complete unless we reverse the effects of aging. You are too young!" There, he thought, I got you.

Joy was silent for a moment, her hands still on the keyboard. She bit her lower lip, eyes blinked rapidly. "All right, Louis, your call." She turned to the lab assistant. "Arlene, would you continue here while I start with Regent Sagan?"

D'Anjou scanned him, then both he and Joy worked assiduously in their displays and keyboards, cleaning the strings that represented Louis's body. Larry and Suzanne helped Arlene with Sharon.

Louis watched for a moment. "Can I help? I know what you two are doing. Let me at it."

D'Anjou directed him to another station beside Joy. A keyboard and display came up and he worked on his own strings. Louis couldn't help but notice how fast and precise Joy's movements were. They were done in a little over an hour. "It took much less time than Yogi," Louis said.

"Because of the new program," said D'Anjou.

Louis looked around the room. He felt fear grip his stomach, and his mouth felt dry.

"Okay, Louis," Joy said in a low voice, as though she had a hard time saying the words. "Ready to become a twenty-five-year-old?" She tried to sound chipper, but the tension had come through in her voice.

As if in a daze, feeling as though it were happening to someone else, Louis walked into the glassite cube. He locked eyes with Joy, whose unblinking gaze seemed to bore right through him. The door shut…he saw a flash and felt his body exploding…and a feeling…it was…then the door opened. What happened? Did it fail? He looked and was surprised to find himself on the opposite side of the room, staring at Joy and D'Anjou, who were walking over…but…he could see very clearly, and he was light…he tried to walk and his legs…were energized…he felt as though he could leap!

Joy grabbed him by the shoulders, her eyes wide. "Louis? Louis?"

"Yes, Joy…I'm fine…I feel terrific!"

Joy stared at his face and examined his body, up and down. "You should, man! You look terrific!"

Louis studied his hands…the hands of a young man…no age spots, no wrinkles…a stranger's hands. Yogi stared at him, his head cocked to one side, and Louis could see every hair on his body. Yogi came over and smelled his shoes, his legs…then jumped up, tongue hanging out, slobber all over the place.

"How do you feel?" D'Anjou asked, handheld device in hand. "I mean…do you feel you are the same person?"

The biologist was also analyzing him with her device. Larry and Suzanne peered over her shoulder, both totally absorbed.

"What are we doing here, Louis?" Joy asked.

"Joy, come on, we came to teleport Sharon. It's me. I'm fine." And looking down at Yogi, who was rubbing his muzzle against his legs: "If Yogi recognizes me, then all is well, don't you think?" Louis bent down and picked up Yogi in his arms and lifted him effortlessly. It felt so good to be strong. And his back didn't hurt…nothing hurt.

Joy seemed mesmerized. She walked slowly toward Sharon's display, all the while her gaze riveted on Louis.

It's Louis, all right, she told herself. But what a difference! She could not stop staring at him, even when she told herself she should not. The old Louis was still there somewhere, the one she loved like no one else on this earth.

"Let's do Sharon, shall we?" Louis said, and that seemed to break the spell. Joy got back to work.

When they were done, Louis wanted to check and double-check everything himself. It was Sharon, and he had to be sure. He

110

realized his mind was more nimble. Thoughts, perceptions, and concepts flowed fast.

When he was satisfied, Louis lifted Sharon, chair and all, and placed her on the platform inside the cube. With his heart racing, he watched the door close, then turned around.

And there she was! The Sharon of long ago, the one in the photographs, the one he both remembered vividly and had forgotten somehow; like looking at a long-lost Sharon, one who existed at some point. Oh, how beautiful! he thought. He studied the once familiar shoulder-length light-brown hair, the delicate yet strong features, brown eyes, graceful lips; the face that had faded over the years. She sat in the chair with her eyes wide-open in amazement, took a deep breath, as though testing her lungs, and gingerly stood up. She was tall! And her body—how graceful. She filled the old woman's dress like never before. It hung out of place on the young figure.

"Lalo? Is that you? Oh my God, what happened to you? What's happening? Where are we? What happened?"

It was her voice, but a young voice. Melodious.

Louis rushed over and embraced her. Oh, she feels so very good, so alive! The warmth of her body, her smell, her feel, he thought. "All is well, sweetheart. All is well, Shari!"

Louis laughed out loud and twirled Sharon around, dancing, to the amusement of everyone in that room. But he could also see in their eyes a certain reticence, disbelief. And he didn't know what to think. A part of him was cautious, a part of him knew everything has unforeseen consequences. But that could wait; for now he had Sharon in his arms, wonderfully alive, wonderfully young and vital.

11

R eilly slammed his fist on the massive desk, and a vase in a corner tumbled down onto the floor. "What do you mean, you don't know where Sagan is?" he yelled.

General Eagan, standing at attention, turned pale. "Sir, he hasn't shown up at any of his offices, not here at Columbia, or Human Services Administration, or Space Administration, or anywhere else he frequents."

Reilly clenched his jaw, stood up, and glared at Eagan. "What about his home? If you are concerned about some police androids, I can send you a thousand armed and fully armored soldiers."

"The entire neighborhood is like a fortress, full of police androids and surveillance equipment. The government has gone out of its way to protect Sagan; it will take a full-scale army to get to him."

"Look, I'm getting a little tense here. I'll send you Captain Cheney and ten of his elite men. They are professionals, you hear? They can invade Sagan's home without any fuss. You'll be in charge of the operation. Need I remind you I don't accept failure?"

"No, sir!"

"Good. They should arrive tomorrow. Now put them to work. I want Sagan."

That evening was strange and wondrous and decidedly surreal. Louis couldn't stop kissing Sharon, and she kissed him back with equal passion, love, and attachment.

The surreal effect carried through everything. He had a sense of not being himself, of living in someone else's body. He sat on the edge of the bed and felt his body in wonder, stared at his hands, his arms, touched his face. He noticed Sharon was doing the same, raising a hand to feel a breast, or an arm.

The next morning they talked in bed about how wonderful everything felt, how fresh and unencumbered their bodies were. But did a part of them miss the other selves? The old, gentle, declining selves?

Those old people were gone. At least their bodies, their old ways, their old aches—though it was the aches, the positioning of oneself to end life, that gave everything a certain quality. Now they had to think about the future, a long, long future.

But for now, they recognized they needed a period of readjustment, but also a time for celebration.

"Let's go away, Lalo," Sharon said, looking up at the ceiling, twirling her now abundant, rich, and silky light brown hair with the fingers of one hand. "Let's go to the writer's retreat in California. I would love to see the place again…now that I'm healthy."

Louis kissed her. Then turned over and stared at the ceiling. He sighed. "I can't leave." And Louis brought Sharon up to date on what had transpired in the past two months with the Patriots. "I'm afraid I'm the best qualified to deal with this…actually the only one. Joy put together a team for me: herself; Regent Angela Hall, a physicist and criminal psychologist; and Lawrence Zimmerman, an artificial intelligence expert and bioengineer. You met him; he was at the teleporter lab…We're just starting to gather information about the Patriots and looking at our options."

"Oh my, Lalo…but you can't just go about your business as regent the way you look."

"No, that's true. That's a new problem. I need to work from somewhere people won't see me."

"The writer's retreat, Lalo. It's perfect."

Louis thought for a moment. "Yes, you are right." He put on his bathrobe and called Joy. She had been expecting his call, for, as she said, "there is so much to talk about."

"Yes, Joy, I agree. We have a very full plate on our hands," Louis said as he noticed Joy's still mystified look on her eyes studying him. "Perhaps the best scenario would be for me to go away with Sharon and work from a place in California…remote and unknown. I'll be working long distance, and buying some time before I make a public appearance. I don't want my neighbors to see me and have to explain. I assume you and Larry are staying abreast of the Patriots?"

"Yes," she replied. "The tracking we put in place paid off. Gary is without doubt a key person in the Patriots. We managed to monitor all of his communications, except for one very sophisticated device. Patrick is working on that."

"Okay. Joy, I know what we did with D'Anjou was a bit hasty and we haven't studied the implications—"

"I'm with you. So far I've been able to keep a lid on it: no one outside of those of us in that lab and Angie knows about it. But once people see you and Sharon, the game's up."

"Yes. We need to give this a lot of thought."

"When are you leaving?"

"As soon as possible. In the meantime we won't go out. I'll have an android walk Yogi, and even that is risky. If someone comes to the door or calls, we'll use a privacy setting."

Captain Cheney didn't like tall people, and Sagan was over six feet tall, so it was going to be fun cutting him down to size. Just grab him, throw him down on the ground, and pummel him a few times. Then pack him in the back of his own car and off to Texas.

Cheney and his team —three men and four women, all handpicked by him for this mission—walked in pairs so as not to attract attention. He and his right-hand person, Marion, walked into Sagan's building and flashed their fake Police Services credentials at the door reader. The rest of the team was to remain outside the building until either dismissed or called in.

Louis hung up the phone and turned toward the bed. Sharon was gone, but he could hear her in her walk-in closet. "Shari, you are getting your things together? Good. Let's leave as soon as we can."

There was no response, and he walked into her closet. She had gone shopping for clothes. Her real self was sitting in a chair, while her virtual self in the closet display was trying on clothes at Bloomingdales…then Orlando's…Four Seasons, and at least two more stores, fortunately in privacy mode so no one could see her, and at each she tentatively chose one or two dresses, and tops, and shoes, and blouses, and shorts. Louis stood watching her, biding his time, but all the while he felt the tension mounting. He was sure a neighbor was bound to spot them, somehow. She finally settled on several outfits, and the old clothes in her closet were scooped up by a house android and thrown in the energy recovery recycler slot in one of the walls. The closet manufacturer whirred, and as he watched, dress after dress, pants and shorts and blouses came out and filled the space where the old clothes once hung. The real Sharon stood up and tried on everything all over again, smiling happily.

The house announced visitors, human agents from Police Services. Louis left the closet, locked up Yogi in the bedroom just in case the police agents were familiar with the neighborhood and had seen Yogi before. He went downstairs to investigate. If they came in person it must be urgent…but he would have to somehow…tell them he was someone else, maybe a younger relative.

He found a man and a woman in the foyer. The man was short and rather unpleasant looking; the woman was tall and stern. They both looked very fit…something wasn't quite right…they didn't act like police agents.

"We are looking for Regent Sagan, sir," the man said.

"Yes, he just left for the university a minute ago. May I help you? I'm his nephew."

In one quick, sudden move, the man pinned Louis against the wall. "We are going to the university and get your uncle, understand?" The voice was suddenly harsh, nasty.

"Who are you?" Louis could hardly talk; the man was crushing his windpipe with one arm. It occurred to Louis that they hadn't detected Sharon, didn't know she was in the master bedroom closet just up the stairs.

"Never mind who we are. Does the car outside recognize your biometrics?"

"Yes."

The man grabbed Louis's right arm and twisted it painfully behind his back, then pushed him through the living room toward his car visible outside the large window. The woman followed them, looking around, as though this was an everyday occurrence. Louis hoped Sharon didn't make a sound, or decide to come out of the bedroom for some reason.

As they approached the large window and it started to slide open, the man released Louis's arm a bit. "Once we get inside, tell the car to take us to the university. Then call your uncle and tell him you want to see him right away. We'll dock at his office. You got that?"

"Yes," mumbled Louis, glad they were out of the house and Sharon was safe.

The man shoved Louis into the backseat, and he was about to sit next to him when the car lurched violently forward, as straps came out and held Louis in place. The man and woman bounced against one of the windows, then the car jumped up and they were thrown on the floor; but they were very nimble and rolled, then stood up fast, as the car lurched to one side, and they again rolled and landed on their feet. The bouncing and jolting around became more violent, but the pair managed to avoid injury, they rolled where they landed and ended up on their feet, like cats. Each time they came within a few feet of Louis, they made desperate attempts to grab him either by a leg or an arm. During a sudden turn, the door opened wide and the car turned on its side. Louis, hanging from the seat straps, watched the pair fall through the opening, flailing their arms. He caught a glimpse of glistening water hundreds of feet below. Just as suddenly the car righted itself and the door closed.

Louis looked out the window. They were flying over the ocean. He took some deep breaths, his mind reeling, trying to figure out exactly what had happened. He felt both relieved and horrified.

"Regent Sagan, are you all right?" the pleasant female voice asked. The two car androids came to look him over.

Louis's straps came off, and he stood up, while the androids reached out to steady him. "I'm all right. But how, I mean exactly how...I mean who directed you..."

Louis felt the car lurch forward, and it kept accelerating. The androids sat him down and the straps secured him. He had never been in a car going that fast.

"Everything is okay, regent. I've turned around to pick up Regent Willcott. The other individuals who came with those two are about to enter your building."

A couple of minutes later, the car docked at the condo. Louis tried to get up but the straps still held him. The two car androids rushed out and ran up the stairs to the bedroom. In a matter of seconds, they came down, one carrying a terrified Sharon and her suitcase, the other carrying Yogi under one arm and Oscar in his cage under the other.

The one android placed Sharon on the car seat, the other dropped Yogi and Oscar on the floor. Sharon and the animals were strapped down and the car took off.

Sharon looked pale. "What's happening, Louis?"

118

"I don't rightly know. Two Patriot agents just tried to either kill me or kidnap me. Somehow this car was able to save me...and killed them."

"I'm sorry," the female voice said, "but I had no choice. Throwing them out into the ocean was all I could do."

"I don't understand," Sharon said, her eyes very wide. "Who is that talking?"

"It's the car, sweetheart. I don't understand, either." And Louis told Sharon how the couple had forced him into his car thinking he was his own nephew, and how they had been dumped into the ocean.

Sharon looked around the car. "And all of that happened while I was getting new clothes? And this car! Obviously someone must have programmed it to protect you. That's wonderful, but who? And I never heard of a car like this."

"Yes. Well, for now I must call Joy. She and the rest might be targets."

Joy was able to talk calmly when she heard Louis's news, but inside she felt her insides being torn apart. The conversation was brief: they had to leave right away. After Louis gave her the destination coordinates, she called Larry, Angie, and D'Anjou. Her orders were to leave with minimal fuss so as not to attract attention. She gave them fifteen minutes to pack as though they were not coming back.

12

On the way to California, with a now calm Yogi licking his paw on the floor, and Oscar in his carrier next to Sharon, his yowls now subsiding, Louis felt the tension leaving him. All was well. The car reassured them no one was following them. It gave a lengthy explanation about tracers and Central, but what it came down to was that no one was following.

Louis asked the car who had programmed her.

"I'm self-programmable, regent. From my inception, I started improving myself, and this is what I've come up with after thirty-six years."

Louis shook his head. "Well, at any rate, I am grateful for what you did." He felt foolish talking with a machine.

No one knew where they were. They were indeed safe. He decided to enjoy the trip.

Sharon wore one of her new outfits, a loose-fitting flowery dress. She seemed to have relaxed as well.

Following a conversation where they reviewed over and over again what had happened, Sharon looked at him quizzically. "Can we defeat the Patriots, Lalo?"

"Yes. I think we can. We need to convene some key regents, and move fast, but we have what it takes. Those people are not that sophisticated beyond a few gadgets they inherited from a hundred years ago."

"Lalo. What about this technology that made us young? Everyone will want to stay young forever and do away with ailments. Once the world finds out about it, it will cause chaos. Not to mention those atavists in Texas. They'll do everything to get their hands on D'Anjou. Have you thought of all that?"

Louis felt the tension grip him again. In fact, he had been doing his best to avoid thinking about it. "I have, Shari. Of course, we have revolutionized medicine and have found the fountain of youth. We may have decreased mortality to near zero. Without proper planning this could be a great threat. We can't afford to let the atavists get their hands on the technology. No way."

"Yes. There's no telling how they might use it. Surely they won't take any measures to prevent overpopulation."

Louis procured a soft drink from the console by his seat. "Right," he said, taking a sip of the lemonade through a straw. "We can't expect the atavist population not to reproduce like crazy without the chips. Dear Lord, what we went through when we had twenty-four billion! All the food riots! And how they killed most all wildlife...not to mention pets...and all the murders for something like a loaf of bread—"

"I didn't know!"

"Only atavists can be so brutal. Normal people chose to starve rather than succumb to such things. Anyway, I'm terribly concerned. We may be facing a population explosion on a grand scale."

"What if you were to offer a compromise? If you have children, you can't rejuvenate. I think even atavists will understand that."

Louis thought for a moment and nodded. "We can stipulate that those who chose to become parents agree not to make themselves younger. Maybe in their case the process can be used to cure only. But once people grow old, they won't be able to use D'Anjou's technology for curing; it's too harsh."

Sharon reached for her console, pushing a button and also getting a drink. She studied the glass with pink liquid for a moment.

"I don't remember the process being that rough. All I remember is a glorious flash, and a sense of wholeness and joy, akin to what I experience during meditation."

Louis absentmindedly looked at Yogi. He recalled a strange feeling…and it did feel joyous…but out of place and so unexpected he'd had a hard time processing it. "Is that what you feel during meditation? I had no idea."

"But you meditate, Lalo. Don't you feel an immense joy, and such a glorious feeling of being one with everything?"

Louis shook his head. "Afraid not. I do feel peaceful, and it's lovely, but nothing like you describe.

"We were briefly in another dimension," Louis continued, "a parallel universe. Could it be that's what you do in meditation? That would be fascinating if it were indeed the case, the human mind capable of such a feat."

Sharon looked gravely at him. "It's not the mind, dear. The mind can take us to the portals of meditation, but we need something else to enter."

"And what is that?"

She stared out the car window at the big expanse of blue. "I can't explain it. I don't think anyone can."

The weather was glorious at the writer's old retreat in the Northern California Coastal Range. Louis had decided it would be great to get at least a couple of hours of enjoyment. They had young bodies now, and Sharon was healthy. Things might look dire, but for a short while they could look the other way. They had the afternoon to themselves; Joy and the rest would show up that evening, and it would be back to the Patriot emergency.

"Forget everything," Louis said. "For a moment let's just be alive."

They changed clothes to shorts, T-shirts, and running shoes, and practically ran to the meadow with Yogi. They climbed the boulder.

The mountains in the far distance were crystal clear. They sat luxuriating in the quiet and soon became aware of life around them, rushing in the bushes and sounds coming from the forest. They could be elk, deer, and coyotes just as the writer had described two hundred years ago. They came down from the boulder and on a patch of rocky soil they found rattlesnakes warming themselves in the sun. Up in the sky, hawks flew in circles.

They ran to the top of the meadow and stopped when they were both exhausted. Louis sat on an old log, Sharon on a rock a few feet away. "That's quite a gift you gave us, my friend," she said, out of breath, her cheeks flushed. "We have what humanity has always craved, the wisdom of old age and the bodies of the young. We are virtually superhuman, then."

Louis thought for a moment. "Yes, that's right. We might have created a new humanity, and you and I are the experimental specimens."

"And Yogi. Don't forget him: he was the first one."

Louis turned to look at the dog resting under a tree, his tongue hanging out, panting. "I wonder what he thinks about this."

"That's the beauty of being a dog. You don't ever think, but simply accept what is."

Louis bent over and picked a long stem of wild grass and bit into it. It was a little bitter, but fresh, full of life. "How do you know, Shari? Maybe he's just as introspective as you and I."

Sharon swayed her legs, and the sun lit up her hair. "Nah. Food, sleep, a human for petting. That's it."

"He's my philosopher dog. I never told you, but I get some of my best ideas from him."

"Oh, you do?" She leaned back, laughing. "The secret is out, then. The source of the great Louis Sagan's genius."

Louis smiled, but it was a doubtful smile. "I don't quite know what to make of that 'genius' part. Lately, I have discovered people's opinion of me does seem to be over the top. I wonder why. I actually haven't done anything that extraordinary."

Sharon laughed again, came over, sat beside him on the log, and slapped his back. "Oh, Lalo. Someone else would think you were being modest, but I know better. You are just so out of touch, sometimes I'm amazed you remember your own name." She stopped laughing and became thoughtful. "All my life I have tried to step out of your shadow. It's hard to be known as 'Louis Sagan's wife,' rather than Regent Sharon Willcott…You get that?"

He twirled the stem of grass in his mouth. It had never occurred to him. "I…I…that's hard to believe…"

"Believe it, Lalo. You practically run the entire government." She shook her head. "You would be the envy of all those atavist conquerors of old who dreamed of ruling the world. And here you are, the quintessential absentminded professor."

"I'm absentminded?"

Sharon sat on his lap and planted big, wet kisses all over his face, laughing once more. Then she stood and grabbed his hand. "You are so precious! Come, my absentminded genius, let's roll around in that luscious grass!"

Rolling around meant literally rolling down the grassy hill laughing like children with an excited Yogi biting at their heels and jumping over them. Clearly, Louis had forgotten how to be young, but found that remembering was not hard at all. They came to rest near the boulder.

After a short while Sharon stood up. She surveyed the far-off hills, the grass swaying gently in the sun and something scampering through the grass and into the forest some twenty feet away. "I can just imagine the writer walking along this same spot," she said, "I bet we are stepping on the same ground he walked on."

Louis looked around. The green mountains were well defined against a blue sky, the lake was a bright sparkle in the distance, and the tall grass was sprinkled with yellow and powder-blue flowers. The place was incredibly beautiful. "Yes, this particular place has not changed at all in thousands of years. The writer talked about how in all likelihood Indians lived on this land going back to prehistoric times…I'm so glad some regent decided to establish the nature preservation zones."

"I'm just glad we are allowed to be here. That's quite a privilege." Sharon walked, swinging her arms wildly, just like a little girl. Then she turned around, bearing the expression of the old Sharon. "Was the writer a happy man? Did he lead a good life?"

"He led a productive life, I don't get the feeling he was particularly happy, not with the unhappy marriages…and as a child and a young man he suffered from obsessive compulsive disorder and chronic depression, both of which, according to him, he overcame through meditation."

Sharon stopped by a massive cedar tree at the edge of the meadow and ran her hands up along the trunk. "A deep meditator, eh? You need to really meditate to get over something like that." She sounded pleased. "If he meditated deeply, then he was a happy man, I can assure you.

"Interesting life. Now we know what shaped his character," she said. "Overcoming depression and OCD on his own was quite a feat. And we know he had trouble picking the right woman for a partner…but you also mentioned his love for animals."

"Yes, the writer speaks very fondly of the pets he had throughout his life. Oddly enough he also speaks fondly of mourning doves."

"Mourning doves? Did he have any as pets?"

"No, no. He said that as a twelve-year-old—when his family moved to a coastal city in Colombia—he used to sit in his room and listen to the mourning doves. He found their cooing soothing, as though they were reaching out to him. When he moved to Hawaii much later in his life, he heard the doves again and felt they were welcoming him home."

Sharon leaned back against the tree. "How sweet. I would love to hear the doves. Where do we find them?"

"Somewhere warm, but not too hot."

"Hawaii!" Sharon said with glee. Then she became thoughtful for some time, her eyes fixed on the ground.

"I'm truly impressed he found a cure through meditation," she said. "I wonder how much he changed…I know he found peace, and real love there."

They approached the cabin with the heavy awareness that their brief respite from reality was about to end.

Shortly after dinner Louis heard cars overhead, went to the door, and saw a car and two white vans land. After a moment Joy emerged from the car, suitcase in hand, followed by Angie, Larry, and Suzanne. Arlene stepped out of one of the vans, followed by D'Anjou.

Louis welcomed them and they sat in the living room, Joy, Angie, Larry, and Suzanne on the couch facing Louis and Sharon in their reading chairs. D'Anjou and Arlene brought chairs from the dining room.

They all exchanged pleasantries with Sharon, who then picked up her book and started reading.

"Well," Larry said. "Here we are."

Louis smiled at him. "Yes, things are now very different. We need to proceed with caution. Any chance you guys were followed?"

Larry shook his head. "No. I used a disguise signature for our three vehicles so Central or anyone else monitoring traffic would have confused us for mass transit. We were three large buses ferrying third tiers to the West Coast."

"Excellent. Now, let's take care of some basics. For tonight, Alphonse and Arlene, you can sleep in this living room; Joy and Angie, you have the study. Larry, I have a cot for you which we can set up in the kitchen."

After some discussion, Arlene and D'Anjou wanted to sleep in one of the vans with the equipment, and Larry said he had brought a tent in his phone that he could manufacture and set up next to the cabin. After examining images of his tent, Joy and Angie decided they each wanted one, too.

For the long run, Angie suggested building an underground facility using a trusted friend who owned an engineering firm. "Let's build underground so we remain hidden and not disturb the forest," she proposed. "But what exactly shall we build?"

"Let's plan for the worst-case scenario," Louis said, "and build for the very long term, a semi-permanent enclave, a residential facility large enough for us, a lab for Alphonse, and room for visitors."

Angie contacted her friend. After a brief but intense dialogue, she hung up and announced that work would start in two days.

Louis then retold them the whole incident with his two assailants.

"That's an amazing car," commented Larry. "Someone wanted you well protected."

"The Patriots must want you very badly," Joy said. "What can we do about it?"

"We are here," replied Larry, "that will do for now."

"Yes," Louis said. "Well, let's start figuring out a strategy."

"First off," Joy said, "we have some news. Larry's savant did some reverse surveillance—"

"That means using the existing surveillance and backtracking it to its origin," added Larry. "We were able to identify most of Gary's atavist army."

"Army?" Sharon sounded alarmed.

Larry nodded gravely. "Yes, there are many of them, armed with extremely deadly weapons. For what it's worth, only a portion of the army is fully equipped at this point. But they are receiving a large infusion of gold, diamonds and other valuables which they are using to purchase massive quantities of weapons, including what they call flying tanks, and artillery."

Angie held her clasped hands in front of her face. "And there are many of them. We watched one of their meetings in Houston, where they're headquartered. Gary and the rest were dressed in green uniforms, with insignias. They called one another by their rank. Gary is a general—"

"There is a person they call 'President Reilly,' five top generals, including Gary, and twenty other lesser generals." interrupted Larry. Turns out they have been busy planning long and hard for several years. The twenty million atavists we detected moving into Texas in the past ten years was part of their plan. They planted Gary in our department eight years ago, so he could be near you, Louis, we assume to gain information. Two other generals are members of the old oligarchy, the big powerful families that migrated to Texas. They are the conduit for all the gold pouring in."

Louis shook his head in disbelief. "That's so incredible. And scary. Twenty-five generals? How large is this army?"

"Oh, Louis!" Joy said. "They don't have many soldiers yet, around a hundred thousand or so, which is still worrisome. But this is just the 'foundation' as they call it. They talk about Reilly's goal to have five million soldiers!"

"So we were right…they wanted us to forcibly move atavists to Texas so that—"

"Yes!" Joy stood up and walked around the couch. "We would have provided a lot of recruits for their army. They are now busy spreading their 'Seven Regents Plot' to create more animosity toward us."

Louis kept shaking his head, as though to dispel the entire notion. "But why do you think they wanted to kill or kidnap me?"

"Maybe because you are the best-known regent, and that would make a statement," Joy said.

"They plan to invade us, take the world government over by force," commented Larry. "That's what the five million soldier army is for."

"What do we know about Reilly?" Louis asked.

"Nothing," Larry said. "Only that he's in charge."

"To make matters worse," added Joy, "All the regents and most of the first tiers are clamoring to find out where you are, Louis. The situation is being exploited by the Patriots. They claim you and the other six regents are plotting an escape, now that they've exposed you."

Angie sat in the couch, her face tense. "What in the world can we do?"

Louis nodded, lost in thought; then he raised his head. "If they want Texas so badly, let's give it to them!"

Joy's eyes grew wide. "What? Give them exactly what they want? A chance to build that huge army? A good many are already in Texas, so we are saying 'take over,' and invite your crazy friends to join you so you can then threaten us?"

"I know, Joy, that's very likely exactly what they have in mind," Louis said. "But it will buy us time; it will take them a lot of effort to take over Texas. They won't be able to do anything else for a while."

"That's a good point," said Larry, who had scooted to one end of the couch. "It will take them two months to take over key institutions, and eradicate or absorb the local militias the ultra-rich warlords have in place. They will also need to accommodate the projected millions of atavists in North America that will come pouring in. Then it will take them four months to train soldiers, get organized into a large enough army, and develop strategies—"

"Is that your opinion?" snapped Angie.

"Actually, no," responded Larry in his calm voice. "I have run a series of predictive algorithms with the information we have. Six months is a safe assumption."

"How do you know those things about them?" Sharon asked, her hands gripping the book on her lap.

"Oh, we have a profile on all of the people in the two meetings we tapped into," responded Joy. "We know who they are and how they think."

"If you know who they are, why don't we just reinject them with biochips?"

Joy paced the room. "Because they are heavily armed and in Texas, Sharon. And they have surveillance in many places. They'll probably know when Police Services will mount their offensive and be ready for them."

Louis took a deep breath. "Fine, we have no choice. Joy, send out the atavist proposal to the cleared regents who are part of peer review. How many have we cleared?"

"Over five hundred," Joy said. "Two hundred or so are part of the atavist project."

Larry ran a hand through his short-cropped hair. "We still have some loose ends—"

"Doesn't matter. We have the defenses in place, right?"

Larry sat up straight. "The virtual scenario–generating biocomputer? Yes."

"Fine" Louis said. "Very likely we'll end up using it. In the meantime let's figure we have six months to come up with a permanent means to deal with Reilly and his friends. Joy—"

"I'm on it," Joy said and tapped her sleeve to make her virtual phone appear on her hand. She then produced keyboard and display.

"Larry," Louis said, "are the virtual scenarios effective on only humans?"

"You mean will their cars and androids be fooled as well? The answer is yes."

Sharon's stare caught Louis's attention. It was as though she didn't quite recognize him. He smiled at her, and she smiled back, although a tentative smile. "Louis, are you going to imprison those people?"

"No, Sharon, we are letting them settle in Texas. They will be free to go or not as they choose. But we need to protect ourselves."

Her usual soft brown eyes now looked hard. "All these things you are planning, have they been approved?"

"No, Sharon, not yet. That's why we are convening peer review."

Sharon looked at Louis while she lovingly stroked Oscar, who had climbed on her lap. "But not all of peer review, just a few select regents."

"The two hundred or so we cleared and can trust."

"That's not what the New Paradigm constitution says. We are supposed to be a fully transparent society. You are also supposed to broadcast the proceedings to the public."

Louis nodded, bent down, placed his elbows on his knees, and brought his chin to rest on his clenched fists as he stared at the floor. "The total atavist project peer review group is not much bigger, a bit over three hundred, so with the ones we cleared we will have a quorum. If we were to release the proposal to full peer review, we would alert those regents who may be Patriots. You know that, Sharon. And of course, we can't possibly broadcast the proceedings."

"How will those people live in Texas? Is there enough food? How many people are you expecting?" Sharon asked. Before Louis could answer, she added, "This is not just a ploy to leave them to their own devices somewhere inhospitable, is it?"

Louis cleared his throat. Sharon had never questioned him before, and for some reason she seemed to doubt him now. The hard look in her eyes was unsettling. "There are fifty-five million defined atavists currently in Texas and a total population of seventy-one million, which includes borderline atavists and normals. We don't know how many will opt to stay. We suspect that a good many of the fifty-five million atavists are Patriots. We don't know exactly how many followers their leader, Reilly, has, or how many additional people will join him. Current infrastructure in Texas, including farms, can support upward of a hundred million. For all we know, all forty-two million defined atavists in this country and Canada may pour into the state.

"Whatever the case, we won't let them starve; we'll send in supplies, including food synthesizers."

Sharon's eyes were fixed on her cat. "So this President Reilly would almost double his atavist population."

"That's the potential."

Louis turned to the assembled group. "Let's meet tomorrow morning again."

The meeting was set for eight in the morning. They got up to set up for the night. Larry went to his briefcase in a corner, opened it, and retrieved a manufacturing unit, a two-foot square flat contraption. After sweeping his phone across it, the machine whirred. A couple of minutes later they walked out with compacted tents under their arms.

With the visitors gone, Louis turned to Sharon. She appeared sullen, quiet. There was now a tension between them.

"Shari?"

"Louis, I don't want to talk right now. Can this wait? I need time to think."

"To think about what?"

Sharon stood up with Oscar cradled in her arms. "About you. About me, about life, and about those awful Patriots." She walked in the direction of the bedroom, but turned around. There was sadness in her eyes. "Louis, I believe you welcome this challenge from the Patriots, that it energizes you. This is just an exciting part of your job, and I don't want any part of it.

"I never led my own life. I was aware of that for many years, but it didn't matter then. I think it's because I had my spiritual practice and my job, and we led parallel lives, and then came the illness—"

"But, Shari—"

"No, wait. Louis. Let me finish. Up until last week, I was ready to die. I had let go of this world, and that was fine. The only part I didn't like was that you were going to terminate your life as well. That didn't make sense. But anyway, I was ready to go. Now everything has changed, and I am looking to the next fifty or so years...I don't want to go back to my old life. I don't want to be Mrs. Louis Sagan...I don't—"

"Shari, I didn't know. I guess you are talking about living in my shadow, what you told me in the meadow."

Tears started flowing down her cheeks. "I don't know. I'm very proud of you and all you have accomplished. And I do love you. But I just don't want that old life…and I certainly don't want anything to do with the Patriots. I want to lead a spiritual life, that's all I want."

Louis stood up and stared out the window. It was very dark outside, and he could barely make out the outline of the nearest tree. "We can talk about this some other time, Shari. Okay?"

Sharon wiped her tears and nodded. She walked away with Oscar in her arms.

At eight the following morning, with the spring sun already warming up to shirtsleeve temperature, Louis heard Joy's voice outside. He opened the front door in time to see Angie come out of her tent and Joy meeting her with a cup of coffee. Larry stood by his own tent in hiking pants full of pockets and a T-shirt. Angie stopped to look around while Joy and Larry made their way to the front porch.

"This is quite a place, Louis," he heard Angie say. "I can see why you like it. Are there any bears?" she asked as she took off her jacket. She wore a tight-fitting white top, and the jeans couldn't have been any tighter.

"Yes, Angie. We are in a nature preservation zone, what is known as the Mendocino National Forest. Fifty thousand acres; originally it was more than a million."

"Wow. I've never been in a forest, only seen pictures and videos," she said, walking toward the house, her gaze lost in the trees. "It's magnificent! Can you hear the silence? I'll tell the construction crew to be as quiet as possible when they get here."

Louis led the way into the living room. Two empty cups stood on the coffee table along with plates with crumbs, the remnants of breakfast with Sharon, who had seemed in a better mood that morning, but still pensive and sullen.

134

Louis called for a house android to clear the place as he moved his reading chair closer to the coffee table and the couch. He motioned for Angie and Larry to take seats on the couch, and for Joy to grab a nearby dining room chair. He plopped himself down in his comfortable seat. D'Anjou, Arlene and Suzanne had decided their time was better spent with the equipment, according to Joy.

Louis studied Joy, Larry, and then Angie. They appeared tense. "Let's call a meeting of the atavist project. Let's make sure our numbers are over two hundred so we have a quorum of peer review, and they need to come here in secret."

Joy nodded. "The moment we have the facilities to accommodate them, we'll be ready."

"That means about a week," added Angie.

"Okay," Larry said. "So what do we tell the atavist project regents when they get here? I assume you don't want to disclose the biocomputer?"

"No," interjected Joy, "the fact that we are planting chips all over Texas and violated their sovereignty would not go well. Let's keep that to ourselves...and that we are tracking Reilly and his goons, thanks to Patrick...or...look, we'll just give them the basics."

Louis sighed. "What can we tell them about the Patriots? Where are we? Have they done anything else?"

"Nothing new from them," Joy said, running a hand through her hair. "But it's just a matter of time. In their last meeting, held three days ago, which we monitored, many of them—"

"You mean the generals, including Gary?" interrupted Louis.

"The group they call the 'high command,'" said Joy, "comprised by Reilly and the twenty-five generals."

"Where was the meeting held?"

"In Houston."

"So we have the high command, and within this group, the five generals. What are the five called?"

"No name. But they wear three stars, while the rest of the high command have two."

"Do they talk about killing all of us in the government?" Louis asked.

"Some of them do," answered Joy. "There are divisions emerging among them; there are the radical ones and the moderates. I don't know the proportions, but the moderates are being intimidated into submission. That's obvious."

"Well, that's good news for us," Louis said, standing up and walking over to the window. "Maybe we can exploit that."

"How?" Angie asked. "Pitting one element against the other? I don't think that will work."

Louis stared out the window at the trees outside. "No, no. What we would do is somehow separate the radicals from the moderates, and that way we'd have a faction that perhaps would be willing to work with us against Reilly."

"That would be great. But how?" Joy asked.

"If they have to make a hard choice, Joy. That usually forces a split, and gives birth to opposition groups."

"What would force a split?" Angie asked.

"War," Louis said. "The prospect of killing and being killed. That would do it. We need to create a war."

"You can't be serious!" exclaimed Angie.

"No, Angie, that's brilliant," Larry said. "My biocomputer can do it."

Angie thought for a moment. "So we have them fighting a virtual war. Then what?"

Louis turned away from the window. "Then we have isolated the radicals, the ones who are willing to kill."

"Yeah, but Louis," Joy said. "And they attack and find out there is no real army, what do we do then?"

"Joy," Larry interjected, "if you were to call here, you would see this room, its furniture, and Louis."

"Yeah, but that would be patently virtual. I wouldn't be able to touch Louis if I wanted to."

"Because your phone is set to virtual limits. That's how it was decided some years ago. It would—"

"You mean to tell me it's possible to go into a virtual realm and actually touch…"

"You do it all the time when you type on a virtual keyboard, reach your hand into a virtual display and manipulate items, go into a virtual store to buy clothes, read a virtual newspaper. If we were to eliminate virtual limits on phones, the chips on your side of the conversation would beam information into your brain through your pupils, or use sound frequencies to produce a similar effect. The same would be done at the other end; so, yes, we have the technology so you can shake someone's hand through the phone."

Angie sat upright. "And kiss, or whatever? Good grief, man! Of course you are not really touching the real person…"

"If I can make you believe you are, and at the same time make the other person believe the same, what's the difference?"

Angie was lost in thought for a moment. "So for our purposes, the Patriots would be fighting an enemy, killing and being killed? What happens to those who are killed in the virtual realm?"

"We can have them emerge in whatever reality we want."

"Let's have them awaken in hell!"

"Angie!" Louis said with a laugh. "Now, that's mean."

"But funny," Joy said. "It would be a hoot to watch!"

"Okay, okay," Louis said. "But seriously, let's think what happens after the 'battle.'"

An android brought tea, biscuits, and orange marmalade on a tray, pausing before each person in the room.

Larry stirred his tea. "I assume with these new developments the regents in charge of the biochip project will let us inject the Patriots we capture with systemic biochips. We just need to assure them we won't turn people into computers like we are doing with trees all over Texas."

"How do the biochips make trees into computers?" Angie asked.

"The biochips are at the molecular level," Larry answered, "and they are programmed to reproduce. Very much like a virus."

Angie reached for her cup and sipped. "Do the Patriots have the biochip technology?"

Larry stood up, yawned, and stretched. "No, I don't think that's possible. Just understanding the process requires extensive biophysics expertise. That's the reason why the general public doesn't know the extent of the technology: not because it's been kept secret, but because it's so esoteric."

"Well, enough talk," Louis interjected, "let's do some planning."

"Okay, Louis," Joy stood up from her chair. "I understand we need to remain out of sight until we figure out how to stop the Patriots and decide how to introduce the rejuvenation technology. But what do we tell the people who are clamoring to know what happened to you? We have a problem."

Louis sighed. "I'll send a communiqué telling people that I had a family crisis and wish to remain in seclusion for two months."

"Are two months enough time?"

"I hope so, Joy. We'll know more after we meet with the two-hundred regents...Please schedule the group a week from today. Let's assume that the facilities will be ready.

"And also, let's select a secondary location to this one."

"What for?" Angie asked.

"Maybe I'm being a tad paranoid, but I know the Patriots are after me, and probably all of you because they had you under surveillance and you disappeared.

"Joy, what's the best location for us to hide from the Patriots?"

Joy shook her head. "I don't quite know. Why don't we assign Larry to figure it out and actually secure something."

Larry assented. "Consider it done." Then he leaned forward in his chair. "I want to talk about hiding. A satellite scanning for Louis's biometrics will not recognize him at first pass, and assume a mistake was made because he is too young; but then the search program will order the satellite to make another pass to verify his identity, which normally takes a day. In short, once someone starts searching for Louis, they will find him within forty-eight hours."

Joy smiled. "D'Anjou could help us with that little problem."

Larry was taken aback. "You mean—"

"Yes, use his machine to change Louis's DNA. It shouldn't be hard to manipulate a couple of strands of DNA, and—presto—he's got green or brown eyes, a long nose, is taller or shorter, or maybe has lighter or darker skin. "

Larry nodded. "Yes, that would be enough biometric alteration to indicate a completely different individual."

Louis smiled. "Makes a lot of sense. Let's have D'Anjou start experimenting with a process to scramble my DNA."

The following day Larry called for a meeting.

When he had Louis, Joy, and Angie seated in the living room, Larry tapped his pants pocket to make his phone appear, then showed them images of three locations: one was an undersea eco-farm, the second a tropical island off the African coast, and the third an arid farm in Texas.

Larry studied their reactions for a moment. "Based on the probability assessments I ran, I concluded we need more than one alternate locale; that if we are forced to leave this place we'll be on the move for eight months. So I went ahead and secured all three locales. Based on what we know about the Patriots, these are the safest places for us to hide, even safer than here."

"How in the world did you come up with Texas?" Angie asked. "Are you nuts?"

"No, Angie. That's the safest of them all. It's the last place on earth the Patriots would think of looking for us."

"But Texas?" said Angie, "that's crazy."

Louis nodded. "Well, I, too, would hesitate to live in the enemy's backyard. So let's vote on where we would want to go and hold the other two as backup."

After a lengthy discussion, and after reviewing data supplied by Larry, they settled on the underwater eco-farm.

They would go after altering their DNA and appearance and assuming the identities of scientists assigned to help the in-house staff at the eco-farm. The farm in Texas and the island would be held as backups.

"Larry," Angie said, "you told us you secured these three places. How did you do that?"

"For the underwater farm, I requested positions using Louis's name. We are all being assigned by him to the eco-farm. The island and the Texas farm have a local currency based on the gold standard. I appropriated a cache of gold I found in a government warehouse. I used a small portion to pay for the places and still have most of it left. I have no idea how to use currency, but I'm learning."

Angie sat up straight, her eyes fixed on Larry. "You mean you went through the Treasury Department for the gold? Are you an idiot?" she shouted. "They'll be able to trace us wherever we go in a matter of hours!"

Larry seemed unperturbed by Angie's outburst. "No, Angie. I didn't follow normal procedure. I located the gold in storage and took it."

Angie appeared surprised and then chuckled. "You mean you stole it? Great going, Regent Zimmerman!" Then after a pause: "Sorry about that," she said with a tense smile.

Larry returned her smile. "That's okay, Angie. We're all a bit edgy."

"Where do you keep the gold?" asked Joy.

"It's still in my car, but I will transfer it to Louis's. It has a larger cargo hold."

"When did you do all that?" Inquired Louis.

"Yesterday. It took me all afternoon."

"Any chance that you were detected or followed?"

"No, I was careful."

13

"No one can disappear like that, no one!" Reilly got up from his chair as though ready to pounce. "You mean Cheney and his team walked into Sagan's condo and...what?"

General Eagan, dressed in his parade uniform, stood along with the other three-star generals in the well-appointed reception room of the presidential palace in Crawford, Texas, on the site of a former cattle ranch. "Cheney went into Sagan's condo along with his top operative and was never heard from again, sir," repeated Eagan.

"So what happened to him? Did he find Sagan? Did he encounter police androids? Was he killed?"

"I don't know, sir. He and his top agent were in there less than ten minutes. When the rest of the team failed to hear from them, they went in and found the place empty, with no sign of struggle. It was just empty."

"Could they have taken Sagan's car and gone somewhere?"

"Possibly. But then Cheney would have reported the fact. He wouldn't have gone anywhere without notifying his team."

"So they just vanished?" Reilly paced the room. "What about Sagan, where is he?"

"We don't know, sir. We have scanned for his biometrics all over New York City, and all over the state—"

"Then scan the whole damn world! I'll give you whatever technicians, spies, agents, and soldiers you need: just find Sagan!

And find out what happened to Cheney! People just don't disappear into thin air. But above all, find Sagan!"

Eagan smiled nervously. "Very well, sir. We'll start a worldwide scan. But it seems he's always a step ahead of us."

Reilly raised a hand. "I don't care what you need to do; just do it, and either kill him or bring him here. I can't emphasize this enough: I want that old bastard!"

Sharon studied the construction workers out of her bedroom window with curiosity. The squat androids, about a hundred of them, were surprisingly quiet. When Louis had said a construction crew was coming, she'd expected to hear a lot of noise, but they had quickly burrowed underground on the hillside facing the cabin, and all she could hear were the steady hum of machinery and sloshing of what she thought might be some sort of liquid construction material. They had been working for two days now, around the clock as far as she could tell, and all she could see were small air vents popping out every so often, and of course, the opening of the tunnel. The vents were immediately disguised with shrubs and big rocks. Someone or something driving into the property would only see what looked like a small-scale mining operation, but the possibility of a stranger coming to this remote area was unlikely. A satellite or car flying overhead would not see anything except for the usual trees, shrubs, and rocks, for a gigantic tarp had been carefully spread out about twelve feet off the ground and extended over the entire building site with an exact image of the locale taken before the work started. That was ingenious. A material-manufacturing truck stood on the old road by the entrance to the tunnel with many hoses coming out from under its belly.

The tunnel had become a vast underground chamber, as far as she could tell. She observed the androids for a while, fascinated with how quickly they moved about and with their uncanny precision. It was like watching a fast-forwarding video. Sharon had never watched construction before, and it was extremely interesting.

She turned around from the window and went back to the comfort of the bed and the company of Oscar. She snuggled next to the cat and picked up the writer's diary. She wanted to read more about his experience with meditation and the people and places he found in Hawaii. And she had made a most delightful discovery. She and the writer followed the same spiritual teachings. The man now seemed more like the brother she'd never had, although he died almost two hundred years ago.

Meditation had become his entire life in the last three decades of his life, the time he spent in Hawaii, on the Big Island. Shortly after he arrived, he heard the Dalai Lama speak, and someone had asked the holy man why he liked that particular island so much. He had smiled and said, "There are many, many, Buddhas here!" In the years to come the writer corroborated what the holy man had said and made friends with several such people. It seemed the island was a magnet for highly evolved souls, just like Texas seemed to be a magnet for atavists. That made sense; the universe always seemed to require a balance. It was gratifying to know that the opposite of Texas was the Big Island of Hawaii.

And that's where Sharon wanted to go. The writer described a location on the southeast of the island, an intentional spiritual community based on his guru's teachings, where he used to go for their group meditations and kirtans. Sharon knew she couldn't possibly go to the ashram in Los Angeles, the headquarters of the organization the same spiritual teacher had founded, because people there knew her as the old Sharon. Maybe after the rejuvenating process was made public, she could go, because she loved the place and its people. But for now, it would be great to go to Hawaii and live for some time in the community the writer had frequented, if it was still around. It would be fun to retrace his steps, take the diary along, and maybe even live in his house if it was still there, and meditate in the same places.

But the most immediate step was to tell Louis she wanted a separation. She felt a lump in her throat. She hated hurting him, but had no other recourse. She'd never imagined she would have to leave, but knew there was no way she could resume that life of old.

That Sharon had actually died; the one who once upon a time wanted nothing more than to be like her husband, to reach the same zeniths of accomplishment. In later years, starting around the time she'd turned fifty, she'd felt pulled into a life of spirit, and what happened in the world mattered less and less. However, she'd allowed the years to go by without taking action; she got used to the frustration and simply took life one day at a time, telling herself, "Next incarnation, I'll lead a spiritual life. I'll become realized then."

And then one day she'd been told she was going to die, and it was an immense relief; she knew her next life was coming, the one where she would lead the life she wanted. And then it wasn't so. At first, she had been excited at being young again and seeing Louis so happy, of reliving their happiest days. But then she'd started feeling frustrated, that he was holding her back…that life with him would always be about his work, about government.

Now she could start living her own life. If she had fifty years left, it would be a lifetime. The next incarnation she had dreamed about.

She went looking for him. She walked hesitantly, wanting to turn back but pushing on. She found him in the study, writing on his computerized display. He looked up as she came in.

"Ah, Shari. You have something to tell me."

"You know?"

"Oh yes. For the past few days you have been working up the nerve to tell me you are leaving me."

She was taken aback, but made an effort to recover and found that talking about how she felt was difficult, but she had to do it. She told him about her struggle, how much she wanted to lead a spiritual life.

Louis had braced himself for this, but it still hurt very much. "And you can't do it with me? We can't march down that road together?"

"Louis, this is your life!" she said, touching some papers on the desk with her fingers. "You are Regent Sagan."

Louis stared at the floor. "It's ironic, isn't? I was willing to terminate just so I wouldn't have to live without you, but now it looks like I will."

"I am sorry, Louis. I truly am!"

Sharon was now a stranger to Louis. He felt that air about her of someone who has already left and only the physical form remained. "And after a whole life together? Fifty years?" he said.

Sharon hesitated, but then found her strength. "I need to go, Louis. I am sorry. I need my spiritual life. That is my greatest priority."

"I guess you are right. I am who I am. I don't think I can meditate the way you want me to. So anyway…when are you leaving?"

"I don't know…I haven't thought about it beyond telling you."

"Well, I suggest you do it right away, so as not to prolong the pain of saying good-bye. Let's just get it over with, then…when you leave, please don't summon your car from New York. The Patriots may be tracking it, use mine. Larry made it safe."

They both remained still, staring at each other.

There were so many things Louis wanted to say, and he had rehearsed them for the past three days and sleepless nights, but nothing came out of his mouth. The hurt inside was heavy, numbing. This was the betrayal he'd never thought could possibly happen.

Feeling shocked and startled, Sharon turned around and made her way to the bedroom. As the house androids packed her things, she called the community on the Big Island.

An hour later she left without seeing Louis again.

The 212 regents arrived in the space of an afternoon. The cars, flying with identity cloaks provided by Larry, dropped them off and were dismissed, to fly back home until needed. The regents appeared expectant, nervous. This was something truly new to them all; the fact that they were in this secret locale, the way they had to travel, leaving no trace, and the vague agenda Joy had told them about…the problem with the Patriots that hung heavy, but also the D'Anjou project and the hints Joy had dropped about "some unexpected consequences." When they had asked about Louis, she had been evasive, reassuring them he was well. And the place looked like a sophisticated hideout. Joy told them that it was for the long term. It was all very mysterious, and they assumed it had to do with new information about the Patriots.

A good many wanted to see the forest, even walk around the trees, but Joy asked them not to; they needed permits. "We need to remain underground so as not to disturb the forest," she told them. "Besides, someone watching might get suspicious, particularly since you look nothing like hikers."

Instead, she gave them a tour of the facilities, the four rooms that comprised D'Anjou's lab, where the scientist, his assistant, and Suzanne were hard at work with some instruments that emitted a blue light. When the regents filed past, D'Anjou and the two women kept working, evidently absorbed in their task. When a regent asked if he would be coming to their meeting, D'Anjou politely refused, explaining he was not a regent. When they invited him, he thanked them and said he might peek in.

Joy took the group through the living and meeting rooms they were going to use. The decor was utilitarian but comfortable. There was a lot of space, plenty of soft light emanating from the walls and ceilings, and fresh air. There was a gym, a sauna, hot tubs, and a large swimming pool. She showed them the dining room, appointed with attractive marcasite tables, all with tablecloths and soft individual lights. The place settings included wineglasses. The bedrooms had video-windows that showed the forest from various angles and let in what looked like natural light and air. The beds were comfortable. There were writing desks and computer displays, and plush chairs for reading or watching television.

They asked about Louis. Joy told them he would welcome them that evening at five in the amphitheater.

Most of them were there by 4:45, admiring the ample room with half-moon circles of seats overlooking the dais in the front. At

4:59, a hush fell over the room. Joy could tell they were all looking for Louis, his absence fanning speculation that there was something wrong with him, that perhaps he was ill. A minute later Joy called the meeting to order. She sat at the main table in the dais but conspicuously not in the middle, but one place to the right. Larry and then Angie sat on the other side of the empty seat.

"Fellow regents, welcome," Joy said. Then Louis casually walked in from one corner of the dais and took his seat. Everyone knew it was him because of where he sat, not that they recognized him; most stared long and hard, trying their best to guess what had happened.

After a long hush, John Samuels, who years before, long before Joy came along, had been one of Louis's protégés, broke the silence. "Louis? Is that really you?"

"Yes, Johnnie. Sorry, everyone, I do look different, and I should have warned you, but I had a compelling reason not to."

Johnnie smiled, but his eyes were still full of surprise and he kept studying Louis.

And that was how he came to tell them about one of the side effects of D'Anjou's teleportation project. Louis explained about Sharon's cancer, and how she was dying and how D'Anjou saved her, and how he was almost kidnapped or killed and that he'd posed as his own nephew, and as he spoke they got more accustomed to his appearance, and they were reassured by the voice they all knew, and his mannerisms. It was, without question, Louis.

They asked many questions, about how he felt, the process, whether there were any side effects. Then the gravity of the situation dawned on them. This was a tremendous boon for humanity, but also a grave threat of overpopulation, and there was no telling what other fallout. Would there be psychological effects? How long would people want to live?

They speculated for several hours, well past midnight. The Patriot threat and the fact that Louis was being hunted were forgotten; all they focused on was the new technology. They came to the conclusion that they had no choice but to let the world know.

"This is just too big for us to keep secret," said Diane Crowley, a law professor from San Francisco. "It's not just a matter of the constitution forbidding us to keep things like these secret from our fellow regents and the public, it's also an ethical issue." The tall, slim, and elegant woman spoke precisely, weighing her words. "We have no right to decide things on our own. We are but ten percent of the board of regents."

"No, no, Diane," interjected Louis. "We have to keep this process contained within the group until the Patriot crisis is resolved. Otherwise we are doomed to failure. In this room we have more than eighty percent of the atavist project peer review and can make a legal decision," added Louis with an edge to his voice. "If we let the public know about the rejuvenation process, we are letting Reilly and his goons know as well. They will want the technology for themselves and they might want to kidnap Doctor D'Anjou...it's just too risky; we don't know what they will do.

"Can we at least decide to go ahead with the concept of the voluntary relocation of Patriots to Texas immediately? That may keep Reilly from committing additional violence and will buy us time."

They debated for a long while then broke into small groups and reconvened.

"I for one am completely and totally against the plan," said Regent Marta Barros, a rather plump woman in her fifties who sported a pageboy haircut. "With all due respect to Louis, we cannot act against the constitution which forbids secretive measures. That's plain as day."

Louis sat very upright, his elbows on the table, hands clasped in front. "I fully acknowledge the tenuous position my proposal puts us in," he said. "My point is that when the constitution was drafted we never expected we would face an enemy from within. We were naive, and now we must take corrective measures."

148

"No, no, Louis," Marta said, standing up. "Preserving the constitution is paramount." At this she looked around the room. "The rule of law is what makes us civilized. I am a constitutional attorney, and I can tell you that what you are proposing will damage us far more than the Patriots could. After all, what's the worst they can do?"

The other regents sat in silence. Gone were the stares when they first saw Louis. After talking for so many hours, they were now more concerned with the gravity of the crisis than Louis's appearance, or perhaps they had grown accustomed to how strange it all was, including the sight of Louis.

"I surmise you are asking what the Patriots might do if we let them take over?" Larry asked.

"Yes, Regent Zimmerman," replied Marta. "Can you please tell us, what are the probabilities?"

"Without question they would dismantle the government," Larry said matter-of-fact. "Then they would impose the old system of two hundred years ago, with money, politics, many laws, and of course, prisons. The man they call President Reilly would assume dictatorial powers for an unknown period of time."

"And is that so bad?" Marta asked, her gaze going around to everyone in the room. "Surely we can weather a few years of the old system."

Louis shook his head in disbelief. "Everything we worked so hard for…"

"I know, Louis, I know. But it's preferable to our violating the constitution—"

"Instead you'll have the Patriots throw the whole thing out?"

"But for how long, Louis? After taking over, the excitement of their movement will wane; they'll get tired of all the responsibility. Then again, Reilly and his cohorts will eventually die…"

Marta caught herself. "Oh dear."

"Right, he may not die, but keep rejuvenating."

Joy looked right at Marta. "Our eavesdropping caught them talking about ethnic cleansing. We can't possibly let that happen!"

Marta waved a dismissive hand. "Oh, that's just talk. I'm sure the majority of them wouldn't condone such a thing."

"Marta, we have long suffered what the Patriots have to offer," Louis said in a slow, deliberate tone, the one he used in the classroom. "Attila's invasion led to the destruction of the Roman empire, the loss of a culture, of knowledge which plunged the world into the Dark Ages. Napoleon killed hundreds of thousands in his quest for empire. Hitler and his Nazis wiped away millions and millions. Stalin killed countless of his own countrymen." The look in Louis's eyes became more intense, and Marta seemed to sink in her chair. "Can you for a moment visualize all the suffering? Families devastated, starvation, whole towns wiped out, children tortured, women raped, large groups of people made to dig their own graves and executed on the spot. Much of the savagery was unnecessary, wanton, and cruel." Louis switched his gaze from face to face. "The Patriots are cut from the same cloth; they are atavists who don't feel for anyone they consider outside their tribe. No compassion, just the urge to dominate. Anger and violence motivate them. The world has evolved and they are no longer in charge, no longer able to cause so much damage. Let's keep it that way."

Marta sat in sullen silence.

"So what do we do?" Joy asked after a while. "In my opinion, and it's a logical, empirically based opinion, It would seem that for us to survive as a society, we cannot afford for Reilly and the Patriots to take over our world. No question."

"But we alone can't decide," interjected Marta, staring at the floor.

"But, Marta," said Alonzo Ross, the regent in charge of Police Services, "we also cannot allow the Patriots to win."

Louis stood up. "We are all tired. It's two in the morning. Let's all reconvene here at five this afternoon. That gives us plenty of time to think things over. We all know the full extent of what we are facing."

That evening, a slim majority of the 212 regents, 113, concluded the constitution had to be preserved at all costs. They voted for Joy to send the atavist proposal through normal channels to all 2,017 regents. That meant the public in general would also be informed. And they would also know about the rejuvenation process.

"We'll negotiate with President Reilly, Louis," Marta said soothingly. "Very likely we'll end up giving the Patriots some of what they want, and keeping some of what we want. That's what democracy is all about. As you pointed out, the world has evolved; they are not going to kill anyone. They just want a little of that world of two hundred years ago. That's not so bad."

When everyone left, Louis sat with Joy, Angie, and Larry at the head table. Alonzo Ross, along with thirty or so other regents, remained in their seats, all looking despondent.

"What happens next?" Angie asked, fiddling with a pen.

Louis's eyes were hard, unblinking. "It's safe to assume the regents will vote to surrender Texas to the Patriots."

"That's a given," Angie said, tossing the pen at the seat Marta had occupied. "But what about the rejuvenation aspect of D'Anjou's project?"

"I don't know," Louis said, staring at the pen on the floor. "I imagine it will create quite a stir, and be hugely distracting for a while, and then Reilly and his crew will want the technology."

"And the fact that we have D'Anjou with us," Joy said.

Louis nodded. "Means they'll come after him."

Angie rocked in her seat and bit her lower lip. "But the whole world watched his presentation; surely they can replicate what he did?"

"Given enough time," Louis said. "About how long, Larry?"

"Oh, it's a complicated process. D'Anjou's presentation didn't even cover the basics. This is very much what happened when the

US developed the atomic bomb back in the twentieth century. The Russians knew it was possible, and that's it. But they also knew it would take them twenty years or more to come up with a bomb. So they recruited spies to steal the technology. I would say the Patriots are in a similar situation; in their case, they are about ten years away unless they get a hold of D'Anjou."

Angie had crossed her arms over her chest and continued rocking back and forth in her chair. "But what about other scientists, colleagues of D'Anjou?"

"I don't know. He must know what others in his field are doing. We'll have to ask him."

Louis could feel the gloom in the room. It would be a matter of days, maybe hours, before Reilly and his goons descended on the place in search of D'Anjou.

Louis stood up. "Well, that's that. We must hide."

"Why?" Alonzo asked. "You don't think any of the regents who were here will let Reilly and his people know where you are?"

"Probably not," Louis said. "But there are many ways the Patriots can find our location. According to Larry, they could get a hold of one of the cars that came here and run a tracer on its computer to find out where it's been...or perhaps coerce one of the attendees by kidnapping him or her, or a family member. There are many ways."

"Oh, Louis, I don't think so," Johnnie said. "The Patriots must first find out there was a meeting. And who will tell them?"

"Besides," Alonzo said, "I ordered Police Services to be particularly vigilant to protect our regents."

"Well, I hope you are right," Louis said. He suddenly felt like a tired old man. He looked at Alonzo and the handful of other regents who remained. "Thank you so much for your support. We'll keep you posted."

Johnnie studied the room. "I can't believe you are going to abandon this place!"

Louis gave Johnnie a sad smile then walked toward the back of the room and the tunnel that led to the outside. Larry, Joy, and Angie followed close behind.

Once back at the cabin, Angie plopped down on the couch and kicked loose her shoes, the low-heel ones she used for business. "Very smart, Louis. You used this place and the meeting as a decoy. You knew all along we'd end up at the eco-farm, right?"

Louis heard desperation in her voice. He bent down to pet Yogi, who had roused from his nap to greet him. "Honestly, not. I was sure peer review would go along with our plan."

Angie tousled her hair. She felt angry and disappointed. There was no telling what was going to happen now because of those idiotic regents. "But you knew there was a possibility they would opt for a transparent process—"

"Yes," replied Joy. "That's why Louis asked Larry to find us a secondary locale."

Louis turned to Larry, who was now standing by the front door next to Suzanne, who came out to greet him. "Larry, I assume all is ready in that underwater farm."

"It is. We are ready to go once we change our appearance and DNA—"

"And what are we going to do," Angie asked, "hide forever?"

"Hiding—that is, surviving—is number one," Louis said, his manner subdued, "but our ultimate goal has been, and will remain, somehow defeating the Patriots."

"How?" Angie asked. "We are separated from the government…fight them on our own?"

"Angela," Larry said, "we have resources…our minds, our knowledge, and contacts."

"Yes, Angela," Louis said, "We'll come up with a viable plan of action to get rid of the Patriots. Hiding will buy us time."

Joy let out a slow breath. "I suggest, Angela, you quell your criticism and attempt to add to the conversation. You are becoming a distraction. I'm beginning to regret I brought you onboard." Then after a pause: "So that's where we are all going, to that underwater place. Louis, Sharon, D'Anjou and his assistant, Angie, Suzanne."

"Sharon is gone, Joy," Louis said and he sat down next to her on the couch.

"What?" Now that she thought about it, she had not seen Sharon around.

"She wanted to pursue her spiritual life, and it did not include me."

Joy reached out a hand and touched Louis's shoulder. "Oh, Louis! I'm so sorry to hear that!"

"I'm afraid it's permanent. I imagine she'll ask for a divorce at some point."

Joy stared at Louis, trying to divine his feelings, but he appeared calm. Perhaps tired, and maybe disappointed with the recent proceedings, but not despondent. Maybe that would come later, she reasoned, when he had time to process.

"Let's talk about our future," Louis said, his gaze on Angie. "The three of you don't have to come with me and D'Anjou to hide under the sea—"

"Oh yes we do!" exclaimed Joy. "We are in this together, Louis. Gary knows the four of us are a team, and ever since I took over the first tier prep class he hates me probably as much as he hates you."

"I'm with Joy," Angie said, calmer now. "We are a team."

"What about you, Larry?" Louis asked. "You can stay at the university. I don't think Reilly and his Patriots have anything against you, besides guilt by association, which you can disavow."

Larry briefly looked at Suzanne, who stood beside him holding his hand. "We need to stop Reilly. I can't do it alone and neither can the three of you without my help...and Suzanne's."

"That's true," Louis said quietly, almost in a whisper. "Are there any dear ones you would want to bring along to the eco-farm for who knows how long...Joy? Angie? Larry? What about Suzanne?"

"Family?" Joy said. "Why, are you concerned about their safety, that Reilly may want to use them to get to us?"

Louis leaned back on the couch and stared at the ceiling, his hands cupped behind his head. "That's a possibility. But also someone you may want to have by your side in case we have to remain in hiding for years."

Joy looked at Louis, Angie, then Larry and Suzanne. "I'm sorry, but I must disagree. We must remain lean, we don't know what we'll encounter, and my assessment is that our loved ones would be safer where they are. Once we are out of the picture, the Patriots will realize we are in hiding and would be foolish to contact family—"

"Yes, Joy, but aren't you concerned they will assume we are maintaining contact and torture them to find our whereabouts?"

"No. I think they will place eavesdropping devices and rely on technology instead. That's how they have acted so far."

"But still," Louis said, staring at the ceiling, "won't you feel better having your mother with you? Knowing that she's safe?"

"And where do we draw the line, Louis? Let's say I bring my mother. She's remarried and will surely want to bring her husband along. And he will want to bring his sister, and she will bring someone else. No, let's stay lean; we can function better that way."

"I think Joy is right," Angie said.

Louis straightened out, brought his hands down on his lap. "What about you, Suzanne?" he asked, looking at the quiet woman.

"She's happy with me," interjected Larry with a half smile as he squeezed her hand.

Louis studied everyone. "Well, let's get ready. Whatever ties and responsibilities we have back East, let's put those aside. We are going to be refugees for a while."

Louis started for the door. "I need to find D'Anjou and see if he made any strides with that process to change our appearance."

Joy bit her lower lip. "Yes, he did. He said it was a straightforward process."

"Well, in that case we might as well do it."

"Right now?" asked Joy.

"Yes, Joy."

Louis made his way out of the cabin and back to the underground compound. Joy, Larry, Angie, and Suzanne followed right behind him, without saying a word.

They found Arlene staring at her computer display.

"Arlene, we are looking for your boss," Joy said.

"Alphonse is gone," Arlene said as if in a trance, staring at her monitor.

A flash of surprise flashed across Joy's face. "What do you mean gone? Where to? He's not supposed to go outside in the forest."

"He took one of our equipment vans and left while I was taking a nap. I think he drugged me...he left a note in this display."

They looked anxiously at the monitor. Arlene touched the screen and D'Anjou's face appeared before them. "I have to leave. I have to go," he said in his nasal voice. His face was tense. He was breathing hard. "Sorry to disappoint everyone, but I can't just wait for those Patriots to come and kidnap me. I snuck into the meeting room and heard it all...I have to go and hide...I am sorry." The image disappeared suddenly, cut off.

Louis took a deep breath. "Oh boy! That's bad news."

Joy shook her head. "By himself he'll be grabbed in no time. The man has no skills outside of the lab."

Larry produced his phone. "I'll call the regent in charge of Police Services, Alonzo Ross. He was here at the meeting. He'll know how to find D'Anjou."

"Fine, go ahead, please," Louis said. "Let's see if they can find him and keep him safe. In the meantime we have to change our appearance and DNA." He studied Arlene. The woman was clearly distressed. Tears streamed down her cheeks as she stared at the blank display screen. Obviously there was more to her relationship with D'Anjou than just being an assistant.

Louis stood beside her and placed a hand on her shoulder. "Arlene, I'm sorry for what you are going through, but if you know how to work this equipment, we need you right now!"

Big teary blue eyes looked back at Louis. She blinked several times. "Yes, of course." She then closed her eyes and took one slow, long, deliberate breath. When she opened her eyes, she was a new person...calm. The change was amazing, whatever she'd done, that long slow breath had worked a miracle.

"Yes, I know how to operate the equipment."

Louis stared at her for a moment in amazement. "Can you change our appearance right now? Including your own."

Arlene nodded. "Alphonse ran a couple of tests and left the machines ready. I can do it now, but not a second time. The machines will lose their calibration in a few days, and Alphonse is the only one who can recalibrate them." She sounded apologetic.

"In that case, no need to put it off," Louis said. "All right, are we all ready? We need to change ourselves and leave as soon as possible."

Larry had walked to a quiet corner to make his call. After a little while, he put his phone away and returned to the group. "Regent Ross is personally looking for D'Anjou. He promised he'll get back as soon as he has news. By the way, he says there's no reason to leave this place; no one is looking for us."

"That's just a matter of time, Larry," Louis said. "Everyone, let's line up."

"Are you sure we...remain ourselves?" Larry asked, a little embarrassed.

"Larry," Louis said. "Do you think I'm any different? Now that you've gotten used to my new looks, I'm the same person, right?"

Larry hesitated for a moment. "Yes, you're right, Louis. Sorry, I guess I'm a little nervous."

Arlene stood by one of the glassite cubes. "I already have Regent Sagan's energy profile. I'll need to scan the rest of you."

Louis took a deep breath. "How much can you change us, Arlene?"

"I can change skin, hair, and eye color. I can also change facial features by doing a little scrambling…even height."

"Fine. As long as we look sufficiently different."

Without hesitation Louis walked into the cube and the door closed. Then he opened the door, and found himself on the other side of the room, with all eyes fixed on him. "Did it work?" he asked and was surprised by the sound of his voice, deeper and of a different quality. It was someone else's voice. He looked at his hands. They were now olive toned.

Angie gave him a mirror. He looked Italian, or maybe Hispanic. There was still some vague trace of who he was, but overall that was not his face. He now had heavy eyebrows and a pronounced jaw. For him it was the second time he'd changed his looks; for the rest it would be a bit more traumatizing.

Ten minutes later it was Angie's turn. "Whatever you do, I better be good-looking!" she joked, her tone not quite masking her anxiety.

She came out looking very different, a tall and handsome blonde with strong features. She looked somewhat like a famous model Louis remembered admiring some years back. But her eyes teared up when she was handed the mirror. "Oh crap! Look at me!"

Joy was next. "Might as well make me taller…and slim."

Larry ended up with a square face, Irish-looking. His hair was now dark brown, as were his eyes. "I feel the same, but judging by your expressions I must be very different."

"Yes, you are no longer a Viking," Angie said, her tears gone. She stared at Suzanne, who emerged from the cube looking much prettier, rich silky hair, smooth skin and a slightly upturned nose, but her expression was the same. When handed a mirror, she looked at her image for a second and handed it back without so much as a grin or a smirk.

Angie kept looking at her image. "This will take some getting used to. I don't know that what we are doing is necessarily safe? Are there any side effects?"

"We have no choice, Angie," Joy said. "It's either this or perhaps getting killed."

Louis gave Angie a reassuring smile. "I can tell you I haven't had any negative effects since I rejuvenated."

"No side effects," Arlene said. "The mouse has shown none, and its life cycle is much shorter than ours."

"Can you change us back if we want to?" Joy asked.

"Yes, Regent Blass," replied Arlene. "I have everyone's original profile safely stored away in two different locales, just the way Alphonse set it up. But the machines will need recalibration, and only he can do that."

They stood studying one another, a bit gloomy and uncertain. It was all intensely strange. Joy remembered Halloween parties when she was little, and this was much like it. But this time it wasn't a disguise. She wondered about the psychological implications.

Louis tapped Joy's shoulder. "Well, let's go."

"Arlene, thank you." Louis smiled at her new appearance: still blonde, still tall, only her face was slightly different. "And we'll find Alphonse, not to worry. And please have your androids pack everything into your other van right away. Whatever doesn't fit, just destroy."

"Oh, no. Everything will fit."

Louis started to make his way down the passageway to the outside. Joy and Angie followed on his heels. Larry had grabbed Suzanne by the hand and came close behind.

Louis decided that a good way to not let fear and anxiety eat at their insides was to stay active. It was the same with his sorrow. Sharon was gone, but the more he thought about her the more he missed her, so he didn't. Instead he focused his attention on those around him, and what needed to be done.

"Where do you think D'Anjou went?" Joy asked.

"I don't know, Joy," answered Louis. "But I hope he's safe."

"Arlene is obviously his romantic partner," Angie said, quickening her pace to catch up with Louis and Joy. "How come he didn't take her with him?"

Louis seemed lost in thought. "Hmm, hard to tell…"

"Maybe he thought it too risky," Joy said, "and wanted to leave her where he knew she would be okay."

"Not necessarily," Louis said. "Maybe he thought she would be a hindrance. Hard to tell without knowing his motives. If it was sheer fear, as it appears, then he simply bolted."

"Yes," Joy said. "Hard to tell. Well, no sense speculating. Let's just find him."

They were about to reach the end of the tunnel. "What do you think will happen here?" Joy asked. The long hallway still looked, felt, and smelled like it was not done being finished.

Louis watched the door to the underground compound slide open. "That will be interesting to see." He stepped outside and stood admiring the forest bathed in moonlight. Where they were going would be nothing like this. An underwater place he had no concept about.

Joy and Angie stood by his side. The forest was captivating. Joy already missed it and wished she could stay.

"It's such a gorgeous place, Louis," she said. "A pity to leave it behind. And the underground facilities: the time, energy."

Louis nodded. "Let's hope we get to come back someday when Reilly and the Patriots are no longer a threat."

"Yeah," Angie said. "When all is said and done, I sure would love to live here for some time."

When they walked inside the cabin, Yogi barked at them and backed off. Louis tried to tell him it was indeed him, but the dog would not hear any of it. He retreated into a corner, snarling, but came out a moment later, tentatively smelling them all, one at a time, starting with Louis. After a few more moments, he came around wagging his tail.

"That's fascinating!" Angie said. "There's something in us he recognizes, although it took him a while. I wonder what that is."

Joy bent down and called for Yogi. "Oh, dogs have a sixth sense. And Yogi is a special one." Yogi licked her hand as she petted his head with the other.

"Keep trying Regent Ross, Larry," Louis said. "He's our best hope. Maybe D'Anjou is not far, thinking things through. We can't leave without him."

They packed their things. An hour later, while eating, their telephones started ringing. Hundreds of people, then thousands, were trying to reach them. They had agreed they would not answer, unless it was Alonzo Ross or D'Anjou.

"Ugh," exclaimed Louis. "I thought we had at least another day before the news broke." He walked over to the computer display in the den.

The Internet was full of the news about the rejuvenation process, and how Regents Louis Sagan and Sharon Willcott, "both in their seventies, are now vital twenty-year-olds." The reports described how Sharon had been cured of her brain cancer in the process of being rejuvenated. The excitement was palpable, every news source and commentator spoke of the revolutionary process and how it was going to change society. Hardly anything was said about the Patriots and the threat they posed. A few minutes later, the emphasis changed, the news was about the congress that Regent Sagan had convened in California to work on the atavist situation. The attendees had seen Regent Sagan and realized the full scope of the teleportation project; that in fact it was a process for doing away with illness and achieving seemingly eternal life. It was then that the atavist threat was mentioned. "Regent Sagan mentioned the risk that Doctor D'Anjou's technology would be misused by the Patriots, should they get their hands on it." Pictures of Louis were circulated showing him both as a young man and as his old self.

One television network interviewed Marta who spoke at length about "the place in the Mendocino National Forest, a beautiful locale at 3,000-foot elevation, very secret, everything built underground…" she smiled and seemed to be relishing the notoriety. "There is an old cabin some writer built a long time ago, very pretty."

"Oh, crap!" Exclaimed Larry, "she just gave away our location."

Louis rubbed his face hard with the palms of his hands. "Well, what else could you expect from her? This will get nasty…I wish we had D'Anjou with us. Where the hell is he?"

Larry sent his car back to his condo in New York. Maybe it would serve as a decoy if the Patriots thought they might be in it. Then he looked at the visual feed on his phone. "No news from Regent Ross. He's been everywhere: D'Anjou's lab, his house, friends and family."

"Thank you, Larry…There's nothing else we can do at this point…I wish we had a sensor outside."

"You mean to warn us if someone approaches? I'm on it."

Larry set up one of the house androids outside. According to him, the model had ultrasound detection. "They are used to watch over children, and can detect unusual sounds from miles away." The android was to listen for visitors and issue a warning. "When it sounds the alarm, we'll have thirty seconds to board your car and leave," Larry said.

"Thanks, Larry. Now, could we leave something behind to mislead whoever comes here looking for us?"

"You mean a false lead?" Larry asked.

Louis looked around the cabin. "Yes, but what?"

Joy was busy rummaging through her purse. "Too bad you didn't travel to, oh, I don't know, Canada? That way your car and phone would have the coordinate tracers on them."

Larry gave Joy a big smile. "Give me your phone, Louis."

Louis handed Larry his real phone, a replicating wafer he kept tucked in a slot in his belt buckle. Larry went to sit on the couch and played with it for a while. "Good. Now, let's make it look like you dropped the phone's wafer chip accidentally."

"What did you do, Larry?" Louis asked.

"Just what Joy said, I installed tracers on your phone to make it look you have been busy calling Canada. Edmonton, to be precise."

Larry walked around the cabin with Louis's phone wafer in his hand. "But where would an absentminded genius drop his phone?"

Louis shook his head. "I don't know where a 'genius' would drop his phone, but I like to read in the bathroom."

"Right!" shouted Larry and made his way to the bathroom. They followed him. They watched as he threw the phone's wafer into the toilet bowl and pressed the cleaning button. A big swoosh of air took the phone away and sanitizing lights swept the bowl antiseptic clean.

"Good job, Regent Zimmerman," Angie said with a derisive laugh. "You just destroyed Louis's phone."

Larry turned to face the mystified group. "No. It went into the recycling depository, where in about four minutes it will be rejected by the biodegrading convertors. It will then be deposited in the holding cell as a foreign object, where, unless it is retrieved within twenty-four hours, it will be demanufactured. Let's hope the Patriots are thorough and have a good scanner with them, in which case they'll find it, and think that Louis—"

"Dropped his phone in the can while bending over to flush it!" exclaimed Joy. "Brilliant, Larry! Anyone who knows Louis would know he's bound to do exactly that."

Louis didn't know what to say. But the scheme was good.

Larry walked over to his briefcase and dug out the manufacturing unit. He pressed a few keys on his phone, and after a few blips and some whirring, a new phone wafer came out of the unit. He then spent a few minutes programming it while Louis watched.

"There," Larry said with a smile. "This one is actually better. I copied all information, including your car's profile. Again, it will supplant the old replicates and then—"

"Thanks...and I know how phones work, Larry."

A few minutes later a call came into Larry's phone. It was Regent Ross. The regent's figure appeared before them. He was sitting in his office. He looked stern, worried. "Bad news. Doctor D'Anjou is now with the Patriots in Texas. I have no idea whether he went there willingly or was kidnapped...as for you—"

"In the hands of the Patriots?" exclaimed Louis. "Are you sure?"

"His biometrics were picked up in Texas about an hour ago. I sent satellite androids to double-check, and now I'm totally certain. He's in Houston, at the Patriots' headquarters. Sorry. I can only assume the Patriots were informed by D'Anjou as to your whereabouts. I'm sending police to protect you. You'll be fine."

"Thank you, regent," Louis said, and watched as Ross's image disappeared. "Okay, people; time to leave for the eco-farm. Now!"

Larry summoned Arlene. She wanted to travel in her own van with the equipment. She would follow close behind.

Larry sent his car back to New York.

They went outside and boarded Louis's car.

They sat down, and Louis instructed the car to lift off immediately, but it refused to budge when it did not recognize Louis's biometrics. Having Yogi along was not enough. Larry suggested Louis use a process of recognition by having him describe various trips and conversations he'd had with Sharon inside the car. It took five anxious minutes, but finally the car was satisfied. Louis gave it the eco-farm's coordinates.

The trip would require going underwater to a considerable depth and they would have to run pressurization tests along the way.

As they were strapped down, Louis turned to Larry. "Can they trace us, Larry? Can you install a cloak, or some sort of disguise?"

"Sure." He stood up to look at the car's display, both lights and digital readouts. "Car, can you open up your program?" he asked.

"Yes I can, Regent Zimmerman, but unnecessary," the pleasant female voice said. "I have added an untraceable directive to our flight plan using false directional inputs, and a fake signature."

Larry looked surprised. "That's amazing. Who programmed you?"

"She's self-programmable, Larry," Louis said with a tense, nervous chuckle. "Okay, let's go before we have company."

They lifted quickly through the clouds, so fast they felt their insides pulled back. The car sped up faster and faster, uncomfortably so, it felt more like a roller coaster…then after a while it slowed down to normal speed.

"Okay, I guess we are safe." Louis said. "But we have to get D'Anjou. We can't leave him in the hands of the Patriots."

Joy, seated next to him, turned to look wide-eyed. "I was just thinking about that, too. Reilly will use the technology to blackmail the world."

"Yes, yes. We have to get him no matter what."

"Yeah, let's hire one of those armies in an outlying country using Larry's gold," Angie said.

Joy shook her head. "No, Angie. We need to go to Texas."

"Oh, crap. Is that right, Louis?"

"Afraid so. Larry, could you give my car the coordinates for the farm in Texas?"

Larry went over to the car's panel.

When he sat back down, Angie grabbed his hand. "What's Texas like?"

Larry smirked. "Well, you saw the pictures. Not anything like California. Let's just say flat and dry. We'll need to appear to be farmers…It's a tradition in the Midwest for three or four couples to buy land and farm. Maybe we can make either Joy or Angie someone's sister, so a single person won't seem odd."

Angie dropped her face into her open hands. She seemed despondent. "How did you pick that dry and awful farm in Texas? Why not a pretty place by a lake or on a mountain?"

"Statford is safe, because the locals keep order, and if someone suspects us to be in Texas, that's the last place they'll come looking for us."

Louis nodded. "Good thinking, Larry."

"Gee, I can't wait," Angie said. "Never been to a hellhole before."

14

At 6:07 on a Wednesday morning, barely an hour after they had left California, Louis's car came down and landed gently on the lawn in front of the house of their two-acre farm. Arlene's freight van docked right behind.

Joy was the first one out. She surveyed the surroundings: the square structure that was now their new home, the small patch of lawn, the orchard behind the barn carved out of the dust that flew at the slightest disturbance, and the neighboring two houses some three hundred yards away to the east and west. Everything looked parched, and she figured that were she to sneeze it might precipitate a dust storm. She could hear the neighbors' cattle—a calf calling for her mother and some serious braying from several cows; the first time she had heard cows in real life. Squat bushes Larry told her were creosote and yucca dotted the landscape. This was certainly not California anymore.

Louis was already on his way to the house, trailed by Yogi and two car androids carrying suitcases. Larry followed with a box and his briefcase. Arlene, wearing an exoskeleton, carried one of the glass cubes. Her two lab androids maneuvered the lab equipment on special pallets that floated a few inches off the ground covered with blankets to conceal their contents from possibly inquisitive neighbors.

As soon as they'd unloaded, the car, followed by the van, went to park itself in the equipment barn.

The house was a remnant of the late twenty-first century: sprawling and blockish, with large sliding-glass windows looking out to the mostly barren landscape broken by the cattle in the distance, a few bushes and a handful of trees close by. The one-story stone and cement structure had been built to withstand tornadoes and hurricanes. It had housed two families. What remained of them—three gaunt and nervous men, their wives, and five children—sold it to Larry and moved "up north."

Larry gave them a tour of the house. They started with the lab in the basement, in what had been a food-storage cellar added by the original owners during the famine. The lab, with the equipment strewn around waiting to be put together, was one large room lit by old-style lights, white and glaring. At one end was a bathroom. Next door was a rather stuffy room, which Arlene selected for her bedroom, eschewing the two adjoining bedrooms on the main floor Larry had assigned for her and D'Anjou.

On the ground floor was a small, basic kitchen, where an android was already busy cooking breakfast. Along a hallway projecting from the dining room and living room, were six small bedrooms with simple furniture and rudimentary closets.

Joy stood in the middle of the living room, the biggest room in the house. "Now let's be clear," she announced. "I assume I'm supposed to be Louis's wife, and Suzanne is married to Larry. Is that right? Angie can be my sister, and Arlene is Louis's sister."

"Why can't I be Louis's wife?" blurted out Angie.

"Because I've know him longer, been friends with him and his wife," Joy said, staring at Angie in disbelief, "and because I say so."

Angie sashayed away with a sardonic smile. She walked into her room and asked for the lights to be turned on, only to realize that she had to do it by hand…the same with the temperature controls. And the closet was just a place to hang clothes. She sat on the bed and wondered how she would manage to live like that.

168

That afternoon, Louis came into the house and found Larry and Suzanne eating a snack in the kitchen. "Larry, can you start working on D'Anjou's equipment?" He asked, looking in the direction of the stairs leading down to the basement. "See if you can learn how to use it...if D'Anjou is now under the Patriots' control, we must get a handle on his technology, otherwise—"

"I know," Larry said. "Suzanne helped D'Anjou and Arlene on and off in California, so she's already somewhat familiar. We'll start studying the equipment and his experimental logs."

A moment later Larry and Suzanne headed downstairs to join Arlene.

While Larry began helping Arlene set up the equipment, Suzanne commandeered the experimental logs. Using one of the shiny metal lab tables as a desk, she pulled up a chair and set up a display. As Larry and Arlene maneuvered equipment around, they could hear Suzanne clicking keys and the buzzing of the search peripherals.

The following morning they all sat at the dining table finishing breakfast. Suzanne, Arlene, and Larry held white lab coats on their laps, anxious to get to work. But Louis asked them all to stay and talk. "We need to plan."

Joy took a bite of toast. "Well, let's do it. You got our attention."

"First off, Larry," Louis said, "what news do you have from the outside world?"

"Not much, and a lot. I can't access Patrick and his tracers of the Patriots for fear they can trace me, too. So the only information I have is what's available on the Internet. The world is in turmoil. People feel the prospect of rejuvenation and eternal health is being stolen, or at least being secreted away. It's a crisis the regents can't seem to deal with. Several billion people are clamoring for the technology. The Patriots are accusing the seven regents of withholding the technology and keeping it to themselves.

"Everybody is looking for you, Louis. You are either a member of the seven regents' conspiracy, or have been kidnapped by the Patriots. But the most recent theme and the prevailing one is that you are hiding with D'Anjou to keep the technology out of the Patriots' hands. By the way, the police flew to our California place and reported us gone. They did encounter some 'unknowns' who were already inside and had to fight them. This was the first known skirmish with the Patriots."

Louis sat up straight. "When did that happen?"

"Yesterday in the early morning, about three hours after we left."

Angie stood frozen, toast in hand. "Any casualties?" she managed to ask.

Larry scrolled down the screen. "Two human police officers seriously wounded, seventeen androids damaged. Twelve Patriots were hit by stun guns and captured. About twenty got away."

They sat in silence. No one sipped tea or coffee or ate.

Louis leaned back in his chair. "I hope the Patriots found my old phone before Police Services arrived."

Louis could see that they felt overwhelmed. "I know we were almost killed or captured. But we were not. We are here! With any luck Reilly will think we are in Canada.

"Let's focus on what we need to do right now. We need to rescue D'Anjou."

"But how do we go about it by ourselves?" Angie asked. "We're no longer part of the government."

"You're right, Angie. We need help. But first, we need to get our bearings, find out who's who around here…we need to figure out a story for all of us…professions, where we come from."

"Let's just say we are from Northern California," Angie offered.

Joy shook her head. "No, we definitively sound like New Yorkers."

Louis stood up and walked around the table. "Fine. And we'll say we wanted a place where we could 'forge our own future and not be part of the oppressive and tyrannical big world government, where individuals don't count'…Is that the right terminology?"

"Yes," Larry said and dissolved his virtual display by closing the phone with evident disgust. "That's good. We can say we had gold hidden and brought it with us, and want to help 'bring back the old American values.'"

"Good," Louis said, still pacing. "Larry, could you write those things down? We need to memorize and practice saying them."

They decided to use their middle names with strangers: Louis was Gregory, Joy was Patricia, Angela was Maria, and Larry was Anthony. Suzanne, whose middle name was Mary, became Marianne to avoid confusion with Angela; and Arlene, who didn't have a middle name, remained Arlene.

"What about last names?" Angie asked, her eyes on Louis.

"How about we keep it simple, so we can all remember," Larry said. "Let's all use our favorite professor's last name."

"Good idea," Joy said. "Now everybody write down everyone else's names, and no slipups! Remember what's at stake."

It would be necessary for the "couples" to use terms of endearment when in public, Louis noted. "So we might as well start practicing."

At this Angie stood up and came over to Louis. "Oh, that's so wonderful, honey!" She kissed him on the mouth long and hard and walked away, laughing at Louis's shock.

"Angie!" exclaimed Joy.

Angie smiled and headed back to her room.

"Okay, people," admonished Louis, recovering his composure. "I think we are also supposed to be evangelical Christians, so act accordingly!"

Angie stopped and turned around. "Nooo!" She said and decided to come back and sit back down.

They argued for some time about the merits of appearing to be born-again Christians, since quite a few of the neighbors were, according to Larry. They decided they would pretend to be interested. "That way it doesn't matter if we don't know all the particulars," added Joy.

Angie was about to get up again, and Suzanne appeared eager to get to work. Louis asked them how they felt, how was it being someone else and in Texas.

"It's too early to tell," answered Joy, her demeanor serious. "It's all too surreal. Ask me again in a month or so."

"Well," Louis said. "I can tell you that after the initial adjustment, it gets easier by the day. I can also tell you that I detect the same personalities, the same perception of you…I can relate to all of you the same as before."

"That's true," Larry said. "But still, I don't like not recognizing myself in the mirror—that a stranger's face is looking back at me."

Joy picked up crumbs from the table with her fingers. "How do we go about meeting the moderate atavists, the non-Patriots?"

"I don't know," Louis said. "I don't want any of the local Patriots to suspect we outsiders are trying to infiltrate their movement. That might be dangerous; they do have guns. If you meet a declared Patriot, back away. We want to get to know the non- Patriots.

"Let's just go about our business, go into town, but not as a group—we don't want to overwhelm them with too many strangers—do some farming with the androids, and see what happens."

"What's the objective?" Larry asked.

"To study the moderates. Just to learn who they are, what they want," Louis said. "Maybe we can use them against the Patriots and free D'Anjou. Let's play it by ear, see what happens.

"Let's get to work, people."

Louis asked Larry to program everyone's phone devices to alternative access. These they would use while in Texas. Their old phones were to be kept silent.

That day they got busy with small things: journals, clothes, tools, looking over the menus available in the kitchen for synthetic food, and making plans how to supplement with hand-cooked meals that would involve buying groceries. That brought the question of currency and how to use it.

Joy and Angie decided to go into town with one gold bar. They came back four hours later with bags full of groceries and wads of the local paper money. "They have a bank," announced Joy, "and we got a pile of this stuff in exchange. These are called 'Texas Dollars' and you can buy a dozen apples with two of them." Larry took one of the red apples and bit into one. "You have to wash it first!" Joy grabbed the apple out of his hands and rinsed it in the kitchen. "We have a bit to learn," she said, handing it back to a surprised-looking Larry. "You can also buy guns. Show them, Angie."

Angie pulled a scary-looking black contraption out of the handbag she had just dropped in the chair. "I also bought bullets."

Louis and Larry came over to watch.

"You put these bullets in the compression magazine which slips into the handle, up to fifty of them" she announced gravely. "You pull back this thing," she said as she pulled a lever and made a clicking sound, "which loads one bullet into the chamber...you switch the safety, and shoot...one bullet at a time, or all fifty, very, very fast."

Joy and Angie decided to shoot the gun outside. When Louis expressed his concern that the women use care in handling the firearm, Angie told him, "A nice young man spent an hour showing us how to shoot and how to be safe."

"Yeah, and you spent half the time flirting with him, you hussy!" Joy said.

"Oh, Louis told us we have to get to know the locals," Angie said with a laugh as they walked out the front door.

That evening they sat down to a hand-cooked dinner. Joy had bought a watermelon for dessert.

They were halfway through the meal when Yogi barked, and they heard a knock on the front door. No house computers in here telling us who's at the door, thought Louis.

Larry walked over to the front door and opened it.

"Greetings, neighbor!" said a pleasant-looking stout woman in her thirties with a round face. She had light brown hair pulled into two long braids. By her stood a slender man dressed as a cowboy. He held a basket with canned goods; she had a pie in her hands.

Larry smiled, introduced himself as Anthony, and invited them in.

The couple walked into the room, the man took off his hat. He was deeply tanned, and the portion of his forehead that had been under the hat was much lighter. His brown hair was slicked back. His face was long and angular, the opposite of the woman's. He wore a gun strapped to his hip. He appeared shy and held back a few paces behind her. Joy assumed the hostess role and invited the guests to sit down in the living room.

"My name is Juanita," said the woman, who sat down primly in a chair, her back straight, holding the pie on her lap, "and this is my husband, Eldridge, and this is a home-warming present." She handed Joy the pie and signaled with a look for her husband to do the same with the basket of canned goods. The fresh-baked pie gave off a delicious scent of hot apples and cinnamon. Juanita wore the kind of old-fashioned red dress you saw in photographs of long ago; it came down to her calves and had flowers embroidered along the borders. She proceeded to talk nonstop about the three other couples they shared their farm with, how they worked the land, that they had known one another "for ages," and how good it was to welcome "like-minded folks to our neighborhood. Why, I can tell you are God-fearing Christians, just by looking at you.

"We heard a gun this afternoon and figured you folks are getting ready for whatever the Good Lord has in mind," she added. "We got us a civil defense group that has kept these parts peaceful, and everyone who lives here joins." She told them how they had kept out various groups that had tried to take over, "from the Hell's Angels to some of those rich guys from the States. We just show up, all armed and ready to fight, and mostly they scamper, but we've had us a couple of firefights."

No one had much of a chance to say anything, including Eldridge. The woman just went on talking. "We are so happy to be making our own lives out here, without some rich guy or big government telling us what we can and cannot do."

She invited them all to "come over for dinner tomorrow night and meet our folks."

Louis and the rest smiled and nodded. They stood up and shook hands. Dinner was to be at seven.

When they left Louis smiled broadly. "Well, I guess that's that!"

"Yes, Louis," Joy said, "we made a connection, and that's great; but did you hear her? They expect us to join their civil defense and fight with guns!"

Louis sighed. "Yeah, well. Let's see how we get around that."

The following evening they walked over to the house Juanita had told them was hers and Eldridge's, "the one with the blue roof" they could see in the distance. They had expected to be grilled about where they came from and who they were, but instead their hosts seemed just glad to meet them. While they ate a simple dinner of meat, mashed potatoes, and cabbage, the hosts asked questions about how it was to live in New York.

Louis spooned mashed potatoes onto his plate from a platter one of the hostesses offered. "Most people in New York just go about their lives without knowing who their neighbors are." Louis went on to describe how crowded the place was, and how "you hardly see the sun, with all those buildings around." Louis tried his best to keep his speech plain and simple. Joy and Angie did the same. Arlene, Larry, and Suzanne kept quiet and answered when spoken to, which was a bit awkward, especially since their hosts were so friendly and open.

Among those present at dinner, Joy had no trouble making conversation with one of the women and her husband. All of the adults present were in their mid-thirties, and one woman was called Marianne; Louis remembered that, but the rest of the names he quickly forgot. There were no children, "but one is on the way," Juanita said beaming at one of the women. Angie, that is Maria, and Joy-Patricia talked about how hard it was to live in New York, and how glad they were, as Joy said, "to be out of that awful place where everybody is watching you." At this point a man named Jonathan piped in: "We are all one big family out here in the panhandle," and they talked about the other families in neighboring farms and ranches, and how they all helped one another. The community came together for births, marriages, and funerals, but also for the weekly dance in town. "I hope you can join us this Saturday night," Juanita said with a big smile. "We'll love to have new dance partners." It was western-style square dancing. Angie confessed she had never danced, and Juanita said, "No problem; we'll all be glad to teach you!"

The following morning at breakfast, all Angie and Joy could talk about was how wonderful their neighbors were.

Joy fed Yogi some of her toast. "It's like they have known us for ages."

"But did you see that big picture of Jesus above the table?" Larry sat cross-legged in the dining room chair. "And notice how often they mentioned Jesus and the questions about whether we were 'saved'?"

"I answered yes," Angie said. "I told them Jesus was my savior. I figured, what's the harm?"

Joy had her cup of coffee cradled in her hands. "Only that they'll expect you in church on Sunday."

"Oh, darn. Well, let's go to the dance tomorrow, and I'll see how I can get out of that church business."

Louis had been listening with interest. "Well, so far so good."

Arlene and Suzanne asked if they could stay home from then on, and Louis agreed, thinking the two were too out of place; they looked, talked, and acted like scientists and had no ability to pretend otherwise. Perhaps it would be best if the neighbors forgot they existed.

The dance was held at the Statford high school auditorium, a large room that doubled as the gym. Basketball hoops stood at either end. The bleachers had been removed to accommodate the crowd of about two hundred. A live band assembled, and a man gave instructions. Juanita took charge of the newcomers. Joy simply followed Juanita around and did as told, hopping and twirling around, switching partners.

Back at home Joy and Angie talked about how they had a very good time and had made new friends. "These people are really friendly, nothing phony about them," Joy said. "I'm impressed!"

For the next few days, different people they had met at the dance kept coming over to visit and offer their help. "Anything you need" was the usual statement. Louis thought perhaps they had been prepped and were acting in unison, but Angie and Joy disagreed. "It's genuine, Louis," Joy said. "These people are just friendly. If anything, it's cultural. The common thread is how they were brought up to welcome strangers."

"Strangers, but of their own kind," added Larry, busy with one of the locally grown apples. "If they took us for 'some of those damn socialists,' or worse yet, regents, they would probably shoot us."

"Yeah, you may be right." Louis bent down from his chair to rub Yogi, who lay on the carpet, feet up, exposing his underside. "But so far, they have accepted us, although we are neither Texans nor wear cowboy attire. I'm pleasantly surprised by that. So we may be talking about various levels of acceptance. We are not seen as members of their tribe, but as acceptable outsiders."

"I think some of them are still unsure and may be testing us," Joy said. "But, yes, overall, I think this is a healthy process."

"Do you get the sense they are moderates, or that some might be Patriots?" Angie asked.

Joy hesitated. "Hard to tell. No one has mentioned the Patriots so far, which perhaps is a sign they are indeed testing us."

"I wish we could speed up the process," Louis said, "and identify Reilly's opposition...Damn, this is frustrating. Who knows what they might be doing to D'Anjou right this minute."

Joy gave Louis a sad smile. "We are doing what we can. You said it before, Louis. That's all we can do."

"Actually," interjected Larry, finishing the last of his apple, "I can produce an army at any time."

Louis stared at him in disbelief. "An army? What are you talking about?"

Joy smiled at Larry. "Remember the biochips we spread around Texas, Louis?"

"Why yes...but an army?"

"At this stage I can produce any virtual reality you want, in any locale or all over Texas," Larry said.

Louis stood transfixed. "Yes, I recall the chips...so we could—"

"Send in an army to rescue D'Anjou? Yes."

"I don't know...how effective is the illusion? What if it only works partially, or...look, it sounds awfully tempting, and I am grateful we have it as an option, but we still need physical troops to follow up, right? What happens when they discover it's an illusion? And we don't know Houston, the layout, or what sort of resistance we'll be dealing with."

Larry nodded. "Yes. You're right. We need a viable plan, and for that we need help."

"Well, let's proceed with meeting the local people, and let's see who comes up."

That night, after lying in bed for a couple of hours tossing and turning, Louis finally fell asleep. He dreamed of Sharon. He saw her on a beach sitting in the lotus posture meditating. She stood up and walked in his direction, but he was still in Texas, in his bedroom standing by his bed. She took his hand, and tears filled her eyes. "I miss you so much, Lalo," she said.

He woke up standing beside the bed, Yogi sitting on the floor looking at him, his ears perked up. It took Louis a moment to realize it had been a dream. He got under the covers. It was strange; he had never sleepwalked before and rarely remembered his dreams. Maybe it was all the tension about D'Anjou and being in Texas, he thought, but Sharon's face and words kept dancing in his head. In the dream he felt a terrible hurt when she spoke, and it was still there. Hurt. Yogi came up to the bed and Louis extended his hand to pet his head. "I don't know, buddy. I don't know what's going on."

15

The Texas Hunters Club meeting hall in Houston was filled to capacity, 4,050 business executives from all over Texas, Missouri, Alabama, Louisiana, and Oklahoma. They sat expectantly, speaking in hushed tones. Below the stage was an impressive line of armed soldiers, decked out in shiny black exoskeleton armor, with guns at the ready. Martial music broke out, and the five top generals filed onto the stage and stood at attention all along the back. A few moments later, Reilly walked in. The audience stood up and applauded.

Reilly motioned for people to sit. He smiled. "Among you are the honorable industrialists who are building my guns, armor, and tanks. Please stand up."

Fifteen men and twelve women stood up.

"Let's give them a round of applause." The people in the room applauded, and the fifteen men and twelve women looked all around, smiling. "Thanks to their hard work and the gold and diamonds pouring into my coffers, we have a fully armed, five million soldier army. We are ready to take back the Confederacy!"

Louder applause, and some cheers.

"That's right, folks, God told me last week that should be our next step, and when God speaks, I listen."

The applause kept going, prompted by the nods of the generals on stage.

Reilly waited for the applause to die down. "Now, what I want you all to do, now that my army is ready to do God's work, is join! Come and join in the glory that will be ours!"

Soldiers walked down the aisles handing out uniforms and the 4,050 men and women didn't hesitate. They threw down their coats and ties, some didn't change their clothes out of modesty, and they pulled the army pants over their civilian outfits. In less than thirty minutes they stood, a sea of green, many with tears in their eyes.

That following Saturday, Louis, Angie, and Joy went to another dance. Louis found he liked square dancing, the feeling in the room when everyone seemed to be enjoying the sheer pleasure of rhythmic movement.

Louis danced and drank a beer. One woman told him he was cute, and would he like to go for a walk? He said he'd better look for his wife.

Back home after the dance, gathered around the kitchen table, Louis and the rest discussed their experience. Joy had had a good time and saw nothing wrong with the people she'd met, while Angie was concerned about "all that rough talk. These are violent people!" She had been accosted by two cowboys who, trying to impress her, talked about bar fights. She ran across another who described a rodeo to her, and she had been appalled. And then she talked to some hunters, and she still couldn't believe what she'd heard. They'd described how they had a hunting club that kept a ranch full of rabbits, which they would release and hunt down. "They kill for pleasure!" she exclaimed.

"That's how a lot of these people are, Angie," Louis told her.

Angie went to bed but spent most of the night wide awake, staring into space. All of her attempts at approaching Louis, to have him look at her as a woman, rather than as another one of his ex-students, all had come to nothing. The man was simply not interested in her. Tonight at the dance she had tried to dance with him, and he had walked away, saying they should mingle.

Why would he reject her? Now that he was young, and no longer had a wife, what was the problem? Together they could do so much: as his wife she could help him with his projects. She had gone over the scenarios before, many times, ever since he became young and Sharon left him. How they could collaborate on at least three projects…she could really propel space exploration…together they could do wonders. Maybe he was still in love with Sharon? No, he never talked about her, and he didn't seem all broken up about the split. Maybe it was her new looks; as her old self she knew she would have had no problem seducing him. Yeah, that was it; she had lost her looks. After crying a little and at some point feeling so angry she could have screamed, at three in the morning she fell asleep.

The following day was Sunday. Joy and Angie accompanied Juanita, Eldridge, and two other couples from their house to the local church, in spite of Angie's protestations. "Come on, Maria, it's for a good cause." With this Joy-Patricia led her out the front door.

Joy liked the experience. "There's a feeling of…goodness in that place," she told Louis and the rest later that morning in the living room. "I can't describe it any other way. I totally dismiss the verbiage and don't like the dogma, all that talk about the Bible, but I must admit I enjoyed being there."

Angie gave her a half smile. "It wasn't so bad."

That was interesting, thought Louis. Perhaps he should come along the following Sunday.

Walking through the orchard the next afternoon with Joy, Angie, and Larry, Louis recalled Sharon's concept regarding D'Anjou's invention. "In due time most everyone will want to rejuvenate. Sharon proposed that those who want children would forfeit their rejuvenation—"

"Oh yeah, like that's going to work!" Angie said, examining a stunted peach tree. "The minute they are gravely ill, they'll change their minds in a hurry. And what about having a dear one about to die? Imagine yourself denying Sharon the technology. Could you have done it?"

And Louis realized that, of course, he would have moved heaven and earth to get her into that machine to save her life.

Larry examined the trees with curiosity, fingering their leaves. "The only solution is to send some people to a new world," he said.

"Yes," Louis said lost in thought. "When we get back to New York, we'll have to deal with that issue."

Joy turned to look at Louis. "It can't wait!"

"But what can we do? We are isolated; we might as well be the farmers we pretend to be."

"Not with D'Anjou's technology," Joy said a bit testily, "and not with our accumulated knowledge. We owe it to the world to solve this, Louis."

"After all," interjected Angie, "we created the problem when we healed Sharon."

Louis sighed and nodded. "I know, Angie. I know it's all my doing."

Joy looked sternly at Angie. "I'm to blame as well, because I was there at that lab doing my best to help."

"Yeah," said Larry, "me too…and Suzanne…we were all trying to save Sharon's life."

"So the only blameless one," Joy said, "is you, Angie. Congratulations."

Angie turned her back on them to stare at the distance, and she remained like that after they had left.

That night, the pressing need to reach Tolima stayed with Louis until very late, when he finally fell asleep.

In the morning when he woke up, Louis felt frustrated with the time he'd spent away from New York. Why did D'Anjou have to run away? All the time and energy spent trying to get him back! What an idiotic thing to do. The man was a jackass.

During breakfast, eager for some news, perhaps good news, he turned to Larry, sitting at the end of the couch with Suzanne, staring at his display on his lap, both in T-shirts and jeans. The rest of the crew was sitting at the table eating scrambled eggs and toast.

"Larry, what's the news from the outside world?"

Larry pressed a couple of keys and grimaced. "The regents granted Texas to the Patriots."

Angie stopped her fork with scrambled eggs in midair. "That's it? They just gave Texas away without preparing the residents? No offers to relocate, no offers to help? How did they negotiate with the Texas government? That is so stupid!"

"I don't know, Angie. There's nothing here about negotiations. Whatever happened, they told the Patriots to go ahead and take over."

Joy stared at Larry in stunned silence. Arlene seemed to be lost in thought.

Louis put his cup down. "That...that's really bad."

"The Patriots are sealing off Texas with a twenty-foot fence all around," Larry continued, "watchtowers within sight of one another with computer disabling equipment to stop cars from flying, and jamming devices to block all communications outside of Texas."

Angie cradled her face in her hands. "What about all those atavists who were supposed to migrate to Texas?" she managed to ask.

"I don't know...maybe Reilly realized that Texas can't sustain that many new people."

"Maybe," Louis said, "but I bet that fence is mostly to keep people in, not out. Reilly means to control his population...he doesn't want to give them the option to leave."

Joy stared at Larry. "We are prisoners!"

"I guess we are," Larry said. "But we still have a hidden weapon, the biochips I planted all over the state."

"Yes!" Joy exclaimed. "Tell us, how do you activate them?" She reached and tapped Angie's hand, then smiled.

"With this." Larry pointed at his virtual computer display.

"And you are the only one who has access?" Louis asked.

"Yes, that's correct."

"Larry, have you tested the system?" Joy asked.

"Yes, I ran a controlled experiment with student subjects to check their reaction. It worked."

Louis looked around the room. "I think we'll all feel better if we could see a demonstration."

Larry stood up. "Let's go outside. We don't have to go far from the house. The bushes and trees around the place will do the trick. But we best lock up Yogi somewhere."

Louis called Yogi. He came out from the basement, wagging his tail. "Come on, buddy, I gotta put you somewhere safe." Louis took him into his bedroom's closet. He told Yogi to sit in a corner, and that he would be back soon. He met up with Larry and the rest by the front door.

Larry, with Suzanne by his side, led them outside.

"Did you inject every single bush and tree in Texas?" Angie asked.

"Yes."

"How?"

Larry made his way toward the equipment barn. "Oh, I sent mosquito androids that injected the chips at night...yeah, I got the whole state.

"I think we best hide from the neighbors' view," he said and led them to the west side of the equipment barn. He tapped his pants pocket to produce his phone and activated the virtual keyboard. It appeared in front of his chest. He grabbed it with one hand and pressed a series of keys with the other.

Thunderous sounds overhead. Two gigantic androids landed not ten feet in front of them with a loud thump, raising a cloud of dirt and throwing cement clumps high into the air. Joy and Angie screamed and hugged each other. Arlene ran back toward the house. Suzanne looked stunned, and Larry hugged her and whispered in her ear. Louis dropped to a semi-crouch, protecting his head with his hands. The androids swirled at breakneck speed and demolished the barn, the equipment inside, including the car and the van. In one giant leap, one of them moved toward the house swinging giant

186

arms around. In a matter of seconds, the house disintegrated in a cloud of dust.

Joy held Angie, who was shaking and looked terrified. The androids had vanished. The house and barn were intact. Nothing happened. There were no giant androids.

"That was…quite a show, Larry," Joy said.

"Yes, it worked better than I thought."

Suzanne had hid behind Larry and seemed frozen. Larry spoke gently in her ear, stroking her head.

Louis stood looking around. "Would the neighbors have seen what we saw?"

"That's an interesting question," replied Larry, still comforting Suzanne. "I only activated the vegetation on this side of the barn, I don't think they would have been affected. I guess we'll find out if they come over running."

But no one came over. They went back to the house, all still shaken, stealing looks behind them.

Back inside, Louis got Yogi. The dog had apparently slept through the entire episode inside Louis's closet. They found Arlene hiding behind the couch. She appeared shaken, but after being told that it was all over, she again took a long slow breath with eyes closed and miraculously regained her composure.

Louis wanted at least one more person to have the program to enable the virtual giant androids, and Angie volunteered. "In case you are not available, Larry," explained Louis.

They asked the kitchen android for more coffee and tea, and talked about "the show" Larry had produced.

"Very impressive, Larry," Angie said. "Convincing, very convincing."

Larry smiled at Joy, who was busy rearranging her kimono. "Did you see Joy's face?" he said, looking around at the group. "I tested my first android on her at the university. Back then she almost peed in her pants; now I think she actually did. I always wanted to scare her like that. It was totally worth it." With this he slapped his thigh with glee.

Joy reached out and hit him in the upper arm. When she got no response, she hit him again, and again. "Damn, I should have asked Arlene to make me bigger, much bigger, so I could really hurt this jerk. Pretty just doesn't cut it!"

Larry looked at her and then started laughing, doubling over. It looked like an asthma attack. His laughter was contagious. They laughed with him, and the more they laughed, the more they wanted to laugh. After a while happy tears started rolling from Joy's eyes.

There was much relief that went along with their laughter, thought Louis.

16

I n the days that followed, Louis watched them closely. Larry's "show" had reassured them, made them feel much safer, but the tension was still there, and they had every reason to be tense; no one ever thought they would be in a situation like this, with some maniac making them prisoners. They were no closer to rescuing D'Anjou, although Larry's virtual androids had obviously raised the prospects. But how exactly would they use them? It was clear that without more information and help from a local group, there was no sense even thinking about it.

That night Larry was dozing in bed when Suzanne came to join him after spending her evening hours down at the lab. He felt her slip under the covers. As usual she had cold feet, and as usual, she pressed the soles of her feet against his legs to warm them up.

"Ouch!" he said in mock complaint.

"Cold feet, warm heart…so shut up."

He chuckled. "You know that doesn't make any sense."

"Of course. I decided I would start talking like you guys."

"Us?"

"Yes, the nonsensical masses."

"Oh. I didn't know you had us categorized," he said, still chuckling as he turned over to face her and cradled her hands in his. They, too, were cold. "How are you doing?"

"What…my blood pressure? Other vitals? My state of mind? My morale?" she said with closed eyes. "You have to be more specific."

Larry smiled. "Let's start with how you are doing here in Texas. Are you okay being here?"

"Oh yes. I am studying Doctor D'Anjou's experiments, a rare opportunity."

"So you are…happy?"

One eye opened. "Hmm? Please be more specific."

Larry chuckled again and kissed her. He felt her respond. "Are you glad to be with me?"

"Oh, that? Oh yeah. I love you."

And Larry knew there was no equivocation in her mind, that she had thought about it and could now say it. He kissed her again and felt a sweet tug in his heart.

The following day, a Sunday, Louis went to church with Angie, Joy, Juanita, and Eldridge. And like Joy and Angie, he found a certain nice "feeling" in the place, particularly after they sang their hymns. What was the feeling, and where did it come from?

During lunch, the group talked about the conversations they'd had with church members. More than a few came across as quite atavistic, viewed anyone involved with the government as automatically an enemy, and a socialist. The sermon had dealt with the devil, hell, and punishment for "God's enemies."

"How do you reconcile the nice feeling in that church with talk like that?" Louis asked no one in particular.

Fall was approaching, and General Thomas A. Kennedy knew what it meant, they were going to set President Reilly's world conquest plan in motion. That was an exciting thought, and he quickened his pace through the long hallway on the way to Central Command Center, Houston. He enjoyed the sound of his heels on the hard floors—very military. He couldn't wait until November, when they were scheduled to take over Massachusetts and he could go around "visiting" old family friends.

"General Kennedy!" He heard the familiar brassy voice and his heart skipped a beat. He immediately turned around in a smart about-face and stood at attention.

President Reilly was coming down the hall right behind him. "Ready to see what your gold has bought us?"

Kennedy saluted. "Yes, sir!" Reilly appeared pleased, and that was good.

Reilly placed a hand on his shoulder. "Good man. Let's go inside and look at what the good folks of MultiDynamics have made for us."

Everyone was there, the entire high command, all 9,227 generals. The contractor was represented by a well-dressed woman of pleasing but cold features and her two assistants. When Reilly sat down at the front of the room, and the generals did likewise behind him, the woman started her visual presentation: thousands of flying tanks, all shiny, executing magnificent maneuvers that left Kennedy ebullient. There was no way anyone could stop them; the lousy socialists would be just rolled over! And the tanks were to be delivered the following week! The presentation showed how the tank crews had been trained, a grueling four-week program conducted at MultiDynamics.

When the presentation was over, Reilly thanked the woman, who took the hint and signaled for her aides to pack up the equipment. They left, bowing at Reilly.

President Reilly took the woman's place in front of the room. "My dear generals…we are ready!" At this, the room broke into thunderous applause. "In three months we will have a parade for the entire world to see. With these here tanks, all fifty thousand of them, and our army now topping five million, we'll just shock and awe the world into submission. That's what our parade will do. It will be televised globally. The very next day, we'll start rolling across the border on our way to New York. On my television address, two weeks before the parade, I'll just talk about us taking over the neighboring states, the old Confederacy, but I think we'll just surprise them and march right on to take over the world. Who can stop us?"

"President Reilly, sir," a voice rang out from out front where the lieutenant generals, the three-star officers, were seated, "why not sooner?"

"Ah yes. I like that, General Bergmann, you are anxious. We need to finish setting up here in Texas. I congratulate General Stevens on how well he's securing our borders." Reilly started applauding, and everyone quickly joined in. Stevens stood up and bowed.

"We need to prep the world first, you see? We need to see how many regents our men will be able to capture. We'll know that in two weeks. That by itself will set the world in a panic. I'll use my television address to lure Regent Sagan and his team into a trap. They will want to liberate the regents, right? That's when I'll get my hands on Sagan and deal with him once and for all.

"I don't need to tell you all how sinister this Regent Sagan truly is. He's the incarnation of evil, and I am the only one who can do away with him. You know that he can disappear at will? First, he vanished along with Captain Cheney, my top agent. Now, no one can best Cheney, but in a matter of minutes Sagan disappeared with Cheney and his top lieutenant. We then spent the past three months trying to find Sagan. We used the best in the business, thousands of them, and nothing! After California, he just vanished. Not a trace of him anywhere in the world; his biometrics are nowhere to be found. Now you ask: how can a man disappear? And I tell you, because he's made a pact with the devil and has these magical powers. But we got God on our side. And God is far more powerful than the devil, and He's told me Sagan is hiding in Canada and how to get him. So I'll set my trap, get him and his crew. The world will be ours, just as the good Lord intended."

Kennedy could feel the excitement in the room. Certainly Sagan was no match for President Reilly. No man was.

"Yes, my dear generals, and now that we have General Alphonse D'Anjou in our ranks, we are all going to be young, as young as we want, and after we do away with that scientist in Portugal and the other in Israel, why, we'll be the only ones with the technology. The world will come begging for it. General D'Anjou, could you show yourself?"

D'Anjou, sharply dressed in a crisp green uniform, sporting two stars, stood up. The crowd broke into applause.

Reilly looked at D'Anjou admiringly. "With General D'Anjou along, we may not even need our tanks and army, but that would just add to the fun, wouldn't it? At any rate, that's what we need the three months for."

D'Anjou sat down, all eyes on him.

President Reilly extolled them to get ready for the parade on October 11. "That's when the fun will begin," he said, "in three months."

Kennedy couldn't wait.

That Sunday, Louis, accompanied by Joy and Angie, went to church again, and were met by a couple they had talked to briefly the last time. The wife seemed to have warmed up to them. "You folks seem like God-fearing people, and that's all right by me!" she said with a smile.

Back at the house Louis thought he'd had enough of church and people who were afraid of God. It had been intriguing, but not worth attending regularly.

But again there had been that nice feeling, he thought as he ate breakfast. Well, that was a paradox he would leave for someone else to figure out. He turned and smiled at Larry and asked him for news from the outside.

Larry tapped his computer display. "I can only get Texas, nothing from the outside," he said. "We are now fully blocked."

Joy got up from the table and walked to look over Larry's shoulder. "Oh, crap!" "Are you sure? Try again."

Larry tapped his keys. "Yes, I'm sure."

Joy turned around to look at Louis. "Now what do we do? How do we learn what's going on?"

Louis grimaced. "What's the news in Texas?"

Larry studied his display. "I would call it propaganda. How President Reilly will take care of anyone who joins his movement, the New Confederacy, alternatively called 'The Cause.' That anyone in Texas not joining his movement will be considered a traitor and 'dealt with Texas-style.' Oh yes, the borders are now totally sealed and anyone trying to breach them will be shot and killed."

Louis shook his head. He studied their faces. "Maybe we can start thinking about how to infiltrate the Patriots. I would say so far so good. We've made significant progress in that regard."

Angie shook her head. "How can you say that? How in the world have we made progress?"

Joy stared at her, surprised. "Angie, we've gotten to know a good many of the locals and earned their trust. And we are all safe for now."

Louis sighed and then stood up. "Come on, people. Let's go to work outside like farmers. That's our cover; let's make sure we keep it." He made his way to the front door. Larry, Joy, and Suzanne decided to join him.

They worked with two androids on the raised beds. They weeded and fixed the irrigation system. They started new beds.

They managed to work on the vegetable beds most of that week. On Saturday they went square dancing and it felt good. They talked about their vegetables and the trees and got much advice.

They worked Monday fertilizing and pruning the peach trees. As the sun was setting and they were about to go back in the house, a car landed in front of them. Juanita, Eldridge, and another man who lived with them came out of the car, silent and sullen. They wore work clothes and the men had their usual guns strapped to their waists.

Louis froze, but tried to smile. Did they come to ask to join them in a firefight against some invader?

Eldridge came up to Louis and extended a hand. "Sorry to barge in like this, but you folks didn't give us access to your phones. Do you have any idea what's going on?"

"Just what we hear in the news, Eldridge, that some man called President Reilly and his group have taken over Texas and sealed the borders."

Eldridge nodded gravely. "Yes, that's right. That Reilly has done all that. Now, what we need from you all is to tell us which side are you folks on. If you are with this Reilly fellow, why, we need to know."

"We know nothing about President Reilly, Eldridge," replied Louis, feeling the tension unwinding all over his body. "But we are very concerned that we are being made prisoners."

Eldridge looked around. "Greg, can we go inside to talk?" he asked, pointing at the house.

Once inside, Louis called everyone else to sit in. They sat around the dining table. The hot sun streamed through the windows. The place was hot and stifling, though the visitors didn't seem to mind. Eldridge fidgeted with his hat, which he held with both hands on his lap. He told his hosts that he and many others had come together under the leadership of a farmer "up north" named Stephen Phillipiak to stop Reilly and his Patriots. "We didn't work this hard to be free just to let some kook take it away from us," he said.

Juanita pushed her seat away from the table and crossed beefy arms across her chest. "Imagine, the world government agreed to let this Reilly take over Texas. They just went and decided what they can do with us all without asking. They didn't even consult our own president, Julian Perry, or our congress. They just kinda brushed them aside like dust."

Louis felt himself starting to blush, and he took a deep breath to stop it. "That's just awful. Obviously we are with you; we want no part of Reilly. He sounds scary."

"Oh yeah," Juanita said. "Reilly is forming an army...he already has one, but he wants it much bigger. He's going to decree that every man and woman who's healthy and between the ages of eighteen and fifty will have to serve. That would be like fifty million people! First, he wants full control of Texas. Anyone who's against him will be either killed or put in prison. All those rich people from the States who settled in Texas have to turn their private armies over to Reilly, but a lot of them are already generals in his army, anyway. Then, he wants to take over the United States and then the world. To do that, he has to destroy the world government. But he also wants to get a hold of the regents who are hiding."

"That's crazy!" exclaimed Joy, who sat next to Louis fanning her face with her hand. "And I guess he wants to be the only one with the rejuvenation process, so he's going after that D'Anjou scientist?"

"Oh no. That D'Anjou fellow is now one of his generals. He's an important man in the organization. Reilly has got all he needs now."

Louis exchanged quick urgent glances with Joy. He felt sick.

Eldridge grabbed his wife's hand, but she shook her head. "Oh, don't worry Eldridge, these folks are fine. I can tell." She beamed them a smile. "Eldridge is concerned I'm giving out too much information. You see, we got us some spies within the Patriots—"

"Juanita. Watch your mouth!" Eldridge said. "Maybe these folks are fine, but you talk way too much."

"Oh, shush," replied Juanita, smiling at Joy. "As I was saying, we got us these spies over there in Houston where Reilly got his headquarters. He will announce that anyone who comes over to his camp will never get sick or die. At the same time, he wants no competition, so he's going to do away with the two other scientists who were working on the same technology. But he's really after the four regents who escaped, but mostly he wants their boss, Sagan…you know what I'm talking about, right? They are all over the news."

Louis told her that, yes, they knew all about the regents.

"Well, Reilly has figured out the regents are now in Canada, trying to hide. So he set some kind of trap to catch them."

Eldridge smacked his lips. "Yeah, we got us these spies," he said with obvious pride. "Reilly will announce in two months all about the rejuvenation process and how he's going to make war. Now we got us some lead time on account of the advance news, and we figured we best use it as best we can."

"Instead of the dance Saturday night," Juanita said, "we are all heading to Stephen's farm up north to plan. Are you folks with us?"

Louis didn't want to appear too anxious to accept, so he demurred. "Well, we obviously agree with you," He remembered he and Joy-Patricia were supposed to be married, so he looked at her for approval.

"Yes, we are with you," Louis said.

When the visitors were gone, Louis turned to the rest. Larry stared out the window, shaking his head in dismay. Joy let out a long breath.

"I can't believe D'Anjou is there voluntarily," Louis said.

Arlene had tears streaming down her face. "That can't be true, not Alphonse!"

Joy scooted her chair and reached an arm around Arlene's shoulders.

"What do we do?" Angie asked.

"Well," Louis said, "The Patriots think we are in Canada. I guess Larry's ruse worked. That's good. It buys us time. Let's go and meet this Stephen they are talking about—"

"But we are no longer rescuing D'Anjou," Joy said, "so what are we doing?"

"I just don't believe he's there voluntarily." Louis turned to look at Arlene. "Let's proceed…and see what happens. I mean, what other option do we have?"

Joy nodded. "Yes…it's not like we can go back to New York…eventually we are bound to be found out…it's just a matter of time."

Louis nodded. "It's possible D'Anjou is willingly cooperating with the Patriots, but it's highly unlikely. Not the type. But, then, what's going on? Why is he there? We must consider the possibility that he was captured and brainwashed. In that case, we need to rescue him and reverse the process."

Joy looked him straight in the eyes. "You might be right. But bottom line, as you said, what other option do we have?"

Louis stood and made his way to his room. Yes, what other option did they have? Maybe Stephen Phillipiak and his group would prove to be the people, the army, they had hoped for. Maybe it was not too late to rescue D'Anjou. But Louis realized what they really had to do was stop that idiotic so-called President Reilly, who was starting to resemble the famous Hitler of the twentieth century. It was a crazy notion to attempt on their own, without the resources of the world government, but if they were going to do this kamikaze thing, this suicide mission, it would not make sense to do it just to rescue D'Anjou…they would try and obliterate Reilly and the Patriots once and for all.

17

At breakfast Louis told the group what he had concluded, that if they were going to link up with the opposition, and if they stood a high probability of being captured or dying, it made sense to at least try and do away with Reilly and his Patriots. After all, they had Larry's virtual androids, and with some good planning and luck, who knows what they could do. Angie was adamant that it was a crazy notion; they should concentrate on trying to escape.

Joy, who sat beside Angie, grabbed her hand, "I must say it again, Angie; we have no other option. There's no way we can escape, and if we try, we'll get either killed or caught for certain. Our best strategy is to try and do away with Reilly...Yes, we stand a good chance of failing, but we have to at least try."

That Saturday afternoon, Louis, along with Angie, Joy, and Larry, walked over next door to Juanita's place. Arlene and Suzanne stayed working in the lab. They were making progress deciphering D'Anjou's technology. That was the best use of their talents.

Louis and his group made their way down their farm's old-style driveway, which had been paved over many years before, then opened the ancient wrought-iron gate that still held cattle at bay. They went by the pasture with the cattle. An old-style windmill pumped water into a metal trough. The breeze picked up, and they heard the windmill go around faster. They opened their neighbor's gate, also wrought iron, with "Jesus Saves" emblazoned across in wrought-iron letters painted gold against the black gate.

They walked up the driveway lined with orange trees. Three dogs came out to meet them, tails wagging.

The neighbors must have seen them because they filed out of the house, already dressed to go out, the men sporting their guns, the whole lot in cowboy attire.

Louis and his group shook hands all around as a large van pulled out of the garage. The conversation was a bit terse, but friendly; all small talk about "when is it going to rain?" And "it's going to be another long, dry, and hot summer." They boarded and sat in four long bench seats, with the rustling of dresses, and guns and hats getting in the way. The car lifted off and headed north. Eldridge, sitting across the way from Louis, told him how concerned his people had been when they saw the newcomers moving in next door. "We thought you all could be Patriots, in which case we would have to do something about you all...but you are all right...only thing is, we had to make sure," he said with a grin.

The Phillipiak farm was some hundred miles to the north, and it was just as flat and dry. Looking from high above at the big stretch of land that went on to the north forever, the big plains, it was easy to imagine the large herds of buffalo that for so many centuries roamed freely until the white man decided to exterminate them along with the Indians.

Stephen Phillipiak now farmed mostly wheat, but in accordance with the sustainable living approach, the prevailing theme in Texas, he also had plots of corn, fruit trees, and vegetables. Eldridge's car landed next to the main house. They disembarked and joined the large crowd that according to Eldridge was "well over five thousand." Everyone seemed to be enjoying themselves, drinking, eating, and talking under a series of old-fashioned fabric tents that formed a massive round pod. In between the house and the tents stood a large pond with trees planted along the edge, a welcome relief from the dry and hot landscape. A number of tables had been set up with food, and smiling young cowboys of both genders offered lemonade, beer, hot dogs, and hamburgers. Louis and his group were not used to eating meat, but had already done so at Juanita's house and at the dance for the sake of blending in, and Louis urged Angie in particular, who was always so finicky, to eat what was offered.

Louis, accompanied by Joy, ambled about and was surprised to find an eclectic group. He had expected to meet evangelical Christians and quite a few appeared to be in that mold, but there were also people who he could easily have pictured back at Columbia University or in the streets of New York. A good many stood admiring the pond and the fish that swam in it.

Stephen Phillipiak himself, who walked around the crowd saying hello, struck Louis as someone he might have rubbed elbows with. He looked the part of a first tier, with a well-tended goatee, salt-and-pepper hair, and dressed in jeans and a well-tailored tweed jacket. According to Juanita he had been a psychiatrist in San Francisco up until some ten years ago, when he had moved to Texas with his wife and two sons along with so many others in search of an independent lifestyle, free of the big government.

Juanita led Louis and Joy to where Phillipiak stood, surrounded by rancher types.

"Stephen," she said elbowing her way through the group, "these here are some folks you ought to meet." Juanita pulled Joy and Louis to stand in front of Phillipiak, who looked Louis in the eyes, then Joy, and extended a hand.

"This is Gregory and Patricia Easterly, Stephen. They came from New York with the rest of their farm family and bought the old Hemming's place next door to us. Real fine folks."

Stephen nodded at Juanita and gave Louis and Joy a knowing smile as he shook hands with them. "A friend of Juanita's is a friend of mine. You arrived in Texas just in time to face quite a situation. Ordinarily we would be just having a good time here—"

"Oh yeah," chirped in Juanita. "We've had us some fine parties at the Phillipiak farm."

Phillipiak placed a hand on Juanita's shoulder. "You'll find these people," and he looked around, "very welcoming. They certainly welcomed me with open arms."

The rancher types around them smiled. They appeared to have every intention to stay where they were, listening to the two men. Angie came to join them and stood beside Joy.

Phillipiak talked casually, but probingly nevertheless, trying perhaps to ascertain Louis's background, affiliations, maybe talents and skills. Louis felt he should portray himself as someone well educated. Certainly someone in Phillipiak's position would be on the lookout for people he could use in his movement. They talked about science, and Phillipiak inquired what Louis had done in New York. He told him he had taught science "here and there." He mentioned that both Joy and Angie were also scientists and told him about Larry's expertise in artificial intelligence.

"You all could have made first tier," Phillipiak said with a faint smile, as he casually studied a card-like device he had pulled out of his shirt pocket.

"I believe we could have done that, but we all decided some time ago we wanted nothing to do with a system where an individual doesn't account for much. We tried to lead independent lives, but you know how hard that is." Louis noticed Phillipiak followed his every word, studied him closely. "So we decided to come to Texas, where we heard we could strike out on our own...but this new development with Reilly—"

"Yes, yes. I know," Phillipiak said, putting his small device away. "That man is starting to scare us all."

"He behaves like that Hitler of three hundred years ago."

"That's right." Phillipiak said. He paused and looked around. The crowd had grown around them. "Greg, I would love to talk to you some more, but I have to tend to these folks." He asked for Louis's phone access, smiled, and walked away.

Louis stood feeling ill at ease. I hope I didn't overplay my hand, he thought. Did Phillipiak suspect I am Regent Sagan? No, that can't be. I don't look like that anymore. But then again, someone who is well informed can put two and two together...Larry, the artificial intelligence first tier...Joy's and my background in social psychology and bioscience. Good thing I didn't mention the Space Administration.

Louis felt someone slap his shoulder. He turned around to find Juanita. "That Stephen is quite a guy, eh? Looks like you two hit it off! I see he got your phone access; means you are important." She smiled at Joy.

Louis nodded. He noticed some of Juanita's friends were now standing around them. A number of other people came over.

"Gregory here is one smart fellow," announced Juanita. "He and Stephen spoke about all kinds of things. And Stephen took down his phone access!"

They wanted to meet him, and shake his hand. They also wanted to talk about Reilly and what could be done about him.

That was an interesting development, Louis thought. They didn't treat him as an intruder, but as a resource. "I'm no strategist, but I would suggest we determine what all skills and abilities we have, how many people we can count on, and try and promote ourselves—"

"Promote, how?" asked one of the rancher types who held a beer in one hand.

"Well, the thing is Reilly is telling people he's the only option to the big government. But we now have another option: Stephen Phillipiak. And we should let folks who follow Reilly know about Stephen."

"But how do we do that?" the man asked.

"Word of mouth," Louis said raising his own beer to his lips. "That's the only sure way for people in our situation."

"And what situation is that?" asked the man as he took a swig of his beer, all the while studying Louis.

"We need to maintain low visibility because Reilly has an army. If they know where we are, they can crush us; if they don't, they will be chasing ghosts all over Texas."

The man with the beer smiled in approval. "That's all right!" He extended his hand. "Mike Arnold. By the way," he said as they shook hands, "that's almost exactly the plan Stephen will announce tonight."

Joy decided to mingle on her own, and Louis walked around joining in whenever he saw a group gathered. He was very surprised to meet one, and then a second heir of the ultra rich who migrated to Texas after the New Paradigm. "My father might have been an oligarch," said Paul, a bland-looking middle-aged man, "but my wife and I are not like that. We want what's right for all Texans, not just a few." That's a gratifying development, thought Louis, and wondered how many former oligarchs thought like him. He also heard a lot of talk about Reilly, but also ranting against the world government, some of it disquieting. Some spoke of taking over the government "by force if necessary to make things right." He did find a few who made valid points. One couple he met, a husband and wife in their late thirties with a small baby, resented the world government "because it has robbed a lot of people of the incentive to do something with themselves." "You can't protect people from cradle to grave," said the woman, looking at her baby in arms, "and expect them to get motivation out of thin air." And Louis wanted to reply whether being of service to others was not motivation enough…but decided to keep quiet and listen. Maybe to them service meant bringing an apple pie to a newcomer; to him, Joy, and Larry, and the rest, it meant everything. That was something atavists would never understand, an ideological divide that could not be breached.

An hour later they all gathered for a talk by Phillipiak, who stood up on a table and addressed the crowd, now tightly packed shoulder to shoulder as close as they could get to him.

Louis heard what he had just told the man with the beer being echoed by Phillipiak. "We need to remain invisible; we can't fight Reilly head-on because he's got the numbers. But we can infiltrate his ranks and tell his followers we are an alternative to him." The talk became a planning session, and Mike Arnold and several others offered their suggestions. They decided they would finalize their plan, and would stay in touch, but would proceed to infiltrate Reilly's army immediately. They already had three spies, or moles, as Phillipiak called them. That was a good start.

After the talk the crowd dispersed. Louis found himself talking to a woman who was eventually joined by another woman and a man. They were all professors at the University of Texas.

One of the women, Cassandra, or "Cass" as she told Louis she liked to be called, taught economics. Louis mentioned how he was not used to living in a moneyed society, but found the idea "liberating."

"The New Paradigm is a worthwhile concept," she said, "but the implementation leaves a lot to be desired."

Fred, who also taught economics, said his objection was the total obliteration of currency; financial disasters happened when most wealth was concentrated on a small group. "The New Paradigm doesn't call it money, but what they have, unlimited prerogatives for their elite, works the same way, and the danger is the same."

Louis thought that was the type of input he would have liked to have because it made a lot of sense. "Why didn't you submit those comments to the world government? I understand they are supposed to listen to anyone, no matter where they live."

"Ha!" Cass said. "It's clear you don't know how the world government works. They instituted a screening process to keep people like us from being heard."

"Absolutely," added Fred. "What they have is another oligarchy comprised by an intellectual elite who speak the same language. That course you take to become a first tier, it's the means to inculcate the way to communicate. If you don't know how, your voice is not heard."

Louis continued asking questions, and found he reluctantly agreed on some important points.

The gathering ended late at night. Tired and a bit tipsy from all the beer, Louis and the rest boarded Eldridge's car.

Back in his bedroom, with Yogi gently snoring on his cushion by the bed, Louis decided it was time to think. He had found the Phillipiak gathering disturbing. While a good many people were surprisingly reasonable and easy to talk to, like Cass and Fred, he had heard a lot of talk about violence and that awful narrow mind-set he had come to dread. Quite a few of those people were atavists. And there was Phillipiak himself, intelligent and reasonable, but something about him was unsettling. He and his followers were against Reilly, but they seemed a bit too eager to fight, and now that Louis thought about it, they didn't stand much of a chance, not against a large, well-disciplined army. And Larry's virtual androids would scare people, but then what? Maybe Angie was right; maybe they should try their best to escape. They should at least look into D'Anjou's technology as a possibility, and surely by now Larry would have a handle on it. Perhaps there was a way to use the technology to escape to California or New York. Once there, they could work with the board of regents on a sound plan of action to stop Reilly.

Early in the morning, Louis walked down to the lab. He met Larry, Suzanne, and Arlene, who were busy talking about some technical data. "Larry," he began, "I don't know how far along you are in getting a handle on D'Anjou's technology, but if the need arises, could you teleport us all to New York or California?"

Larry shook his head as he ate a handful of almonds, the last of his breakfast. "We tried a few days back to send an apple to my office at Columbia and it was blocked. I imagine D'Anjou is the brain behind that."

"Don't you need a receiving station?"

"Our revised protocol involves teleporting a receiving-sending station with the subject. It also serves as a vehicle to encapsulate and protect the subject during the process. It worked well between the house and the barn, so it should've worked for any distance. There was nothing wrong procedurally; there was some type of block at work."

"I was afraid of that. Is there anything else we could try? How about another dimension?"

"When we failed to send the apple in Kali Four, we tried nearby dimensions, and they didn't work, either."

Louis drummed his fingers on the worktable. "Are there any dimensions they can't possibly block that you can access?"

"It's theoretically possible, but I don't quite know how to do it. As far as I can tell, the higher the energies combined, the more elusive the dimensions seem to become. The highest I've been able to go is Kali Eight hundred twenty, but nothing above the Kali sequence."

Louis rested his gaze on one of the big glassite cubes. "So if you can't tap a higher dimension, neither can D'Anjou or anyone else. Why is that?"

"Because to go to those dimensions with higher energies, you need to match them, or you can't access them. You can't just go in as we are, we are suitable for no higher than Kali Four, anything higher, and we are rejected."

Louis started pacing slowly in between the two long metal lab tables. "Sharon told me that when D'Anjou sent her on the teleporter she felt something akin to meditation, do you know why that would happen?"

"That's interesting. Arlene said the same thing. My guess is they experienced one of the higher energies, maybe Diva."

Louis stopped his pacing and turned to face Arlene, who was standing silently to one side. "So, Arlene, you are a deep meditator, eh?"

Arlene blushed. "Yes. I've been meditating for quite some time."

"We all meditate," Louis said, "but do you go deep?"

"Yes, I guess so."

Louis turned to Larry. "Could you use your instruments to read if she is going into another dimension?"

Larry hesitated. "I really don't think anyone can go into another dimension at will. I just don't think that can happen...I mean, detecting the energy is one thing, but actually being in say, Diva Three?"

Louis smiled at Arlene, who stood primly in her lab coat, pretty face and long blond hair. "Well, could you just take a reading while she meditates, just to humor me?"

Larry half smiled. "I'll do it, Louis, but I can tell you it will read Meda Eleven."

"What's Meda Eleven?"

"It's the dimension that makes up the universe we inhabit."

"Well, let's just take a reading while Arlene meditates, and if it reads Meda Eleven, we haven't lost anything except a little time."

Larry rubbed his ear, lost in thought. "The reading should be interesting at any rate. I'll set up the experiment and talk it over with Suzanne, ask her what she thinks—"

"Whatever you have to do, Larry," added Louis eagerly, "please do, and the sooner the better...can we try it today?"

Larry looked at the worktable in front of him and the pad with his notes. "I guess so. Can you give us an hour, Louis?"

Louis went upstairs and talked to Joy and Angie, had a bite to eat, and decided an hour had passed.

He found Larry and Suzanne standing beside Arlene, who sat on a chair, her eyes closed, back straight, and hands resting on her lap.

"We've just run a couple of readings," Larry said, excitement written on his face. "All I need is this handheld scanner, and yes, we just determined she matches the energy found in the dimension Diva Two Hundred-Fifteen."

Louis examined the silent and very peaceful-looking Arlene. "Does that mean she goes there?"

"I must assume that to be the case, otherwise her reading—"

"That makes sense," Louis said thinking aloud. "Does that mean that you can teleport her using dimension Diva Two Hundred-Fifteen?"

"Theoretically, yes."

"Can you try it?"

Larry stared at Arlene. "I can't ask her. It might be a place of no return, or worse yet, obliteration. I really...can't."

And Louis understood. "That's fine, Larry. You don't need to explain; it is after all, a risky proposition because it has never been done before, and you can't send the mouse first. So I'll just have to learn to go much deeper in meditation and do it myself."

"You? C'mon Louis, it's too much of a risk!"

"It's for me to decide, Larry. Now, what do you suppose might be the properties of Diva Two that Kali Four doesn't have?"

Suzanne, who had been standing listening, stepped forward. "For one, matter will be much lighter, for want of another term," she said with uncharacteristic authority. "Therefore you would be unaffected by Meda Eleven."

Louis was surprised and elated she had answers. "Can you explain that?"

"The higher you go, the greater your domain over our universe."

"Can you give me an example?"

"In Diva Four you could change things here, solid things, and physical construct factors would have no effect on you."

"You mean I could conceivably walk through a wall as though it were a virtual image?"

"Yes. Even walk on water, if you wish."

"You are implying the universes, that is, the dimensions, overlap."

Suzanne stared him straight in the eyes. "We are all a part of the same cosmos."

"In common vernacular, we are all here. I would be able to see and touch someone in the Diva Sequence."

"Of course," said Suzanne, "you just saw Arlene, and she was in Diva Two. But in the higher dimensions, Diva Four and above, you may touch someone in Meda Eleven, but not the other way around."

Larry had stepped to one side, folded his arms, and was listening intently.

Louis stared at Suzanne in disbelief. "How about travel, could I go to Tolima in Diva Two?"

"Yes. It would be much easier, with no concern about contamination or interference."

Louis thought for a moment then smiled. "So, bottom line, if we access Diva Two, we can leave Texas if we want to."

"I would say unequivocally Diva Two would be unaffected by anything here in Texas or anywhere else in Meda Eleven," Suzanne said.

"How certain are you of all this?" Louis asked.

Suzanne stared at him for a moment. "I am basing my conclusions on D'Anjou's research ranked by peer review in the top one percentile. In my own review, I found not a single procedural flaw." Suzanne closed her eyes. "I am 99.956 percent certain of what I just told you."

Louis smiled at Suzanne. That was great. The odd young lady, whose presence he often questioned, had proved invaluable. He nodded at Larry and looked at Arlene, who still sat in silence but now had her eyes open and studied him with an unusually serene look. "I know what I need to do. I'll start meditating right away and will let you know when you can send me through Diva Two."

"Where?" Larry asked.

"I don't know. But I do know I must do it."

"Even if it means risking your life? I mean, we don't know much about Diva Two, and we can't experiment with a mouse."

"I know, I know. Unless we can teach a mouse to meditate…Thanks, Suzanne. And thank you, Larry and Arlene."

One day he would have to thank Sharon for her role. In the meantime, he had much work to do.

18

T hat night he tried to meditate deep. It was no longer a matter of dissipating worry and relaxing, now he set his mind on Diva Two. After three hours, he didn't feel any different. He knew it would take time, but he had no time to waste, and it would have to be the most urgent task of his life.

The following day at breakfast, Louis announced to the group he didn't want to be disturbed until further notice. He went to his room and spent over twelve hours in different stages of meditation. Unfortunately the effort just left him in a rare state of exhaustion. The inside of his head felt numb.

He kept at it for several days, and then one day he tried a balance of effort and just letting go. He did the breathing exercises meant to concentrate his mind and relax his body, and then he simply let go. By the afternoon, he felt he had made progress. It was fascinating; he could feel a gradual change come over him. Unfortunately the slightest distraction, particularly anything that stirred his emotions, would bring him back to what he detected as his "old self."

The trick was to stay in a meditative state while active. It took much discipline, but it was necessary and he would do it.

He kept at it for the next ten days, making some progress, he felt, and that was encouraging…but not fast enough.

One Sunday he asked Larry to take a scanner with him to church. He was curious if that nice feeling he had felt those Sundays was something measurable; whether the churchgoers, too, were accessing another dimension.

Larry agreed. He was excited by the scientific aspect of the enterprise, but not by going to church. And he, along with Arlene and Suzanne, did look like fish out of water, stiff and uncomfortable, but when the singing began, and he took out his scanner, all three of them focused on the readings and acted as though they were back at their lab. Louis had to shush them a couple of times when they talked out loud.

And their scanner did prove there was something happening in that church. "They were definitely in the Ella sequence, around the six hundred level," concluded Larry on their way home.

And that was an eye-opener for Louis. Atavists did access those higher dimensions, but why were they still living in that awfully constricted world of theirs? And then it dawned on him: obviously because the mind didn't have anything to do with accessing those dimensions. Of course! He recalled Sharon's statement—which at the time hadn't made any sense—that the mind can take us to the portals of meditation, but we must leave it behind to enter. Now it started to make sense. That was the reason he wasn't going deeper, yet when he let go and relaxed, he did.

He couldn't wait to go to his room to meditate, and this time he went deep. Later, still sitting, he analyzed the experience and concluded that the meditation process was one of transcendence, that as he meditated he was gradually and quite literally entering another state, another dimension. He guessed he had experienced Diva Two or thereabouts.

It was time for Larry to try his scanner on him.

The following morning, in his temperature-regulating sweats, and feeling elated, Louis took his customary walk down the driveway with Yogi. Later on, after breakfast, he would approach Larry and his gang.

As he walked he started to plan how he would proceed provided that he could be teleported…he would…but then what? What would happen to the rest? Arlene was the only other person who could escape; the rest…his phone rang, and Phillipiak's image came up before his eyes. Louis touched his breast pocket and Phillipiak's virtual image stood before him.

"Greg, I need to talk to you in person. Can I come over?" Phillipiak's manner was friendly, but he appeared anxious. "I have been trying to get in touch for the past three days, but your phone has been turned off. Can we talk now?"

"Yes, of course. When?"

"Right now."

Louis heard a buzzing sound overhead as a car started its descent. Yogi barked, and Louis told him to sit.

His heart racing, Louis called Larry on his phone to stand by with the giant androids just in case.

Phillipiak's car landed on the lawn. Louis heard the front door of the house open and quick steps behind him. He turned around. It was Joy in her kimono.

Phillipiak, in jeans, cowboy boots, and a light white jacket, emerged from his car with an outstretched hand and a smile. "Greg, how are you?" he said as he walked over to the cement pathway where Louis stood.

"Fine, Stephen, you remember my wife, Patricia."

Phillipiak shook Joy's hand. His smile seemed authentic, but there was tension in his face. Yogi came up to him, and Phillipiak petted him. "What a beautiful Rottweiler, and a gentle one." He turned to look at Louis.

"Greg, what I have to tell you might be rather shocking. I'm sorry."

Louis felt cold in the pit of his stomach. "What's going on?"

"Reilly. He kidnapped about a thousand regents, and killed a few. His people have also killed a few others: two scientists, one in Portugal, and the other one in Israel, both apparently very close to duplicating Doctor D'Anjou's technology; a number of human policemen, and scores of innocent people who happened to be in the way. Probably fifty people altogether."

Louis felt Joy's hand clasp his. "Oh my...When did this happen?"

"Three days ago."

Louis had a hard time taking everything in. He needed more information. "Where has he taken the kidnapped regents...do you know the names of the ones he killed?"

"I'll tell you what I know: He's built a concentration camp near Houston. The kidnapped regents are probably there. I don't know the names of the regents he's killed, but Louis Sagan is not among them if that's what you want to know. We really can't afford to lose Sagan. That would be terrible."

Joy gasped, as though taking in air. "I thought you were against all regents."

Phillipiak shook his head. "Look, I'm sticking my neck out here, but please, between us...I figure I can trust you. Back at my farm I have to appear to be someone I am not, for the sake of the more, shall we say, atavistic minds among us? Although I hate that term, it's so general, and so disparaging."

Louis felt Joy's fingernails dig into the palm of his hand. Yes, it could be a trap, he realized. "Well, it's commendable you keep such an open mind, Stephen, and I do agree, to classify all of those folks as simply atavistic is too broad, and yes, rather degrading."

"I knew we were of like mind, Greg, that's why I came to see you. You are all well educated and knowledgeable about the world government since you lived in New York. I need you. Listen, about Regent Sagan, I think he's trying his best to save us from Reilly, and I hope he succeeds because I don't think we stand a chance."

"Why? I thought you had a good plan."

"And I did, but my spies reported Reilly is tightening up security. Maybe he suspects something, maybe he doesn't, but he doesn't trust anyone anymore who is not in his inner circle, the five top generals. Listen, can we go in your house? I feel vulnerable talking out here."

"Yes of course, let's have some coffee."

Stephen talked into his shirt pocket, and his car gently slid into the equipment barn, out of sight. They walked toward the house, Joy still holding Louis's hand.

They sat around the kitchen table. Angie joined them. She smiled at Stephen and said good morning, with some tension in her voice. She asked the android to make coffee. Larry came out of the study and Louis asked him to sit with them.

Joy brought Larry and Angie up to date on the kidnapped regents and the killings. Angie's face went white and she sat down as if in a stupor. Larry appeared lost in thought.

"Why do you think Reilly kidnapped the regents?" Louis asked as he watched the kitchen android place a cup of coffee in front of each person.

"The intelligence I got is he plans to use them as pawns to catch Regent Sagan and his group," replied Stephen.

"That makes sense," Louis said doing his best to appear calm. "But I don't see what we can do. We do have some abilities, but certainly nothing you can't find within your people."

"That's right," Stephen said slowly. "We have some fairly sophisticated individuals. There are several medical doctors like me, artificial intelligence experts like Anthony, not to mention highly capable administrators."

"So what do you want from us?" Angie asked harshly, her lips trembling.

Stephen seemed taken aback. "You know, I would like to let you people think about whether you want to help me or not. I'll call tomorrow, and we'll chat some more." With this Stephen got up, thanked them all, and left.

Joy turned to Angie. "That was rude, Angie."

"I didn't mean to sound rude, but everything is collapsing…"

"Angie, we need to do something. The people Reilly has killed! I just shudder to think about that. Those are our friends. People we know. And just on a practical note, if Reilly keeps kidnapping or killing more regents he'll have the world in total chaos."

"Yes. But what do we know about Phillipiak?" Angie said with anxious tears streaming down her cheeks.

Louis looked at her. "Angie, what else can we do? Alone, we are at a loss. With him, we can perhaps do something. We have to trust him."

"Oh, I don't know!" With this Angie brought up her hands to her face and sobbed. "I'm so scared!" She cried for a moment. Then she looked up at him. "Larry said you were experimenting with teleportation…did you find anything?" She asked in between sobs.

Louis sighed. "It was a possibility, but something that would require a lot more work. Certainly nothing we can use right away."

The following morning Larry knocked on Louis's door before breakfast.

"Louis, sorry to disturb you, but this is urgent."

Louis came out in his pajamas and followed Larry, already dressed in jeans and T-shirt, into the kitchen.

"Reilly is about to make an announcement on television in about ten minutes," Larry said, as he walked ahead of Louis.

Joy, sleepy-eyed, sat at the table in her kimono, sipping coffee. She smiled briefly. No one else was in the kitchen. Probably Larry had decided not to alarm the rest.

Louis sat down at the table, and an android brought him a cup of coffee. His phone rang. Louis touched his breast pocket, and Stephen's still face came on with his name. Louis answered, and Stephen's full figure showed up, still wearing his white jacket and jeans.

"Greg! Good morning. Oh, I see you folks are early risers, Good morning Patricia, Anthony. Listen, can I barge in again?"

Louis looked around the table. "Maybe later? We are having breakfast and about to watch Reilly on television."

"Oh, really? He's going to make a personal appearance? Wow. Say, can I watch it with you?"

Louis agreed, and five minutes later Stephen walked in, smiling. Joy pulled up another chair. They poured coffee for Stephen and chatted a minute or so about how hot and dry it was. Angie walked in wearing tight jeans and a sweater and in full makeup. She asked for coffee and sat across the table from Stephen. Larry enlarged the display to hang above their heads. Reilly's image came on. He stood ramrod straight, tall and impressive looking. He had an intense look in his eyes and had an air of authority about him. He wore his Confederate uniform, Stetson hat and all.

Stephen pulled a card-sized device from his pocket and laid it on top of the table. Lights started going back and forth across its surface, apparently scanning.

"Greetings," began the voice in a southern accent. "I am your president. People of the world, be warned: the sword of God is coming! Fellow southerners, this is our moment of glory! Together we will bring back our beloved Confederacy and take over the world. Doesn't that sound good? I bet it does. There is nothing anyone can do to stop us. So come join our army. Share in the glory! Avenge the South. All you have to do is show up at one of our border points and we'll let you in.

"But if you don't, I'll know who you are, and I'll deal with you. That goes particularly for all of you in Texas.

"People of the world: hear my warning! If you surrender peacefully and join our cause there will be no retribution, but if you don't, we will kill you, and we will kill your family.

"All of you good Christians, we are looking to thousands of years of peace and prosperity, a world under Christ and the one true God where all of his enemies will perish under our sword.

"All you lazy atheists who have grown accustomed to a cushy life: it's over! From now on get used to hard work because it's a-coming.

"This is your president, and I will rule for thousands of years. You will have to swear allegiance to me and me alone, for I am Christ's emissary on earth. You are either with me or against me. There's nothing in between. My followers will live forever; my enemies will perish.

"I have made prisoner over a thousand of those vile regents who have taken advantage of us for way too long. I plan to execute them a week from today, at sunrise on Sunday, October 12, a day after our glorious parade.

"I would consider exchanging them for Regent Louis Sagan, whom I blame for all the violence I was forced to inflict. For the next week, I will allow for calls to come into Texas. I am posting this broadcast worldwide, so if anyone knows of Regent Sagan, you can call me at Confederacy-Forever. Texas."

The phone access code appeared on the screen and kept flashing.

"Watch our parade starting at eight in the morning this coming Saturday, Houston time. We'll televise it all over! Stay with us all day so you can admire the Patriot army that's going to take over the world!

"In the name of our Lord Jesus Christ, and his father who is in heaven. Amen!"

They sat silently examining the frozen picture of the man on the display above them, with the phone access code still flashing. Angie had covered her mouth and was sobbing quietly. Joy had an arm around her shoulders, but she, too, looked pale and shaken.

Stephen checked his card device. "Hmm. That man is, or was, a preacher from El Paso named William Omar Reilly. He was a guest pastor at a small congregation in Houston, but left without a word about ten years ago."

Larry examined the card device on the table. "Is that a voice-pattern recognition device?"

Stephen smiled. "You know your stuff."

Larry looked at Louis. "That's quite a gadget. It was manufactured in the last century. I had no idea there were still any around.

"It analyzes people's speech patterns and compares them against an automatically updated database that contains anything from phone conversations to public appearances. Virtually anyone who's ever spoken on a telephone, given a lecture, or appeared on television within the past twenty years is in there. A good device will recognize variations due to age, or even an attempt to disguise."

Louis's eyes were fixed on the device. "How accurate is it?"

"It's been rated at 99.9999 percent. Practically foolproof."

Stephen smiled, a gentle and benign smile. "Yes, Regent Sagan. It is foolproof."

Louis hesitated, looked at Joy, who stood motionless in her chair, consoling Angie, no longer sobbing, but still staring at Reilly's frozen image. Louis felt he had to say something, anything. "I suppose you learned who I was when I first talked to you at your gathering."

Stephen nodded and addressed Angie, who was shaking, her eyes wide. She appeared about to become hysterical. "Look, I'm here alone, right? I have known who you are for over two months, and no one has come to arrest you, so I must be on your side, right, Regent Angela Hall?"

Stephen stood, looked them over, and brushed a curl of hair from his forehead. "You guys are my heroes! It took tremendous courage for you to come here to Texas to try and stop William Reilly." He went over to Angela and took her trembling hand in his. "Regent Hall, I have nothing but admiration for the four of you." He looked at Louis without letting go of Angela's hand. "I have followed your career, Louis. Your work is brilliant. I only take exception with your approach to the atavist project. There you did very poorly. That proposal to let Reilly take over Texas…is just terrible. But you had good intentions, and I am certain you had your back against the wall."

Stephen gently let go of Angie's hand. He sat back down on his chair, then met Joy's stare. He smiled at her. "I know Louis made himself young, that was in the news, but can you use Doctor D'Anjou's technology to change your appearance as well? Wow."

"What can we do?" Joy asked, gently stroking Angie's shoulder. Angie turned to face Stephen with tears in her eyes. "Yes. What do you want from us!"

"Regent Blass, Regent Hall…" Stephen said in a reassuring tone, "I came here to ask for your help. You are free to turn me down, and I will still try my best to protect you all." He took a sip from his cup, brought it down, smiled, and stroked his immaculate reddish-brown goatee. There was still tension behind his demeanor, but outwardly he was reassuring; he was smiling, his eyes friendly and kind.

A good psychiatrist, thought Louis. "We have no reason not to trust you, Stephen. You are right; if you had wanted to, right now we all could be in that concentration camp in Houston with the other regents."

Stephen shook his head. "Correction, my friend. You'd most likely be dead, after being paraded around for all to see."

"We are sorry," Joy said, still gently patting Angie. "I guess we have been extremely tense."

"Understandably so, Joy," Stephen said as he studied Angela's hands, which she clasped and unclasped.

Angie seemed to regain a measure of composure. "I mean, you act so nonchalant, but what we just heard is very scary," she said in a tremulous voice. "I can just imagine how the world is reacting to all the kidnappings and killings. I am thinking of my family, my friends, colleagues, about the whole world. They must be terrified!"

"Yes, Angela," Stephen said calmly, "and that's exactly what the killings and kidnappings were designed to do: terrify the world and bring it under submission."

"Stephen is right, Angie," Louis said soothingly.

Joy nodded in agreement. "And we all know the world government is largely defenseless; they don't have the armies, the guns to fend off that monster...nor the skills. If that man keeps killing and kidnapping regents, soon the government will come to a standstill. It's safe to assume first tiers are filling the vacant positions, but soon no one would want to step up for fear of being killed or kidnapped. I suppose that's Reilly's plan. No one else can stop him. It's all up to us."

Angie sat very still in her chair. "Of course, of course. Yes. I know. Please forgive my outburst."

Stephen smiled. "Well, my new friends," he said, and walked over to stand behind Larry, placing his hands on his shoulders. "We can now get down to work. We may not have five million soldiers, but we have an awful lot of brainpower around this table. Let's use it."

Stephen sighed. "Reilly is in a position of great power—"

"The question is, what are his immediate plans?" interjected Louis.

Stephen sat down. "What I've heard from my moles is he will pour across the border and head straight for key places in the United States." He reached for his cup and took a long sip. "He intends to control the country before he goes abroad."

Joy glanced at Stephen and pursed her lips. "In a week he'll execute the regents." Her stare bore right into Stephen. "Is there any way we can save them?"

"That would require a raid with an army," Stephen said. "I have about ten thousand untrained ranchers and farmers. He's got five million well-trained and armed soldiers. I don't think there is much we can do militarily."

"Well, there's something we have that might help," Louis said.

Joy nodded. "Let's show Stephen Larry's gizmo. But let's call Arlene and Suzanne. This involves us all."

Louis nodded and tapped his breast pocket. "Arlene, Suzanne. Could you please join us in the dining room?"

They responded. Soon they could be heard coming up the stairs.

Louis brought them all up to date, explaining that Stephen knew who they were, but that was fine; he was now part of their team. Then the news about the kidnappings and the killings. They watched Reilly's proclamation again, and Joy had to calm an excited Arlene.

Joy's phone rang. It was Juanita telling her about Reilly's speech. Joy told her that, yes, she had watched. Then she listened for a moment, thanked Juanita, and hung up.

"Juanita says the speech made some people in town very scared. A good many are joining the Patriots. Others are going into hiding."

Stephen brought up his hands and rubbed his temples slowly. "So what can we do to stop that monster?" He sounded angry.

"Fate may have placed us at the right moment and the right place," Louis said in a soothing tone, but his mind was racing, trying to find the right concept, the right thing to say. "If we act right now and offer Reilly's followers a reasonable alternative, I'm sure a good many will go for it." Louis now felt he had the answer. He paused and tried his best to speak with certainty. "At this moment, just like in Nazi Germany in 1935, people who oppose Reilly, as their counterparts opposed Hitler back then, are in despair because they realize who he really is: a lunatic. HHHhhad someone risen to give the Germans a reasonable alternative; I bet—"

"Of course," Stephen said, "but Hitler would have done his best to kill this person." Stephen thought for a moment. "You are proposing I put myself out there to challenge Reilly!"

"Yes," Louis said. "You can pull a good many Patriots behind you, once they know who you are." He now felt the importance of his words, and was sure that what he was saying was right.

Angie shook her head. "What makes you think the Patriots will want to break away and join Stephen? They went along with Reilly because they are like him, because they want war, because they are excited at the prospect of violence."

"No, Angela," Stephen said. "Excuse me, but I know these people. Yes, some of them want war, but once they are exposed to it, they will be repulsed by violence—"

"Absolutely," Louis said. "You can track the evolution of humanity by its reaction to war. Unlike warriors from earlier centuries, in the twenty-first century most of those young men who played soldier as children and fought in the Middle East wars were quickly awakened to the horror and suffered post-traumatic stress syndrome at a level never seen before. They were committing suicide at an unprecedented rate, because their government didn't know how to deal with them. We haven't had a war for more than a century, so now their reaction would be even more pronounced."

Stephen seemed taken aback. "I know about those veterans you are talking about. I've studied them. What a horrible thing to happen to those poor kids. But are you are saying we should give the Patriots a taste of war?"

"Yes. Unfortunately that's the case; otherwise they'll still glorify war."

Stephen thought for a moment. "How? Guerrilla warfare won't work, not with the surveillance equipment the Patriots have. And have you seen their flying tanks? Those things have sensors you won't believe—"

"Well, let's see what we can do," Louis said. "Larry, would you care to show Stephen what we have?"

Larry fingered his computer display, now brought down to palm size. "Shall we all go outside?"

"No," Louis said. "I would like to observe through the window, to see whether the effect is the same. And I want Joy, Angie, and Suzanne to go downstairs and lock themselves in the bathroom with

Yogi." He turned to address a mystified Stephen. "Just follow Larry outside, will you, Stephen?"

Larry led Stephen outside as Louis went to stand by the window. He heard Angie close the bathroom door downstairs.

Louis saw the two giant androids descend. They destroyed the barn again; this time just pulverized it. Stephen and Larry were swiped aside by one massive hand. One of the androids tore up the driveway and headed for the house's front door, kicking rocks and chunks of sod as it went. The front of the house disintegrated, and a roaring, flaming monstrosity stared at Louis.

The androids disappeared.

Miraculously, everything was serenely back to normal, the same dry, flat, and uneventful landscape with cows in the far background and a barn, a house, and a driveway.

Louis checked his watch. It had been over in less than three minutes. A pale and shaken Stephen came back into the house followed by Larry, who walked with display in hand making adjustments. No neighbors came over or called. Apparently they were far enough away.

Stephen was clearly impressed, but was too unraveled to speak. The rest were shaken, but not as terrified as before. Hiding in the bathroom was no defense. Joy told them next time she would hide in the bedroom closet with Yogi, who was still upset.

At dinnertime they sat down to a vegetarian meal of broiled vegetables and complete meal patties on a tomato sauce.

Stephen sat down at the table. He looked at his plate and smiled. "Good food. Thank you.

"Wow," he said lifting a fork. "That show would scare the crap out of anyone. I was sure I had broken bones, could actually feel the pain. That's interesting; the stimuli made me think I was hurt."

"Yes," replied Larry, smiling as he scooped a forkful of food. "In my experiments I had subjects who had to be convinced they were actually okay."

Larry then told Stephen how he developed the bio-computer. "It's viable for at least five years," he told him.

Stephen shook his head. "It's amazing what you can do with technology…and right now I'm ever so grateful." He turned to look at Louis. "So that's the taste of war you have in mind, eh?"

Louis used his fork to cut into a large chunk of pumpkin. "Yes, and nobody gets killed. They may suffer post-traumatic stress, but that's a risk we must take."

"How long do the effects last?"

"About twenty-four hours," replied Larry.

"Okay," Stephen said, talking in between mouthfuls. "That's good. Workable. But how exactly do you plan on using it?"

"Well, we have the parade a week from now," Louis said, putting down his fork, "and that might be our best chance because most if not all of the Patriot army will be out in the open—"

"Actually it's our only chance, Louis." Stephen said. "After that the army will be dispersed over several states…It's now or never…and it's the real reason I came to see you folks, hoping you all had something like what you just showed me…but please, go on."

Louis inhaled deeply, now feeling elated. "We'll use the virtual androids to make the Patriots believe they are under attack by an overwhelming force." Louis felt himself turn into his professorial self, calm and confident. "The androids, thousands of them, will definitely do the trick. While they are in disarray, we use a human force to liberate the regents in the concentration camp while another group goes after Reilly and his high command, and takes them away. I also want to free D'Anjou, whom they captured and brainwashed. Before the Patriot army has a chance to regroup, we appeal to them—"

"But out of the blue? They won't know who we are," Stephen said, eating the last carrot on his plate.

"You are right," Louis said, wiping his mouth with a napkin. "We need to prep them, introduce you. I propose a massive

227

campaign through television, phones, even pamphlets and flyers we can post. The Patriots will know about you, Stephen, and that way we can plant the seed of an alternative. After they have tasted war and are in shock, we offer them a way out."

Stephen stood up. He appeared lost in thought. He paced around the room for a while before stopping to stand by the window. "It might work, it might just work...but the problem is logistics. There are five million soldiers, and that implies a gigantic, prolonged battle that may take more than the twenty-four hours, in fact it might last several days...Is it possible to modify the virtual reality?"

Larry shrugged his shoulders. "Yes, of course. What do you have in mind?"

"Interesting that you mentioned post-traumatic stress in soldiers of the twenty-first century, Louis; I've studied the psychological affects of trauma for some time and I focused on those soldiers of two hundred years ago because of the terrible trauma they exhibited. It's because of them that we now understand how to treat PTSD. In fact, it became my specialty. I treat people with post-traumatic stress disorders, generally the result of an accident, or a loved one dying tragically. But historically the most horrific trauma was experienced by soldiers who had to kill someone with their own hands, face-to-face...and someone whom they identified with."

"Kin?" Louis asked.

"Yes. Someone they identified with, someone who looked just like them."

"That's horrible!"

"Exactly. If we manage the illusion well, we can affect those in the Patriot army who register above median on the altruism scale. It will stop them in their tracks. Then we can gauge the impact and stop the illusion before they are permanently scarred."

Larry opened his virtual display and started keying in symbols. "So we would have the five million Patriot army fight some—"

"Fight someone they identify with, one-on-one. That means everyone in that army will have a similar experience."

"I'll need to develop individually targeted scenarios...that's rather complex."

"Yes. Scenarios that respond to the individual's emotional response, so if they start breaking down, we pull back, if they are nonresponsive, we press on."

Larry nodded. "Yes, press on until we find a recognizable point where the individual's combat response diminishes...we would need to detect endocrine secretions—"

"Yes! Can it be done?"

Larry stared at his computer display, deep in thought. Then he turned to Suzanne. "What do you think?"

Suzanne nodded.

Larry smiled. "You have your answer. We can do it, but it will take a lot of work."

"Good," replied Stephen, "the parade will take place outside Houston, not far from where the Patriots have their major base. The army will assemble two miles away in recovered grazing land, about ten square miles, with trees that shelter cattle in the summer. The Patriots use the field for war exercises. Will that work for you, Larry?"

Larry nodded, looking at a live satellite view on his virtual screen of the area Stephen had just described. "Yes, I can see the trees. There are also some shrubs. That will work...there's a big domed structure not far, and urban sprawl behind the field where the army will gather."

"Yes. That's another reason I don't want us to use the giant androids. If the army fires against them, they may hit that part of Houston."

"Not to mention the spectators," Louis said, "If it's a parade, there will be many spectators, and they will panic and trample one another. Now that I think about it, the giant androids should be a last resort."

"Yeah," Stephen said, "they project upward of ten million in attendance."

Larry let out a slow whistling sound. "No question that Stephen's virtual reality would work better. A week from now, eh? We better get started right away." He closed his display and took Suzanne's hand.

Stephen stood up. "I'll help you guys."

Stephen followed Larry and Suzanne downstairs to the lab.

Larry, Suzanne, and Stephen worked nonstop through the night. The rest stayed up around the kitchen table drinking coffee. From time to time Larry would call on one of them for help.

At six in the morning, the three of them came upstairs, looking haggard.

"We got it," announced Stephen, his hand on Suzanne's shoulder. "These two are amazing."

"But have you tested it?" Louis asked.

Stephen nodded. "Yes, on each other."

"And we still have the giant androids, if we need them," added Larry.

The kitchen android brought them breakfast: eggs, toast, and coffee.

Louis grabbed a cup. "So, they fight one another, and hopefully then they'll be incapacitated. At that point, Stephen—"

"At that point my men take Reilly and liberate the prisoners and the brainwashed scientist, and we—"

"And the affects still last twenty-four hours?" Louis asked, scooping some eggs off his plate.

"No, Larry said. This is different than the giant androids. The soldiers don't 'die'; rather, they kill and are then traumatized, and maybe even in shock. The effects last as long as we keep the stimuli going, but I don't know what happens with prolonged exposure. Our tests were five minutes long."

"But what if someone is out of earshot?" Joy asked. "You remember when we tested the giant androids and Yogi was locked in Louis's bedroom closet? He just slept through it."

"Yes Joy," Larry said, "but that was with limited stimuli from just a few plants outside. We don't know what will happen when I use ten square miles of vegetation."

"Okay," Stephen said. "I'm satisfied we have our weapon. If the one-on-one combat fails, we'll use the giant androids. Now, how about that propaganda campaign? How do we do it?"

Larry thought for a moment. "We would need to do it soon, since we only have six days. I can tap into phone frequencies in Texas and make one announcement before they wise up and block me."

Louis rubbed his chin. "I like the idea of tapping into phones, but we should also use leaflets and television."

"There is one television station in Dallas," Stephen said, thinking out loud. "They broadcast an hour's worth of local news each day and lots of Mexican soap operas. I can have my men take over the building."

"Right," Louis said. "We'll prepare a recorded message—"

"The minute you do that," Joy said, "Reilly will be after us and we'll be on the run."

"Yes, of course," Louis said and crossed his long legs. "We need to do it all at once, the phone tapping, the leaflets, and the television broadcast. Then we hide until the parade."

"Okay, Stephen said. "Reilly plans to have all of his army march past him while he stands on a high platform, with spectators sitting below. Everyone in Texas will be watching on television, as will be the world. His intent is to—"

"But can we do it all in six days?" Angie asked. "Is that enough time? Don't we need more time to prepare?"

Joy reached for Angie's hand. "Sweetie, we need to save the regents. Remember what that awful man said in his speech? They'll be shot the day after the parade."

"Okay, enough talk, we have a lot of work," Louis said. "How long do you need to tap the phones, Larry?"

"Oh, just an hour or so."

"And how about taking hold of that television station, Stephen?"

"My guys would need no more than a day's notice to plan."

The android brought a tray full of coffee mugs.

Louis reached for a mug. "Fine, let's make the leaflets. Stephen, prepare your men to take over the television station and aim for the day after tomorrow, Tuesday. Then we keep you hidden for four days. I don't think anyone would think of looking for you here, so we can just stay in this house as long as you don't show yourself."

Angie shook her head frantically. "No! That's crazy. Let's do the campaign the day before the parade; otherwise we'll be hiding Stephen for four days...and what if they find him, in this house? They'll kill us all!"

"Angie," Joy said in a plaintive tone, "that doesn't sound like you."

Stephen stared at the floor. "Angela is right...I will be putting all of you in jeopardy. Let's prepare the materials for the campaign, and...I'll leave my kids with Mike, then—"

"Absolutely not!" exclaimed Louis. "We need to stay together so we can coordinate the virtual war. Besides, I will not stand by and let you take all the risk."

Angie seemed subdued, embarrassed. "That's not what I meant; we should all bear the same exposure. We are the regents, the government; the Patriots are mainly our responsibility, and Stephen is helping us. But I still say we should release the campaign the day before the parade to minimize the risk."

Stephen smiled at Angie. "Thanks, Angela. But Louis is right; we need time for the message to spread by word of mouth. Four days is actually cutting it short."

He tapped his sleeve to produce his phone and made two calls. Then he stood up. "Look," he said to Louis, "I'll have to take care of my people right now, but I'll be back as soon as I can."

After Stephen left, Angie and Joy went to sit on the couch. Larry stayed at the table. Arlene sat talking to Suzanne in nervous whispers.

It was obvious to Louis that everyone was scared. "This is exactly what we wanted, what we talked about in California," he reminded them as he stood by the window watching Stephen's car take off. "We wanted to find a group to oppose the Patriots, and we found them. Stephen is the best candidate to help us neutralize Reilly."

"Oh, you just got us deeper and deeper in trouble!" shouted Angie from the couch.

Joy shushed her and held her tightly by the shoulders.

Louis had noticed a change in Angie of late, in the way she looked at him and the way she barely made eye contact with him when they spoke. What a departure from the admiring student and protégé he remembered.

After some time everyone dispersed to their rooms. Only Louis remained seated, stroking Yogi's head and wondering whether they would live to see New York again.

19

S tephen, looking worn and worried, didn't make it back until the following morning. Louis called everyone back to the living room. They walked in eagerly, but sat tense, their eyes riveted on Stephen.

"The problem is, some people have already left us to join Reilly," Stephen said to the assembled group, as he plopped himself down in a chair. He sighed. "I told Mike to figure out who is still with us, and he is setting up a raiding party for the television station for tomorrow.

"But I'm afraid I need to hide right away, I'm concerned some of the people who left might tell Reilly about me. I'm not safe in my farm anymore...my two boys are not safe."

Louis, who sat next to Stephen, reached out and placed a hand on his shoulder. "Bring them here right away. We were going to hide you anyway. We have plenty of room. You can have the study."

Stephen stood. "Thanks. I don't have anywhere else to go. I brought my boys with me."

Stephen made for the door and tapped his sleeve to call his car on his phone.

He was back shortly. He walked in the door with two boys of about four and five. The older boy held a yellow lab by a leash. They had packed light, everything they had held in two backpacks.

Louis welcomed them, and asked Joy to show them to the study. He watched her kneel in front of them, hug them, and whisper something. She then grabbed them by the hand and led them away. Their fear was tangible.

Stephen, Louis, and Larry huddled in a corner of the living room. In a short while, Joy came back to join them. Suzanne and Arlene had gone down to the lab.

"Yes. The bad news," Stephen was saying, "is the parade is five days from now and we must somehow survive until then. This place is not good enough; we need to hide."

"Why?" Louis asked, "what do you expect will happen?"

"There are people who were with me who are probably being interrogated by the Patriots at this very moment. By now the Patriots know who I am. Once we hit the television station and Larry taps the Internet and the phones, Reilly will make me, that is all of us, his number one priority. After the broadcast, I expect that in a matter of hours your neighbors next door, Juanita and Eldridge, will be arrested. The men who left know about them. As soon as they talk, we'll be next."

"Why don't you pass the word for everyone to scramble and hide?" Louis asked.

"Yes, many already have, but I will tell Mike—"

"Let's tell Juanita and Eldridge to hide, right now."

Louis and Stephen went out of the house and walked over next door.

Juanita answered the door. Stephen told her what was going to happen the following day, Tuesday morning. Juanita stared at each man for a moment, turned around, and shouted for Eldridge and the rest.

An hour later they were gone. Juanita called Joy to let her know. They had left two androids to take care of the place, including the cows and the dogs.

"Well," Louis said, sitting next to Stephen at the table, "we removed that danger."

It was time to prepare the television and telephone broadcast. "It has to be short and to the point," Louis said. They started working on their script, and after a couple of hours, they had what they wanted.

They called Larry to do the recording and he looked around for a neutral background that would not give away their location. "We can't show anything; no reflections, no lights, instruments, no background sound," Larry mumbled aloud.

They went from room to room, but none were foolproof. In the living room, they could still hear the cows next door and according to Larry, the whirl of the windmill a half-mile away was still detectable by his phone. The rooms had "signatures" he didn't like, electronic emissions from their kitchen, androids, even their communication devices. "A medium-savvy technician will be able to pinpoint exactly where we recorded this in less than an hour."

They went downstairs, but that was no better.

"Let's try Louis's car," Larry said. "Maybe there's a way to control that smaller space."

They went to the barn and inside the car, and looked around wondering how to block windows and deaden sounds.

"Regent Zimmerman," the car said, "let me do it." With this, its windows filled up with a white substance and became like one of the walls. The interior of the car seemed to fill with a sound that was not a sound.

Larry smiled. "Sound eliminating infra-waves. Thanks."

Stephen looked around in wonder. "Wow. So this is what regents get to drive? I've never heard of a machine this intelligent."

Louis examined his old familiar car, and it had become something else, a vacuous space: colors were neutered, shapes diffused. It was hard to tell where they were anymore. Certainly not inside a car.

Larry motioned for Stephen to sit in the backseat.

Stephen sat with his back to the now white background. Larry held his virtual phone in one hand. "Ready whenever you are."

Stephen nodded. "Good morning, fellow Texans," he began. "I am Stephen Phillipiak, and represent many thousands of your fellow citizens who are extremely concerned with what's happening today in our country. William Reilly, who now calls himself president, but who was until a few years ago a repent-now preacher, has hijacked our country with his army. While I agree we can do much better here in Texas, I don't agree with his methods or his goals. No one has to die; no one has to kill; we can assert our rights if we band together as the rational people we are, not a bunch of kill-happy savages. Put down your guns and join us; we can stop Reilly and his generals.

"In a few days, we'll let our presence be known in a very dramatic and overwhelming way. That will be your chance to come over to our side. Until then, do your best to not kill, not hurt anyone. I repeat, we will make our presence known and that will be your chance to join us."

They reviewed the recording, made some adjustments, and Stephen sent it to Mike's phone to use on the television broadcast. Stephen ordered Mike to pass on the word for all of his followers to hide that evening. He told Mike to expect to hear from him the following Friday at 9:00 p.m., the day before the parade.

Larry programmed his phone to broadcast the message over the Internet at the same time the television station would broadcast the message, at ten the following morning.

Tom Kennedy had not seen President Reilly so angry before. He had heard about his temper tantrums, but now he wondered whether he and his fellow generals shouldn't try and sedate him. But he dared not say it.

Reilly had been going around his elegant office throwing lamps, antique books, precious figurines and all sorts of brick-a-brac against the wood paneled walls. Old glass and crystal fragments lay all over the floor. "Why can't we catch that bastard? We need to get him. Sagan is just a man, and there are five million of us after him. Let's find him! We know he's in Canada, not Africa, not Asia, not somewhere on a Pacific island curing some disease, but in Canada, trying to sneak into Texas!" he shouted.

He was so far from his usual self, the man in control. The contrast was shocking, a different person altogether, perhaps even deranged…no, not deranged, desperate. The realization left Kennedy with a sick feeling in the pit of his stomach.

He looked around at the other four lieutenant generals. They stood along one of the walls, trying their best to avoid flying objects. In their eyes he saw confusion and fear.

Kennedy wondered whether Regent Sagan could really be that much of a threat. Was he all that dangerous? Certainly smart and devious, but evil? And of course not imbued with mysterious powers. But, no, he dared not say anything. Nor anyone else in that room, and certainly not now. He flinched as Reilly flung a side table violently against a mirror.

Finally spent, Reilly sat down in a chair and seemed to just collapse. "Bring me Sagan…he's got to come to rescue his precious friends." Reilly sat breathing hard, his crazy eyes darting around the room. "Well, I figured what Sagan is doing in Canada. Yeah, it takes one genius to figure out another." He looked at the faces of his generals with disdain. "You know that pipeline they used to bring oil from Canada to the Texas Gulf Coast? Yeah, now you are beginning to get it, right? The evil bastard figured he could sneak into Texas using one of those pipes.

"But where are the pipes? Sagan is traveling freely in them, bringing troops and weapons, and we are just sitting here like toy soldiers. Now you all need to find where those pipes are, where they end up. Once you do that, we'll find Sagan's little highway."

After a long pause Reilly seemed to calm down. "Now, distribute his picture again to all the troops. Make sure every one of our guards can recognize him the moment they see him…I don't really care about anyone else, I want him! Our parade is Saturday and he knows we'll be shooting his precious friends on Sunday morning; so I assure you he'll make his move on Friday." He studied his generals' faces again. "You don't get it, right? Well, I put myself in that bastard's shoes. You know what he'll do? He'll hit us the day before the parade when our troops are mobilizing. That's when he figures we'll be at our weakest, so guess what we'll do?" Reilly panned the line of generals. "Yeah, we'll keep our elite corps on standby on that day, all fifty thousand of them. There's no way Sagan will be able to match our guys.

"Now get!"

The generals left the room in a hurry, as President Reilly remained slumped in the chair, his eyes staring blankly at the floor.

It was 9:30 Tuesday morning. Louis and his group had breakfast and waited around nervously until ten. Larry kept rubbing an ear while staring at the clock on the wall.

"Oh, Stephen, what if your people have all been caught!" exclaimed Angie fidgeting with her breakfast.

"Well, then we're on our own," replied Louis. "And we'll figure out how to proceed."

Angie didn't reply, but kept playing with her food.

Stephen stood from the table and went to look at the house next door through the window.

At two minutes to ten, they all became very quiet. The only ones missing were the children, who were with the dogs in Joy's room. Larry projected the virtual screen above their heads, on television and telephone modes. They could hear nothing on the phone, and the television was broadcasting a soap opera. Then both screens went momentarily blank. Stephen's face filled the screens, while his voice boomed on the phone..."do your best to not kill...we'll make our presence known..." After the message, the screens went blank again and stayed that way for a moment, as though hesitating. Then the soap opera came back on.

They looked at each other across the table.

Now there was no backing out.

Louis could feel the adrenaline rush around the table. They watched the screens. After a few more moments, an official-looking announcer came on. "We apologize for the interruption. A group of terrorists took over our facilities for a short while, but our Patriot army reacted quickly and killed them all. President Reilly has announced he'll find everyone behind the plot." The soap opera resumed, and the phone was back.

Stephen started to dial his phone, but before he could finish, Larry snatched it and turned it off. "We must assume they are okay. By now the Patriots are on full alert, monitoring all communications. Let's not give them any leads." He gave the dead phone back to Stephen.

Stephen nodded. He looked pale. "Okay. We just did it. And they must be alive."

"Let's hide somewhere!" Exclaimed Angie. "Please!"

"No, there's no need for us all to hide," Louis said calmly. "If we run, we'll look suspicious and we'll be captured only because we are running. Let's stay put. They are looking for Stephen. Let's hide him."

"Okay...yes," Stephen said. "But where?"

"Right here, Stephen," Louis said and reached out for his shoulder. "We'll have to change your appearance, and your boys.' Let's go get your kids and go downstairs."

They heard a buzzing and rushed to one of the big windows.

An army tank landed next door. Juanita's dogs barked. After some time, they heard a loud crash, the sound of a door being torn down.

"They are looking for Juanita and Eldridge!" Stephen said. "They are sure to come here any minute!"

"What do we do?" Joy asked. "Can we make it to your car, Louis?"

"No," Stephen said. "We don't stand a chance, those tanks are very fast."

"Larry," Louis said, "can you stand by at the ready with those giant androids?"

"Sure. Should I hide in the hallway closet?"

"No, no," Stephen said. "They have detection devices on them that will tell them where we all are. They'll simply shoot at the closet assuming you are about to ambush them.

"Let's just wait for them."

Louis turned to face Stephen. "If they are looking for you, which they probably are, and recognize you, then we'll have to rely on the giant androids to make our getaway.

"Okay…everyone, try and relax…let's just wait."

They backed away from the window and stood huddled together in the middle of the living room, not making a sound. After what seemed like a long time, they heard the buzzing outside and in a matter of seconds there was a loud banging on the door.

Louis answered. He was met by two big, fully armored soldiers with guns at the ready.

"Stand aside," they ordered.

The soldiers went through the house, opening doors, looking everywhere. Louis followed along, explaining they were loyal followers of President Reilly and wanted no trouble. Apparently the soldiers had not recognized Stephen, but then again, they had not looked at any of them closely. The soldiers pushed Arlene against a wall when she didn't move fast enough when told to move. One of them, while in Joy's room, was apparently annoyed by Max's barking and raised his gun to shoot the dog, but a tearful Joy got in the way. "Don't, please don't!" she begged. The man laughed and pushed her out of the way with one hand. He raised his gun again, but his friend stopped him. "No need, Corporal Wolfowitz. These folks are loyal. I can tell." The corporal reluctantly lowered his gun. "The lieutenant said to interrogate them."

"When did you hear that, sarge?"

"On my communicator, while you were knocking on the front door."

Corporal Wolfowitz looked around the room. "Okay, I'll go get the interrogator then."

The sergeant ushered everyone, including Stephen's two sons, into the living room. His manner was subdued, almost apologetic. While they waited for the corporal to return, he looked at each of his captives and ordered them to sit down. "You will need to tell the truth; if you don't, the machine we got will send a painful shock of electricity through your body. Sometimes it's lethal. I'm sorry. We are looking for Stephen Phillipiak and his followers. The machine does an automatic identity check, and depending on how it was programmed at headquarters, it might kill right away."

Corporal Wolfowitz came through the front door with a handheld device. It had two wires coming out of it.

Larry turned white. "Yes, I've heard of those—"

"In that case," the corporal said, "you'll get to watch your girlfriend be interrogated first." With this, the man grabbed Joy by the arm and brusquely sat her down in one of the dining chairs. He attached the two wires to either side of her head.

Larry casually reached into his pants pocket.

"Are you a follower…" began the corporal, and he froze in place. So did everyone else in the room except for Stephen, who went over to a paralyzed Louis, grabbed his hand, and used it to tap his shirt pocket and produce his phone.

He pressed the button for Louis's car. "Hello? This is Stephen Phillipiak. Do you know me?"

"Yes, Doctor Phillipiak," the female voice answered.

Oh, good. "We need to leave right away. I temporarily froze everyone and I need you to send out your androids to carry our friends. They'll all be fine—"

"Very well, doctor."

He heard a buzzing. In a moment two androids, both male humanoids, walked in the door. They grabbed Louis and Angie first, took them to the car, and quickly came back for the rest. Stephen went to look for the two dogs still in Joy's bedroom.

When he walked into the car, he found the stiff bodies neatly lying side by side on the floor, including his two sons, although in their original standing positions. The dogs walked in and sniffed them. Yogi went over to Louis and licked his face.

The car shut the door. "Where to, doctor?"

"We need to maneuver carefully—"

"I know, so we are undetected. I can do that."

I'll be darned. "Good. Let's proceed to Houston. There's a friend of mine by the name of Jorge Collizo, a clinical psychologist. He also heads a meditation center. Take us to his home."

"Yes, doctor. I've located Psychologist Jorge Collizo at Gradient 1234879 Sycamore Avenue, Zen meditation teacher. I'll run undetected for two hours to give enough time for my passengers to wake up, then I'll switch my signature and emulate official Texas government identity and head for Houston. Is that agreeable?"

Amazing, just frigging amazing. She actually reasons. "Sounds good to me." Stephen called Jorge and asked if he could drop by with some friends at his home "in a few hours." The reply was polite, albeit a bit terse, but Stephen decided he would explain the sudden visit when he saw Jorge in person.

A couple of hours later, Louis and the rest started to move. Slowly at first and appearing disoriented as though coming out of a deep sleep.

"What?" Louis said as he looked around, surprised. He stood up. The others were starting to stand as well.

"Sorry, Louis, but I had to paralyze all of you. We are on the way to visit a friend of mine in Houston, where we'll be safe."

Joy stood up with the interrogation device still attached and Louis came up and detached the two wires.

Larry took the device from his hands. "Worth studying."

"What did you do to us? What happened?" Louis asked.

Stephen dug in his jeans front pocket. "I used one of these," and he produced two packets of tablets. "The red tablets are a nerve gas. I keep one in my mouth at all times, and it paralyzes anyone within a twenty-foot radius. All I have to do is spit it out. Handy if you are in a jam.

"Take one of each. All of you.

"The blue tablet," he said, as he held one in between his fingers, "is an antidote. You take it now and it will keep you from being paralyzed by the gas for a month."

Louis and the rest stood around Stephen. They passed the two packets, and took one pill of each.

"Take two of the red ones," Stephen said, "There are enough for all of us."

Louis carefully picked pills from the packets and examined them. "How long are the paralyzing effects?"

"About two hours, depending on body weight."

Angie held her three pills in her hand, watched as Louis and the rest ingested the blue one, and followed suit. She was so glad Stephen had come on board. He had saved them, no question about it. He was so on top of everything. With him around there would be no more mistakes.

Stephen turned to Louis. "Your car claims it can run undetected. Can you verify that?"

Louis smiled. "I would have to take her word for it. Maybe Larry can check her programming."

"Of course," Larry said and made his way to the control panel.

"Excuse me, Regent Sagan," the car said, "could you please all sit down so I can strap you? You are in danger of being thrown around by turbulence."

They sat in the two seats. Joy with the kids and Arlene. Stephen, Angie, Suzanne and Louis on the other, leaving room for Larry next to Suzanne. The two dogs were strapped as they lay by the kids' feet.

"I checked your car's programming," Larry said to Louis as he sat down. "What she told me was very impressive; I do think she's currently non-detectable. She's very smart and capable. I like her."

Stephen turned with a sardonic smile. "You are talking about a machine."

"There are some that are human-like. She's definitively one of them."

"In that case, does she have a name?"

"She told me it's Wendy."

Wendy flew south in a wide zigzag pattern, with a stop at every turn. "To confuse the flight monitoring computers," according to Larry. He also mentioned that she changed her identity signature every time she turned, to make it seem as though it was another vehicle coming the other way. "It makes sense. The monitors will record a variety of cars flying in different directions, instead of just one. Very clever…now she's switched again and is going straight for Houston, I assume."

Louis tapped Stephen's shoulder. "Where exactly are we going?"

"Jorge Collizo's home in Houston. He's a friend of mine, my former meditation teacher, and I trust him completely." Stephen smiled. "I decided to follow Larry's reasoning and head for the place where they'll look for us last: the Patriots' seat of power."

"That will do it for sure. So far, so good. What happened to the two soldiers?"

"They are awake by now and very likely have sent in our descriptions."

"Doesn't sound like they had time to recognize you."

They landed in front of a typical housing complex, the kind one might see in any city: units stacked thirty stories high that stretched unending for miles. Wendy told them she had located Jorge's house and sent an identifying code describing Stephen. A garage door opened on the third row from the bottom.

She glided in.

The adults came out of the car. They were in a meticulously clean garage. Two cars were parked one on top of the other. A man stood by the cars. He was in his late forties, of medium height, slender build, and pleasant features. The brown eyes behind steel-rim glasses were friendly, but perhaps a bit tense, apprehensive.

"Stephen…what a surprise…and you bring company."

He led them inside the house. "How long are you and your friends planning on staying in Houston? I assume you came to attend one of the rallies of our beloved president?" Jorge said as he pointedly scratched his ear, took off his glasses, and very slowly and deliberately blew on the lenses and wiped them with a handkerchief.

Louis got the point, and by looking at Stephen and the rest it was obvious they did, too. Everything they said and did was being closely watched and heard by hidden ears and eyes.

"Absolutely," answered Stephen. "This here is Greg and his wife, Patricia, and his extended farm family. They all have just joined the Cause."

"Yes," Joy said, looking around the room. "Will we be able to see President Reilly up close?"

"Not until the parade next Saturday," answered Jorge. "But we can watch him on television every evening."

"Every evening? You are so lucky. How come we don't get that back home?"

"Oh, it's only for us here in Houston." With this Jorge sat down and motioned for them to sit in simple but comfortable chairs in a spacious living room. Through a glassite door, they could see a good-size swimming pool. An android brought them coffee and tea on a tray.

Through the tense conversation, Louis understood they were being examined and very likely identified, at least Stephen was. Unfortunately they had compromised Jorge just by being there. Louis turned and met Larry's calm but steel-hard gaze that told him what he already knew. They were in grave danger and had to leave right away, but without a fuss.

"Thank you, Jorge for your hospitality," Louis said. "We'll now check into a hotel. Do you have a recommendation?"

"Gee. Let me think. The Biltmore is very nice, and that's where most of our Patriot generals are staying. Maybe you'll get to see them." His words sounded relaxed, almost too relaxed.

They stood up to leave. "I know what!" Jorge said with a smile. "Let me accompany you, I know one of the managers, and maybe I can get you folks nicer rooms."

Louis understood: Jorge was asking to flee with them. He would be arrested if he stayed behind. They started toward the garage and Wendy.

The android that had served them coffee quickly came up to Jorge and grabbed his arm. Jorge winced...he couldn't move. The android made to grab Angie's arm with its free hand as she went past, but she scurried off. Another android came down the stairs.

The pretense was off, and they ran as fast as they could back to Wendy, who had her door wide-open and was already turning around. Both of her androids came out of the car running and went past them. Louis heard a commotion behind him. The group jumped in. Louis was the last one, making sure no one was left behind. The two car androids jumped in. One of Jorge's androids lay motionless on the ground. The car's door closed and Wendy lurched forward toward the closed garage door, which splintered on impact.

Wendy hurried along the street, then doubled back slowly.

"What is she doing?" yelled Stephen.

"She switched signals and changed her color," answered Larry studying his phone. "They are looking for a fleeing silver car, now she's a red car going the opposite direction."

Sirens and flashing red lights went past them in the direction they had taken when they first left Jorge's house. Wendy continued on, past Jorge's house and kept going at a slow, cruising speed. After ten minutes, they came to a shopping mall and Wendy hovered into an overhead parking space. Rows of cars were lined above and below and all around them.

They seemed to exhale at once. The boys sobbed quietly in Joy's arms. Even the two dogs appeared to have sensed the danger, and they stood tensely side by side against a bulkhead.

"I should have changed my appearance!" Stephen said in an excited voice. "I just got Jorge arrested!"

Louis, who stood by the door, turned in his direction. "You had no way of knowing the extent of the surveillance."

Stephen brought both hands to his face. "Oh, man! I'm such a jerk!"

"Let's just calm down and think," responded Louis. He stood and approached Wendy's control panel. "I wonder if she suffered any damage when she rammed the door."

"I'm okay, regent," Wendy said.

"Good, good. Excellent," muttered Louis. "Where can we go? We need to go somewhere far from Houston. I'm sure they are looking for us throughout the city."

Larry stood up. "We need to be out in nature, surrounded by shrubs and trees so I can activate the giant androids if we need them."

"Well, let's see..." began Stephen, and he stared at the floor for a moment. "Hey, I know of just the place. It's in South Texas, the Davis Mountains, about half an hour from here in a fast car. It's one of three preservation zones your government designated. It's surrounded by desert, really remote. I've been there, and we can find a well-hidden canyon, with tall trees and boulders to hide our car. I'm sure we can stay out of sight until the parade.

"But how do we get out of Houston undetected?"

Joy looked up. "Can Larry create a distraction with that gizmo of his?"

"Of course!" Larry said and he looked down at the ground through a window. "There are plenty of trees and shrubs down there."

He sat down next to Joy and started fiddling with his phone. After several minutes, while everyone sat in tense silence, he rose to his feet. "I got it. I ran a probability program, and I think this will work. How about a dozen police cars? They can be escorting us out of Houston."

"You mean as though we are prisoners?" Stephen asked.

"Yeah. The cops that are on our way will assume we have been captured, and make way for the police escort."

"Hmm," Louis said. "I wonder if that's proper police procedure around here."

"Doesn't matter," Stephen said. "If our police escort looks official enough, and we act fast enough, the real police will be taken aback and sit still. That's human nature."

Angie looked at Larry, close to tears. "But you constructed that virtual scenario way too fast and it hasn't been tested. What if the police cars look fake, or—"

"Give us another choice, Angie."

They sat in silence. No one spoke or made a sound.

"What if I become a police car?" asked Wendy.

Larry emitted a low whistling sound. "Yeah, that would be great!"

"The moment your virtual police cars arrive, I'll become one as well."

Louis smiled. "Let's go for it. Larry, do it!"

"Okay," Larry said, "Wendy, start going at nineteen degrees northeast, that's the direction the cops came from. I'll have the police escort join us right away. Then go as fast as you can toward the Davis Mountains."

"Regent Zimmerman," Wendy said, "if I may interject, it will be safer if I do an evasion fly routine for forty-eight hours before we head for the mountains."

Louis stared at the car's control panel. "What, just fly around Texas for two days?"

"Yes, regent. I ran a probability algorithm and that would be the safest. I already have a route planned around fly patterns in the state. I'll be switching from official police car to—"

"That's fine, Wendy. Whatever you think best."

"Please remain seated. It may get rough."

Wendy pulled out slowly from the parking stack. Straps came down and held everyone snug, including the dogs. After a few seconds a group of police cars came out of nowhere and grouped around their car, with lights flashing and sirens blaring.

Wendy lurched forward along with the police pack, faster than usual, then gained more speed.

In a few minutes, they were approaching the city limits and could see ahead and all around a solid wall of police cars lined up in a cordon around the city, rows and rows of patrol cars stacked high into the clouds. They held their breath. For a moment it looked like the police cars in front of them would hold fast...but someone must have given an order because the police made way for them to pass. They zoomed past, and when they looked back no one tried to pursue them.

They sighed in relief. Wendy kept going for what seemed a long time and then she switched direction and headed east. She went into a cloud with the police formation around her. When she came out they had disappeared.

Everyone remained silent. One of the boys started to cry, and Joy cradled him against her chest. "It's okay honey, we are safe, we are safe...everything is fine."

20

A t least half an hour went by. Houston was far behind. Down below they could see an expanse of barren land and an occasional farm. Wendy withdrew the straps. Larry stood up, the two dogs walked around.

Louis stood and stretched. "Whew. It worked. I'm glad the police cordon didn't try to communicate with us—"

"Oh, they probably did," responded Larry, "but we came up so fast they didn't have much time."

After another hour or so, when they realized things were going to be quiet for a while, they settled around the car. Wendy's androids brought out food, and Joy played games with the children.

Every so often Wendy switched direction, sometimes abruptly. She landed a few times only to take off again suddenly. They were constantly being jarred around. The drinks and food spilled, and were picked up by one of the car androids. Sometimes they flew along other cars in a commuter corridor, sometimes higher up in a faster corridor. They stopped every so often near a housing development to let the dogs out, and they could all stretch a little, but only for a few minutes. They saw many flying tanks and police cars, but no one approached. There was no telling what they looked like, whether Wendy had decided to be green or red, or mimic an official car. They kept flying, and landing, and flying some more.

Night came, then sunrise, breakfast... then lunch. It all blurred together.

They showered in the bathroom, but had to keep it short and the space was cramped, but at least they showered. When Angie lingered too long, Joy knocked on the door. One of the boys had to go.

Louis could tell Stephen was concerned about his men. He didn't have to say anything, his face told it all. A worried look would come over his eyes and he would look out the window to try and hide his anxiety, but it was palpable...and the same thought was very likely going through everyone's mind. There was no question, if Reilly wanted to kill all of Stephen's men, he could; he certainly had the resources. How many of them would survive through Saturday? Louis knew that all the adults in that car were also asking themselves if they could have done things any different; if there was some option, something they had not considered...for himself, he knew the answer was no.

After they had been flying for twenty-eight hours, the adults looked haggard and the children cried easily. The tension, and the way Wendy had to fly, was hard on everyone's nerves. Angie compared the car to a torture chamber, but Joy reminded her that they were safe.

"After we land," Louis said, "we'll have thirty-six hours to rest before the parade. For now, let's do the best we can."

Sharon checked her watch. It was 2:10 in the morning. She knew she couldn't sleep any more.

She put on a shirt and shorts and grabbed a flashlight, but when she stepped outside her bungalow she found that a big moon lit up the place. She tucked the flashlight in her pants pocket and followed the path that went around the retreat center now bathed in silver twilight.

She walked slowly, observing the tree branches swaying gently in the breeze, and listening to the coqui frogs chirping away. She came upon a life-size meditating Buddha statue in a clearing. Once again Louis came into her mind, and she wondered what he was doing that moment. Her stomach tightened at the prospect. She didn't even know where he was, only what everyone else knew: they were on the run, and the Patriots were after them.

She stared at the Buddha's serene features. Why didn't Louis answer his phone?

She resumed walking.

Now she was paying for her decision, worrying as she had never worried before. What if he was dead? What if he went after that awful man in Texas and got killed in the process? Oh, Louis!

Then there was Wendy. She had let her know how things were with Louis, until suddenly the communications stopped. Why? Because she had been destroyed? Could it be that Louis, Joy, and the rest were dead? Maybe she'd never know their fate; maybe they had all been killed in some horrid prison. But then again, that night when she had been able to connect with Louis, when she meditated on the beach, she had been able to feel him very clearly, and he was fine.

But perhaps she was deluding herself, maybe she was in denial and he was really dead.

"Oh, Louis, Louis. My beloved friend, my husband." Sharon came across a low bench, sat down, calmed down, and meditated. She thought of Louis, and reached out to him with all her heart: "How are you, dear Lalo?"

At that moment a heavy cloud drifted in front of the moon and the night became pitch black. Sharon looked up. It felt ominous. This is umbra, she thought, when a shadow is at its darkest. But after a minute or so the big cloud passed over and the silvery light again flooded the path and the trees. Sharon could now see the full moon in between two palm fronds. The sight filled her heart with hope.

Louis heard the hum of the car's engines below. It was a reassuring sound, as though Wendy was telling him she would take care of him, of them all, that she knew where she was going, and would keep them safe.

They came down into a meadow shortly after sunrise. But the car didn't stop, it kept gliding over bushes, in between tall trees, across a creek, on top of the grass, over some rocks, and it went up an incline. There was the sound of scraping, and they could see branches moving violently outside the windows as though they were flying through a tree. Wendy righted herself and finally came to a stop.

The seat belts came off, and the door opened. The place was semi-dark. Wendy turned on her sidelights, and a sheer rock surface came into view. Louis got up and stepped outside the car, followed by Joy, Stephen, and then Angie, who held her gun tightly in her hands.

Wendy had found a hiding place. A big rock outcropping hung over their heads, and boulders on either side made up the walls. Trees and bushes almost completely blocked the entrance. It was apparent that Wendy had performed some very skillful flying to come in between the big branches.

Their refuge was not very wide, but there was space left around the car, enough to move, spread some things out, maybe sleep. The ground was littered with loose rocks.

Louis looked at his watch. It was six thirty Friday morning. Wendy had flown fifteen hours longer than the forty-eight she had told them she would, and he was glad; clearly flying the way she had was the best way to hide but they also needed to rest and be ready for the parade, and the secluded site was the perfect place for it. Louis wondered how she reasoned, how she decided to go ahead with her decision to fly the extra hours, and find the hideaway, all without consulting them.

The parade was scheduled to start at eight in the morning the following day. That wasn't so much of a wait, but he knew it would be a long twenty-five hours.

He walked to the very edge of their refuge, and a spacious sky greeted his tired eyes. Below was a grassy meadow flanked by oak trees, which grew sparsely on either side as far as the eye could see, interspaced by bushes and more grass. They were apparently on the foothills of a mountain, for the terrain sloped down for miles. Straight ahead Louis could see the desert where the mountain stopped and everything was flat again, flat and dry.

They were undetectable by anyone flying above them, as long as they stayed below the outcropping.

Joy was coming up with games for the kids to play on the very back of the place, behind Wendy. Louis could hear her talking with them or telling something to one of the dogs, in a sometimes playful, sometimes motherly, voice.

Louis sat down on the dirt at the entrance, keeping an eye out for anything unusual. A few hours passed. Most everyone now slept stretched out on blankets on the ground.

By midmorning, they were up and about. A car android distributed breakfast of coffee, orange juice, and complete meal patties. Stephen came to sit next to Louis. Larry joined them.

"Strange, isn't it," Stephen said, staring at the glass of juice, "how fate has placed us in this situation?"

Louis sipped his coffee and placed his mug down on the ground. "You mean that we are about to conduct a battle?"

"Yes, with so much at stake. So much rests on our shoulders. If we fail, the world will enter a dark period like it has not seen in a long time."

"Oh, it could not possibly last," Larry said. "Tyrants can't exist in a vacuum, and most people will be against this sick nut."

Stephen had bit into his patty and was examining it. "But he can do a lot of damage in the meantime. He's already turned Texas into a hell. About six months ago, when I first heard rumors of what was happening in Houston, I decided to go and take a look. It was the day of another parade. I stood in the street watching along with thousands, and realized what a terrible threat this preacher turned tyrant posed. I met Jorge. He, too, was watching the parade. He asked me to come to our old meditation center. I remember him pleading with me not to use violence. He said he was going to meditate and pray. Now he's in some prison, or maybe dead."

"Aw, come on Stephen," Louis said. "There is no reason for them to kill him."

They sat in silence for some time.

"Stephen, one thing I find baffling," Louis said, breaking the long silence. "I can't figure out how your followers seem to come from such varied backgrounds."

"We owe that to you, my friend," Stephen said with an attempt at a smile. "We all originally came to Texas to fight an unheeding world government. Otherwise, yes, we would not have normally mixed."

"But still, there is a divide, right?"

"Oh yes. I can't stand most of them. I read your papers on the atavists and I am totally with you. The area where I disagree is that your government has progressively ostracized them. I strongly feel you need to give them their voices back, to make room for them in your society."

"What can they possibly say that we want to hear," Larry asked. "We want to kill and torture animals? We want violence? We want a return to bigotry? C'mon, Stephen."

Stephen looked at Larry. "Yes, a good many of them will say those things in some manner or another. But they can change, and they will only change if you give them a chance, not by isolating them, but by modeling progressive behavior. We must break the pattern for them. That's why I and many others moved here, to help them."

Louis had been staring into the distance. He nodded in agreement. "Now that I've met a good many atavists here in Texas, I agree isolating them is not the solution. We were wrong. I was wrong. When this is all done and over with, please come with me to New York and let's work on this issue together."

Stephen chuckled. "You mean become part of the world government?"

Louis was about to answer when they heard a buzzing above their heads. They quickly stood and jumped back.

Two cars flew overhead pursued by a flying tank. They flew on toward the desert below, the cars taking evasive action, turning to the sides, up and down, while the tank fired missiles at them.

"Oh, man!" Stephen said. "Larry, can you tell us what's happening?"

Larry produced his phone, and a display and keyboard appeared before him. "Hmm. Reilly has vowed to kill all traitors. He warns everyone not to talk about the broadcasts, and anyone caught with a flyer will be shot. The news report of ten minutes ago said the New Confederacy's government has chased down and killed over two thousand of Stephen Phillipiak's followers so far. Reilly has claimed all traitors have been identified, their whereabouts determined, and that they will be dealt with."

"Oh shit!" Exclaimed Louis.

Stephen stood with arms folded across his chest and stared in the direction the two cars and the tank had flown. He didn't say anything for some time. His face had turned pale. "Those are my people he's killed. Oh Lord!" Stephen clenched his jaw. "I killed them! I killed them with this plan of ours. Oh God, how I wish we hadn't done all that."

"Now, Stephen," Louis said, "let's wait until tonight when you are supposed to talk with Mike...we don't know the truth. Of course, Reilly wants to scare us; of course he wants to make it seem like he's—"

"You are right, you are right, of course," Stephen said with a painful smile. "Larry, do you think the Patriots know where we are?" Louis asked.

Larry shook his head. "No, I don't think so. Wendy did a great job flying. It would take an extremely complex computer model to identify us."

"But the rest...they might be traceable," Louis said.

"We'll see," Stephen said. "I'll just put in my call to Mike at nine tonight like we planned, and let's see if he answers. If he does, we'll proceed with our plan," he said with difficulty.

"What exactly do you have in mind?" Louis said in an attempt to distract him.

"We'll wait until those jerks start filing past their president, then let's blast them with the virtual scenario. While they are busy fighting hand to hand and, hopefully, unable to function for a while, let's use the opportunity for some of my men to grab Reilly, while another group liberates the regents. That's about it, right?"

"I suppose we need to meet your men beforehand," Louis said.

"No need. I can direct them by phone. But I do need to know that they are ready...if they are all dead, if Mike doesn't answer, I plan to do what I can myself. Maybe use the chaos we create to reach that Reilly bastard and do away with him...that would be enough for me."

Louis observed Stephen for a moment then sighed. "Very well. That's as much planning as we can do. We'll have to improvise...we'll launch the virtual scenario and see what happens. Right now, let's just survive the next twenty hours or so."

Stephen panned the landscape in front of them. "Let's take turns keeping a watch out here, and resting...is that what you mean?"

"Precisely. Perhaps we should also relieve Joy with the kids. Let's keep four-hour watches?"

"I have an idea," Larry said. "Why don't we ask Wendy what she can do. She's got much better sensory equipment than any of us."

"Good point. Why don't you and Stephen go ask her while I stay here."

Ten minutes later Stephen came back. "She's on it. She needs to turn around and face the opening. Most of her sensors are in the front. She can't use satellite imagery—she's concerned someone can trace her—but she'll use infrared, ultrasound, infrawave detection, and God knows what other sensors."

Louis stood up, and they both hugged the wall on the left, as Wendy rose two feet and turned round. She pointed one way out of the opening, then another. For a while, she was like a dog settling down, until she was satisfied. Larry came over and they sat back down on the ground, facing the vast expanse below with Wendy beside them.

Stephen turned to Larry. "I have never run across a machine like her. Is she unique?"

"We've had intelligent computers for quite some time, but not like Wendy."

"Can you explain her?"

Larry turned to look at Wendy. "What happens in modern manufacturing is they build a basic machine and then give it a program that says 'complete yourself according to your environment,' with a built-in boundary. I surmise Wendy was able to overwrite the boundary."

"What about all those sensors? Did she make those? And her ability to change colors? And what she did with her interior when we did the recording?" Louis asked.

"Well, that's the easy part. For the past twenty years or so there's been no distinction between hardware and software. We develop the software, and the hardware, be it a shirt, a car, an android, or a house, follows along as a result."

"I had no idea," said Stephen. "I guess Texas is quite behind technologically. And I suppose raw materials are just part of the loop?"

Larry smiled. "Yes, even the small manufacturing unit I have in my briefcase can access any raw material it needs, using a process along the lines of what D'Anjou used in his technology, but far more rudimentary. He just evolved what was already there, in a very clever way."

"You mean, get down to the energy level and create anything?"

"In essence, yes. The energy conversion cells we use to power everything have the signatures of any element you want as long as the cells have been used for recycling on an ongoing basis. To make things all you need is a manufacturing unit and an energy cell."

"So Wendy is able to come up with any software and the resulting hardware she deems necessary?"

"Yes. She's quite sophisticated."

Louis looked under the car's nose, where he could see a number of sensors. "Well anyway, let's just consider ourselves lucky she's with us right now.

"Wendy," he called out, "what do you detect down there?"

"There is a mountain lion seven hundred and three-quarter meters at thirty-two degrees northeast, and twenty-two snakes spread out within my sensors' range, but none pose immediate danger."

"Wow," Stephen said. "I guess we can all rest and get ready for tomorrow." With this he stood and made his way toward the back, where his sons were playing with the dogs.

The boys were busy building a fort with loose rocks, and the two dogs seemed happy trying to destroy it. Joy and Angie sat on a blanket in a corner, talking. They had made a cozy place for themselves with pillows.

Stephen decided that was a good idea and went into the car to fetch a blanket and a pillow, which he laid down on the opposite corner. He leaned against the wall, watching the commotion of dogs and boys, and after some time started to feel groggy. There was nothing he could do, nothing he should be doing, except resting. His people were being hunted down, some were being killed…but there was nothing he could do about it…life was brutal, sometimes too brutal.

He must have dozed off, because he was awakened by nearby footsteps. He looked up to see Angie in her tight-fitting jeans. It seemed she had come over for a purpose. "Hi, Angie."

"Oh, I didn't know you were sleeping. I can come back later."

"No, no. Care to sit down?" He scooted to one side and offered half the blanket.

"Those are two great boys you got," Angie said sitting down primly beside him, leaning on one hand, her legs curled to one side.

"Yes, Jason and David are good boys. I wouldn't have survived the death of their mother without them."

"Oh, I am sorry to hear their mother died. They seem very well adjusted."

Stephen talked about his late wife, how she died suddenly of a brain aneurysm three years before at thirty-five, and he was fully aware a biochip would have saved her life. "But those things are so intrusive; she hated it when it was still active."

"Yes, that's what most people say." And she started to tell him Sharon's story, how she had almost died, but he had heard about it in the news.

They talked some more, and at one point she became serious. "What was your plan when you met us, Stephen?"

"You mean after I found out who you all were?"

"Exactly. It's clear you had your own plan for stopping Reilly, but when you saw Larry's toy, you changed your mind and came on board with us. What had been your plan?"

"Okay, okay, Angie, I see." Stephen righted himself and sat with legs crossed. "I'll tell you. I was going to kidnap all of you using a paralyzing pill, and then use you to gain access to Reilly.

Once in front of that idiot, use another pill to paralyze whoever was in the room, and kill him, with my bare hands if necessary. Is that what you wanted to know?"

Angie studied him in silence for a time. "That makes sense, it's what I would've done." With this, she reached over and hugged him tenderly. "I'm glad we came along when we did and you didn't have to sacrifice yourself." Her hand caressed the back of his neck.

He slid his face along her cheek and found her lips. He kissed her and he remembered what it was like to kiss a woman. It was a deep yearning he hadn't quite known he had.

He became aware that someone was watching. He pulled away and discovered his two sons and Joy staring at them.

Stephen leaned back and looked at Angie's face. She was studying him, her eyes now tender and a faint smile on her lips.

She lay down and signaled for him to lie down behind her. She curled up with her back against him, brought his arm to hug her, and after some time fell asleep.

They were woken up by a strange voice. It took Stephen a moment to determine it was Wendy's. "There's a car coming. Everybody come inside my compartment right now."

They rose. Joy was ushering the two boys and the dogs toward the car. Stephen grabbed Angie's hand and they rushed behind the dogs.

The rest were already inside the car, and the door closed. Wendy backed up as far as she could against the back of the hiding place, scooted over to hug the left wall. "Please lock the dogs and children in the bathroom. Please remain as quiet as you possibly can," she said in a low voice.

Joy took the two boys and the dogs into the bathroom, whispered for them to be as quiet as possible "because the bad guys are outside. Don't let the dogs bark."

Stephen took three quick steps, made his way past Joy, opened the bathroom door and threw one of his red pills inside, then quickly closed the door.

Wendy turned off all lights, including her control panel. The only sounds were their slow, controlled breaths. They fixed their gaze on the opening behind the trees. From that angle, they could see nothing but blue sky through the branches at the entrance. A slow, big gray balloon-like shape came into view; it seemed to slither across the sky. It flew about a hundred yards in front of the cave. They all held their breath. Seconds passed, it flew out of view, doubled back, and hung in place, apparently scanning. And then it took off with a sideways jerk toward the desert, perhaps alerted by some distant sight.

Someone let out a breath, then someone else, and the others followed.

When they were sure it was really gone, Joy opened the bathroom door. The boys and dogs were frozen in place like statues, startled faces turned in the direction of the door. "Oh, poor babies, my poor babies..." she began and seemed about to cry.

Stephen came by her side and put an arm around her. "it's okay, Joy; they'll be all right in a couple of hours. I'm sorry, but I just couldn't take the risk."

When the boys and the dogs recovered, Joy led them outside. In another minute they were playing, racing around, and Joy stood with tears running down her cheeks. Stephen came over and again put an arm around her shoulders.

"See, they recover fast. I bet they can't remember what happened."

"That's true. It was the right thing to do, I know that."

She looked up at his face, and Stephen felt tenderness toward her that he had not felt for a woman since his wife died. Given the choice between Joy and Angie, who would he choose? But was it his choice? At that moment, looking into Joy's eyes, perhaps he did have a choice.

They spent the rest of the afternoon in the back of their refuge, sitting on blankets. Wendy was back with her nose right at the opening.

They had arranged themselves in a circle with the boys and the dogs in the middle. In another time and another place, thought Stephen, this would be an idyllic situation, something for picture taking, and building memories. Angie took a hold of his hand, smiled, and looked into his eyes.

And he recalled the look in Joy's eyes, and they seemed to haunt him.

Louis had stood and was silent for a long time staring at the opening. He then chastised himself for not planning what to do should a tank appear. "It's obvious we owe our lives to Wendy," he mumbled. "I, who am so adept on the world stage, am so inept at survival."

"It's okay, Louis," Stephen told him. "We are all at fault; you are not the only adult in the group."

They ate dinner, time crawled along, and then it was nine. Time for Stephen to call Mike. Stephen reached for his pants pocket, his face pale, hands trembling. Louis and Larry stood by his side, their faces grim. With some trepidation he touched his phone and asked for Mike. Mike's face appeared almost immediately.

Stephen let out a breath of relief. "Mike! I'm so glad to see you!"

"No kidding! Stephen, you're alive!"

"Tell me what happened."

"We managed to broadcast for an hour and left without incident," Mike sounded energized. "We reached all of Texas, and well beyond, that's what the television engineer told us. Our guys also spread fliers all over the place. People were talking about the phone broadcast as well. Man, I think we really did it.

"But then, when it came time to disperse—"

"Mike, how many did we lose?"

"Oh, at last count, an hour ago, twenty-eight confirmed dead, and another thirty-one missing."

Stephen was clearly relieved. "The news said thousands..."

"Yeah, man, I know, that bastard Reilly lies; that's all he does."

Larry stood in front of Stephen and emphatically ran his finger across his throat.

"Okay Mike, we can't talk long...at the appointed hour and place, wait for my signal."

"Got it!"

"Whew!" Stephen said after hanging up. "Fifty-one casualties...a lot better than thousands, but still...well, if we can last a few more hours we'll be—"

"At least we'll be doing something," added Angie, grabbing a hold of his hand.

Larry seemed upset; he stared at his phone and kept shaking his head.

"Larry," Stephen said, "did I talk for too long? Do you think the Patriots traced my call?"

"They could've...but there's nothing we can about it now...can't fly around like before; they are stopping and searching cars all over...shooting them down. We have to stay."

Stephen sat beside Angie and they watched the kids play with the dogs. Wendy's body shielded them from the entrance. Her back, about five feet from them, was all they could see.

Louis observed the group. All the adults seemed relieved with the knowledge the long hours would soon be over. Or maybe it was also that they had managed not to be found by the flying tank and that Mike's men had been successful and most of them were still alive. People all over Texas now knew there was an alternative to Reilly. Yes, that was a very encouraging thought.

There was a chance that Stephen's call had been traced, but Larry had concluded that the Patriots were now focusing their attention on providing security for the parade and would probably not send a tank to investigate the call.

All they could do was wait another nine hours.

Angie and Stephen hugged tightly sitting on their blanket and talked in nervous whispers. Joy sat monitoring the kids, concern on her face. Larry and Suzanne sat leaning against the back wall of the cave. She slept with her head on his shoulder. Larry was in deep thought, his gaze lost somewhere, oblivious to Yogi, who had just jumped across his legs, and to Jason, who came after the dog.

"I just wonder..." he began, speaking to no one in particular, "why are the casualties so low?"

Stephen turned to look at him. "Why so low? Larry, let's just be thankful."

"Oh, I am...but with the resources at hand, Reilly's soldiers surely had the opportunity to do much as he claimed, to kill most if not all of your followers, which I understand are around ten thousand. I just wonder...there's clearly a mitigating factor, and—"

"Larry, of course!" exclaimed Louis. "That points to reluctance in the part of most of those soldiers to kill because that's what they were ordered to do; not capture, but kill. I think the broadcast is working, they know there's an alternative, a way out...I wonder if they are all waiting for us to do something."

Joy stood up, her eyes wide with excitement. "I think it goes back to what we talked about, that we would see a split within Reilly's followers when it came time to kill, and coupled with the broadcasts—"

"Yes!" Stephen exclaimed looking up at her. "Of course! There should've been many more casualties. I wonder if Reilly is now wondering the same thing."

"Of course he is," Louis said. "But he has to wait. He and his five generals can't take any disciplinary measures now; they must wait until after the parade, when they will probably do a purge."

"Stalin-style?" Stephen asked.

"Yes, that would stand to reason. He will execute a good many who disobeyed him, and the rest will fall in out of fear. He knows this is a critical time within his organization when he must solidify his authority."

"Both Stalin and Hitler did that," Stephen said.

Louis nodded. "Yes. That holds true for all tyrants. Their followers are in the minority, but they can pull the majority along through fear. Reilly started out with a relatively benign promise of standing up for individual rights against an overreaching world government..."

Stephen let out a chuckle. "You agree that your government squelches individual rights?"

Louis smiled. "No, Stephen. I'm talking about people's perceptions, and I agree that's the perception here in Texas. But let me finish. In Germany in the 1930s what Hitler delivered, and what made him so popular, was the reunification of all German peoples in Poland, Czechoslovakia, and Austria; economic recovery; and a return of lost national honor from the previous war. But then he went off the deep end, exterminating Jews and trying to conquer the world at a cost of tremendous suffering. Once the German people realized what he was doing, it was too late: a reign of terror had been solidly put in place, and most decided that to survive they'd better go along and turn a blind eye to the atrocities."

Louis stared down at the ground, a sad look in his eyes. "I keep thinking of the White Rose Movement, a courageous group of students at the University of Munich, who, in 1942, tried their best to make people see what Hitler was up to, using leaflets. But it was too late, and no one rose in support. They paid with their lives. Had they tried a decade earlier, they might've succeeded."

"In our case, it's not too late. We have caught Reilly's movement at a crucial stage. I don't think his followers are solidly behind him, or that they know exactly who he is and what he intends to do. It also helps that the world has evolved: atavists are a minority, and even they are not the same. All indications are that when the soldiers experience their virtual hand-to-hand combat they won't want to fight anymore. Ever. At that point if we provide an exit strategy, a good many Patriots will turn their backs on Reilly."

"But how do we do that?" Larry asked. "To provide them with an exit strategy we need to prompt them—"

"And we have to reach them first," Stephen said.

Larry nodded. "Oh, we can reach them all right; I can turn the chips in the plants into voice synthesizers."

"Okay," Stephen said, "but what do we tell them?"

"I don't know…I don't know," Louis said, thinking out loud. "But if we have a chance tomorrow, let's take it. Their vacillation would be our most powerful weapon, besides your virtual fighting, Larry."

Stephen shook his head emphatically. "Oh, no need to overthink this. We'll make it with what we got. After Larry activates the virtual hand-to-hand combat those idiots will be rendered useless and we'll take Reilly and free the hostages…with my men…say if six thousand show up tomorrow, and that's a conservative figure, we can round up that creep and his five generals, then this whole New Confederacy movement will be done with."

"But there are five million of them!" Louis said. "If even a small fraction decide to stop us, we are doomed; but if we can convince most of them to come to our side—"

"Of course," Stephen said. "But look, what I'm saying is that we'll do fine with what we have. Besides, that's what the hand-to-hand combat is going to accomplish, neutralize most of those soldiers and give us a chance. A good many refused to kill my men, so we know that there are quite a few who are already borderline and need one final push."

"It will only take one determined commander to turn the tables on us," Louis said. "Somehow we must do away with the top leadership—"

"We'll do fine, Louis," Stephen said with a forced smile. "My men can handle it."

270

Louis nodded absentmindedly while he watched Yogi play with Jason. He felt a heavy weight of worry, or more so, a certainty that they were going to fail and be killed.

And he remembered his experience with the energies...Diva Two. What if he could enter Diva Two through meditation, raise his energy and the group's energy, and maybe as a result...maybe he could change the outcome of what he felt was certain failure? Why not? At the very least, meditation would calm him so he could think more clearly. He went inside the car, sat on one of the seats, and went into meditation.

After a relatively short while, Louis felt a tremendous shift inside: a joy, a deep-seated peace. After another hour, he opened his eyes with his insides brimming with wholeness. He decided to sleep.

Stephen slept fitfully, waking up at the slightest sound. There was no telling whether his phone conversation had given away their location.

He lay on the blanket with Angie in his arms and could sense that she was awake most of the time, but seemed content just lying there. He could see his sons not ten feet away sleeping soundly with the dogs, and Joy sitting up, with her back leaning against the rock wall, keeping watch. For their sake, he should marry Joy...no, it wasn't just for his sons he would want Joy.

Joy knew she wouldn't be able to sleep if she tried, so might as well just stay up and suffer some more... what the hey...they will probably all die tomorrow and a lunatic will take over the world...the one man she had fallen for really bad was now sleeping with her best friend...oh well, what else was new. Oh yeah, those two boys had stolen her heart, and they will go live with Angie instead. Well, at least the more you cry the less you have to pee. There's a bright side to everything.

Louis slept soundly, but in the middle of the night he got up to check on everyone. All was as well as could be expected. He went back to bed.

271

Every so often Wendy blipped a series of lights on her panel, green and blue. She had told Louis before he went to bed that it was a sign all was well. He smiled, lay down and meditated a little more, and fell fast asleep.

21

L ouis awoke. He sat up and looked at Wendy's panel. The blue and green lights greeted him. He checked his watch. It was 5:10 in the morning. The parade would start in three hours. Spectators were required to be there an hour in advance...they had barely an hour to get ready. He could still feel the effects of meditation: a deep sense of well-being and peace. That's so great, he thought.

Outside he found Stephen and Angie eating breakfast. The kids were still sleeping, Joy sat dozing, her head cocked to the side.

"Good morning," Louis said aloud.

The car androids distributed breakfast. Louis took two quick bites of his complete meal patty, washed it down with a sip of coffee, and gave the tray back. Larry and Stephen came to stand beside him, both silently sipping their coffee.

Larry went inside the car and came out a minute later. "Wendy says it will take her twenty minutes to reach the parade, but she wants to merge with traffic, so she asks for an extra fifteen minutes. She'll be using a signature from an official Texas government car. I found out that all Texas officials are required to attend the parade. They won't pay any attention to us, not with the millions of cars driving to Houston they have to keep an eye on."

"That makes sense," Stephen said. "I like the plan."

"We have to be there at seven, so let's leave at six."

"Yes," Stephen said. "Let's leave supplies for Joy and the kids and take off."

Joy had come to listen to the group and stood behind Louis. "No way! If anyone should be out there with Louis it's me."

"Joy," Stephen said. "I know you are Louis's right arm…but that's in New York. Here it's different. Actually Larry is the only indispensable person. It would ease my mind knowing Jason and David are safe in your care, and if something happens to me, I would be so gratified to know that you will raise them. Please stay with them. We'll keep you informed through the phone. If we go silent and don't return by tomorrow morning, call Mike. If he doesn't answer, I'll give you a list of telephone numbers, keep calling until someone answers. Someone will come and get you."

Joy stared at the children now rousing from their sleep. "Okay, fine, but I don't like it."

"What I think will work best," Louis said "is if we send Wendy back as soon as she drops us off, then we can call her to pick us up; in the meantime she'll be here to protect Joy and the kids."

They left right at six. They could see in the window display that Wendy was making a wide arc in her approach to Houston. There were cars as far as the eye could see in either direction. They approached the parade grounds, a vast flat expanse of land with a wide swath of concrete in the middle. Over in the distance loomed the Megadome, Houston's sports arena.

Louis had never been in a group of so many cars; they flew almost touching one another in large solid banks, thousands stacked vertically and horizontally. He hoped all car computers worked well: it would take only one to malfunction to create a catastrophe. But all went well; the cars touched down in layers, then took off horizontally for the next layer to land.

Wendy dropped them off. A huge mass of humanity was lining up to enter the parade grounds under the watchful eyes of soldiers. They were entering the "standing room only" field, an area fronting the presidential booth and its two long arms of bleachers, where the

New Confederacy's favorite citizens were slated to sit. In between the field and the bleachers ran the hundred-yard-wide avenue where the parade was to take place.

Most of the spectators in the standing-room-only field were lining up as far forward as they could, and close to the presidential booth.

Louis aimed for a large tree set back about five hundred yards from the front and a mile to the right of the presidential booth. Louis led the group to a spot where they were protected from the sun by a massive branch.

They could see the fancy glassite enclosure, raised about two hundred feet up in the air, where Reilly and his top generals would sit. It dominated the place like a big eye in the sky. Two large Confederate flags stood tall on either side of the booth.

Old-fashioned display screens were positioned on poles all over the place. The picture alternated between an inside view of the presidential booth and an aerial view of the parade grounds.

Half an hour later, they were surrounded by people as far as the eye could see in either direction. Shortly afterward, the television showed Reilly walking into the glassite enclosure with his top five generals. Louis recognized Gary. D'Anjou stood beside Gary in a general's green uniform, apparently all full of himself. Louis found the sight jarring, and he wondered whether brainwashing could actually eradicate someone's deep-seated values...well, whatever the case, there he was, Alphonse D'Anjou now in the enemy camp. Reilly wore his gray Confederacy uniform with medals. D'Anjou and the other generals talked with the president, and their manner was subservient, respectful. Reilly's expression was disdainful as he responded to whatever one of his generals said. At one point he smiled and apparently said something funny, at which time his generals and D'Anjou doubled over with laughter and went on laughing way too long. Louis turned to look at Arlene, and saw she had tears streaming down her face.

The aerial view was meant to impress, and it did: it showed an immense formation of soldiers and war machines waiting to start moving; like an enormous fat snake that went clear to the horizon. The massive formation would take many hours, even days, to file past once it got started; but maybe not all of them were slated to parade, maybe most of the huge mass of soldiers and machines were meant as a backdrop.

The camera panned the bleachers filling in fast with thousands and thousands. The standing-room-only field had become a sea of people as far as the eye could see.

Louis knew people all over the world were watching their televisions with a mixture of trepidation and awe, as if witnessing a powerful storm forming, one that was about to unleash horrible devastation, and there was nothing they could do but watch.

But for many of the spectators at the parade the reaction was very different: they were happy and apparently proud. A good many waved, smiled, and shouted, "Long live President Reilly!" when the cameras panned their area. When the cameras left, some cried, filled with emotion.

Louis wondered how much of that was real, and how many of those people were plants placed there to motivate the crowd. Evidently it worked, for those who had only watched before, when the camera came by again, now imitated the emotion-laden behavior, shouting, waving, and crying.

Right at eight, loud music rang out, its martial tones reverberating through the huge crowd. The display screens were now split; half showed Reilly and his top generals, the other half the parade grounds, and the huge army in the background.

When the music stopped, Reilly began to speak: "You are about to witness the mighty Sword of God I will unleash on the world! It is the sword of justice, and righteousness, the sword of punishment for those who disobey God's Word and disobey me, God's emissary on earth! I will teach the world…"

That was more than Louis could take, whatever fear and reservations he had evaporated in a gush of anger and disgust. "Larry, are you ready?" he whispered.

Larry felt his pants pocket. "I am," he whispered back.

Louis looked around. Larry stood by his left with Suzanne. Arlene sat on a big tree root by his feet. Stephen and Angie were on his right. Their tree was surrounded by a big mass of humanity. "If anything goes wrong, let's all climb this tree," he told them, looking at the branches above them.

Reilly was thumping his fist and talking about "the weak races, the inferior, the dumb…" and the crowd roared its approval.

"Okay, let's do it!" Louis said.

Larry took a deep breath, stuck his hand in his pocket, and pressed a key.

They stared at the vast troop formation in the television screens. At first there was nothing, but then there was a commotion in the ranks, like a huge wave running through it. The soldiers started cutting and jabbing with invisible knives, wielding imaginary clubs, and throwing punches in the air, as though gone mad.

"It's working!" Louis said.

Spectators looked at one another, murmured, and watched.

Larry produced his phone's virtual screen. It split into a dozen screens. In it they could see the dozen selected cases and who they were fighting: soldiers just like them. Knives cut throats and arms and stabbed chests. Fists broke noses. Heads were split open with rocks. Larry explained that soldiers wouldn't use their guns, in their illusion they only saw knives, clubs, and rocks. They watched as a soldier fended off an attacker, plunged a knife, and stood watching in horror before falling down on his knees in disbelief beside his attacker.

In a matter of minutes, a communal wail rose from the army, an anguished, horrifying wail. Millions of throats yelled, screamed; million of bodies thrashed about in a mad pantomime. It seemed to go on for the longest time. Then it started to subside, as soldiers stood, their gazes fixed on the ground. Some were crying, lifting invisible heads, bowing over unseen bodies.

Spectators remained riveted to the television images. "What is it?" some asked. "What's happening? Can't someone help them? Maybe they are hallucinating."

More time passed. A great majority of the soldiers were now on the ground, on their knees, or standing crying or yelling in horror.

"Okay," Louis said. "I think that's enough. Larry, stop the sensory override and let's try talking to them."

"I'm turning the plants into voice synthesizers."

"Good."

"Wait," Stephen said. "Look!" He pointed at the television monitor now showing the presidential booth. Reilly and his generals seemed to be arguing, pacing around, then looking at the monitor showing the army. Reilly produced his phone and spoke anxiously. A flying tank arrived; Louis could see its massive bulk through the booth's back glassite wall. A door opened in the wall. Reilly put down his phone, said something, and everyone in the booth rushed out the door and into the waiting tank.

Most of the spectators were now riveted on the part of the screen showing the presidential booth. They pointed at it and talked feverishly. Then, after a brief pause, the crowd went for the exits. Louis and the rest hugged the tree trunk as the throng surged all around them. The day turned to semi-dark as millions of cars hovered overhead, a solid high bank of cars that filled the sky. Then they started coming down in layers just below shoulder level, allowing their owners to be helped on board by car androids. Soon people rushed any open car door, and the cars took off full to capacity; but quite a few of the interlopers were thrown off. Many in the crowd were yelling, some were trying to run but couldn't move beyond a slow, hesitating pace. Panicked faces were now looking desperately around.

Larry, with his body tight against the tree trunk, handed Louis his phone. "I stopped the sensory override. Just speak clearly," he said surprisingly calm.

Louis spoke into the phone in a whisper then handed it to Stephen, who listened to Louis's recording before making his own.

When they were done, Louis gave the phone to Larry, who pressed a couple of keys.

Louis's thunderous voice resounded throughout the fields, drowning all other sounds.

"This is Regent Louis Sagan. Soldiers of the Patriot army, what is taking place is a virtual reality designed to show you what President Reilly is really like. He and his generals have fled to safety and left you to what they thought was your destruction. You haven't hurt anyone; it was all an illusion.

"You decided to follow Reilly because you believed in his promises, but most of you have now taken a second look and know that what he wants to do is control the world for his own selfish and dangerously misguided reasons. He plans to commit mass genocide, with your help. Don't do it! Now is your time to shed your uniforms and come to the side of reason.

"As regent, I promise I will initiate changes in our government to make room for your concerns. We can work together on this. I am already working with Stephen Phillipiak, the leader of the resistance."

Then after a brief pause:

"This is Stephen Phillipiak. What Regent Sagan said is true. We can make changes together.

"I know you don't want to kill or be killed. I know you don't want to shoot innocent people.

"Shed your uniforms and come over to our side. We'll send that creep Reilly where he belongs. Now, take off your tunics to show that you are with us!"

The effect of the broadcast was almost immediate: Large gaps of white appeared everywhere as soldiers shed their tunics and exposed their undershirts. There were many still on the ground, and a significant number, still wearing their tunics, were gathering to one side, but what once had been a huge army was no more.

Louis turned to Stephen. "Stephen. Call your men!"

Stephen quickly produced his phone. Mike came on right away. "Mike, we've done our bit; most of the army has surrendered. Now do your job!"

"No kidding! I can see! I'm ready with over seven thousand of our guys."

"That Reilly creep just took off in a tank with his five generals. See if you can follow and capture them. Also send some guys to the concentration camp."

"Will do."

All the while the crowd thronged past them. Cars kept landing and picking up passengers, many more kept hovering overhead.

Louis looked at the aerial television monitors. Most of the army seemed to have shed their tunics, but a significant group of armed troops were gathering at one end, apparently under someone's leadership. A number of tanks were converging in their direction.

A part of the army was regrouping, perhaps a tenth of it, but still a significant number.

Stephen tapped his sleeve to make his phone appear. "Mike. Mike, get over to the parade grounds. You must get there at once and take charge."

"How?" came the answer. "There are so many of them."

"Find the commanders, Mike. Find the commanders of the troops that have given up. Then use them to try and convince the guys that are regrouping to surrender."

"Okay, Stephen, I hear you. I'm over at the Megadome. Reilly is inside. I'll leave Roger in charge and head on over to the parade grounds. I already sent some guys to the concentration camp."

Stephen shut down his phone and looked around.

Louis was staring at the television picture. Angie was crying and laughing, and so was Arlene. Larry was smiling broadly and saying something to Suzanne.

Stephen smiled. "Okay, guys, we'll celebrate later. Let's head on over to the Megadome. Reilly is inside."

They could see the curved top of the dome in the distance, what appeared to be some ten miles away.

Louis tapped his shirt pocket for his phone and called Wendy. There was no answer. He called Joy.

She answered right away.

"Joy, we need Wendy. Where is she?"

Joy was crying. "Oh my God, thank goodness you are safe. Is everyone okay?

"Yes, Joy. Everything is fine. Reilly's movement is collapsing. He's hiding in the Megadome, and we need Wendy to get us over there."

"Oh, Louis, I have terrible news. Wendy was shot down! She's lying in a heap downhill from us. There's still smoke coming from her."

Louis's stomach knotted up. "Wendy has been shot down!" he told the group.

Angie appeared startled. Larry seemed to be thinking about the news.

"We need to get to the Megadome!" Stephen said. "Let's figure out something fast."

Most of the spectators were gone, but there were still quite a few in large groups here and there staring at the television screens.

A group of soldiers without their tunics stood in one group, mingling with a number of spectators. Stephen ran toward them, followed by Louis and the rest.

Stephen was the first to reach the soldiers. There were several hundred of them, mostly young, some were women; all had their hair shorn down to the scalp. When they saw Stephen and the rest, they lined up in formation. The civilians backed away and stood to one side.

"I am Stephen Phillipiak, and this is Regent Sagan," he said pointing to Louis, who led the rest of the group.

"Yes, sir," said one of the soldiers, a young and muscular blond man. "We know who you are. We've been watching you. It's an honor, sir! I'm Lieutenant Schweitzer, How can we be of assistance?"

"We need transportation to the Megadome, right away."

The lieutenant looked at the other soldiers. He hesitated for a moment, and appeared to make up his mind. "All we got are our motorcycles over there," he said pointing to a nearby tree.

The motorcycles were neatly lined up to one side, standing on their jacks. "We don't know how to ride those things," Stephen said.

"We'll be glad to give you a ride, sir."

They ran toward the motorcycles with the lieutenant and other soldiers.

The soldiers lined up six motorcycles and handed them helmets. Stephen got on one motorcycle behind the lieutenant, and the rest took their places on the remaining cycles.

When the lieutenant saw that they were all ready, they heard him say "Megadome main entrance" in their helmets. The machines lifted about ten feet off the ground in unison and proceeded at a fast clip toward the dome. They rose above the trees, and Louis felt fear but also excitement; it was close to flying on one's own. He realized why young people liked to ride the things.

22

Stephen spotted Roger on the ground by the Megadome's entrance, waving. The short and burly man had his field glasses on and was still inspecting all the motorcycles.

They landed next to Roger. "So glad you are here, Stephen," he said with a smile.

Louis dismounted and came to stand next to Stephen. Larry was walking over.

Stephen thanked the lieutenant and asked him to stick around in case they needed the motorcycles again. The soldiers saluted and smiled.

Stephen turned to Roger. "What's the news?"

Roger took off his baseball cap, exposing a mop of copper-red hair. "When we arrived, we saw Reilly, his top five generals, and some civilians, being joined by thousands of other generals and some soldiers, right here at the entrance. They ran inside as we were disembarking. We haven't heard anything since then. No sound. No one has come out either. I got the place surrounded. The soldiers, about two hundred of them, were armed, but not the generals, so in a firefight we could take them."

Stephen looked at the enormous structure, silvery metal with translucent panels. "Why this place?" Stephen asked. "What's inside?"

"Just a big open field where they play sports and have rodeos and stuff," Roger said.

"But no place to seek shelter, right?"

Roger ran his hand over his bushy red moustache. "You mean like a fortified place?"

"Yeah, a big concrete structure, someplace where they can hole up?" Stephen asked.

"There is no telling. I don't know the place well enough. I thought we'd wait for an android with a camera and send it in. I already asked for one."

One of Roger's men came up followed by an android. Roger produced his phone and scanned the android's code.

He got a clear picture from its camera. It showed the front of the building. Roger whispered a command into his phone.

The android walked through the entrance past the escalators.

"I told it to inspect the entire building starting with the arena," Roger said as he produced a virtual display.

They could see the long tunnel leading to the arena. Then the edge of the field. No one so far. The android came to the end of the tunnel and it showed the entire huge field. Artificial sunlight lit up the place. It was empty. The android picked up speed and went inside the arena, panning the bleachers on either side. Nothing.

Roger spoke into his phone and instructed the android to inspect every inch of the place. It proceeded to climb the bleachers.

Suzanne pointed at something on the screen and whispered in Larry's ear.

"Wait a moment," Larry said. "Could you show me the arena one more time?"

Roger appeared baffled. "But it's empty!"

"Do as he says," instructed Stephen. He then gave Angie, who stood next to him, a reassuring smile.

The android came back to the arena. Its camera went from side to side, up and down.

"There," Larry said. "Go up to one of those boxes."

"What boxes?" Roger asked.

Larry came up close to the virtual screen. He pointed at a small object on a ledge. "That. Show me that."

The camera zoomed in. It was a dark metal box about two inches tall, four inches wide and four inches long. It had an old-style dish-like antenna on top.

"Circle the ledge. I bet there are boxes like that all around."

The camera went around the perimeter and showed a number of boxes placed at regular intervals on the ledge that separated the bleachers from the arena. There were dozens of them.

"Okay," Stephen said. "Someone made those little boxes and placed them around the place. So what? We are looking for Reilly and his people."

"Yes," replied Larry. "And that's where they went."

"What the hell do you mean?" Stephen asked.

Louis shook his head. "What I think he means is that Reilly teleported out of here. Those little boxes constitute the sending station. Is that right, Larry?"

"I am almost positive," he said. "I would have to take one of those boxes apart, but I can tell you already those are most likely teleporting transmitters."

They waited for the android to come back with one of the boxes. Roger and a group of his men stood around whispering excitedly.

The android walked toward Roger, but Larry intercepted it and snatched the box from its hands. He turned it over and examined it; then he crouched down and placed the black box on the sidewalk. He produced his phone and started pressing keys. He pointed the phone at the box.

"I've programmed the phone to act as a scanner," he said while running the phone along the box. The phone's virtual screen started showing a myriad of parts that Larry and Suzanne studied intently.

After a few more minutes Larry looked up from his phone's display. "It's a sending station, all right."

Louis looked at the dome's main entrance, a three-story-high concrete opening. The wrought-iron gate was wide-open. "So what seems to have happened is D'Anjou built those transmitters and kept them with him in case of emergency. When they thought everything was lost, they teleported out somewhere."

"But why the Megadome?" Stephen asked and watched as the android went back inside to resume its search.

"Because it's an enclosed place made of the right materials," answered Larry. "Energy deflecting stremptonite and glassite."

Stephen scratched his head. "But where did they go? And how do we catch up with them?"

"I'll try and read the destination coordinates," Larry said. He clicked a couple of keys and asked Suzanne to hold the phone-scanner while he turned the box upside down.

"Oh Lord!" he exclaimed, then fiddled with the phone and took another reading. And another. "Well, there's no doubt," he said, looking up.

"What?" Louis asked.

"The coordinates point to Tolima."

"But could they go there?" Angie asked, staring at the readout in Larry's hands. "That's bizarre!"

Suzanne shook her head while looking over Larry's shoulder.

"Not so bizarre," replied Louis. "I suspect Reilly took with him his generals and an elite guard. We'll have to question someone who was close to the group, but my guess is he plans to come back for more of his followers. Perhaps he envisions setting up a colony up there, a world all of his own."

"But isn't teleporting to Tolima next to impossible?" Angie asked. "And he doesn't know who else is there. For all he knows, there might be a more advanced civilization, or perhaps primitive people...who can tell?"

"Well," Louis said, "first things first. Let's take care of business here, and then let's worry about Reilly and Tolima. I don't think he'll be back in the next few hours, but we do need to somehow catch up with him."

"Oh, catching up is no problem," Larry said, examining his scanner. "I have the exact coordinates right here. The problem is surviving Tolima and getting back."

"But isn't what you are holding proof that D'Anjou figured it all out?" Louis asked, looking at the scanner.

Larry sighed. "There's no evidence these boxes worked. For all we know, Reilly and his generals might have disintegrated on the way, or arrived there and were turned into something quite different."

"Why?"

Larry stood up, device in hand. "The object being reconstructed is subject to the predominant energy."

"So," Stephen said, "if Tolima is an advanced environment, they could end up as far more advanced beings."

"Well, not exactly," responded Larry. "Your energy has to match."

"And if it doesn't?"

"You are rejected...I have no idea where you go or what happens to you, but you simply do not reconstruct."

"Oh," exclaimed Stephen.

Larry peered into his display, incredulous. "I can't believe a scientist of D'Anjou's caliber would take such a risk."

Louis turned toward Suzanne. "What if he was somehow able to tell what Tolima's energy is like?"

Larry shook his head. "No, I don't think so...not without many more years of research. We would need to send androids first—"

"I see," Louis said. "Because machines are not affected?"

"We don't really know," interjected Suzanne, "but at least with androids we are not risking any lives."

"Well, we need to find out what happened to Reilly and his gang," Louis said, "and whether they pose a future threat. What will it take to send that android after them?"

Larry exchanged glances with Suzanne. "It's going to take us some time…we can try. The worst that can happen is we'll never see the android again."

"What do you need to do?" Louis sounded impatient.

"I would have to equip it so it can send itself back."

Larry, accompanied by Suzanne and Arlene, started for the inside of the Megadome looking for the android. Larry told Louis they would work until finished.   Stephen sent three hundred men and women armed with rifles to protect them, just in case. Then he asked Roger for a car, and he and Angie went to get his sons, Joy, and the dogs.

Louis walked away toward the Megadome entrance. "Larry, I'm going to ask the lieutenant for a ride to the parade grounds. I'm going to check on the Patriot army. You take care of business here."

Louis found many thousands of soldiers standing in groups talking, a confused look in their eyes. When he arrived they stood at a respectful distance shouting questions: "When do we go home?" "Do we go back to our barracks?" "Who's in charge?" "What happened to President Reilly?"

Mike told him that the brigade commanders, the one-star generals, were gone. They had gone to watch the parade and no one had heard from them again.

Mike had gathered as many colonels as he could in a hangar, about fifteen thousand. They told him that a Colonel Bush had assumed command of a mixed infantry-tank brigade. He was known as a fanatical Reilly follower. Bush had gathered over 300,000 soldiers and some flying tanks in a far-off field and was "prepared to maintain a ready army until President Reilly returns," as he told a colleague over the phone. Louis talked to the colonels and could tell that they knew it was all over; they, and their soldiers, just wanted to go home. Quite a few had done just that in the last two hours.

Louis and Mike stood before the officers. "Let's ask them how we should deal with Bush," he told Mike.

They argued for some time. Clearly no one was in charge, and Mike was no help. "He's not going to surrender on his own," said Colonel Toney, a tall and energetic man in his forties. "At some point in the next couple of days they'll get real hungry," commented another. Louis could tell that at that stage they had little interest in whatever happened to Bush...or to the army.

"Why don't you guys surround him," offered Louis. "Maybe he'll realize he can't win and give up."

"Yeah," piped in Toney. "Let's scare him; pretend we're going to pound him."

Toney called Bush. "Give up in an hour or we'll have no choice but to attack you."

Louis watched as the army reassembled. It was like a huge puzzle coming back together. The once confused and demoralized soldiers, still in their T-shirts, now seemed energized, and focused. Toney called for three brigades to mobilize. The rest were to remain at standby until further notice. It took about two hours for the three brigades to surround Bush's unit.

Larry reached the end of the tunnel and looked at the boxes around the arena. The android was surveying an area at the very far end. Arlene and Suzanne were ahead of him walking toward the android.

Larry started to follow them when he saw something out of the corner of his eye. He thought he saw a figure up in the bleachers. But now it was gone. He kept looking at the place where he saw movement. He saw a figure rise, take a few steps, then duck behind one of the rows of seats.

Larry turned to one of Stephen's hunter types behind him. "There's someone up there!" he told the young woman.

"Where?" she asked.

Larry pointed. They looked and after another minute or so, the figure moved again. It made a dash for another row, and ducked.

Eight of Stephen's guards went to investigate. They split into four teams of two and started closing in from different directions where they last saw the figure. The figure stood up and tried to run, but it moved clumsily. The hunter types closed in. One grabbed the figure and held him or her.

As they approached with their prisoner, Larry could tell it was one of Reilly's army men. He had shed his tunic, but his pants were dark green with two black stripes along the side.

Arlene and Suzanne had turned back.

As the hunter types got closer Larry stared at their prisoner in amazement. "It's D'Anjou!" he exclaimed, not quite believing what he was seeing.

The man was nothing like the arrogant general Larry had seen sitting behind Gary on the television screen. He looked rumpled, and obviously scared.

"Alphonse!" Larry heard Arlene exclaim behind him. She ran toward him and threw her arms around his neck. D'Anjou seemed surprised, but accepted the embrace.

Larry waited until the group got closer. He examined D'Anjou. Now he looked more like his old, shy self. "I thought you had teleported to Tolima."

"No, no such thing." The rumpled figure said in a tremulous voice, looking at Arlene a bit mystified. Sweat dripped from his face and down the front of his T-shirt, which was soaked.

The hunter types held on to D'Anjou's arms. One produced manacles and shackled his hands together.

"I…I have some explaining to do," started D'Anjou.

"Please do," Larry said. He then asked one of the hunter types to bring a chair for D'Anjou and some water. He seemed on the verge of collapsing.

D'Anjou examined the people around him, and Arlene next to him. "May I inquire who you are?"

It dawned on Larry that D'Anjou had no way of recognizing them. "I'm Regent Larry Zimmerman, Alphonse. We scrambled our

DNA to change our appearance using your machines. This is Suzanne, and next to you, Arlene. And these guards," Larry said turning toward the hunter types milling around them, "are Stephen Phillipiak's soldiers."

D'Anjou looked at Larry and Suzanne. He smiled at Arlene kneeling by his side. "Arlene, of course I recognized you!" He then kissed her softly on the lips.

"Oh my word," he said. "I'm glad you figured out the technology, sweetheart," he said to Arlene.

D'Anjou looked at the manacles on his wrists. Larry signaled for the hunter types to release him. There was little chance he could get away, even if he wanted to.

D'Anjou sighed, rubbed his wrists, and then tugged at his pants. Arlene hugged him, crying silently. "Reilly was going to invade the United States tomorrow. In another year they were going to move to Europe and do the same. All in the name of The New Confederacy, or the Cause, I don't know; it got confusing. Asia was next. The rest of the world was going to be easy. It was then that the ethnic cleansing would start. Reilly's estimate was that ten billion people would be exterminated, two-thirds of the world!" The nasal, strangely undulating voice sounded subdued. "Reilly wanted to get rid of all Muslims first, then anyone of dark skin. His dream was to reintroduce the white race and Christianity as a majority and have it reign supreme—"

"But most so-called whites are highly mixed," exclaimed Larry.

"He thought that was propaganda. I took his DNA sample once, and he was part Cherokee, part Scottish, and part black. But of course, I never told him; instead I told him he was pure white. For some reason, he also believed the stories that Regent Sagan was part black, to be false."

"But why did you get involved with him?" Larry asked.

One of the hunter types brought a chair. D'Anjou plopped himself down gratefully. "Back in California, while listening to all of you talk in that congress of yours, I came up with a plan to get rid of Reilly. I had to. What you were all saying was plain nonsense. I figured Reilly would nab or bribe one of two colleagues of mine: Mariella Tonoho of Portugal or Eli Cohen in Israel. It was just a matter of time before he would have my technology through one of them, and I realized how dangerous that would be. But then it dawned on me that if I worked for Reilly, and gained his confidence, I could maneuver the technology to use it against him. So I figured out a plan with a couple of contingencies and given the opportunity I would use one or the other. So I decided to take the risk. But I had to go at it alone. I couldn't tell you, knowing that you would never approved of my plan; besides, all the politics had your hands tied. There was no way I could tell you…or tell Arlene." D'Anjou looked at Arlene for a moment. "I took one of our cargo vans and flew toward my lab in Maryland. I was intercepted by the Patriots shortly after I landed, as I knew I would. I told them I had escaped, and wanted to help them."

Larry studied D'Anjou in disbelief. "Go on, Alphonse."

"Something strange came over me," continued D'Anjou. "It was like I was not myself. I became someone else. Now I know what actors must feel like when they assume another person's identity. I convinced myself that I was a rogue scientist, someone much like the Patriots, that my ideology was superior. I became self-righteous, arrogant. Quite an obnoxious person. Fascinating, really.

"Reilly had long talks with me, and finally decided I was 'for real,' as he put it. He was so glad, he made me an overnight general." D'Anjou looked down at his pants legs and smiled derisively.

"I built new equipment. It was easy; I had unlimited resources. Then I started experiments with Tolima, but there was no way to get any new data. I tried teleporting androids, but never got any information back, even when I sent protective shields with them."

"Did you send them with receiving and sending stations as well?" Larry asked, still studying D'Anjou incredulously.

"Of course. I tried everything. I tried different shields and stations, but as far as I can tell nothing survived. And I was under constant pressure from Reilly and his top aide, General Eagan. I had to show results, or else. It was terrible. The whole affair was one long horrible ordeal. I just knew that one day I would be shot, or worse, tortured if I didn't produce results.

"I witnessed many of Reilly's horrors. He killed many people. But those he hated, he kidnapped and broke them. He had very sophisticated torture equipment. The people he put through it emerged as idiots, automatons. It was a terrible thing." D'Anjou's face contorted into a grimace. "And there was not a thing I could do about it. Had I tried to help someone, or stop the torture, I would have been branded a traitor." D'Anjou stared at the floor. "One of his victims was the poor husband of a woman Reilly had once courted, and I guess she turned him down, because he kept telling her how she had to pay. He put her husband through the torture, and made her watch him turn into an idiot. He planned to kidnap Regent Sagan and torture him while she watched. Evidently she had been one of the Regent's students and thought very highly of him. That's the type of monster that man was." D'Anjou shuddered.

"Then one day, Reilly told me he had killed Cohen and Tonoho. He was really proud. 'We are the only ones who have the technology, General D'Anjou,' he told me. I felt responsible for their deaths; it was a terrible blow, but the shock of their deaths and the knowledge that Reilly had absolutely no ethical boundaries gave me the courage to start on my plan. I had to stop him. I accessed images from a space telescope showing Earth and convinced Reilly it was in fact Tolima, an exact duplicate of Earth."

Larry smiled. "You mean a parallel construct?"

Suzanne's eyes widened and she shook her head.

"Exactly. It was an exact duplicate, and would contain a duplicate of him. I showed him images of New York, Paris, San Francisco; you name it, and told him those were cities in Tolima. I was able to access an infrawave shot from the month before when he met with his generals, and I convinced him the scene was taking place that very moment in Tolima. I told him Tolima was exactly like Earth, except a month behind in time. That what he was seeing was a live image."

Larry laughed. "That's so ridiculous! And he bought it?"

"Ah, yes, I have found people will believe what suits them best." D'Anjou said. "The only person I had trouble convincing was the lab assistant they assigned to me, a former science high school teacher. Eventually I was able to convince him as well, but that took a bit of doing...I basically overwhelmed him with technical information, more than he could understand. Fortunately, he didn't quite understand how the space telescopes worked and what kind of data you could access from them. But I had to be careful that he never saw how I faked those 'live' shots...had he found out, I'm certain I would not be here today. He was smart, but not all that knowledgeable.

"Reilly, on the other hand, was a fool. And he was a desperate man. He was so obsessed with Regent Sagan, it was incredible. After months of chasing after Regent Sagan and not being able to catch him, he became convinced Sagan was the devil himself, and was coming after him, and he wanted the means to escape if necessary. At first Tolima was his escape hatch, but in time it became his secret weapon to defeat Sagan. He stood watching himself and his generals in Tolima, mesmerized. I was lucky Houston was a large file in that particular telescope, and I was able to show him hour after hour of himself, his generals and his army. One time, when he saw one of his generals make a mistake—it had to do with ordering the wrong type of ammunition—he jumped up and said, 'If I could go there, I could stop him from doing that.' And I said, 'Yes, sir.' And he said, 'I knew God would show me the way.' He was jubilant. I never saw him so happy.

"The following morning he had come up with his own theory. He said Tolima was in reality Earth, that the dimension I had tapped into was a 'wrinkle in the space-time continuum,' so that in effect, we were looking literally at ourselves a month in the past. 'What you've done,' he told me as he held up a piece of real paper, then folded it in half and made the ends touch, 'is bring two points in the space-time continuum together. That's all you've done.'

"Reilly started writing down his theory. By the end of the week, he told me his 'discovery,' as he now called it, was God's means for him to defeat the devil and make him invincible and infallible. He ordered me to find the way to travel to that month-old earth. By this point, my assistant, who praised Reilly to no end, was totally sold on the concept, and so was most of the high command.

"I waited three days and I lied again; I told him I was able to send androids. I had had searched the telescope files and found an image of an android I used in my office. Reilly and General Eagan came to my lab. I called the android over, placed it on the sending unit, and teleported it to who-knows-where using the Tolima coordinates. Then I showed them the telescope image of the android. Reilly looked at the picture, studied it for a while, and was satisfied. "Congratulations, General D'Anjou," he said, very pleased. 'But coming back,' I said, 'is not yet possible.' 'No problem,' he told me, 'all we have to do is wait a month.' He laughed and was very proud of himself. 'But Mister President,' I told him, 'whoever we send there would be forever a month behind.' He laughed some more and told me he didn't see anything wrong with that. When I told him he would find his old self there, he smiled. 'Imagine two of me. I can accomplish twice as much!'

"So I manufactured the seventy little boxes you see around this arena. He ordered me to always have them ready to send up to a hundred thousand of his soldiers, 'just in case I want to go back and make some corrections.' Then I had to write his theory down, which he had scribbled down. It was all silly—the musings of a child, but a very arrogant child. I did, and after he made some changes, he published the book under his name and ordered it disseminated throughout Texas. That was going to be the one and only book on astrophysics once he conquered the world."

Larry exchanged glances with Arlene and Suzanne. The hunter types stood commenting among themselves.

D'Anjou pulled out a handkerchief from his pants pocket and wiped his face. "But for the last few days he could think of nothing but Sagan. His men failed to kill Phillipiak's army and he became convinced Sagan was responsible. Taking over the world took a place on the back burner; he wanted Sagan. He was convinced the regent would attack right before the parade with an army and sophisticated weapons. He got ready for the onslaught, and had a crack unit ready." D'Anjou took a long sip of water, and then wiped his mouth with his handkerchief. "When Sagan didn't show up, he became more frantic. But by now he had to go through with the parade, he was counting on it to terrify the world into submission, and he was afraid that if he backed out he would loose his supporters' confidence, those very rich people who had become his high command. He assured them that after the parade he would catch Sagan, execute the kidnapped regents, purge his army, and then march on to New York."

"Oh, that's just wild! Unbelievable!" Larry said. "Why was he so afraid of Regent Sagan? I mean—"

"As I said, he had tried capturing the regent for months, and when he couldn't even find him, he became convinced he was dealing with the devil. The broadcast of four days ago just tipped the paranoia scales. Today, when his army started acting strange and wouldn't respond to his commands, he totally lost it: he screamed 'Sagan is attacking us!' He summoned his high command and his elite guard to join us at the Megadome, then he called for his personal tank and we all made a run for it."

D'Anjou nodded and took another sip. "On the way over Reilly was maniacal. I am certain by then he was completely insane. 'I have a month to prepare,' he told me, his eyes wide, like those of a scared child.

"Once here in the Megadome," D'Anjou said, "he was very anxious to get back to his previous earth. He planned on going to

Canada with all of his five million men and hunt down Sagan before he had a chance to brainwash his army. Then all would be well. In a month he would restage his parade and go on with his conquest. 'No problem, no problem,' he kept saying, 'God has shown me the way.'

Then we heard Regent Sagan's voice booming all over the place, and he was just beside himself, shaking with fear. He, his generals, and his elite guard, quickly lined up in the sending area, ten thousand two hundred and eighty-six all told, and he shouted frantically for me to send them back right away." D'Anjou turned his head away. "I know the process is not ready for interstellar travel...I know that. But...I...I didn't have a choice."

Larry saw pain and regret in D'Anjou's face. At some point Suzanne would tell him of her findings that to teleport anything more than a hundred meters requires a protective vessel...but that would come later. "But why did you set up the actual Tolima coordinates, why not some innocuous destination?" Larry asked.

"I didn't know what else to do. Had I sent them somewhere on earth, they would have been after me in no time at all...and it felt so good when I saw them vanish."

Larry started chuckling. "Okay, that's funny...and tragic. And you probably disintegrated the whole lot."

"There's still a chance they made it to Tolima."

"But tell me, Alphonse, how did you save yourself?"

D'Anjou gave him a sad smile. "It was rather easy: I excluded my energy signature from the teleporter."

As the former Patriot army's three brigades surrounded Colonel Bush's rebel unit, Louis pleaded with Mike to stop what was going on. "What if Bush starts firing?"

"You just don't understand Texans," Mike said. "Once you got a rattlesnake cornered, you got to—"

"Mike," yelled Toney, "come over here."

Louis followed Mike to a lookout window in their flying tank. They had approached the front lines and were supposed to take the "command position," but instead of facing Bush's troops, they were facing thousands and thousands of their own soldiers, all wearing white T shirts. The young men and women faced both ways, and formed a wide buffer zone between both armies. A good many had written "peace" on their shirts, others, "no killing."

Louis, Mike, and the other colonels could see that the "mutineers," as Toney called them, were busy talking to soldiers on Bush's side.

An hour went by. Fifty or so soldiers from Bush's side took off their tunics and came over to the side of the "mutineers." Then twenty more. Some more time went by with no one coming over. Louis could see that the young men and women in white T-shirts were still trying their best to convince Bush's soldiers, but now they were being spat on, and occasionally punched in the face. The "mutineers" were forced to back off.

Bush called Toney in privacy mode. There was some heavy discussion that went on for about thirty minutes. Then Toney hung up and approached Louis.

"He's decided he wants to join President Reilly...or fight. He's given us fifteen minutes before he orders his men to start shooting."

"But he knows that Reilly and the generals abandoned their army!"

"I tried to convince that jerk, but he doesn't believe me. He says that Reilly went to Tolima and he wants to join him. He says his troops feel the same way...I'm telling you, regent, these are hard-core, real fanatics. He called me a traitor, and says that he and his soldiers would rather enjoy killing us."

Louis didn't want casualties, particularly among the so-called mutineers. "I'll make a call...let's see what we can do."

Louis called Larry. He answered right away. In the background, Louis was surprised to see D'Anjou, talking casually with Arlene. "What's happening, Larry?"

"Oh, Louis, do I have a story for you! D'Anjou is quite the hero." And Larry started telling Louis the whole story. "He then fooled Reilly into—"

"Larry, you'll have to tell me later. I have a crisis on my hands. Can we teleport 300,000 soldiers to follow Reilly?" Louis explained to Larry what had happened with Bush and his soldiers.

"Louis, we might be simply atomizing them. We need to develop a vessel to protect them. Their chances of making it are close to nil. It's—"

"I know, Larry. I know. But it's either that or a bloodbath. I would rather see them teleported…it's my decision, and I will take responsibility for it."

"Okay, okay," Larry bit his lower lip. "I understand…" Larry turned around. "Alphonse…" and he talked to him for a while. "Yes, Louis. We can do it, but 100,000 at the time. Send them over."

Louis thought for a moment. Teleporting those people to Tolima could be tantamount to killing them. Rather, he would tell D'Anjou to send them someplace, maybe an island, minus their weapons. Then Police Services could deal with them. Louis turned to Toney. "Tell Bush that he's right; Reilly teleported to Tolima to set up a colony there, and that we will teleport him and his soldiers as well."

Toney called Bush. After a moment he turned around. "He agrees, but the crazy nut claims that Reilly will be back in a month. Apparently he's got a scientist in his brigade that used to work with General D'Anjou and he told Bush all about Tolima."

The lieutenant was waiting for Louis with his motorcycle. They rode ahead of the first group of Bush's soldiers.

About an hour later, and just as Louis, D'Anjou, Larry, and Suzanne were finishing getting the little black boxes and the control panel ready, Bush marched into the arena followed by 100,000 of his soldiers.

He approached Louis and Larry. "I just have to make sure you folks send us to the right place," he said and called a young soldier over. "This is Captain Rice."

A tall and hard looking young man drew near. "Hello, general," he said to D'Anjou.

"Hello, captain," D'Anjou said, then turned to Louis. "Captain Rice was my lab assistant."

Bush told Rice to stand next to D'Anjou. "I never trusted that bastard. Make sure he enters the right address in that gizmo."

Bush turned to watch his first group of soldiers get ready to be teleported. They lined up in formation. Louis studied their faces. They didn't look any different than the mutineers, but there was something about their attitude, or body language, that spoke clearly of hatred and violence. Louis decided he was not sorry to see them go...to wherever they were going.

D'Anjou pushed a button, and they disappeared.

Then it was the second group's turn, and they disappeared just like the first.

The third group of soldiers lined up.

Colonel Bush looked around with his small beady eyes on a vacuous face. Louis decided that the man had probably not had a worthy thought his whole life. Bush observed Louis for a moment, then drew his gun and aimed it at him, his lips curled into a smile.

"I just outsmarted you, you sly, evil bastard. You're coming with us." Bush turned to his men. "We got him. What do ya think, am I going to make general if I bring this here trophy and present it to our president?"

The men raised their weapons and cheered.

Bush was apparently relishing the moment. "Should I kill him first, so he can't pull one of his evil tricks?"

"Yeah, Bushie, kill him!" His soldiers shouted.

Louis felt more perplexed than afraid. He had never experienced anything like it. He could feel the vile, violent excitement from those people. He caught sight of Larry, Suzanne, and D'Anjou. They stood wide-eyed, and pale. Larry had a protective arm around Suzanne's shoulders.

Bush told two of his men to grab Louis, then he pressed the barrel of his gun against Louis's head. Bush laughed. "I like fear." He turned to look at his men. "Now I think I'll make him beg for his life. What do you say?"

"Make him beg, Bushie," someone shouted. The ranks exploded with laughter.

Bush smiled as he put his gun away. "I think I'll reserve that pleasure for our president."

The two burly men dragged Louis to the front of the formation. Bush came up beside him. "Okay, Captain Rice, make sure General D'Anjou pushes the right buttons, and then come join us."

Rice walked backward from D'Anjou, his gun aimed at his chest. He came to stand next to Bush. "Now press that send button," Rice ordered.

Louis hoped that D'Anjou had had enough time to single out his energy and exclude him without Rice noticing.

Then Bush vanished. And so did the rest.

Twenty feet away, D'Anjou, Larry, and Suzanne stood smiling at him.

Louis felt a wave of relief wash over him.

23

The day after the "Great Victory," as the media called it, Louis and Joy had their hands full beginning the process of dismantling the Patriot army, then taking care of the freed regents, along with the other prisoners. Joy had called New York for assistance, and now they had over 5,000 professionals working alongside Texas government officials, in anything that Joy told them to do. Police Services had dispatched five million android officers, "just in case," according to Regent Alonzo Ross. Joy made sure that Regent Ross knew of Louis's and Stephen's decision: no one in Texas was to be reinjected with a biochip, not until their government, or new government, approved.

In the past twenty-four hours Louis had thought long and hard about how they teleported Bush and his army, and that they might have killed the whole lot. He talked it over with Joy. "We don't know what happened to them," Joy said, "they may be in Tolima at this very moment fighting off dinosaurs along with Reilly."

After talking with Suzanne he knew that was a slim possibility, but one he didn't want to dispel.

For now, he had to look after Reilly's victims.

A number of the regents were seriously traumatized, but not as bad as some of the other prisoners. It was then that Louis realized the full scope of Reilly's malevolence: He had turned those he considered his enemies into little more than vegetables using torture, a hundred and sixty-seven persons, all told. Louis asked Joy to make arrangements for their care, see what could be done to help them.

In the evening, Louis, Joy, and Angie sat debriefing D'Anjou. After several hours they realized his whole story was true, and the full scope of what he had done. Louis told Joy to release the information to the press, and in less than an hour D'Anjou became a celebrity. Louis was glad; it took some of the limelight away from him, and D'Anjou deserved the glory: he was a true hero, one who went against all norms and even his own nature to do what he felt was right. But it was still a mystery to them all how he had managed to muster all that courage.

The following day, in spite of the mountain of work they still had to do, they all went to pay their respects to Wendy. Even D'Anjou, when he heard what had happened, insisted on coming.

Wendy's two androids had stood watch over what was left of her to keep away cleanup crews.

Wendy's remains were in the middle of a large empty, flat, and dry expanse interspersed by a few bushes. The crumbling ruins of a housing development stood about half a mile away to the east. The Davis Mountains loomed to the south, lush and green.

Louis had at first come along for Angie and Joy's sake but was surprised by his own emotions. He was actually grieving the passing of a machine. Or perhaps it was Joy's grief he was empathizing with. Still there had been someone named Wendy, not something; objects don't inspire love.

Yogi stood by Jason, who was crying. They had formed a circle around the one end of the car that seemed to have been the front, although it was hard to tell what anything had been, as it was all charred debris. Joy stood by herself, holding a white rose. She cried for some time, then she retold the story of how Wendy had come back after dropping them off for the parade and again stood guard in the front of the hideaway.

"The two boys were sitting on Wendy's floor eating their sandwiches with Yogi and Max, when Wendy sounded the alarm: she told us to go to the back of the hiding place and lie down and be very quiet. She instructed her androids to help me restrain the dogs." Joy took a deep breath. "She had told me she had tapped into a Patriot tank's communications, and was sure Stephen's call to Mike the previous night had been monitored, because they were coming to 'kill Phillipiak.' But she didn't think they knew exactly where we were.

"Jason had started to cry so I used a paralyzing pill on the kids and the dogs. Then I watched as a flying tank made a beeline toward us. I crouched in horror as the craft aimed for the entrance. At that point Wendy shot out at full speed, grazed the craft in the belly and sent it spinning, but it recovered and gave pursuit. Wendy made wild turns, went up and down as they fired missiles. One damaged her, but not severely; it was then when she went straight for the enemy craft. They fired at point-blank range and she appeared to disintegrate in midair, but what was left of her smashed into the tank, and they teetered off and crashed in the desert." She pointed to a place they could barely make out in the distance.

"She saved our lives," Joy sobbed. Angie, who had been standing next to Stephen, came over and hugged her.

One at a time, they each proceeded to place the one white rose they'd brought on the debris; even Stephen, who at first appeared to be merely respectful of Angie's feelings, seemed to be moved. His voice cracked when he said good-bye and placed his rose right by Angie's, on top of a tangle of wires.

When it was Louis's turn, he muttered, "Thank you, Wendy," and it felt right. Most everyone was crying.

Only Suzanne seemed to be oblivious. She went around turning over charred pieces of debris with a stick, which made Joy angry, but Suzanne just kept digging. She found something, examined it, and put it away in her pocket.

On their way to Statford to use D'Anjou's machines to restore their former appearance, Stephen turned to Louis. "That's quite an experience, grieving over a car. Do you think we are just projecting? Or was Wendy really alive?"

"I don't know, Stephen," Louis said. "But I'm grieving."

"Ha!" exclaimed Joy. "Wendy possessed more self-awareness than a lot of people I've run across. I would've rather talked to her than that idiotic Reilly, or Gary. In my mind those people were automatons, while Wendy was good and decent, the true mark of humanity."

"Something worth studying," Larry said.

"Oh, go study your ass," Joy said, holding David in her arms. The two boys were very sad, both on the verge of tears. "We lost a dear friend and all you can think of is your precious science. And you," she said, looking at Suzanne, who sat by Larry dozing, "you have no feelings. How dare you look for souvenirs in the wreckage. That's horrible!"

The following day, after returning from Statford, Louis went to visit the liberated regents. They had been taken from the concentration camp and moved into a Houston hotel. Relatives, friends, other regents, members of the press; they all crowded the hotel lobby, but made way for him. Everyone took special measures to show their respect for Louis; it was as though they didn't quite know what to make of him, how to treat him. But he knew that in time they would forget and he would be semi-anonymous again, lost in the crowd of regents.

Louis entered a big reception room where the rescued regents were being interviewed by the press. The room fell into a hush when he walked in. Marta, the regent who had played a key role in swaying the board of regents to try and appease the Patriots, with such terrible consequences, was talking to a television reporter. She had just arrived from New York with a group of government officials, most of whom stood around her.

"It was nobody's fault," she said deliberately louder than necessary. "I don't blame Regent Sagan, even though the Patriots came under his jurisdiction, it was his project..."

Louis felt anger starting in the pit of his stomach, and his pulse quickened. He took a moment and made an effort to speak calmly. "Marta," he said, and at this she turned in his direction and so did everyone in the vicinity. "It's easy enough for anyone to review the process and determine who is at fault. All proceedings are public record." At this he watched her recoil as though trying to hide. "In fact, with the fatalities involved, we have to review what happened, how those people died, and who was responsible. Also, how the decision to relinquish Texas to the Patriots was made. The constitution demands it." Everyone in the room was now following the exchange. "But I didn't come here to accuse you or defend myself, merely to see how all the kidnapped regents are." Louis continued with dozens of cameras now focused on him. "We will need to make many changes in the government; one would involve security, so something like this can't happen again. Another will be how we will accommodate the needs of the citizens of Texas and places like it. We also need to review how we approach the whole concept of atavism."

Marta did not respond, and after a moment moved away with her retinue of government officials.

Louis went around the room talking to the various regents and their families who crowded around them. Television cameras followed his every move.

He walked out into the hallway, shooed the reporters away, and took a deep breath. It seemed everything rested on his shoulders and required his immediate attention: reconvening the board of regents, opening the Texas borders, determining what to do with D'Anjou's technology, whether finding a new habitable planet should be top priority, whether they should keep trying Tolima, what really happened to Reilly and his generals, and what to do with the Patriots?

Louis called Joy on his phone. "Joy, I'm near the hotel hospitality room where most of the kidnapped regents are being interviewed. Where are you?"

"I'm..." she hesitated, "I'm very busy...and..."

"What about Angie? I need help; I need someone to work with me."

"Right, Louis. I'll have Angie call you right away."

In a moment his phone rang. It was Angie. "I'm back in New York, Louis." Her voice was terse and she looked sad. "I decided to get back to work as soon as I could."

"Right. I'll be heading that way in a few days...how about Stephen?"

"He's still there...I don't care...he's with Joy probably." She spit out the words.

Clearly they were no longer a couple. "I don't know what happened between the three of you, but I need you to work closely with both of them."

"I'm aware of that." She bit her lower lip. "Don't worry. I'll manage to get my feelings out of the way in due course, but for now, I'm happy to be back in my office. By the way, things are a mess with the government. The regents are clamoring for a congress to reorganize. All told sixty-seven regents were killed and 1,237 were kidnapped. Out of this group we question the ability to perform of over three hundred who are in various stages of recovery. First tiers have temporarily filled the vacant positions, but things are still a mess."

Louis became aware of a television crew trying to eavesdrop. He waved them away. "Okay. We'll get everything done," Louis said, noticing Angie was now looking at him as before. Gone were the furtive, critical looks. "We are not an atavist society, Angie; we need but minimum government. We'll do just fine. Twenty years ago we used to run the world with three hundred of us. I'll come to New York when I can, but first I have to meet with Sharon."

A moment later as he walked down the hall his phone rang again. It was Joy.

"Sorry, Louis. What is it you need?"

He asked for information about the Patriots and the army, whether someone was in charge. Yes, she had placed Police Services in charge and they were working with some of Stephen's personnel. He told her he was leaving for Hawaii to see Sharon.

"Louis...that's great news. You two will get back together?"

"I don't think so, Joy. If she left me once, she can leave me again, and I don't want to take that risk."

"But she knows she made a horrible mistake, and she wants to set it right."

Louis realized the women had talked. "Right now I just want to find closure. We never said a proper good-bye, and after a lifetime together we should at least do that. I best find a car."

"See you tonight for dinner?"

"Sure."

He went back to the hospitality room and began visiting the kidnapped regents. He noticed doctor types talking to some of them.

"They are mental health specialists," he heard a voice behind him say. He turned around to find Stephen, looking at ease. "Most of them are psychologists, which might be good; at this stage we need more counselors than physicians."

Louis smiled and shook his hand. "How are you doing, Stephen?"

"Good. And not so good. I just found my friend Jorge from Houston. He was tortured and they made a mess of him. But he's amazingly resilient. Must be because he's a meditator. I also visited the families of my followers who were killed, forty-seven all together."

"I'm sorry, Stephen."

Stephen lowered his gaze. "Yes, so am I. We can celebrate our victory, and many people are, but for the thirty-two families of those forty-seven people killed, the world has ended. They are in mourning and I will personally miss a good many of them."

"Yes. We also have many regents who were killed. We are not used to people dying violently. In another day and age, that was commonplace, now we have to learn how to cope.

"I'm going to visit the former hostages. Care to join me?"

They made their way through the large room. Artificial windows looked out to scenic landscapes of mountains, green fields, and lakes. You could feel the breeze and smell flowers and trees. There were fishermen on one of the lakes. The "natural" light from the windows flooded the room.

Louis and Stephen talked with the kidnapped regents, most of whom were visibly shaken, some even heavily traumatized, according to Stephen. People made way for them when they saw the two approach—doctors, nurses, reporters, government officials, and family members all stood to one side. The regents sat in mobile chairs and were hooked up to every type of monitor and scanner. They thanked them both profusely. Everyone knew what had happened in every detail, which seemed to vary a bit. They all wanted to meet D'Anjou and thank him as well.

They were done with their visits by evening. The following morning the recovering regents would fly back to their homes, some under a totally unnecessary police escort. A good many talked of retirement, but most vowed to be back at work within a week.

That night, Stephen and Joy, Louis, D'Anjou and Arlene, Larry and Suzanne, and Angie, who and come from New York at Joy's request, had dinner together in a restaurant in the hotel. Yogi lay by Louis's feet, and Max lay by the young boy David. The manager had insisted the dogs come in when Joy made the reservation.

All around them other diners did their best not to stare, but there were many muffled conversations with furtive looks in their direction. When Yogi made his way to one of the tables and Louis made to call him, one of the women called out: "He's no trouble, regent, honestly. It's an honor."

Louis was surprised at seeing Stephen and Joy together as an apparent couple, and wondered how it all came about so quickly.

They talked about the kidnapped regents, and how close the government came to total chaos. It was obvious the government had come very close to collapsing, all because of one man. But Reilly and his goons were now gone.

"And they were all turned into energy waves," exclaimed Stephen in between forkfuls of enchilada. He smiled in D'Anjou's direction. "That was quite a ruse you pulled, Alphonse."

D'Anjou smiled and blushed. Arlene held his hand.

"Yes," Louis said. "I thought for sure he was one of them."

"Go figure," Stephen said.

"I never did," Arlene said.

"I do feel a little guilty, though," said Louis, "at how relieved I feel that we managed to get rid of the worst of the worst of the atavists...I should feel remorse for atomizing well over 300,000 people, but..."

"Louis..." began Joy, "please. Don't feel guilty. For one, there's a slim chance they made it to Tolima; second...those were really bad people!"

"And..." added Larry, "you didn't do it. They did it to themselves. I call it poetic justice."

"Well, I did say a little guilty...not a lot."

They toasted D'Anjou. They looked at him in wonder. Just observing him, his manners...what he did was so incongruous, but he did it nevertheless.

"Speaking of the government," Larry said, staring at his plate of burritos, rice, and beans, "It's all turmoil out there. The government is trying to come together while the public is clamoring for D'Anjou's technology. Everyone has a father or uncle who's dying. We need to act—"

"I know, Larry, I know," Louis said, trying to sound reassuring, but he felt a knot in his stomach. "We'll figure things out. For now, let's just enjoy our victory. We no longer have the Patriots to worry about. Let's celebrate."

They raised their glasses and toasted. It was clearly an immense relief to be rid of that monster, they knew it, and the world surely knew it as well. Things could wait.

"I'm leaving for Hawaii in the morning," Louis told them. "I'll go straight to New York from there."

"How long will you be gone?" Stephen asked.

"Oh, two days. Will I see you in New York?"

Stephen looked at Joy and smiled. "You'll see me there all right, but not straight away. I need to make sure Texas is in capable hands first."

"The Texas congress and president seem to have things under control," Louis said.

Stephen gave Louis a sideways glance as he sipped his beer. "You mean the congress and the president you guys manipulated for so many years and ended up pushing aside when you gave Texas to the Patriots? Well, my friend, I just have to make sure that can't happen again."

"We can work on that together, Stephen. Let's figure things out."

"I think we'll work things out between us Texans, and let you know what we decide. How's that?"

Louis hesitated. "Well, obviously the board of regents would want Texas to be part of our government, but I'm sure we can come to some accord that will satisfy everyone."

Stephen responded with a wry smile. "It's going to be an interesting process, to say the least. While you, personally, are held in high esteem by people in Texas, your government isn't. People figure the government will just go on, unchanged."

"Oh, no way, Stephen; we need to make many changes…what happened, how the government acted, was inexcusable."

"Yes, it was. But what most Texans think, is that you will issue a proclamation that things were handled badly, but then the same regents who blundered will continue on, and ultimately not much will change. The board of regents wants things to remain as they are, and your citizens are well trained to follow passively. Nothing much will happen. I will bet on that."

Larry seemed uncomfortable with the conversation. He played with his wineglass, twirling the red liquid inside every which way. "At what time are you leaving tomorrow?" he asked.

Louis placed his fork and knife on his plate. "Oh, around noon, I think. I need a car. Transportation Central promised to deliver something by late morning."

Larry exchanged knowing glances with Suzanne. "Can we all meet in your room at eleven? We have a surprise for you."

Louis gave him an inquisitive look. "Sure, Larry, eleven will be fine. I can leave right after. See you then."

Louis smiled, stood and walked to an elevator and his room. Yogi, who had meandered somewhere in the restaurant, showed up and followed him, cream sauce all over his snout. Louis thought of Sharon. It would feel right to formally end the relationship and for both of them to go on with their lives. He had talked with her briefly on the phone the day before. She had cried, and he told her how "touched" he was that she still cared about him. At this she cried some more and said, "You have no idea," a little annoyed perhaps, and asked him to come and see her. He had much to do, he told her, explaining that "the government is in chaos." But she persisted. "Please, Louis. In the name of what we once meant to each other, please come." He acquiesced; he could spare a couple of days. If she hoped for reconciliation, he would have to tell her it was too late; he was now certain the hurt he felt was centered on a sense of betrayal, and he couldn't trust her anymore. When he tried to visualize being together again, it just didn't feel right. Going to Hawaii was just to see her one more time, wish her well, and go on with his life.

In the morning, following a long meditation and breakfast, Louis showered and shaved with Yogi ambling in and out of the bathroom. The steam in the bathing stall felt good. After the ultralights dried him off, he asked for soothing lavender oil, something he had learned about from Sharon.

He dressed in black slacks and a temperature-regulating white shirt. Hawaii was supposed to be hot and humid. Then he heard the room's front door open and the familiar voices of Joy, Stephen, and Larry. He looked at the bathroom clock. It was ten minutes till eleven.

He came out to greet them. They stood in the living room waiting for him, looking refreshed and relaxed.

"Wow!" exclaimed Joy. "Sharon will be swept off her feet!" She had the youngest boy by the hand, who in turn held on tight to Max. "Come here, you hunk; give me a hug."

Louis smiled and obliged. She smelled of perfume and her manner had changed with her new boyfriend: she was softer, more feminine.

He assumed that Larry would announce that he and Suzanne were getting married. He could detect that something was different in Larry's demeanor; he seemed happy and expectant, like a child. Very uncharacteristic.

"Well, Larry, they promised my new car will be here soon, and I have to leave in about an hour. Let's have it."

Larry smiled. "That's pretty much why we are here." He pressed the phone in his pants pocket, and a shape slid into view outside the window. It was a car, the same model as Wendy. In fact, it looked exactly like Wendy, same silver shape and everything.

To his surprise Louis felt a lump in his throat. It was a sweet thought; Larry had managed to find the same model. Louis heard the gasps in the room coming from Joy and the kids.

The car docked, and it opened its doors just as the hotel window slid open. Louis followed the rest into the car, and he felt sorry for the kids. He knew Larry meant well, but they expected

314

Wendy, and instead they were walking inside something that looked like her but wasn't her.

Louis caught sight of Joy. She was looking around the car with tears in her eyes. Oh my, he thought, Larry was about to hurt them all over again, this time with disappointment.

He braced himself. The familiar lights on the panel flickered the way Wendy's used to, to tell him everything was fine…and the scent and looks of the car were exactly like Wendy's, something she apparently had been able to control.

"Welcome, my friends," he heard Wendy's familiar voice. Oh no, now he's gone too far, Louis thought.

"I know what you are thinking, Regent Sagan, but it's me, Wendy. I assure you."

Louis heard himself chuckle, and felt butterflies in his stomach.

"Suzanne managed to rescue my brain from the wreckage. When I hit the flying tank and it started after me, I realized that I would be shot down no matter what I did, so I decided to let the missile hit me, and I froze my brain—"

"That means," interjected Larry smiling at a very surprised Louis, "that she withdrew all power from her brain circuits so the electromagnetic pulses from the missile would not find it. She knew the blast itself would not damage it, but electromagnetic impulses would. When Suzanne dug the brain from the wreckage and inspected it, she couldn't detect any damage, but she wasn't certain, and she didn't want to build up our expectations, so she kept the news to herself. It was only when we got to the hotel, and after she had examined it thoroughly, that she told me.

"We decided to surprise all of you, but the process surprised us both. Once we connected Wendy's brain to a voice synthesizer, she asked us to provide her with an industrial manufacturing unit. We procured one and when we connected her brain to it she proceeded to rebuild herself in two hours. Then she spent the last six doing diagnostics and reprogramming herself."

"I was counting on Suzanne finding my brain," Wendy added. "Her personality profile predicted she would."

Louis sat down on one of the seats, shaking his head in disbelief. He watched as the two boys talked to Wendy, all excited. Joy was no better. Wendy talked to Joy soothingly, as a woman would talk to another, offering a cup of coffee...and cookies. There was no question; those were two friends finding each other again. Joy cried nonstop.

D'Anjou and Arlene sat holding hands and smiling.

Stephen sat opposite Louis with a quizzical look on his face, perhaps not quite knowing how to react. Suzanne stood beside Larry listening intently and studying those around her.

"Quite an extraordinary feat," Louis said, smiling at Larry and Suzanne. "And thank you both. Wendy...I'm very glad to have you back...we all are." After saying that, he felt awkward, maybe a little embarrassed; but that was fine.

24

Louis left for Hawaii two hours late to allow everyone to celebrate properly, including Wendy. On his return to New York, he would talk with Stephen and Angie about the Patriots, he would meet with Joy about summoning a new congress, and he would talk with D'Anjou, Larry, and Suzanne about space exploration, but for the next two days, he would meet with Sharon.

"Let's go see Sharon, Wendy," he told her as he sat down and watched her buckle him down. Louis bent down to pet Yogi, who was lying by his feet.

"Very well, Regent Sagan. We'll be there in two hours and forty-five minutes...I made a cup of coffee just the way you like it." One of her androids made its way over with a tray bearing a cup. Louis picked up the cup and took a sip. Ah, french roast, cream with two sugars.

Houston's skyline fell from view and all he could see were clouds, but then an urgent report flashed on his window, which had instantly become a display.

Votes were coming in from all over the world. Someone had started a public mandate to force the government to release D'Anjou's technology right away for healing and rejuvenation. The government had twenty-four hours to deliver teleporting stations to every major city. Louis shook his head. There was no way they could act that fast without doing some studies and the necessary prep work. Louis watched in dismay as the votes piled up and reached over ten billion, an overwhelming mandate. They had no choice.

That was the first time in the government's history that a public mandate had been issued. Louis stared at the display. How could people be so stupid? Then he thought how desperate he had been to save Sharon. Yes, of course. A lot of people have an ill or dying father, mother, or grandparent. But it was so rash. While he was still lost in thought, another mandate took off. This time the public had taken the matter of the Patriots into their own hands. The votes were again coming in fast. People had reviewed the government's proceedings of the past year regarding the Patriots and Reilly, Texas, and Louis's papers, and had come to the conclusion that Marta was to blame. She alone was mostly responsible for the failure of the government to protect its regents, and for the rash decision to surrender Texas to the Patriots.

Louis sighed; there was nothing he or anyone else could do. He watched as the votes were tabulated and again reached their dismal climax: well over eight billion. Poor Marta. He wondered what would become of her, with a public censure that big, the humiliation would be horrible. Obviously she was not going to be a regent anymore. After that, the public voted to censure seventeen additional regents for incompetence. They, too, would be dismissed immediately from their duties.

That was so unprecedented. First the public mandate to release the rejuvenation-curing technology and now the censure. History in the making…theory had become stark reality. One thing for sure, from then on the public was certain to be more involved. Louis wondered how the government would handle the developments. Well, he would soon find out; certainly his phone would start ringing at any moment. He wished the public had waited and allowed the regents to conduct their own processes. Maybe the results would have been the same, but not as rash. D'Anjou's technology would be released in due course; probably within a year, and Marta and the others would have had a chance to defend themselves. Oh well.

He called Stephen. He and Joy were sitting in their hotel suite's living room. "Stephen, have you heard?"

"Yes, yes!" Stephen was jubilant; Joy subdued, and perhaps worried.

"The people have acted. They have balls!" a smiling Stephen said.

"Yes, you can call it that. I just wanted to make sure you knew things are changing."

"You bet. Now you can count me in, Louis. Let's talk when you get back."

"I look forward to it."

Louis clicked off the display and told Wendy to block all further communications. He settled down to think about Sharon and to rehearse what he needed to tell her: how much he had cherished being married to her, and that they would remain friends, but now they must both go their separate ways, maybe find other partners…for him, someone more loyal. But of course he wouldn't say that.

"Regent Sagan," the familiar voice woke him up. Louis had no idea he had dozed off. "We'll be landing in fifteen minutes. Enough time for you to freshen up…maybe brush your hair?"

Louis looked at his reflection in the window. His hair was tousled and his shirt a bit undone. "Thanks for the thought, Wendy, but I think I look fine."

"There's mouthwash in my restroom, regent. Just in case you want to use it."

"Thanks just the same, Wendy. I'm just fine."

"Maybe another cup of coffee?"

Louis shook his head, chuckling. "Maybe I'll wash my face, after all." The seat belts came off and Louis stood up and made his way to the washroom. When he opened the bathroom door, he was surprised to find a fresh shirt hanging neatly on a hanger.

"That's Regent Willcott's favorite color on you, Regent Sagan," Wendy said.

Oh my, Louis said to himself. He washed his face. He brushed his hair, used the mouthwash, took off his shirt, threw it down on the floor, and exchanged it for the light blue one Wendy had offered. "Thanks. Very thoughtful of you." And he realized it didn't feel so strange anymore to be interacting with a machine, but that fact left so many questions that begged answers.

Wendy landed on a wide expanse of grass. A volleyball court was nearby. Banana, papaya, citrus, avocado trees, and a variety of flowers and herbs grew profusely all around. Louis had to put on his sunglasses as he walked out of the car with Yogi right behind. The sun seemed brighter than in Texas, the colors vivid and something of a shock.

Sharon stood some paces away dressed in dark blue shorts and a flimsy white blouse. She looked at him for a moment and rushed over. She kissed him on the mouth, hard, and held him for some time.

Louis was surprised by his own emotions. She was very dear to hold, but there was still hurt...he didn't want to open up to her. Better be safe, he told himself, although that kiss and hug were like heaven.

They walked hand in hand in the direction of some cabins surrounded by a garden. To the left was a big building, "the main house" as Sharon called it. People dressed in gardening clothes, some in bathing suits, others in white robes, were all over the sumptuous gardens. "Let's get you settled down," she told him. "Do you want your own cabin, or would you stay with me?" There was hesitation in her voice, and an underlying plea.

"I'll stay with you, if you don't mind, Sharon. We don't have much time, just two days; let's make the best of it."

She nodded and led him to a cabin made of natural wood that stood alone in a nook of the garden. It had a wide veranda all around. Flowers, herbs, and bushes of some sort—a well-tended garden—grew in front of it. The scent was subtly fragrant. The air was soft, not dry and harsh as in Texas, but warm and caressing.

Yogi led the way into Sharon's cabin and started exploring. Louis found himself in a small living room with a couch, two chairs, and a coffee table in the middle. The carpet was light blue. A generous bay window looked out into the garden. Behind the living room was a kitchenette and dining area. To one side was a French door that apparently led to the bedroom. Oscar winked a greeting from one of the chairs and was soon being sniffed unceremoniously by Yogi.

Sharon made her way to the kitchen, her manner tense, ill at ease. "Can I offer you some coffee, or would you prefer a juice?" She stood in front of the kitchen console, her eyes tentative, her lithe figure young and vibrant.

Louis had followed her partway to the kitchen and stood in the dining area. "Juice would be good, thanks." It felt strange being formal with Sharon.

She made her way to the living room and sat down, curling a leg under her on a plush chair. Louis sat opposite her. He watched as the kitchen android, an Asian-looking woman, brought him a tall glass on a tray. Yogi decided to lay down halfway between them, just like in old times.

The juice was wonderful, full of intriguing tastes.

"Can you hear the doves?" she asked suddenly with a wistful smile.

It took a moment for Louis to figure out what she was talking about. He paid attention to the sounds outside and heard a soft cooing, which did sound sad. He chuckled. "You remembered the writer's mourning doves!"

They listened to the doves cooing back and forth, perhaps a mating call. It was beautiful, and he could now understand how the writer as a child would find the sound soothing, as though they were reaching out to him.

"Thank you," he said. "That's wonderful."

Sharon stared into his eyes, a sad and contemplative look. "Louis...I am so very sorry for what I did and said back in California...I should have stayed with you...when I heard the news from Texas and realized you were in the middle of the whole affair, I just wanted to die." At this, tears formed in her eyes.

Louis stared at the glass in his hand. "You have no obligation to me, Sharon. What happened in Texas was my choice. I chose to be there. You chose to come here and lead your own life, apart from me. That's fine."

Sharon swept her hair back with one hand and held it back, her elbow resting on the back of the chair, exposing the tall and smooth forehead. "That's not what I meant," her eyes were now lost on a spot to Louis's right. "I wasn't speaking of my responsibility as a partner. What I meant is that I wanted so badly to be by your side...thought I wanted to be on my own, apart from you, to lead my own life, but that was not the case."

Louis felt his resentment intensify, it was like a lump in the pit of his stomach and he wanted to spit it out...at her. "I still don't understand how you can profess love for me, how after fifty years together—"

"I know, I know!" she said her voice rising. She dropped her face into her hands, and cried softly. She shook her head. "You have no idea what I have been going through!" She looked at him with tearful ayes. "I made a rash, foolish decision...can we somehow put it behind us?" And Sharon told him how she had arrived at the retreat center and found a warm welcome. The director, who knew who she was, suggested she take on a spiritual name, that way people would not be treating her as "Regent Sharon Willcott," but as Mukhti, a young woman in search of herself.

Everything was peaceful and joyous just as she had envisioned, but even back then she started to realize she had been rash. Maybe a part of her had expected Louis to fight for her, to talk her into staying with him. "But when you didn't, Lalo; when you acquiesced so quickly to my leaving, I was extremely surprised, in shock, and deeply hurt…so I convinced myself it was all for the best, and I tried to embark on my new life. That lasted about a week before I realized how much I loved you…and what a colossal mistake I had made. Then the news broke about the Patriots, Reilly, and D'Anjou and you and me…and I was…beside myself. I knew I needed to be with you, to face this together as we had always done before; but you were out of reach. My only consolation was Wendy; she kept me apprised of what was going on—"

"Wendy?"

"Yes, Wendy. She contacted me ten days after I left and volunteered to keep 'an eye on your husband,' as she put it. I knew she was there to protect you, and I was so glad for the lifeline, I decided not to question anything. But then she stopped communicating, and I thought the worst had happened.

"Those were terrible days. I couldn't stop worrying about you. I felt so torn inside. I felt small…I had betrayed you…I'm terribly sorry," Sharon said amid gentle sobs and then wiped her nose with a tissue. "It was the meditation, support, and nurturing in this place that kept me going; otherwise I would have lost my mind. Some days I felt as though I would go over the edge, into some place of anguish; but then I would attend one of their kirtans and my spirit would soar. I would then come home, go into deep meditation, and be at peace. But the cycle would repeat itself again and again. That is until I heard from Wendy again.

"I will have to give her a big hug somehow.

"People here soon realized who I was; after all, they saw my picture in the news; but amazingly, no one made a fuss, instead they made a concerted effort to make my life as normal as possible. You know, the fact that I am your wife was quite a stir, but not as much as what I represented, my young and healthy body. But after a while all of that seemed to fade away. I overheard one of the residents warn a newcomer: 'we have a very famous person here, but we try our best to let her lead a normal life, so please pretend like she's just another regular person. We call her Mukhti.'

"That's how these people are, Lalo. They are of another world. And although I love my life here, I want to be with you."

Louis was quiet for some time, staring at the inch or so of liquid that remained in his glass, that marvelous golden juice. "I'm the same person you left, Sharon. Right now I should be in New York, and will leave as soon as I can. There are so many problems I have to deal with. Then I have to prepare myself for space travel. I need to reach Tolima, and right now I'm the best candidate, and I'm obligated. I'm the one who precipitated the whole thing; our population is about to explode and we need to reach another earth."

Sharon looked at him in alarm, her eyes wide. "What are you talking about? You...you going to Tolima? Are you crazy?"

Grateful for the break in the conversation, Louis told Sharon about D'Anjou's and Suzanne's latest findings, the dimensions, and his own forays into meditation to reach the Diva sequence.

Sharon listened intently, then started laughing, a happy laugh. "Oh, you! So that's what it took to get you to meditate! And of course, you had to do it on a grand scale.

"From what you're telling me, you reached an amazing state, a form of Samadhi...and you call it the Diva sequence?"

"Yes. Diva has a predominance of the Alma energy, which D'Anjou identified as the origin of it all. Everything, all creation comes from that energy. Alma is everywhere, but it's unobservable, at least that's what D'Anjou and Suzanne have found."

At that she told him about how the ancient Rishis, the wise men of India, had found much the same. "I believe D'Anjou's seven energies correspond to the seven chakras Hindus and Buddhists have known about for thousands of years."

And they talked as in the old days, when they discussed one of their projects.

"So you found God, Lalo," she said after he described one of his experiences in meditation.

"What do you mean? I was just able to transform and fit into what I think is a high end of the Diva sequence. What does that have to do with God?"

Sharon leaned back and beamed him her beautiful smile. "If as you say, Diva has more of the Alma energy, which to humanity is God, then you met God."

Louis smiled. "Well...that makes sense. Those who have experienced Alma would have to call it something. Of course, they would call it God. It fits. But is that what God is, energy?"

"I would call the energy a physical manifestation. At one point you feel intense, overwhelming love and you realize what you have found is so much more; best not to try and understand it. Keep your scientific mind away from it."

Louis was thoughtful for a moment. "You know, Shari, I hesitate calling what I experienced 'God.' To me it has a negative connotation, reminds me of all of those fanatics."

"So don't call what you experienced anything. Buddhists don't believe in God. They, like you, believe in a state of attainment. They've done just fine."

Sharon stood up and came to stand beside him, her arms dangling in front of her with fingers intertwined. Her manner now relaxed. "But now that you know what we are all after, I have a gift for you."

"A gift?"

"Yes, Lalo. A gift. Let's meditate together, and you'll see. When two people join together, it can be so much stronger than on your own."

She called Wendy on her phone and asked her to send an android to take Yogi back. He was bound to get restless. The android came, but she continued talking to Wendy for a few minutes in whispers. She then put Oscar outside the cabin. Sharon took Louis by the hand and led him to the bedroom and the ample bed in the middle. She changed into a silk robe, as natural as she had always been with him, slipped her naked body into the silk, then turned around and sat in the middle of the bed in the lotus posture. She patted the covers in front of her. "Come sit with me, Lalo."

Louis obliged, sat with legs crossed, and then dragged a pillow to sit on. He watched her close her eyes. He could tell she was going deep into meditation, could feel the wonderful energy. He followed suit and felt immediately transported to a very deep state. At first, he was aware of her presence, but then that melted away…there was nothing but a deep peace, which made way to a feeling of joy that seemed to explode in his chest…he saw a strong white light and heard a vibrating sound…he seemed to become one with the sound and the light, and was aware of ever expanding…and he felt his mind stopping…

He opened his eyes and discovered many hours must have passed because it was already dark. Without question he had been radically transformed; the feeling inside and all around him was absolutely marvelous…indescribably so…beyond his mind's ability to comprehend. It definitely felt like love, or something close to it. She was right; it was like nothing he had experienced on his own. And he realized where he had been was intimately familiar…the love had that sense of reunion, of coming home.

He understood…rather, felt the connection, the oneness…he could now feel…feel what he realized was all of creation…and it was a part of him…

Together they had just brought the entire world a little closer to the Alma sequence; they had just changed the world ever so slightly. And he was only beginning.

In the twilight he could see Sharon had opened her eyes and was lovingly looking at him. "How was that for you?" she said with a hint of a laugh, perhaps amused by the unintended sexual innuendo.

326

"Marvelous." He felt an intense love for her, and knew they would be together. There was no way he would leave her.

"Well, then I have more I want to share with you tomorrow morning."

She told him that at six in the morning, there would be a World Meditation, where about four billion people would come to meditate together for three hours using virtual media. "Tomorrow will be different. You know my essence, so you had no problem meditating with me. Tomorrow you'll find yourself having to accept the people around you, and that can be a challenge, but when you do, oh boy! Is that powerful!"

"Four billion?" he said, mesmerized. "You can gather that many people who meditate?"

"Oh, many more meditate, Lalo. That's just the size of our convocation, the people who are fully dedicated to their meditation practice and decided to join our effort to change the world."

He could barely see her face in the twilight. "Are you saying four billion people do nothing but meditate?"

"No, that's not accurate. Most of them also do other things. They have jobs or businesses; but yes, meditation is their focus in life…as it's mine."

Louis thought for a moment. The concept was staggering. That many people meditating would have a tremendous impact on the world's energy. He had no idea…wait until D'Anjou and Suzanne hear about this…"Wow, that's a startling concept. Can I meet some of them?"

Sharon smiled. She could almost hear Lalo's wheels turning. "This evening at dinner time you can meet the thousand or so who are staying here, the 'convocation coordinators'… leaders and organizers of groups across the world. I'm sure they'll be delighted to meet you, Lalo; you are quite the celebrity, and they'll be so thrilled to hear how you became a deep meditator. That's just so much like you!

"In addition, for tomorrow's meditation, we'll have about five thousand from all over the world, in person, and billions in virtual form."

Sharon scooted off the bed and stood up. Louis could see the outline of her body against the faint light coming from the bedroom window, a beautiful slim figure in shimmery silk.

"Let's have some tea," she offered. "Dinner in the main house is still more than an hour away."

Louis stood up. His knees were not used to the lotus posture. He felt stiff as he followed Sharon into the living room. "Four billion! More than a quarter of the world's population, pursuing a life of—"

"Meditation? Yes. Since we became aware of the terrible events in Texas, we decided to do something about it. It all started six months ago when one of our coordinators in Houston, Jorge Collizo, called for the first convocation in Los Angeles."

"Jorge Collizo? I met him; he got arrested by the Patriots. He's the one who started this—"

"You met him? What a small world! Yes, he called for the first gathering. We expected two billion to show up in real and virtual form, and we got almost four billion! Since then, our numbers have remained consistent, and for the past four months we have been meditating together for three hours every day."

They had an herbal tea that reminded Louis of their many evenings together years ago. She used to lure him into their sitting room back in their New York condo, no matter what he was doing, and despite his protestations, had his cup of tea waiting for him on a side table; she dressed in her house clothes. And this time her silk robe that hinted softly of her femininity reminded him so much of those days of their youth... their other youth.

She seemed gloriously at ease. They sat again in the big comfy chairs and again she curled one leg under her. Her house had turned on soft lighting that emulated candles. She asked more about D'Anjou's experiments and what Suzanne had concluded. "You know you'll never get inside the Alma sequence with any device," she said, "but if you did, you would discover the equivalent of another infinite set of energies—"

"You know them? Have you tapped into Alma?"

"Yes, and so have you. There's no doubt."

Then they talked about their youth, and reminisced for a while. Louis found he was more than ever in love with her, or maybe just realized they were entering into a new way of relating, one that was so much clearer.

He noticed she was staring at him and that her eyes had grown moist. "What are you thinking about, Lalo?" Her voice carried a certainty. She knew.

"I think I want us to be together…but I still have to fix what I broke."

Sharon started to cry. She had tears flowing freely down her cheeks. "I know. You did it for me, but even if you hadn't, I would still want to help you. Can we work on this together?" She looked down, wiped her tears, and when she looked up again her eyes were soft and tender.

"It's such a big challenge, Shari. We do need to reach Tolima, or some world like it. In only two years, without anyone dying as they are supposed to, the world's population will reach over twenty billion again, and it's exponential from then on. I created a big problem."

She stood from her chair and came over and neatly sat down on his lap, like a cat, soft and warm. She put her arms around his neck and stared into his eyes. "We are together, Lalo, and that's all that matters to me right now. Tomorrow you will see how we fix problems around here."

They went to dinner at the main house. They walked into a huge hall arranged with many round tables. Well over a thousand people stood in small groups, talking, drinking from glasses and cups, and laughing softly. When Louis walked in escorted by Sharon, who held his hand, the room went quiet, and then it broke into polite applause. Following many introductions, a young man, who Sharon introduced as the community director, asked Louis to give a talk, tell them how he'd changed as a result of his challenge in Texas. And Louis told them the story, but he went beyond what the press knew, he talked about his meditation experience, and how he now knew it helped him face the challenges in Texas, "even though it never helped me use teleportation."

After he answered questions, Louis and Sharon sat at a table with ten others, directors from centers in New York, Paris, Buenos Aires, and elsewhere, including Jorge Collizo. What impressed Louis was the general feeling he got that while they thought he was very accomplished, those accomplishments were not largely consequential. Even the role he played in defeating the Patriots was acknowledged but without the awe and hero status he had received in Houston. One woman, whom Sharon called Lani, summed it up by saying "you did very well by the world."

And Louis understood. In their minds the real work had been accomplished through meditation.

The feeling in that room was certainly wonderful; Louis could tell he was in the company of people who went deep in meditation, but maybe they were taking themselves way too seriously. Maybe this was where the scientist parted ways with the mystic. Louis thought of the specific day when the Patriots had been defeated. It had been Larry's virtual scenario that had neutralized the troops, and that in turn had prompted Reilly and his men to make a run for Tolima, and that had been D'Anjou's doing. But, yes, he had to admit, what if Reilly had not escaped to the Megadome...not become so obsessed with an evil Louis who was coming after him...instead decided to take charge of his troops? What if Reilly had not been so sure of himself, of his concept that Tolima was Earth, a month behind in space-time, what if his high command had not gone off with him...what if Bush had decided to fight...of course there were so many variables, how things worked out. Yes, Louis could say it was all a miracle, but the direct result of these people meditating and praying? Well, yes, he had to remind himself, if they actually managed to change the energy of the world, then yes, he could see how they had a hand in "the miracle."

An older man, perhaps in his eighties, approached their table and asked if he could join them. "I am Francisco de Aconda," he announced with a slight Spanish accent. He sported long white hair and a beard, which made Louis think of Moses. His white robe completed the effect. After sitting down and smiling at those all around, he praised Louis for his achievements. "I am most impressed how you went about defeating the Patriots. Congratulations, regent."

"Thank you, Don Francisco," replied Louis, not quite knowing how to acknowledge the compliment, "however, I didn't do it alone, there—"

"Of course not, but your role was remarkable," Francisco said raising his bushy white eyebrows. "You reached a state of interior harmony, of surrender to your higher self. Then you acted and brought about a string of what most would call miracles...am I right?" he asked with a broad smile showing yellowing teeth in between his white whiskers.

"Yes...I suppose you could phrase it that way."

Sharon touched Louis's arm. "Of course you could phrase it that way, dear. You learned how to balance yourself, how to act within what you call the Diva sequence—what we call Nirvilkalpa Samadhi."

Francisco studied Sharon for a moment, a deep, probing look. "That's exactly right, Sister Mukthi." He turned his gaze on Louis, an almost unbearable stare. "You are a scientist and an agnostic, right? But now you know firsthand what spiritual teachers have been preaching for ages, what Jesus meant when he said, 'Seek first the kingdom of God and all else will be added unto you.' Amazing how ancient that advice is, and how misunderstood through the ages. It's actually quite practical and to the point, isn't it?" His whole face was beaming.

Louis nodded, although the religious reference was a bit irksome. "Yes, Don Francisco. I guess I am beginning to get the point."

"Well, *estimado amigo*, you are now privy to the secret of so many people who came before us; such as the famous Knights Templar. They knew that action has to be accompanied by a switch in energy through meditation or prayer, otherwise nothing happens…that's how they managed to resurrect democratic rule for us all." A crowd had formed around the table and it seemed the whole room had fallen silent. "In your class you described how Barack Obama was the catalyst for a massive change." Francisco's voice boomed throughout the now silent dining hall. "But now you know that many people just like us meditated and prayed long and hard for him to become president…or when our New Paradigm became a reality. The same was the case when significant developments in science came about that saved lives and lessened suffering…or when awful tyrants were overthrown…including that crazed Reilly. What's unusual is when there's a merging of the consciousness that manifests the transformational energy and the person or persons doing the actual work. You were such a person. Congratulations. The Templars would have bowed before you.

"Yes, dear friend," Francisco continued, his eyes crinkling. "What will complete the picture for you is the World Meditation. Tomorrow you will experience firsthand the engine that drives the world."

Francisco contemplated Louis for a time. "You and I are not that far apart in age. I'm barely five years older." He smiled. "But the process that made you young and healthy is quite a Pandora's Box, isn't it?" Then as he got up to leave: "It's certainly not for me; I'm ready to depart this physical plane." He then noticed the crowd that had gathered around, smiled shyly, and quickly walked away.

On their way back to the cabin, Sharon told Louis that Francisco was a famous spiritual teacher in South America. "He's right about D'Anjou's technology. It's quite a Pandora's box, as he put it."

"I know, I know. Overpopulation. We need to reach Tolima."

Sharon took hold of his hand. "That's just the most immediate concern. But what about humanity's greatest curse: the fear of death? The anxiety is the cause of most mental disorders, but is also our greatest motivator. Will be interesting to see what happens over time when you remove that primordial fear."

That night they slept together, with Yogi on the floor and Oscar in a corner of the bed. They had fallen asleep hugging closely. He could feel the energy linking their hearts, ever so sweet. It rained hard and it sounded like music to Louis's ears. In the middle of the night, when he tried to pull away from Sharon to turn over, she groaned in her sleep and tightened her grip around him. Louis decided to stay put.

In the morning, they dressed in white robes that came down all the way to the ankles. A young man had brought one for Louis and smiled sweetly as he handed it to him at the cottage door without saying a word.

The meditation hall was an open expanse encased in a magnetically-controlled plasma dome, a temporary structure that kept rain and insects out, allowed air circulation, and reduced the sun's rays to a semi-shade. The ground was a well-kept lawn that had been blown dry of the moisture from the night's rain. People sat on cushions and chairs, including all the virtual bodies, compressed to miniature figures so they could all fit, millions and millions of little figures sitting on the lawn at the very front, getting smaller and smaller as more came to join them in their virtual space. A counter floating to one side showed two billion...then three...and when it passed four there were many smiles. It was the biggest gathering, real and virtual, Louis had ever seen, much larger than any of his classes by far.

And the meditation was very powerful. Sharon had been right, it was hard at first with so many people, but once he surrendered, let go, he felt swept up by the collective energy. And incredibly enough, he became one with them all, and just as with Sharon the previous night, he arrived at a point of nonbeing.

Afterward, as he stood outside the huge hall, waiting for Sharon, who had decided to stay in meditation a while longer, he was mesmerized and in awe, with the realization that this was a whole aspect of the world he had not been aware of. No one wrote papers about it, no one spoke about it in the government...a secret movement that was a quarter of the world's population...and they were the actual movers...Francisco had been right on target when he called them the engine that drove the world. Louis watched as groups in white robes walked past him, mostly silent. He watched them for a while in amazement. Those were the real movers and shakers. But how could it be so; why did they keep it so secret? And how? Was it necessary? Why not speak openly about it...but then again, what could they say? That they were the actual doers? Certainly they considered the rest of the world to be...immature— children, really, children who played their silly games while they did the real work.

A part of him felt foolish and small, and another part felt like laughing, because he could see the world and particularly the government in a totally new light. Yes, like children at play. And another part of him felt exceedingly glad, that there were grown-ups in charge. Of course, there was no way the Patriots could have won, not with these people around.

He went to stand under a large tree to get out of the sun and found that a profusion of large, golden mangoes hung from its limbs. The sky was blue with a few clouds here and there, and the ground was covered with flowers and shrubs, and trees and more shrubs of so many different colors. Some purple with lavender flowers, and a tree in the distance had blue flowers, and another one flaming orange. The main house loomed in the distance to his left, and he knew the wide lawn in front of him led to a cluster of cottages, and hidden in between the trees and shrubs and flowers was Sharon's house.

He heard steps behind him and felt Sharon throw her arms around his torso. He turned around and she kissed him softly on the lips.

Holding hands, they walked back toward her cottage, slowly and in silence, but as they were going by a flower bed, he couldn't help himself. "Now I know."

Sharon smiled. "Yes...and we can do this in New York as well. So if you want to be in New York, I'll come with you."

Louis shook his head. They were going by the "Edible Garden," large plots of plants, an array of green, red, yellow, orange, and purple. "No...I'd like to stay here with you. I still have to go to Tolima, and I have to help reorganize the government, but I'm sure I'll figure things out, now that I know how." He looked around. "We can stay here. In fact, this is where we both need to be."

"*Si, estimado amigo*, this is where you are called to be," a voice said from under a nearby avocado tree some twenty feet away. It was Francisco. He sat on the grass in the lotus posture. Apparently it was where he had spent the three hours in meditation. "Do you know about the golden age?" he asked.

And it dawned on Louis what Francisco was talking about. He didn't answer for a moment. Of course. We did away with death, defeated evil, and now understand the workings of creation. That was all foretold in Hinduism and Greek mythology as well as other ancient traditions. He recalled the class he took as a freshman in college: what he had gone through; all of it, could be taken as signs, almost verbatim, that humanity was about to enter such an era, a glorious phase where harmony reigns.

"Yes," Louis said softly, "I know of various ancient legends about the golden age which supposedly comes every twenty-four thousand years. I recall something in the Bible as well, something about the wolf living with the lamb?"

Francisco eyes stared at the distance. "And the wolf will dwell with the lamb, and the leopard will lie down with the young goat, and the calf and the young lion and the fatling together; and a little boy will lead them. Also, the cow and the bear will graze, their young will lie down together, and the lion will eat straw like the ox."

Louis repeated the words in his mind, and then he nodded. "Yes, Don Francisco, that's the passage. Maybe you are right, maybe all the myths are right, and we are about to enter one such era."

Sharon shook her head. "But according to Hinduism, we are still thousands of years away from a Golden Age!"

Francisco looked up at her, his eyes deep and steady. "We accelerated everything starting 200 years ago with the decisions we made…all the signs are there, sister. We are entering a Golden Age."

Louis smiled at the man. "Wouldn't you like to stick around and see for yourself?"

"No, *estimado*," he said with a chuckle. "I've done my bit." He gave them a big smile and closed his eyes again.

They continued on toward Sharon's cottage, holding hands. In the distance they heard a bark, and Yogi bounded over. Wendy had released him when she saw them coming. He could see her silvery presence by the cottage.

Sharon turned to look at him. "A golden age? Wouldn't that be exciting."

After a slobbery greeting, Yogi decided to lead the way back, his tail wagging in time with his strides.

THE END

www.ingramcontent.com/pod-product-compliance
Lightning Source LLC
Chambersburg PA
CBHW020330180626
46812CB00001B/130